WEREWOLF'S EMBRACE

WEREWOLF'S EMBRACE

MICHELE HAUF
CYNTHIA COOKE
KATIE REUS
JENNA KERNAN
ELLE JAMES

MILLS & BOON

Published in Great Britain 2014
by Mills & Boon, an imprint of Harlequin (UK) Limited,
Eton House, 18-24 Paradise Road, Richmond, Surrey, TW9 1SR

WEREWOLF'S EMBRACE © 2014 Harlequin Books S.A.

Moonspun © 2012 Michele Hauf
Wolf Magick © 2010 Cynthia D. Cooke
Protector's Mate © 2012 Katie Reus
First Heat © 2011 Jeanette H. Monaco
Demon's Embrace © 2012 Mary Jernigan

ISBN: 978-0-263-91407-8

89-0914

Harlequin (UK) Limited's policy is to use papers that are natural, renewable and recyclable products and made from wood grown in sustainable forests. The logging and manufacturing processes conform to the legal environmental regulations of the country of origin.

Printed and bound
by CPI Group (UK) Ltd, Croydon, CR0 4YY

MOONSPUN

MICHELE HAUF

Michele Hauf has been writing romance, action-adventure and fantasy stories for more than twenty years. Her first published novel was *Dark Rapture*. France, musketeers, vampires and fairies populate her stories. And if she followed the adage "write what you know," all her stories would have snow in them. Fortunately, she steps beyond her comfort zone and writes about countries she has never visited and of creatures she has never seen.

Michele can also be found on Facebook and Twitter and michelehauf.com. You can also write to Michele at: PO Box 23, Anoka, MN 55303, USA.

Chapter One

Shifted into werewolf form, naked and glistening beneath the moonlight, his wife's body glided above Creed Saint-Pierre. Her rhythm grew faster, frenzied. The soft black fur at her shoulders, hips and thighs gleamed like moonspun hematite. Nearby, faery lights danced within the thick foliage surrounding them on this cozy moss-covered dais within the forest.

She squeezed his cock with her powerful muscles, forging him into hot steel, pulsing and ready—so close. Creed dug his fingers into the moss and clenched his teeth. A fang cut his lip and blood rolled down his chin. His hips bucked and his thigh muscles strained.

And when he could no longer resist the call to lunge forward and sink his fangs into his lover's neck, he instead closed his eyes and surrendered to the wicked union of vampire and werewolf. Exquisite. Dangerous. Blu's throaty growls preceded the orgasm that captured them and shook their bodies together, spasming, clutching, clinging.

Loving. Always and ever.

Creed's groan, long and loud, echoed up through the tree

canopy. He exhaled, his tight muscles giving way to the luxurious fire molting through him.

Blu pushed away from him with taloned paws. His cock slipped from her hot depths and landed on his stomach. The werewolf lashed her tongue across the crimson claw marks serrating his chest above the nipple. Leaping off him, she dashed into the night.

"I love you, too," he called after her. "You gorgeous she-wolf!"

The faeries bobbling overhead swirled in a ribbon behind the werewolf, eager to follow her romping lopes. The wolf's howls echoed up to her moonlight master, a gorgeous silver medallion suspended high in the charcoal spring sky.

Propping up on his elbows, Creed dragged his tongue over the blood pearling on his lip. His fangs always came down during sex, though he could control it if he had the mind to. "I've got to stop doing that." Then he chuckled, because being so lost in the enjoyment of his wife was not something he ever wanted to stop.

He stroked his fingers over the talon wounds on his chest, feeling the skin knit and heal with a tightening that always made him wince. Rolling onto his side, he spied the silhouette of his wife framed between birch trees that had only begun leafing out from their buds to perfume the air with spring. Her body shifted and her wolfish head changed to human form. Luscious dark hair spilled down her slender neck and her shoulders dropped, losing the muscle and bulk she took on when in werewolf shape. A beautiful creature, she, when wearing fur and howling at the moon, yet more stunning when in human form and with moonlight bejeweling her pale, dewy skin.

He watched as she raked her fingers through her hair, causing it to spill out in the dark veil Creed loved to feel sweep across his body. Blu turned and skipped back to him, her bare feet tracking the forest floor still carpeted with fall's soggy, brown leaves. With a giggle, she landed on him, straddling his hips and brushing aside the hair from his face. The glitter in her gray eyes could lead a man through the darkest night, yet Creed would allow no man to follow his wife, for she belonged to him.

"Sorry about that, lover." She kissed the scars tracing from his shoulder to pectoral; the skin would be smooth, scarless by morning. "You know my wolf likes it rough."

"I like you rough, howling, and any way I can get you."

"Mmm, you're so good to me, vampire." She nipped him on the shoulder, but didn't sink in her teeth. Though he bit her on rare occasions, she had not developed a blood hunger, and had never bitten him to drink blood in return. "Race you to the shower?"

"Only if we can do this again. Inside?"

"Hell yeah, I'm not sated yet. And to judge from this hard fella—" She sucked the head of his cock slowly, twisting her tongue about it, then winked at him. "—you're not, either. Go!"

She dashed off, and Creed sat up, chuckling at her antics. He'd let her win. Because she always won. She was faster than him. Faster to tease him, faster to fall into his arms. Faster to love him.

And he was grateful his heart had grown steadfast for his werewolf wife.

Cherry-red fingernails glided over the black satin sheets, clutching, then releasing the slippery fabric. Her lover's tongue performed the same slippery glide over her skin, purposeful and determined to lick every inch, and taste every drop of water following the shower. He meant to devour her and she enjoyed being the feast.

Blu Saint-Pierre purred like a kitten, and the image of a pleased feline curling about a vampire's legs made her laugh.

Creed looked up from her stomach, where he'd been lashing at her navel. Dark hair hung over his brows. "You find this funny?"

"I was thinking I sound like a kitten purring under your expert tongue."

"You do. I love your purrs, my pretty little kitty cat."

"Don't you dare start calling me that." She hooked her legs over his shoulders and redirected his ministrations. "I'm wolf to the core."

"A wolf who smells like chocolate." He nipped the inside of her thigh, right there, where the slightest touch made her shiver in anticipation of where he would next touch her skin. "Even down here. Did you bathe in chocolate syrup?"

"I thought you liked sweet treats?"

"I do." He lashed his tongue across her swollen clitoris, and Blu's body reacted, her hips surging upward to receive more of his delicious torture. He did not disappoint.

"It's bath oil," she said. "Perfumes me even after I've dried off."

"Wear it always." His fingers slid along her folds, firmly, then softer, knowing exactly how to play her to a humming mess of want and desire. Surrender eddied in her core, challenging her to release even though she was already blissfully sated. "Come for me, lover. My beautiful chocolate-flavored wolf."

"Not without you."

Blu shifted her hips, taking Creed by surprise, and flipped him onto his back to land against the pillows with a moan.

She shimmied down and kissed his mouth, his chest, his belly and then his magnificent cock.

He in turn spread her legs and buried his tongue inside her. When she nibbled along his thick shaft, he hummed against her delicate folds, and the vibrations rocketed her pleasure to the stratosphere. His hips bucked slowly, demanding his measure, and she slickened her strokes with her tongue and clasped the base of him tightly with one hand while cupping his testicles with the other.

Her vampire husband dropped his head and forgot his attentions to her. She loved that she could command him so easily. "That's right. You're mine," she purred, and another giggle was unavoidable. "But don't forget about me."

As he growled against her clit and began to come, she relaxed her tight core muscles and surrendered to a matching climax. Together they cried out, harmonizing in ecstasy. Too much—and not enough—and always just right. Blu lifted up on her palms and her husband slickened her chest with his forceful release.

She fell aside, rolling onto her back, and slid a hand over her chest. Licking her fingers clean refocused her thoughts. So much potential for life in this substance. And then she thought about what she always tried not to think about after sex—a vampire could not get a werewolf pregnant. It wasn't the way things worked between their breeds, for reasons beyond her ken. Though certainly a werewolf male could impregnate a female vampire. And she had heard rumors the reverse was possible with great magic, or voodoo, or who knew, maybe some kind of faery boon.

Creed nestled alongside her, nudging his nose into her coal-dark hair and cupping her breast with his wide, warm hand. His hard muscles melded against her softness like a

puzzle piece finding home. He smelled like sex and chocolate and strength. "What are you thinking about, kitty cat?"

"Creed."

"Wild-haired sex kitten?"

"Watch it, pale vampire dude." She reached behind and
over her hip and gripped his soft penis, tightly.

"All right, I'm sorry," he quickly said. "No more teasing."

She released him. "You start that, and I'll have to call you
longtooth."

"My teeth are long." He bit into her shoulder, not breaking skin, though she didn't mind when he did, rarely, pierce
her flesh. "On occasion."

They'd been forced to marry in a match arranged by the
Council, a group that oversaw the paranormal nations. The
marriage had been a means to bring together the opposing
breeds and begin peace talks. It had worked to the extent that
some vampire tribes had gained respect from a few packs,
but Blu wasn't so foolish to believe either breed would ever
drop their prejudices and embrace the other graciously.

Surprisingly to both of them, they had fallen in love, and
the marriage could be counted a success. And after she'd
learned to trust her vampire husband—who had once slain
werewolves in medieval times—Blu had allowed him to bite
her. With Creed's bite, they had bonded in a way vampires
bonded. Yet werewolves bitten by a vampire almost always
developed an unnatural blood hunger. That had not happened
to her yet, for which she was thankful. Probably because he
had bitten her only a dozen times in a few years. She couldn't
fathom drinking blood for pleasure.

"Deep thoughts?" he wondered, tugging a sheet corner
to wipe off her chest. The polite Frenchman to the core, he
was warrior, lover and doting husband, all rolled into one
fine package.

Deep brown eyes she could stare into forever looked suddenly worried in the soft glow from the bedside lamp. She'd mentioned her *deep thoughts* casually before, but had never dared say how much those thoughts haunted her of late. They'd been married two years. She adored her husband. To know she would enjoy centuries with him thrilled her beyond measure.

But something was missing. An innate, visceral call to the maternal.

"I want to have your children," she whispered, feeling as if the confession was so sacred she could only share it with him, and only in quiet tones. "I wish there was a way, Creed."

Feeling the tender, yet insistent, tug in her chest, she blinked, and Creed traced the tear below her eye.

"If I could make it so, I would, lover mine. I hate seeing you unhappy."

"I'm never unhappy with you. It's…well, you lying beside me right now? I was thinking how we're like pieces of a puzzle perfectly fit. Yet a piece of me is missing, maybe fallen on the floor somewhere, and I can't seem to find it."

He kissed her chin, her lips, her eyelids. The reverent stillness allowed her to feel his heartbeats against her chest. If they embraced long enough their heartbeats would synch.

"Wolves are, by nature, family-centric," she said, pressing her palm over his beating heart. "I want to make babies with you, lover. Have a pack."

"What if they were vampire babies?"

"Do you think that matters to me? Honestly?"

"No. The whole hating the vamps thing is not within your nature. At least, not any more."

"I could never hate you. Or any child I had that might have to drink blood to survive. Hell, if I can't have a pack, I'll have a tribe! But our children could be wolves."

"Or half breeds," he said. "I would love a child too. I crave innocence. The wonder of youth."

Blu sighed. Such talk stirred a dangerous fantasy. Because that was all it could ever be. "I thought I heard something about saying blessings to Faery if one desired something with all their heart."

"I'll say them daily, then." He clasped her hand and drew it against his heart. "I would die for you, Blu, you know that."

"Yes, but if you were dead, then who would give me babies?"

He chuckled. "Is this what they call the ticking biological clock?"

"No, it's an instinctual desire to create a family with the man I love." She kissed him, dashing her tongue against his fangs, which she knew gave him a visceral thrill. "Would you be upset if I did some research? Tried to find a means to make this happen?"

"Upset? Blu, I'll help you. After living almost a millennium, nothing could please me more than to finally become a father."

"Are you serious?"

Blu rolled over on the huge beach towel spread next to the pool. Bree, her faery best friend, was teleconferencing her via their iPads and had just told her an old faery tale about a kitsune shifter who had wanted to have a vampire's child. Certain animal breeds could not procreate with vampires. But a faery boon—powerful faery magic—could overcome any genetic obstacle.

"So you think if I asked a faery to help me get pregnant by my husband, it would work?" Creed was inside, lingering in bed, the sun too high to allow him to be out by her side.

"That's how it worked for the kitsune," Bree said. "But Blu, it's an old wives' tale, and who knows if it's true."

"Yeah, but it never hurts to try. Could you give me a boon?"

"Oh no. You'd have to ask a wise faery, a sage, or someone in royalty like a champion or mystic. And you won't find them wandering about the mortal realm."

"So I'd have to go to Faery?" She gripped the iPad as if she could reach through the device and grab her friend's shoulder. "Bree, you have to help me get there."

"Sweetie, slow down. I know you want this with all your heart."

"With two hearts, if I had two."

"No faery will do anything for another being without a return boon."

"So I have to give them something? That's cool. We're rich. I can pay, shower them with diamonds, offer them a condo in Paris."

Bree laughed, and Blu caught her chin in hand. She knew diamonds meant little to faeries. Nor would mortal money bring up a glint in their violet eyes.

"How do I get to Faery?"

"You don't. The faery would have to come to you. You'd have to perform a ritual to call them out. I'll see what I can come up with, okay?"

"I love you, Bree. How's Rev?"

"You mean the sexy vampire who is lying in my bed right now? I'd say about half-mast, and eager for me to get off the screen."

"It's best not to keep hungry vampires waiting. But don't keep this wolf waiting, either. Call me as soon as you find something."

She signed off and set the iPad aside. "Maybe this can really happen."

Filled with hope, Blu tugged off her bikini top and dove into the pool.

"Thanks, Hawkes. Can you email that spell?" Creed asked.

"Yes, but it'll take a day or two to have it interpreted," his friend Rhys Hawkes replied over the phone. Their international connection, from Minneapolis to Paris, was ridden with static.

"I'm glad I contacted you," Creed said. "If this works, I will make my wife a very happy werewolf."

He hung up and propped a leg up on the edge of his desk. From the office window, he could see Blu performing some mermaid moves in the pool. Not only would she be happy, but he would as well. He'd walked this world for ages. It was time to view it through an entirely new and wondrous perspective—that of fatherhood.

Chapter Two

"Fuck yeah."

There were two instances in life that demanded the oath hissed in satisfied tones. Following deliciously mind-numbing sex. And when sinking into the perfect bath, water almost—but not quite—too hot to stand, bubbles frothy but not overwhelming.

Blu stretched up a leg in the bathtub and slicked the bar of cinnamon soap along her thigh. Bliss was an hour to herself in the tub. When they'd rebuilt the mansion, Creed had let her design every room, and this bathroom had been her first project. All white marble, including the tub, it offered her sanctity from the world.

"Sorry, sweetie," Creed said as he strolled in, barefoot but still wearing his Armani suit, and grabbed a toothbrush. "I'll be quick. Or I could use the other bathroom?"

"No, I don't mind." Sanctity breached, she knew it wouldn't take him long and her peace would be restored. But seriously? She couldn't get enough of the man. A few minutes to watch him was like a sweet treat.

His hips shimmied when he brushed. Blu dipped low in

the tub and smiled to herself. She'd heard married couples eventually grew bored of one another, less attracted, too. How that was possible, she didn't know. Every day she found something new to admire about her husband .Tonight it was his silly toothbrushing shimmy.

"What?" his reflection asked in the mirror, his mouth full of toothpaste.

"I've never noticed your toothbrush dance before. Shake those hips, lover boy."

He shrugged, dismissing her request, yet with the last few strokes he offered her a few exaggerated shimmies. Rapping the brush on the sink, he wiped off his mouth then started toward the door. That was her guy: always willing to please, even if it meant giving her some space.

"Wait," Blu said. "I need you to do something for me first."

"Whatever my true love desires." He stood there, arms spread, waiting her command.

And Blu was inclined to command. "Take off your clothes."

His brow arched. "Really? I thought you liked your bath time all private and peaceful."

"Yeah, but you make me so horny. I want to watch you peel away your clothes and reveal the sexy muscles underneath. I always undress for you. It's payback time."

"Very well."

Unbuttoning his crisp white linen shirt, and expertly snapping the platinum cufflinks from his cuffs, he quickly took it off and tossed it aside. The cufflinks chattered across the marble vanity.

"Slower," Blu directed. She stretched her arms along the warm marble tub rim and put up a foot near the faucet. "I like to see your muscles flex. Don't tell me you've never performed a striptease?"

The man didn't blush, but his blinking look from under the fall of his dark hair gave away his surprising hesitance. "Actually, I don't believe that opportunity has ever presented itself in all my years."

With a teasing lift of brow, he unzipped his trousers and slowly pushed them past his hips until the fabric fell to his ankles. As he stepped out of them his abs flexed, highlighting that gorgeous cut muscle that eased along his hip and down toward his loins.

Blu felt the water's heat near boiling. No, that was her body temperature rising. Maybe she could boil the water? Ha!

Her husband, a six-foot-plus warrior, stood in front of her wearing nothing but the form-fitting boxer briefs she'd bought for him. The briefs were black, thigh-and cock-hugging, and went to the tops of his thighs. Normally, she would pull those down herself—with her teeth.

"Turn around," she insisted. "Let me see those powerful delts and obliques. Oh yeah. That's the way to make this wolf growl." An appreciative growl felt very necessary.

Sliding her fingers down her stomach, she strolled them over her cleft, but didn't want to finger herself. The visual was enough. Besides, if she clenched her legs together, that primed her just enough to take this fuck-yeah bath over the top. "Briefs down, big boy."

He turned slightly and tugged down the briefs, letting them drop. Viewed from the side, Creed's powerful frame was wide about the chest and thighs. He looked as though he spent hours daily in the gym, but it was his vampire nature that kept him lean and tight, an iron-strapped god of flesh and bone. And there, his cock, upright and proud, and ready for action. Uncircumcised, the foreskin had slipped down beneath the bold, red head of it, and Blu imagined the feel of it entering her, pushing forcefully to ease into her pussy.

He spread his arms and tilted forward a hip. "You like to look at my cock?"

"Fuck yeah."

"You want to touch it?"

"Ye—erm…no." Tugging her lip down with her teeth, she devised a more intriguing plan. "I want to watch you stroke yourself. Slowly."

With an approving shrug, Creed stepped a few feet closer to give her a front-row view. Grabbing his cock, he moved his fingers expertly up and down what Blu knew must feel like molten steel in his grip. Even though they made love often, she knew he jacked off as well. Didn't bother her. He was a man; it was what men did. And hell, she jilled off, because thinking about Creed when he wasn't around demanded immediate satisfaction.

"That's my big guy," she cooed. "You like it firm and faster?"

"Mm…" he replied, picking up the pace. His gaze had been focused on her, but as his strokes grew faster, his eyelids shuttered and mentally, he turned inward.

Man, she loved watching him do this. So focused, intent, vigorous. Come to think of it, that was a good way to describe how he handled a battle sword. He really gave the thing a workout and he wasn't gentle with it.

Note to self: whack that thing around next time she had it in hand. It could take it, and he preferred it rough.

Her thoughts made her smile, and she slipped an arm over the tub side and rested her chin on the edge to get a closer view of her husband's sex show. His tense abs tightened, shaping skin over hard muscled ridges, his hips shivering minutely. Breaths gasped through his lips quickly, and his fingers raced.

"Going to come?" she asked.

"Soon. You watching me…so good…" He winced and his muscles flexed and trembled.

Blu licked her lips and cooed.

He spurted up over his chest and cried out forcefully, catching his free hand on the edge of the tub. Blu stretched her fingers up through his hair.

"Come join me, lover. Now it's my turn."

"I have to run out tonight."

Creed sat up in bed, stretching out his neck with a smart twist. Usually Blu stuck around after sex, unless… "You going to let your wolf out for a run?"

"Yes, it hasn't been out in a few weeks, and I'm prickling for some laps in the field." She leaned in and kissed him, sliding her hand down to squeeze his cock. "Don't wait up for me. I want to feel the sun rise on my fur."

"All right. I might head out myself. To uh…you know."

She kissed him again. "I know."

If he couldn't bite her once a week, then he had to get his sustenance somehow. They'd come to terms he would bite men more often than women, because it bothered Blu that the bite was a sexual thing, and though she knew it wasn't cheating on her husband's part to take a woman in his arms and bite her, she preferred he keep the intimate embraces with the females to a minimum.

"See you in the morning, lover."

Blu grabbed a strappy sundress fashioned from blue-spangled sari material and pulled it on. She padded out of the bedroom, giving her hair a fluff. She wore her natural, midnight-black hair uncovered more frequently now because she had nothing to hide from Creed. Once she'd been all about the brightly-colored wigs, because she'd thought they kept men at a distance, something she'd needed after growing up with the aggressive males in the Northern pack. Her father had actually given her to the males as a sexual gift, and there had been nothing she could do about it.

Until she'd been forced to marry Creed. And her world had changed for the better. Creed made her feel protected and loved. Always. Nothing to hide.

"Except this one small thing," she thought about tonight's planned foray.

Blu shifted from four-legged wolf to human shape in the center of the forest near the mossy dais. She didn't feel at all self-conscious to wander the forest naked. Wasn't like wolves returned to were form clothed. And Creed owned a couple dozen acres, so she was confident her moonlit peepshow would never be discovered by, say, a hunter or hiker. Not on private Saint-Pierre property. Old man Schmidt's land was a dash away, and she was ever leery of that gun-toting, to-bacco-chewing artifact, but didn't plan to go near his property tonight.

In a few nights the moon would be full and her werewolf would demand release. The werewolf was her half human, half wolf form, and she only let it out during the full moon—and when Creed was in the mood for some real vigorous sex. Sometimes her werewolf wanted sex, and it didn't matter if it was with a vampire. She needed that bond, that joining. She loved him for that, because heaven only knew any non-werewolf having sex with a werewolf did face challenges, such as talons and a big, toothy maw. She tended to go beyond rough when in werewolf form, but the vamp could handle her talons, and he did like her aggression, and matched her every move.

But fore? Her animal nature felt the urge to procreate under the full moon. The only way a werewolf could conceive was while in full wolfed-out shape.

Smirking at their active and delicious sex life, she tiptoed over a thick padding of moss, setting a fragrant crush of oleander perfume into the air. A red fox darted across her path as if hell were on its tail. It sensed her animal nature, surely. A pale moth fluttered before her, and she reached out, allowing it to land on her forefinger like a living ring. Everything was magical this time of night.

"Can I wish upon you?" she wondered, then blew gently to set it on its way.

Bree had video-conferenced her with the instructions needed for this night. And Blu had muttered the ritual all day, making sure she knew it by heart.

Taking a deep breath, she whispered the sidhe words. "Sheimme, shuom, galimmour. Hear me through the veil and know I come with open heart and clear soul."

The air immediately shifted about her, not like wind, but as if it were moving through her skin and swirling in her veins. Suddenly as giddy as bubbles in champagne, she clasped her hands to her chest in expectation and searched the night.

Shimmers danced before her like tiny lightning bugs, and they followed a swaying pattern that twisted into a lush swirl much like the faery lights that hovered above her and Creed when they made love out here, their favorite spot in the forest. Scents of loamy earth, leaves and animals increased until Blu's senses grew mad with desire to pinpoint them all. It was like being overwhelmed in a noisy nightclub by sound, movement and light. Random life pulses fluttered across her senses, tripping up her heartbeats and then shimmering away.

And then it stopped, and the shimmers formed into a faery with violet wings threaded with gleaming dark veins that resembled blackened chrome. Coal hair was streaked with white, but Blu realized it was painted or dusted with pollen. Three blue dashes crossed diagonally from above her left eye, over her nose, and down her right cheek. She stood as tall as Blu—who, admittedly, was short without her spike heels—and her bright violet eyes narrowed. A thin white sheath danced over her narrow frame, exposing remarkable muscles for such a petite figure. At her hip gleamed a crystal scimitar.

Warrior, Blu decided. She'd called a sidhe champion to her. Such luck!

Blu bowed. "Well met."

"Well met, wolf," the faery said in a gruff voice that chastised for disturbing her, while also piqued a question. She slammed a palm to her hip near the scimitar. "For what have you called me?"

As Bree had instructed, she must get right to the point. "I want to conceive my husband's child."

The warrior sidhe walked before her in a wide arc, casting a discerning gaze over her. Blu felt lesser standing before her—she caught herself and lifted her shoulders. She never considered herself lesser, or greater, than anyone. And she would best show her confidence before this woman.

"If a child is your desire," the faery said, "why marry the one man who could not give you that child?" She scoffed. "A vampire?"

"It was an arranged marriage set up by the Council." She'd thought the marriage stupid until Creed had kissed her after they'd recited their vows. That kiss had changed her attitude toward vampires forever. At least toward the one sexy, loving vampire who only had eyes for her. "But I love him more than anything in this world."

The faery's laughter sounded like bells the size of flower

heads. Eerily out of place when measured against her warrior stance. "Did Creed Saint-Pierre not murder your father?"

"No, that was one of my father's men," Blu protested.

Ridge Addison, her father's right-hand man, had taken off Amandus Masterson's head with one swipe of his talons. Blu could never be angry at Ridge, because he'd been protecting her and Creed at the time.

"Creed was...tortured by my father." Her father had ordered the punishment of one thousand talons against her husband. Her heart pulsed as she recalled finding Creed bloodied and near death in a ditch following that awful torture.

"He suffered for me." She let out a breath. Clutching the air with needy fingers, she shifted from foot to foot, jittery with need. "Please. It is all I want, to give my husband a child. To answer my breed's innate call to surround myself with family."

Those were the desires that twanged daily at her very soul. It wasn't right she should be denied merely because her breed was not compatible with Creed's.

"One child is all you ask?"

"Well..." It would be greedy to ask for many. Yet a pack, or even a tribe, required more than a few. "The ability to carry my husband's *children* is what I ask, no matter it be one or more than one. Is that all right?" She winced. *Be firm, positive.* "I want my womb to be receptive to his sperm, to get technical."

With a tilt of her head, the faery's eyes glowed, deep amethyst caught in surrounding stone. "And what do you offer in return for so great a boon?"

"I am willing to give whatever you ask."

The faery's brow lifted. "You are an agreeable wolf. I like that. So often your breed tends to be rough with me." She shivered, setting her wings to a glamorous shimmer.

"I would never harm the sidhe. I'm cool with all breeds. Well, mostly. Demons freak the crap out of me. And vampires still give me pause. The ones I don't know."

"You are honest as well." The faery tapped her fingers against the scimitar. "Another admirable quality."

Blu shrugged. "I am what I am. And if given the chance, I know I'd be a good mother."

"Will you tell your husband about tonight?"

"I, uh…" Didn't want to unless it worked. No sense in getting his hopes up. "I will. But only should my wish be granted."

Another tilt of the faery's head displayed concern. Distrust? Or curiosity?

"Please," Blu said on a breath. So close to having her heart's wish, her body shivered minutely.

"Very well, I grant you the boon to carry your vampire husband's children. And in return…"

Pulse racing, Blu clasped her hands tightly, thrilled this was really happening. She would give anything…

"You will give me your firstborn," the faery said.

Blu's jaw dropped. Her heart stopped beating.

But. The word sat on her tongue. She wanted to blurt it out. She wanted to grab the faery about the neck, shake her and rage at her.

How dare the faery ask such a thing? No mother could conceive of such a sacrifice. Why give away the only thing she desired?

"Do you agree?" the faery asked.

To protest would cause offense. She had to play this carefully. "Will I have more than one child? If I do not, then this bargain would be ridiculous."

The faery shrugged, which set her wings to a flutter.

Blu breathed out. If she could have one child, then she

could have another. Yes? Giving up her first would kill her—
and Creed. No, it was foolish. How could she possibly get
through a pregnancy only to the hand over the babe?

Yet what if she had twins? Or triplets? Werewolves were
notoriously fertile.

Her gut churned, and her throat closed painfully. Tears
wobbled at the corners of her eyes. The faery surely would
not give her something and then take it away with no means
to have another. That wouldn't be fair.

The sidhe did not live by fair or what was right.

"I need a guarantee I'll have more than one child," Blu
said, her voice whispering so its shaky tones could not be
discerned. "Please."

"Your request was only you could carry your husband's
child."

"Children! His children," she corrected. "Do you think me
a fool? I will not sacrifice the one thing I want—"

"Very well, you insipid beast. Children. As far as I'm concerned you can give birth to an entire pack of half breeds.
But the first one is mine."

The sidhe did favor half breeds, and Blu was aware of at
least one vampire who had fallen into the clutches of a greedy
faery because of it.

They had agreed she would have children—as in more
than one. An entire pack? Surely, she could sacrifice one
for the rest?

Blu closed her eyes and fought against the voices begging
her to reconsider, then said, "I agree."

Creed returned from the forest where he'd called out the
faery according to the ritual Rhys Hawkes had emailed him.
Blu was going to be thrilled to learn what he'd done.

He paused, propping the toe of his boot against the chain-link gate that surrounded the immediate grounds and which had once been warded against werewolves and faeries. No longer. He glanced to the mansion. The first pale beams of sunlight burnished the rooftop. She wouldn't be back from her run yet. He could go in and set up a surprise for her.

But intuition told him to keep what he'd done tonight to himself. Telling Blu would only give her hope. And what if it didn't work? He would learn soon enough if the boon the faery had granted him actually proved true. And perhaps he'd never have to reveal what he'd promised in return. It might never come to pass. And if it did, they would handle that together when the time came.

"I did the right thing," he muttered. "We will have family," he said more firmly, to reassure himself. "I just hope it doesn't break Blu's heart."

Suddenly a gunshot echoed in the darkness. Creed twisted, pricking his ears to gauge the location of the shot. He waited. No further sounds.

"Damned farmer," he muttered.

And then he clutched his chest. Blu was out there. Somewhere. He'd best take a walk along the property border.

Chapter Three

Creed walked into the kitchen and smiled to find his wife eating her usual mixing bowl full of crunchy cereal and milk. Today's wig color was hot pink, which matched the latex dress she wore over fishnet stockings. The stripper heels glinted with rhinestones and he was pretty sure they were pushing six inches.

He did love his wife turned up to eleven, as she so often was.

He bent to inspect the brightly-colored, cartoon-emblazoned cereal box. "What happened to Count Chocula?"

She smiled through a mouthful of cereal. "I love the Count's vampy chocolatey goodness, but I was feeling like Captain Crunch this morning."

"You're cheating on me with cereal? Somehow I think I should be offended. That pink milk scares me. It's not right."

"And vampire cereal doesn't freak you?"

"You have me there." He leaned against the counter, heels of his hands on the cool marble behind him. "Were you out running earlier?"

"Uh, yeah? I told you I was heading out."

"I heard a gunshot."

"Farmer Schmidt again. I was in wolf form and strayed too close to the property line. Old dude's got it in for me. Don't worry, I can outrun him."

"Blu, don't be so dismissive of a mortal with a gun. One of these days you won't be able to outrun him, or you won't see him. He's a crafty old hunter. And your breed is no longer on the endangered species list in this state. If not Schmidt, then someone else. Damn it! I'll kill that bastard."

"I love it when you're so protective of me."

He bent to kiss her forehead, pausing to keep her warmth against his mouth, and inhaled the sweet cereal scent. "I would love you more if you took precautions when out running. You can scent out the property line. Don't go near that man's land."

"I try not to, but you know how I get carried away on a run. And I do recall something about a rabbit, but you know, I never remember if I actually made a kill. Which is a good thing."

"I'm going to talk to him."

"Just don't kill him!" she called after his exit.

"I won't go that far, but I will put fear into the bastard's irrational mortal heart."

Creed marched toward the dilapidated red barn set at the back of Schmidt property. He'd spoken to the landowner on a handful of occasions, the last few times to rebuke him for shooting at the wolves in the area. The old man seemed to think a wolf would try to steal one of his cows, which were only six times the size of the local timber wolf.

"Saint-Pierre." The man spied him and, spitting his ever-present tobacco juice to the side, wandered over and shook his hand.

Glad he'd never had the desire to don a pair of blue jean overalls, Creed asked him how the farm was doing, and received the usual pitiful reply. Times were tough for farmers, yet Creed could only relate when he thought back through the ages to medieval times when he'd been living off the land. In feudal France, he'd planted wheat until his lord had called upon him to become a knight and fight against the English in his stead. Things had gone south the night Creed had unknowingly slain a werewolf. But that was a long and different story.

"What brings you over?" Schmidt asked.

"I heard gunshots this morning. And wolf howls."

"Yep. Tracked the damned black wolf onto my property again. I got an eye out for that one. She's a sneaky bitch."

"She won't harm your cows," Creed hissed.

Schmidt spat to the side again. "She'll go for their legs. Wound 'em so I'd have to put 'em down."

"She will not."

"You seem to know the mind of that wolf, Saint-Pierre."

"Wolves do not go after such large prey, and you know it."

"Just when I start believing such nonsense is when old Betsy will get taken down by the bloody she-wolf. The area is infested with them. And now they're off the list, I've every right to protect what is my own."

The man's idiocy infuriated Creed. He couldn't verbally warn the man and hope he would obey him. If he saw Blu in wolf form again, Schmidt would shoot at her. That was not a risk Creed was willing to take.

"Listen to me, old man."

Schmidt lifted his chin and crossed his arms. "Watch it, fella. I've no beef with you, but I don't like the tone you're using with me. You know the value of one of my heifers?"

"Not nearly a fraction the value of that wolf, I'm sure."

"They're bloody predators!"

Incensed, Creed grabbed the man by the front of his overalls and lunged toward his neck. He knew this would not play well, but as he had the thought, he had to carry it through. Sinking his fangs into the carotid, hot blood spurted against the roof of his mouth. He began the persuasion.

Leave the black wolf alone. No wolves will harm you or what is yours.

Shoving the man away, he watched him slump against the stack of hay bales behind him. Bending, Creed licked the wound, which would allow it to heal quickly and keep his indiscretion a secret. Schmidt would come to with no memory of his bite and a newfound respect for the area wolves.

Creed strolled down the hallway and spied Blu shoving the violet damask Louis XV chair out of the bedroom. The thing was heavy, so he rushed to help her, but paused. She was strong, and liked to do things herself.

"Getting ready?" he asked, amusement lightening his tone. "I guess that means we're not taking it outside tonight?"

"It's started to rain. And much as I love sex in the rain, I had candlelight in mind for tonight."

"You think the candles will survive your werewolf?"

She smirked. "Maybe one or two set far across the room. I need help with the picture on the wall. I'd hate to see that damaged."

"I can do that." He followed her inside the bedroom and unhooked the original Mucha lithograph from the wall. Blu caught the end of it to help him carry it out.

"You talk to Schmidt?" Her gray eyes sparkled curiously.

"I did, and he won't be bothering you anymore."

"You didn't…?"

"Blu, please." While he'd never use persuasion on his wife—and couldn't persuade her breed—he knew that she knew what he had done, and hoped she'd leave it at that.

She shrugged, setting her pink wig bouncing. "That's cool. Tonight's going to be special. I can feel it," she said.

The moon was full, and he'd made a bargain with a faery. "Yes, I think it is."

Blu spat out a fluffy white down feather that settled on her lip as she clung to the bedpost amidst a rain of hundreds more feathers. She'd shifted from werewolf to her human were shape and her muscles were slick with perspiration, her arms and legs luxuriously stretched. Her belly was tight and pulsed with the after-tugs of a lingering orgasm. Yet with an inhale, and a clench of her legs, she brought on another orgasm and cried out joyously as she slid down the post to land among the pools of feathers and hardened candle wax on the floor.

Laughing with sheer bliss, she cast her eyes about the room, finding the smaller wardrobe had been tossed against the bathroom door, and the rug was shrugged up against a wall. Not so much damage as usual. Nothing was hanging from the crystal chandelier, nor was anything stuck in the wall, which got a frequent replastering and was covered over with a flocked damask wallpaper Blu kept on order all the time at the local hardware store.

Somewhere within the chaos, her husband groaned and let out one of those happy sighs, followed by a deep growl in his throat that signaled he was pleased.

Ah, there, sprawled at the end of the bed, his arm hanging down and his fingers tickling the air near her hair. A long scratch bled down his bicep. He started to chuckle and rolled over, his hair falling over the side of the mattress.

"I love my werewolf princess," he muttered, "wherever she is."

"Down here." Blu pushed up to sit against the bed. Normally the top mattress was shoved onto the floor, but again, not so much damage as usual tonight. "You happy?"

He lunged over the side of the bed and gripped her head, kissing her from his perch. He kissed her deep and kissed her hard, and ended with a drag of his fang across her lip.

"Fuck yeah."

Chapter Four

Three weeks later...

Creed parked his BMW before the mansion and got out. A breeze wafted the scent of jasmine through the air. After a fire had destroyed the place a few years ago, he'd rebuilt on the land with virtually the same design. He liked the retro feel of the brick-and fieldstone-fronted house. It appealed to his love for old things.

Hell, when a man walks through the centuries, everything eventually becomes old, including his mind. Blu infused him with youth and a carefree attitude he desperately needed. Children? That would put him over the top with new experience and wonder. Too much to hope for? Nothing was ever too much to dream.

He leaned against the car door, checking his text messages before going inside. Once at home, he belonged to Blu, including his attention. He couldn't tolerate her chattering on the phone when he was around, so he gave her the same respect.

The Rescue Project had been slow lately, and that was a good thing. After stepping down as the Nava tribe leader,

Creed had taken on heading the project, which rescued vampires who had been captured by werewolves and then used in vicious blood games. They hadn't had a rescue call in months. Perhaps the wolf packs in the area were finally coming around?

He doubted that. Much as he adored his werewolf wife, Creed still had issues with most wolves. A guy didn't survive the torture of one thousand talons and turn around and embrace all wolves as friends. Wasn't going to happen in his long lifetime.

The front door slammed open and Blu burst through, running toward him in a streak of violet wig and barely-there dress. He opened his arms to receive his wife, and she jumped and body-slammed him. He stumbled, and they collided with the car behind him.

"What is it? You're not screaming, so you can't be injured."

"Oh, Creed." Legs wrapped about his hips, she clung to him and braced his face with her palms. Her heartbeats thundered against his. She didn't say anything else, but that look—those bright gray eyes had never dazzled so brilliantly.

Creed suddenly felt to his very bones the same joy emitted from his wife. "Really? You're sure?"

She nodded eagerly. "I just peed on a stick. I have an appointment this afternoon with a midwife. But Creed, I know it's happened. I know!"

"Oh, my love."

He spun her there in the yard, taking her joy into his heart. The two shouted, "Yes!" and somewhere above their home a glitter of faery dust glinted in the sun.

Three months later...

The cold gel gave Blu a shiver as the midwife moved the wand over the gentle rise of her belly. She was showing much more than she'd expected, but that made everything more exciting. Like it was real. This was happening. She and Creed were going to be parents.

The midwife, Suzanne Walters, had explained werewolves gestated about seven months, so naturally as her baby grew rapidly, she would get bigger faster than a mortal pregnant woman.

Creed, who sat beside her, held her hand and watched the screen. His attention was rapt, and Blu couldn't help but stroke her fingers through his hair as she studied his profile. He was hers, this handsome man who had given her a child.

A child. That she had promised to give away.

Biting her lower lip, she closed her eyes and pushed away the horrible thought. She'd been desperately trying not to think about her promise to the faery since learning she was pregnant. How could she tell him? The more she worried about a confession, the harder it was to actually blurt out her horrible secret.

"So," Suzanne began, "you're going into your fourth month. That means no more shifting."

"What?" Blu propped up on her elbows. "But the full moon is tomorrow night. I have to." She searched Creed's gaze and he offered a helpless shrug.

"The werewolf doesn't have to shift," Suzanne, a werewolf herself, explained. Creed had insisted they hire the best and someone who knew Blu's breed firsthand. "You are merely compelled by the full moon. You and the hubby will have to do something else to ensure you don't shift," she added with a knowing wink.

Creed waggled a brow at Blu, then asked the midwife, "Is it because the baby doesn't shift?"

"Right. As the fetus gets larger, shifting would create problems with Blu's bones changing and her muscles reforming during a shift."

"I get it," Blu said. "Don't worry. No more shifting for me. Creed will have to keep me real happy for the next few months."

"I can do that." He leaned in and kissed her on the forehead.

The midwife started to detail the blurry black and white images on the screen. It was already possible to discern where the head and limbs were.

A new life was really in there, Blu thought. They had done it!

"Well," the midwife said, and looked to Blu and Creed.

"What?" Blu squeezed Creed's hand. *Please don't let it be bad news.*

"Look here." Suzanne pointed to a small, pulsing blob of white near the spine. "That's the heartbeat."

"Amazing." Creed leaned forward to study the screen. "I thought it was that other spot up on the right."

"You're right, Mr. Saint-Pierre."

"What?" Blu sat up to study the screen more closely. "Are you saying…?"

The midwife nodded. "Two heartbeats, and they both look healthy and sound."

"Twins?" Creed nuzzled his face against her neck and hugged Blu. "You did good, princess."

"I think it was you who did good."

"You both have done very well," Suzanne agreed.

"Everything is going to be great now," Blu said. Now she had two babies in her belly, she and Creed would not be left without a child. And while the thought of giving one away killed her, she couldn't deal with that right now. "So good."

"Yes." Creed offered a smile, and then looked aside. "One would have been enough to start our family. We've been blessed."

"Faery blessed," Blu said.

He smirked, but she sensed his joy was forced. It was a lot to take in. "Faery blessed."

"That explains a lot." The midwife winked at Blu. She hadn't mentioned how she'd gotten pregnant, but Suzanne did know Creed was vampire. "I'll leave you two. Congratulations."

"Two," Creed muttered after the door closed. He stood and walked to the window, his back to her.

Two, she thought. But not really. A queasy wave overcame Blu and she swallowed the urge to let loose tears. She was strong. She could do this. She would have to do this.

Two months later...

He had to tell her. It wouldn't be right to keep such a secret any longer. While Blu must have figured out he had asked a faery for a boon, she couldn't possibly know what he had offered in return.

And now Creed's heart sat more heavily than it had those first few months as he'd watched his wife's belly grow and had smoothed his palm over it, kissing her skin and knowing they had created what she was nurturing inside. Now they had two children.

But not really.

Savory scents drifted into the living room from the kitchen, distracting him from dire thoughts. Cooked meat. Blu had been taking her steaks ever rarer lately. Followed by peach ice cream for dessert. There was only one grocery store in the entire Twin Cities that sold peach with the big chunks of fruit, as Blu preferred it, and it was a forty-five-minute drive each way from the mansion.

Last time, he'd picked up ten quarts and stored them in the freezer.

Thinking about the emergency ice cream stores made Creed smile and release his worries. He'd tell her later.

"Soon," he muttered. And he pushed the kitchen doors open and walked in. "Oh, horrors."

The meat on her plate was pink and a pool of blood puddled on the white bone china. Creed was not in the least attracted to the blood, which had come from a dead, half-cooked beast.

"That looks more rare than usual."

"I could rip a cow apart," Blu said, forking in another bite. "I crave blood so much lately."

"Really?" He wondered: Dare he interest her in a warmer, French vintage—like his own?

"It kills me my vampire husband has a problem with me eating bloody meat."

"That blood has no life in it. You know I must have mine hot and pulsing with life."

"You're going to make me puke. And I've already worshipped the porcelain throne this morning. I hate morning sickness."

"You could indulge in the occasional bite of *moi*?"

She waggled her brows. "You tempt me."

"Really?" Now this was fascinating. Creed pulled up a chair beside her.

Blu pushed her plate aside and ran her tongue over her teeth. "I've been thinking about it a lot. Hot blood. Hot blood direct from the vein."

"Is that so?"

She sighed and set down the fork. "You're going to freak if I say this, but I think I want to bite you. In fact, I think I *need* it." Catching her lower lip with her front teeth, she waited for his reaction.

"Oh hell, Blu. I..." He stood, but did not leave her side.

She grabbed his wrist and forced him to sit again. "I know the idea of me biting you turns you on."

"Hell yes. Yet at the same time, I'm angry with myself for giving you that craving in the first place. It's unnatural for a werewolf. Are you sure? You…crave blood? Beyond the stuff from that steak?"

"Maybe it's the babies?" She nuzzled aside his neck and licked the vein, setting him to instant readiness for whatever she had in mind. "All I know is I need it, Creed. I need your blood. Right now."

She'd been feeling the mutinous compulsion all morning. The craving for something dark and sweet that didn't come nestled in crinkled tissue cups in a box. Blood. It smelled so strong as she got up from the table and walked Creed backward against the counter. She hugged her body up against his, her belly making it difficult to achieve a close snug.

He slid his hands over her hips and down her derriere. "Are you sure, *mon amour*?"

"No. Yes. I don't know. The idea of drinking blood—it freaks me out."

"Thanks."

"Creed, come on. You know how hard this is for me."

"Then why did you bring it up?"

"Because. I might *need* it. For the kids, you know?"

She traced the vee of skin revealed between his crisp white shirt lapels. He wore a black velvet coat, which did things to her control. They'd survived the full moon last week by having sex—no shifting. But they hadn't had sex since due to silly things like her sore back, and she'd been sleeping at odd hours lately. But she wanted him now in a way that was going to surprise him, because it really surprised her.

She leaned in and whispered at his ear, "When was the last time you bit me?"

"Seems a while. Before you got pregnant. Do you want me to bite you? Maybe that's what you need instead."

His mouth slightly open, his fangs descended, and she could feel her husband's body grow rigid in anticipation. Drinking blood was the ultimate for him, and drinking *her* blood took him to a place she imagined was like where she went with orgasm, yet beyond, like some kind of nirvana. And yes, she could admit his fangs turned her on.

She breathed against his neck, delighting as his skin goose-bumped at the sensation. He stroked a palm up her thigh, lifting her dress to expose her derrière. Slipping his fingers under her panties, he cooed, "Ruffles? Christ, Blu, you make me so hard."

"That's my job." She wiggled her butt. "Keeping you hot and hard." A dash of her tongue stirred up a wanting moan from him. "You wanna bite?"

He breathed out heavily. And nodded.

Stroking a hand over his erection, she licked his neck, then met his eyes. Sliding a leg up along his thigh, she fitted herself to him, her belly not so round yet they didn't make a nice wolf/vamp sandwich. She tapped his fang, tracing its sleek length, which she knew gave him a similar thrill as if she were stroking his cock.

Kissing him, she drew his hand up over her breast and he squeezed, tweaking her nipple until she moaned and pressed harder against his touch. Her craving was more a feeling for sustenance, she thought—she'd hoped—and yet she wanted to do it this way. All sexy and needy. Blood alone felt wrong, dirty. Blood with sex? Something right about that.

Pressing a hard kiss along his jaw, she then lightly rubbed her lips over the stubble there, loving the roughness, the way it abraded her softness. Raking her fingers through his hair, she dove to his neck and willed down her canines, pressing them to his skin without breaking through. Dancing her tongue over his vein, she tasted his heat and his rapid heartbeat.

Her sexy Frenchman hissed and swore and gripped her ass, crushing her against his erection and rocking his hips against her body to get off.

Without a cautionary thought, she bit into his skin. Creed's growl hummed in his chest. It was, and it wasn't, a sexual noise; she'd hurt him. As his body slid down against the counter, she wrapped her legs about his waist, going with him. She sucked in the hot blood that initially tasted like nothing, and then it spread a metallic tang across her palate.

Heartbeats stuttering, Blu sucked vigorously, feeling her husband's body surge upward and his hips rock faster as she raced his pleasure to a climax. When he growled hoarsely in orgasm, she drew out her teeth from his skin, noted she'd torn large gashes, and then slipped away to sit beside him on the marble kitchen floor.

Head falling back against the glass cupboard doors, she closed her eyes and licked her lips. The blood did not offend, but it didn't taste particularly delicious either. On the other hand, it had fulfilled some crazy craving she seriously hoped had been initiated by her babies because any other reason was too wrong.

She'd done it. Taken blood from another being whose heart beat. Werewolves didn't do that. They had no need to do so.

"Blu." He clasped her hand and drew it to his chest, but she tugged away from the possessive grip. It felt intrusive now.

Bowing her head, she avoided his gaze. The last drops of blood trickled down her throat, tasting not so sweet.

Creed went on his knees and leaned over her. "Blu? What's wrong? I'm okay. It's already healing."

"It hurt though, didn't it?"

"Yes, but I'm a big boy. And man, the pleasure that followed. Look at me."

She twisted her head away from his attempt to turn her chin toward him. The *something right* feeling had fled. "Just leave me alone. Please?"

"Blu, what's… Are you…? Ashamed?"

Tucking her head against her knees, she nodded.

"It's all right, sweetie. I know it's not natural for your breed, but you're safe here with me. We trust one another. Hell, it's what I do all the time."

"Go away!" she cried. "I need to be alone. To…process this."

He heaved out an exhalation. She'd hurt him more than physically. But she couldn't look at him now. Not with the taste of his blood lingering in her mouth. "Fine." He stood and padded out of the kitchen. He called as he left, "I'm stopping by Alexandre's in the morning. I'll kiss you goodnight later?"

She nodded, but didn't reply.

Chapter Five

Sitting on the bed, browsing through the new maternity and childcare apps on her iPad, Blu looked up when a quiet knock sounded on the door. This morning Creed had discreetly crept from their bed. It was afternoon now, and she wasn't sure she was prepared to face him yet.

The blood had come between them. So stupid to have followed that feeling. Nothing in the manuals said anything about fetuses requiring fresh blood. Though she could argue that a vampire mother would infuse her unborn every time she drank blood.

The door opened and Creed popped his head in, followed by Bree's blond locks. "She stopped by," he said. He offered a guilty shrug and pulled the door closed behind Bree after she'd entered, leaving them alone.

"What are you doing here?" Setting aside the iPad, Blu patted the bed and her best friend climbed on beside her. .

"Creed called me earlier. He said you were feeling down and wondered if I would cheer you up."

"I hate that guy."

"What?"

"Oh, Bree. I hate him because he makes it so hard to be angry with him. I love him so much. And when we're not talking he knows exactly what to do by calling my best friend."

"So you two are fighting?"

"Kinda. Maybe. I don't know. Bree, last night I drank Creed's blood."

"Oh."

"I know. It was a weird craving. Rare steak wasn't doing it for me, so I thought maybe I needed the real thing straight from the vein. Tried to justify it by thinking the babies needed it. And you know he let me, because what vampire is going to turn down the chance to get bitten?"

"And you didn't like it?"

"That's the part that is freaking me out. I didn't like the taste of it, but I think I enjoyed it still. You know the whole sucking on him and rubbing our bodies against one another. In the moment, I could relate to what it was like for Creed when he takes blood."

"That's either good or very bad."

"I know, right? And then I made Creed feel like some kind of tick because I couldn't get beyond the wrongness of drinking blood. And I haven't talked to him since."

"You needed time alone to process."

"I did. Though I'm not sure where I'm at with it now. Do you think it's a pregnancy thing? I mean, Creed has only bitten me half a dozen times in the few years we've been married. I have not developed a blood hunger."

"It could be the babies. Look, don't worry about it too much. It's not like you're turning longtooth." Bree smoothed her palm over Blu's stomach. "I brought along a surprise. You want me to bless the babies?"

"Oh, yeah."

She dumped out her purse and told Blu to pull up her shirt to expose her belly. "You tell Creed about the bargain yet?"

"No."

Bree cast her a sideways glance.

"Soon."

"Like some time before the babies are born and some faery warrior comes to whisk one of them away from Creed's arms?"

"Yes, Bree, like—hell. Some time this week?"

"How about today?"

Blu winced and looked aside.

"I can't believe you're running away from this, Blu. You're always upfront about things. In your face and take me like I am. Fuck 'em if they don't like you."

"Turned up to eleven, as Creed says." Blu sighed.

"He'll understand."

"Do you think so?"

Bree laughed, and rubbed a tube of glittery substance between her palms. "Your husband loves you like crazy, Blu. Now, this is going to be drippy, so hold still. You make pregnancy look so sexy."

"Thanks, I needed that. I feel like a porpoise. Which is probably why I spend so much time in the pool. My skin itches, and my bones ache. I want to shift so desperately. You know, shifting is like therapy. A good shift realigns my whole body, tenders the aches and pains. It's a necessity."

Bree patted Blu's growing belly. "You're more than halfway through this, sweetie. You can do it for the kids."

"The kids." Blu sighed and lay back against the pile of pillows, staring up at the ceiling tiled with rococo plaster. "But they're not both mine. Bree, I'm the worst mother in the world and I haven't even given birth to my children yet. What have I done?"

"You will tell Creed about the deal, and he will support you."

"He might. He might not. I'm afraid of his reaction. Even

though we'll still get to keep a child, I don't want him to hate me for having the capability to actually give away one of his children. How awful am I?"

"You were desperate. Mothers ransom things of value all the time to conceive."

"Like what?"

"Like money. Mortals spend untold amounts trying to conceive."

"True. But I wasn't guaranteed to have twins. Though we did agree on children, so I knew I would have more than one. I should be thankful for this small mercy."

"Faeries don't do mercy, Blu."

"I know, and that's what worries me. Fuck, I can't do it. There's got to be a way around the deal."

"You don't want to mess with a faery bargain."

"I know, but Bree…" She sniffed tears.

"Oh, sweetie." Bree laid her head on Blu's shoulder. "I'll look into it. But I fear the only way to change the bargain is to offer something more valuable in exchange."

"What's more valuable than a child?"

"I have no idea."

An hour later Creed knocked and Blu cheerily called him into the bedroom. Bree was finishing the design on her belly, and both women nursed goblets of white wine.

"Come in," she repeated, sensing her husband's reluctance. "I'm feeling much better now. Not so cranky. Thank you for calling Bree. You always know the right thing to do."

"I was feeling badly for how things went last night, but we can discuss that later." He strode over to inspect Bree's handiwork. "Is that like the Indian mehndi designs Blu sometimes wears on her hands and feet?"

"Yes," Bree said, leaning back to let Creed inspect Blu's

rounded belly. "But it's infused with my dust." He veered away at that revelation. Vampires and faery dust did not mix without someone—namely, the one with the fangs—becoming addicted. "It'll dry and crinkle off by tonight, then it'll reveal a pretty, pale woad design beneath that'll last a month or so."

"Nice. The babies must love the attention from their mommy and their aunt."

"I get to be the aunt?" Bree asked.

"Of course." Blu squeezed her hand. "Godparents, too? Will you and Rev honor us with that?"

"Of course we will. Oh, I can't wait to tell Rev."

Blu shifted on the bed and pushed up to kiss Creed when she saw the kiss coming. But Bree's gasp stopped the twosome before their lips could touch.

Creed followed the faery's gaze to Blu's stomach. "What the—? It's all fallen away."

"What?" Blu inspected her stomach. The faery dust concoction, which had been thick and goopy, had dried and fallen away, leaving her skin clean. No trace of the woad design that should be left behind. "That's not supposed to happen."

"Blessed be, I think I should leave you two." Suddenly nervous, Bree shoved her things into her purse. "You know why that happened, Blu."

She met Creed's wondering eyes. Hell, the bargain must be repelling her friend's faery magic. It served as a warning that she had better be honest with her husband.

"What's going on?" Creed questioned as he followed Bree to the door. "Maybe it was a bad batch?" He turned and gave Blu a shrug. "I'll walk her out."

"Thanks." Blu slid off the bed and clasped her hands over her bare belly. At that moment she felt a tiny inner nudge behind her belly button, but sensed it had been an admonishing kick. "I'll tell him. Soon."

Chapter Six

The storage room was packed more with Blu's things than Creed's. Though the man had walked through many centuries, he'd kept very little in mementoes. Their Paris estate stored more of his valuable collectibles, which made sense, because he'd lived most of his life in Europe.

Blu wandered down an aisle and spied the small, brightly colored box she had come to find, partly because she'd wanted to avoid talking with Creed, and partly because right now she needed connection to something that could ground her. Winnie the Pooh danced around the box. He had been her favorite character when she'd been a pup. The memory of her mother reading about Pooh and Piglet's adventures didn't bring a tear to her eye. Instead, she smoothed a hand over her stomach and promised she would read the same to her children.

Child, she thought wistfully.

"You're going to love Tigger," she murmured as she pulled out the box and tucked it under an arm. She'd bring it into the study to look through. It was too cold to remain in this room.

The space behind the small box revealed the front of an

old leather steamer trunk she had not noticed before. Curious, Blu pushed aside some of her cardboard boxes of treasures to check out the old trunk. It belonged to Creed, surely. And there was no lock on the decorative iron flap.

The lid initially stuck, so she had to carefully jimmy it open to look inside. Must and mildew assaulted her nose. An old moth-eaten black cloak was laid over the top, and beneath, a top hat had been crushed, causing the silk to tear in the creases and decay over the years. A few books with ornate, gold-embossed cover designs lay inside, as well as an empty glass flask with an absinthe advertisement pasted on it.

A stack of photographs intrigued and she drew out a few. They were on tin or some kind of metal.

"A tintype?" she wondered, thinking that was what they had been called when photography had been invented in the nineteenth century, though she'd never been an A student in history. That was Creed's forte.

The first featured an image of a man she knew well, yet the label at the bottom cleared declared the bearded gentleman Edouard.

She stroked a finger over his face, which was still fine and handsome after all these years. If anyone was going to age in her marriage, she would develop wrinkles before Creed did. The thought depressed her, so she shoved it aside. He'd worn a beard back then? That gave her a chuckle.

"Edouard, you charmer," she muttered. "Edouard Credence Saint-Pierre."

He changed his first name between Edward and Creed every century or so. Necessity for a man who had lived so long as he. She preferred Creed, though there was nothing wrong with Edward, either.

"What's this?"

Another tintype featured Creed standing next to a woman.

The image was blurred, but it was clear he had his arm around the woman's shoulder with his other grasping across her stomach, very high, just under her breasts. A possessive hold. She had dark hair and a somber mouth. A black ribbon tracked about her neck and the dark Victorian clothing was a smudgy blur from waist down.

"An old girlfriend?"

She and Creed talked a lot at night, before and after making love. He'd told her stories from his past, of his adventures, and pointed out how history sometimes got things wrong. She could listen to his sexy French-accented voice until she fell asleep, which was often the case. He'd mentioned one or two women, but she suspected he'd had many lovers over the years. How could he not?

Tucking the tintypes carefully within the cape's delicate folds, she closed the lid, grabbed her Pooh box, and skittered out of the storage room. What she wouldn't give to be a time traveler who could journey backward to visit her husband at various times in his life. Wonder if faery magic could do that?

Idiot, she chastened as she wandered down the hallway. *Stay away from faeries and asking for boons, girlfriend.*

"Fine," she muttered. "I have learned my lesson."

But, lesson learned, she was gaining something amazing in return. All for the price of a great sacrifice.

Stopping at the open door to her husband's office, Blu spied him sitting behind the desk, and took a moment to breathe in deeply and put her mind in the right place. *Don't think about the sacrifice. Be strong.*

She strolled in, placing her box on the desk before him. "So, Eddie, how's tricks?"

"You're feeling rather feisty after Bree's visit."

She shrugged. "In a much better mood, for sure."

"I'm glad. Come here."

She slid onto his lap and kissed him soundly. "Mood swings, I think. The whole emotional gamut thing that comes with being pregnant is weirder than a pack of monkeys chasing the full moon."

"And nothing whatsoever to do with the fact you drank my blood?"

She sighed and tilted her head against his shoulder. "I was freaked. I'm over it now. Really, I am. For some reason I got uptight about the whole werewolves shouldn't drink blood thing. But you know? It didn't change me, and I think the babies needed it, so I'm cool with it. Probably won't do it a lot, but…"

"Yeah, your teeth are thick, and tend to tear."

"I hurt you?"

"Your canines weren't designed for a delicate bite."

She inspected his neck and found thick scars from her bite. They should have healed by now. Hmm… She wore scars at her neck, a mark of their bonding. Could his be the same? She kind of liked that. "Are these permanent?"

"I believe so. And I wear them proudly. But. Next time," he said, "maybe we'll let me cut a vein, yes?"

"Deal. If there is a next time. We'll let the kids decide that one. So, I was snooping in the storage room."

"I see that. You found something of yours?"

"And yours. Something in an old trunk that didn't have a lock on it."

"Which, in Blu-speak, translates to 'open me up and look inside.'"

She kissed him, dragging her nails down his neck, but not hard enough to break skin. "You don't mind."

"I never mind, and you know that. Kiss me again. You taste good."

She licked his lip and dashed her tongue inside his mouth.

He tasted like icy mint. She wanted to devour him. Dragging up her leg, she couldn't quite hook it as high along his hip as she normally could, and that spoiled the sexy moment. "Oops, babies."

"They're already keeping an eye on their parents," he said with a chuckle and turned her to straddle him and gave her the deep kiss she'd wanted. He gave her his full attention. His hands caressed her growing curves, his body rising to meet her, and his mouth, ever the master of her desires, explored her mouth with luxurious adoration.

"Mmm, cherries," he said. "That case I had shipped from California must have arrived?"

"This morning. I so needed fresh fruit, and in the winter it's impossible to get good stuff here in Minnesota. Anyway…" She tapped his mouth with her red-lacquered finger. "I found a picture of you and one of your old girlfriends. Did you seriously work a beard back then?"

"You saw that in a photo?" he asked.

"One of those old tintypes."

"Ah, a daguerreotype. Must have been during my Victorian phase. Beards were stylish."

"Also black clothes, which, I must say, you kinda got stuck in the black mood, eh?" She dusted the shoulder of his black shirt.

"If I was presented with putting together patterns or colors, you know how crazy I would look?"

"Like a fashion nightmare. Stick with the black, lover, and leave the color to me. So who was the chick?"

"I'm not sure. It's been so long. What did she look like?"

"Dark hair. Dark clothes. No smile. She had a ribbon around her neck."

"Ah, the telltale ribbon. That would be Dasha. She wasn't my girlfriend, more like a BFF."

"Eddie, you are so starting to pick up the lingo."

"One can hardly not when living with you."

"So Dasha and you were best buds? You were holding her like she belonged to you."

"I seem to recall it was more a hurried attempt to hold her still and keep her from giggling while we posed seriously for those interminable camera flashes. Are you jealous?"

"No. Yes. Well, she's dead right?"

He shrugged. "Not sure. But I've not spoken to her since that time."

"Wow. You and your paramours. Makes me wonder what your number is."

"My—seriously?" He stroked her lip and tapped it smartly. "You want to know the number of sex partners *I've* had?"

"I won't judge, lover boy. I know you've lived—"

"Almost a thousand years. I couldn't begin to guess at the number."

"Well, if you figure at least one partner per year." She propped her head on his shoulder. "And being the sexy looker you are, I imagine you had more than one a year."

"You imagine correctly."

"So we'll make it one or two a month."

"Could have been more," he added.

"Yeah, whatever. Factor in all those decadent orgies you attended in the eighteenth century."

"Quite a few, if I recall. And don't forget Marie Antoinette."

"Yes, the queen. You were such a celebrity hound. You're right. I don't want to do that math."

"Probably best you let it be."

Her husband had likely had sex with thousands. And the evidence of his skill was apparent every time they slid between the sheets, or when he pushed her up against the wall, or bent her over the back of the couch. As he'd done to so many previously?

Okay, she wasn't going to think about this anymore.

Sitting up on Creed's lap, Blu pulled the Pooh box before her and opened it. "I found this stuffed at the back of my mother's closet. It's the only thing of hers and mine I managed to rescue after her disappearance."

Her mom had disappeared when she was ten. She'd been told Persia had run off with a lover, but later, recently in fact, Blu had learned her father, Amandus, had murdered Persia in a jealous rage.

So her family wasn't exactly the Cleavers.

She drew out a tiny red dress dotted with white flowers and white bows at the hem. "This used to be mine. Can you believe I was that small?"

"I bet you were the cutest baby."

"I probably wore white tights and little red slippers with this number." She drew out a gray jumper that had a tail and a hood with ears. "My mouse costume! I wore this for my first Halloween. Don't you love the braided tail? I think Mom made this. She used to sew a lot of my things, and she'd hand-bead the gorgeous saris she used to wear."

"Are those your mother's saris that you wear now?"

She nodded, feeling a lump rise in her throat at her mother's memory. All she'd wanted after her marriage was a mom to talk to, someone whose shoulder she could lay her head on and get advice. She'd done fine without her, but she didn't ever want her children to grow up without a mother and a father.

But one would. All alone in a strange land called Faery.

"What's that?" Creed's voice brought her back to the present.

With a sigh, Blu pulled out the next item. It was a tiny

pink knit cap she must have worn home from the hospital. "A little skullcap. I was so kickin' in style, wasn't I? I think I should bedazzle this. Put a heart on it."

"Is that what you call it when you sparkle like mad?"

She did have a tendency to hit her closet with bedazzler in hand. Life was better when it sparkled.

Creed nuzzled his nose into her purple wig and his thumb stroked across her belly. Blu wondered if her parents had ever shared such intimate, loving moments, then couldn't imagine the cruel Amandus being so caring toward another living being. She wished her mother could have escaped his torture, and not through death.

Her lungs squeezed, and she sniffed a tear. Emotions rose and the horrors from her past crashed into the uncertainty of her future. "Oh, Creed!"

"What is it, lover? Blu, don't cry."

"I don't know if I can do this. Can I be a mother? I don't remember much about my mom. And my dad—he was such an asshole. I want to raise my child right. To protect it. To never allow it to fear. But I'm not sure. Is this right?" She met his dark gaze. "A werewolf and a vampire raising a family? That's so wrong, if you think about it."

"How can love be wrong?"

Tears spilled freely now and she tucked her head against his neck, breathing in his spicy masculine warmth. "It shouldn't be."

Her father would be horrified she was having a vampire's baby. Her mother? She would never know. But she so wanted her mother to know, to have her around to help her, to teach her how to raise a child. To approve of her actions, no matter how foolish or rash they had been.

"What if I'm a terrible mother?"

"You won't be."

"What if my child comes into this world with a craving for blood?"

"That won't happen until puberty. And what's wrong with the blood hunger? Wouldn't it be okay if they took after their father?"

"Yes, I'm sorry. You know I've no prejudice against vamps. I will love them no matter their breed. I'm…not in the right place lately."

"You're getting worked up, Blu. You've so much love to give, we'll need to raise a whole pack so you can spread it all around."

"But—"

"Shh…" He kissed her head and hugged her close. "The book was right about emotional mood swings," he said.

And Blu laughed, but didn't feel the humor as she cuddled into her husband's embrace.

If he knew what she had done, he wouldn't call her such a loving person. Now was not the time to confess her dark deed. How could a man like Creed forgive her that crime against his family? But when would it be right?

Chapter Seven

Two weeks later...

After her daily walk through the forest—she had to get out; her nature demanded it—Blu wobbled into the living room, where Creed sat listening to the strains of some symphony he'd probably once seen conducted by the original composer in a fabulous Parisian opera house. His eyes were closed, his bare feet resting on the end of the couch. She sat and placed his feet on her lap and began to massage them with some of the cocoa butter cream they kept on the coffee table. His feet were soft and she loved touching them, easing her fingers over the thick veins and the hard curves of his ankle bones.

He reached for the remote and turned down the music to a background noise. "You have the magic touch."

Easing her knuckles along the arch of his foot, she pressed his toes to her belly. "Feel that?"

"One of them is a real fighter," he said, opening his eyes and sitting up. "Or maybe both. My turn. Pull up your shirt." He dipped his fingers into the cocoa butter and smoothed them over her stomach. "Feel good?"

"You're so good to me, lover." She tilted her head back. The man had magic fingers that seemed to ease every ache she had, and the touch always restored her energy. It was dorky to think, but they really did complete one another. "How will we raise them?"

"What do you mean?"

"We won't know if they'll be werewolf or vampire—or both—until they reach puberty. So how will we raise them until that point?"

"There's much to think about." He gestured to the baby handbook sitting on the coffee table. "We need to start stocking up on diapers and blankets. And you should pick out things for the nursery."

"Bree is giving me a shower after the birth. I'll get plenty of loot then."

And then they would only have to buy half as much as Creed suspected now.

"I think we should raise them as both," Blu said. Nervous now, she felt compelled to confess, but wanted to work up to it slow and easy. "I'll teach our child—er, children—to run free and hone their natural instincts, while you can teach them patience and understanding. Of which you have a lot. And integrity and honor. That is you to the core."

"You will teach them to enjoy life and always see the glass half full."

"You can teach them some incredible history."

"You'll make sure they know all the best music and social networking."

"I want a boy."

"Really? I would guess a woman would desire a girl. Especially a girlie woman like you, who loves to play dress-up. I won't have you dressing our boy in wild outfits."

"Don't worry. But I want a boy and I want him to be wolf, to carry on the Masterson line."

Creed nodded. "I see."

"We could have two boys. One of each," she suggested, but didn't want to say any more than that. It was hard enough not to say *child* when she was supposed to say *children*.

"I will be happy with either," Creed offered, bending to kiss her belly. "A little Saint-Pierre running underfoot. I don't need a child to carry on my name. That feels selfish. You know why I really want children?"

"Tell me."

"I have lived nearly one thousand years. And in that millennium, I don't think I've ever known innocence." She stroked his cheek and he bowed his head to her shoulder. "I want to experience the world through the eyes of a child. I want my child to ask me, 'Daddy, why is the sky blue?' And then I'll have to wonder, 'Why *is* the sky blue?' Can you imagine?"

"I can. I can't wait for you to learn new things about the world through our child."

Blu sighed. She had used the singular again. Maybe it wouldn't be so difficult to reveal her sin to him. A necessary sin, she tried to convince herself. But would the child taken to Faery believe as much?

"I'm ready to get down on my hands and knees and play with blocks and in the sandbox," he said. "Which reminds me, I want to put a sandbox out in the yard."

"And swings."

"And slides and go-carts. Everything. Ah, I should have done that before the snow fell."

"You'll have time in the spring before the little one starts toddling about."

She closed her eyes, imagining chasing after a cooing, toddling child, but her thoughts averted to the very near future. Blu had gotten to know Lyric Santiago during their summer stays in Paris. Lyric was married to Vaillant, a vampire who, two days after his birth, had been taken from his parents, Rhys and Viviane Hawkes, by a sidhe to Faery in order to repay a bargain his father had made centuries earlier. The fact that Rhys Hawkes hadn't been Vail's blood father meant nothing at the time, because no one had been the wiser. Suffice it to say, Vail hadn't returned to the mortal realm until decades later, and he'd been more than a little fucked up and pissed at his parents for giving him away.

Blu needed confirmation that what she had done was right. Hell, who was she kidding? It would never be right. But could it be reasoned she'd had to sacrifice one to save the other?

You had no idea you would have twins.

And she couldn't keep the secret from Creed any longer and feel like she wasn't betraying him. She needed his support.

She needed him.

Creed curled up beside her, head on her shoulder, and hand on her belly. She liked this maternal feeling of carrying life, of carrying on a family line, both hers and Creed's. She was bringing life to this world.

And to the Faery realm.

"I have to tell you something," she whispered. "It's a confession. Something I should have told you months ago."

"You can tell me anything, Blu. Is it difficult doing daily things? You've become so round. I'm sure you're tired all the time. You need to rest more."

"It's not that. Nearly seven months and I look like I'm ready to burst, but surprisingly, I have a lot of energy. You give me that energy. What I need to tell you is…" She huffed out her breath and Creed sat up, turning to face her.

"Whatever it is, you know you can tell me. We can work through anything, yes?"

"Have you ever wondered how I was able to get pregnant?"

Creed opened his mouth, but did not respond. He looked aside. Surely he had figured it out?

"I called a faery to this realm to ask for a boon." She spread a hand over her belly. "The boon of carrying a vampire's child."

He put his hand over hers, and their fingers clasped above a tiny kick.

Blu decided one of her children was giving her the kick because it was about damn time she told Daddy her deed. "You must have suspected?"

"Well, of course, that is how it was able to happen. There was no other way you could have possibly conceived my child—children."

"Creed." Heart pulsing so quickly she thought it would beat the rabbit, Blu spoke quickly, "I had to offer a return boon, and agreed to give the faery my firstborn child."

The room stilled. The orchestral whispers in the background faded. Creed stood, looking down upon her, his expression unreadable. So handsome, his dark European features never failed to make her heart go pitter-patter. But now she was frightened he might react by lashing out. He'd never harmed her. But memories of her past, of being beaten and used by the pack, never left completely.

Wanting to get up, to face him—because she never backed down from anything, most especially the problems she had created—Blu struggled to lift her cumbersome weight, then gave up.

"I'm sorry, Creed. I thought it was something I could handle at the time. The faery said it was a boon so I could carry your child, and/or children, so I knew we could have more."

"You gave up our firstborn?" he said, his tone unreadable. Was he angry? Surprised? Horrified?

All of the above, surely. And it was all her fault. She'd hurt him. She'd inflicted a wound upon their growing family that was only beginning to sink in now.

Blu nodded. Winced. "But everything is going to be okay. I've got two babies in here. Much as I cannot fathom giving one away, we'll still have the other."

Creed tilted back his head. His fists clenched at his sides. Not a pose she saw often. Her werewolf senses, heightened with pregnancy, picked up an acrid anger from his pores—or not. She didn't know how to place him right now.

"Creed, please talk to me. What are you thinking?"

"I need some air." And he dashed away, out the patio doors.

Mouth agape, Blu caught her head in her hands. "I've fucked things up. He hates me. Why did I do this?"

She smoothed a hand over her belly.

"I'm so sorry," she said to her unborn children. "I wanted you so desperately, I had to sacrifice one of you."

Snowflakes blanketing the ground, Creed kicked the fence gate, and charged through it and toward the back of the property. He slammed it behind him, and heard the latch snap off smartly.

What the hell had she done?

He let out an enraged burst, and then thought to himself. *What the hell have I done?*

It was midnight when Blu heard Creed wander into the bedroom and make a beeline for the shower. She sat in bed, e-reader propped on her belly.

Behind the bathroom door the shower stream clattered against the marble tiles. He hadn't spoken a word to her since her confession earlier. Rarely—hell, *never*—did they go to bed angry with one another (save for the night she had drank his blood). They always talked things out, and generally followed with delicious makeup sex.

She wasn't much for full-on sex, being as big as she was right now, but she craved his reassuring touch.

"He won't touch me," she whispered. "I've given away one of his children as if bundle of blankets to a homeless shelter."

The shower stopped and Blu contemplated turning off the light and rolling over to fake sleep. She was no coward, though, and she wanted to talk about this. They needed to talk before she gave birth and all Hell broke lose. Make that Faery.

"I can't do this alone." Tears streamed down her cheeks. She clasped her hands over her belly. "I won't. If I have to battle all of Faery, I won't let them take my child."

Creed wandered into the bedroom, a towel about his hips, and steam drifting from his gorgeous, tight muscles. Blu licked her lips even as she wiped away the tears. She would never tire of that view. An erection bobbed beneath the towel. The fact he was turned on by her now was heartening.

"Want me to take care of that?" she asked lightly as he slipped off the towel and slid into bed. "I've got some mad jack-off skills, as you well know."

He kissed her, lingering on her mouth, nuzzling his nose against hers, and for a moment she believed he had forgiven her. "It's impossible not to be turned on by you, bright one." He smoothed a palm over her stomach. "And to see you round with my children is an even bigger turn-on."

"Seriously? You go in for fat chicks?"

"You're not fat, Blu. You're abundant with life."

He had such a way of putting things, she was constantly reminded why she had fallen in love with the enemy.

"I'm sorry about charging out on you earlier," he said. "That was wrong. I needed some time to think."

"We've both been in the mood for contemplation lately. What's happening to us, Creed?"

He sat facing her, and she wanted more than anything to pull him down to nestle his head against her belly, but she would let him play this one.

"Can you forgive me?" she asked, hating the wobble in her voice.

He kissed her belly. "There's nothing to forgive. Had you not made the boon this wouldn't have been possible. But Blu, I have a confession as well."

"You don't have to be pleased with me, Creed. You can hate me for this. Hell, if you want a divorce—"

He shook his head vehemently. "Don't say things like that. Not ever. I love you , Blu. Good and bad. Thick and thin. Blood, howls and talons. I would never hate you for any of your actions. Don't you know me better than that?"

She shrugged. "Then what's your confession, my vampire husband?"

He clasped her hands in his, and didn't speak right away. It was hard for him, and that troubled her. What dire news was he about to unleash upon her?

"I, too, called a faery to this realm and asked for the boon you might carry my child."

"You did? When? How did you…?"

"I suspect it was on that same night you said you were going for a run under the full moon, and stayed out until the morning. You usually come in before the sun rises, so it was out of character for you."

"That was the night. Sorry to lie to you."

"Don't apologize, Blu. I kept a secret from you as well. I got a spell from Rhys Hawkes, who has access to some faery magic thanks to his business, and the faery agreed to grant me the boon."

"So we had double the power going into this. Go, Creed! Oh." Her breath hushed out. No boon was ever given without a return boon. Now she understood his reluctance and his inability to look at her right now. "Our firstborn?" she tried.

Creed swallowed and bowed his head, and shook it slowly.

"What then? What more could a faery want?"

"I thought it a wise deal at the time. That perhaps it would be a bargain I might never have to make good on. But now it's become the worst thing I can imagine." He met her gaze with watery dark eyes. All his one thousand years seemed to crease upon his face and sadden his soul. "Blu, I promised the faery our second born."

Chapter Eight

His confession out there in the air between them, Creed bowed his head to his wife's belly. She stroked his hair, but he sensed it was an absent gesture for he had taken the breath from her, and neither of them spoke. He'd always enjoyed their shared silences. Now, the quiet felt like a stake to the heart.

They had, each of them separately, promised the faery a child. Neither could have known the consequences. Both must have been relieved to learn Blu carried twins; their hearts would not be completely broken, because one baby would be left in their arms.

Not so.

Why had he not promised the first? Because he'd thought it much better to promise the second. Perhaps then they would only have one child, and never have to face repaying such an unspeakable price.

"What have we done?" Blu's voice shook. "Oh, Creed, both our babies?"

"Blu, I'm so sorry. I had no idea you had also made a promise. Hell, I had thought it my boon that had allowed you to conceive. But I won't let the faery take them both. She can't. I'll do what I can. I'll give myself for the babies."

"No, Creed, don't say that." She bracketed his face with her warm, slender hands. Too fragile, even in her abundance. "I need you. You have to stay here with me, no matter what happens. Promise you won't do something stupid like give away your soul, or even your life? Promise me!"

He nodded. "I promise. I vow it to you." And he took vows seriously. A man was nothing without his word.

He couldn't fathom being away from Blu. To lose a child he did not yet know would be, not easier, but perhaps less devastating. Already, though, he loved both children.

He swept a hand over his wife's belly and she joined him. Blu must see her family line carried on. And he, how would he ever learn innocence if he did not have a child to teach him?

"This one is the fighter," she said, sniffing at tears. Beneath their clasped hands a tiny fist or heel nudged up her belly. "The other is quiet. She's kind of dark."

"She is?" It was the first time he'd heard her label them as boy or girl, beyond fantasizing about it.

"I know she's a girl. My sweet, quiet one. I've been thinking about names lately, but now…"

He clasped her head and kissed her fiercely, wanting to erase all the bad and make it all good. They had committed a grave sin against their unborn children, but now, more than ever, they needed to stand together, to face this as one.

"Tell me?" he asked. "Let's talk about names."

"Like nothing else matters? Like we didn't give away our children?"

He nodded and winced. "Please?"

"Yes, we need to be positive. For the children." Releasing a heavy sigh, she clasped his hand. "I like the name Kambriel for a girl. Kam for short. It's dark yet regal. Girlie, too."

"I like it. And if the other is a boy may I name him?"

"Of course. Do you have a name in mind?"

He hadn't, but now he'd been asked, the obvious choice jumped into his brain. "My father's name was Malakai."

"I love that name. Kam and Kai?"

"Strong, vibrant names."

"Creed, we've got to keep our children. We need to call that faery back and do something. I'll die if I have to give them away. They're mine. Ours."

"I agree." He spread his hands possessively over her belly. "We've been foolish for the sake of our greatest desire. But there's no reason we must be punished so harshly for wanting a family."

"Maybe she'll agree to take one? Was it the same faery?"

"I don't know. She was tall and thin, yet dark, and she had markings on her face. I didn't get a name."

"Neither did I. Creed, if it was the same faery, we might be able to deal with her, but if it was two different faeries…"

"Don't think about it, Blu. Your emotions transfer to the children. We mustn't allow this dire ordeal to affect them."

"I've tried to keep my chin up. Now that I've finally told you I feel as if a weight has been lifted. But, oh…now it's been replaced by a more crushing weight. Creed?"

They held each other's gazes, desperation joining them in a wicked bond. They had betrayed their children, and one another. And yet, love had motivated their selfishness.

"Let me talk to Rhys Hawkes about this," he said.

"Or Bree, she might know more than Hawkes."

"Yes, but Rhys's nephew is Vaillant."

"The vampire who was taken to Faery as a baby. Oh, Creed, we've got to be smart about this. But we don't have much time. A few more weeks, at the most."

He kissed her belly and rested his head there, where a tiny heartbeat called to him. His future son or daughter. He would not suffer the faery to take either from him now. If it brought a war to his doorstep, he would stand and defend his own.

Two days later, Vaillant greeted Creed with a buss to both his cheeks. Frenchmen, Blu thought, as she observed from the doorway. How she loved them.

The sexy vampire with a rock 'n' roll vibe walked over and kissed each of her cheeks, then stood back to look at her. "You've got the glow," Vail remarked. "Gorgeous. How many months?"

"Seven." She rubbed her belly. "I could go any week now. Good to see you again, Vail. How's Lyric?"

"She sends her love and said you're supposed to Skype her later. She wants to stare at your belly."

"Will do."

Vail chuckled. "I think she's ready for another one herself."

"Thank you for stopping by on such short notice," Creed said as he led them into the living room, where Blu plopped onto the couch and put up her feet. "I appreciate your willingness to help us with our situation."

"I was in the area with my brother Trystan—he's here for a snowboarding competition up north—so it was easy enough to stop by." Vail raked his fingers through his short dark hair, causing the silver chain bracelets at his wrist to clank together. "Sounds like you two have made a deal with the devil."

"More like faeries," Blu muttered.

"Even worse," Vail said.

He paced before the coffee table, one hand hooked at his hip and pushing aside his black suit coat to reveal a silver-threaded black silk shirt. The silver studding his boots glinted, and Blu knew exactly what it was about the man that had attracted Lyric. Pure, unadulterated sex appeal.

"So, you each, on separate occasions, promised one of your children to some nameless faery?" Vail asked.

Creed sat next to Blu and took her hand. "Right. Blu promised our firstborn. I promised our second born. It was a foolish bargain, and now we want to know if there's any way we can renegotiate the deal."

"Was it made with the same faery?" Vail asked.

"Not sure." Blu sighed. "Why would the same faery make such a cruel deal with the two of us?"

"Why not? Faeries are malicious and cold," Vail said. "If given a choice, I'd much rather deal with the devil Himself."

"Is there anything we can do?" Creed sat forward. "I entirely expect we should honor the agreement and give up one child. But both? That is asking far too much."

"I couldn't imagine giving away my child," Vail said, his gaze drifting over their heads. He and Lyric had had their first child a year ago.

"How is Johnny?" Blu asked.

"Oh, he's a little booger. And I mean that literally. Who'd've thought kids had so much drippy, runny stuff inside them? And always scampering about and shouting at the top of his lungs. He's started walking, but it's not really a walk, rather a full-on run. I love the guy. I would kill to keep him safe."

"Is that what's required?" Creed suddenly asked. "Do you think the sidhe would accept a sacrifice?"

"Creed."

He glanced at her, but the hurt Blu saw on his face stifled her concern. He was a man who would protect his own, as Vail had stated. Creed had once been a battle warrior, who'd swung his sword to slay werewolves without a blink or a stab to his conscience.

"Sacrifices are looked upon with favor," Vail said, "but

they are not so valuable to the sidhe as a half-breed child. This much I do know."

And Vail did know, since he'd been taken to Faery when he was two days old. The faery had taken him as payment, fully expecting he would be a half-breed vampire/werewolf. Except he hadn't been. His real father's identity hadn't been known at the time of his birth to Rhys and Viviane Hawkes. Vail was a blood-born vampire, but only at puberty was that discovered. Vail had suffered in Faery because of this mistake—Lyric had told Blu—and as an adult he'd returned to the mortal realm an addict. Even now, he had to avoid faeries because one hit of dust would plummet him to some unspeakably dark depths of depravity.

"We're idiots," Blu said. "But surely, if we could speak to someone high up, someone in charge, and explain the deal that was made, they would make adjustments?"

"Someone in charge?" Vail chuckled. "Ch'yeah. No one is in charge of Faery. Though if you knew if you had dealt with Seelie or Unseelie, that could help."

"Unseelie," Blu and Creed said at the same time. They looked to one another.

"I don't know why," Blu said, "I just feel it."

"Me too," Creed agreed. "She had three blue markings on her face, slashed from brow to cheek."

"Yes," Blu agreed, "I think it was the same one. I was thinking she was a warrior or champion because of the crystal blade she wore at her hip."

"Sounds like Unseelie, and you may be right about her being a champion," Vail said. "Crystal blades are rare. My guess? Ooghna."

"You know her?" Creed asked.

"No, but I know of her. She's vicious and cold. Unwavering in battle. Why she would want a child is beyond me, but then, a half breed can be traded in Faery for a great price, or raised and trained."

"Trained?" Feeling a queasiness rise in her throat, Blu swallowed.

"Ooghna is Malrick's champion," Vail said, wandering to the patio doors and shoving his hands in his coat pockets. "He's the Unseelie king. You could appeal to him. Not sure it would do any good."

"We'll do anything." Creed stood. "How do we contact him?"

"You don't. He already knows," Vail explained. "And if he's curious, you'll speak to him soon enough. That's about all I can do to help you two. I'm sorry."

"No, you've helped," Creed assured. "Names are good."

"Yeah, well, be careful with that. You don't want to call upon something that you will regret."

Blu and Creed met gazes.

"Er, right." Vail clapped his hands in the tense silence. "I gotta run. My flight takes off in a few hours. Heading home to Lyric and Johnny."

With a firm tug, Creed helped Blu to stand and she caught Vail in a hug. "Thank you. Give this to Lyric when you see her." She hugged him again, then tweaked his cheek. "And give that to Johnny. I wish we could have summered in Paris, but with my big belly, it was out of the question. I do plan to visit in the spring."

"You'll bring your baby along then," Vail said.

"I hope so," she whispered, then caught a tear against her palm, and had to turn away from him so he couldn't see her heartache.

Blu watched as Creed sank into the pool next to her and stretched out his arms along the tiled edge. For as much as she'd once hated to swim, she'd spent a lot of time in the pool lately. She enjoyed the sense of weightlessness and felt the babies liked the water also. At least someone was happy.

Her husband stroked her cheek. It felt too tender. And she felt too…much.

"What's wrong?" he asked quietly. "I'll find a way to contact the Unseelie king. Promise."

"I know you will." She glanced skyward. "Full moon tonight."

"Ah."

"Creed, I need to shift. It's been months. I need to run, to go hunting. To get all furred up!"

"You've done well resisting the shift. This will be the last month for sure, Blu. You can do it. And you know I'm here to help. Let's make love."

She snorted and swished her hands through the water, sending out waves. "Right. I feel so desirable lately. Not. Hell, I look like a freakin' whale."

"Yes, well, I've fucked a werewolf. I guess tonight I'll have a go at a whale, eh?"

She speared him with a hard glare. "That was not funny."

"So it wasn't." He edged away from her and she felt his chagrin.

"Sorry. I'm so ready to have these babies. And yet…" Sighing, she floated over to him and buried her face against his neck above water level. "I'd hold them inside me forever if that meant I could keep them both. I can't do this, Creed."

"Whatever you have to *do*, we'll do it together. I intend to call out the faery king. There must be a bargain we can agree to."

"I don't want your sacrifice. We've already sacrificed so much. And for what? For selfish greed. We wanted a baby so desperately we were willing to give another away? How terrible is that?"

"Stop beating yourself up about this, Blu. And me. Do you think I don't feel the weight of our mistake?" His chest heaved and she heard him sniff. She'd never seen him cry, and he wasn't now, but it was the closest he'd ever been to showing such raw emotion. "I will make it right."

"I know you will," she whispered, believing, if only for the moment, that he would. "Make love to me so this itchy urge to shift will leave."

He bent to kiss her, and she drew him forward, floating until her shoulder nudged the first underwater step. "You sure about this union between a vampire and a whale?" she asked, forcing a smile.

"You are the most beautiful sea creature I have ever laid eyes upon."

He slipped down her bikini top and her breasts became two islands in the water, her nipples cooling in the night air. He pressed kisses to each one, gently, not rough or hurried as his kisses could sometimes be. Reassuring almost. Claiming. Sweet.

With one of Creed's arms under her back to anchor her to him, Blu closed her eyes and spread out her arms, floating. His mouth felt so soft, at times she couldn't determine if it was his kiss or the slap of the water with his movement. This quiet touch was what she needed when she knew the frenzied energy of their normal moonlight sexcapades would never be comfortable with her larger shape.

He placed soft kisses over her belly, which seemed a vast island in the ocean. She had marveled how her skin could stretch to encompass the lives within, and worried about stretch marks, but hadn't seen any yet. She could probably attribute this to Creed's cocoa butter massages. And hell, maybe the fact that she normally shifted her human skin to wolf fur had something to do with it as well.

She was ready to release this burden. And yet she'd meant it when she said she'd carry the babies forever if only to keep them with her.

She noticed the kisses had stopped and opened her eyes to see Creed holding her gaze. He tilted his head. "Stop thinking," he said. "Slip into that good, sexy space you go to when we make love. Can you do that?"

"I can. I will. I want you inside me, slow and gentle."

"I was just getting to that." He kissed her hip and tilted her body away from him so her elbows landed on the step and her body floated stomach down. He slipped down her bikini bottom and slid inside her. "This is nice. Whale breaching in the moonlight."

"Oh, you creep!"

He chuckled, yet held her secure across the belly as his rhythm inside her kept a slow and languorous pace. "Just kidding."

"You had better be. I can flick out a few claws if I feel the urge."

"I like it when you mark me," he said, laying his cheek against her spine where the tribal tattoo darkened her skin. "If I didn't have the ability to heal so well, I would be a walking canvas of your love scars."

"They are given with love," she said. "As we wear each other's bite marks with pride."

"Mmm, don't mention biting, or I might need a nip."

"I can dig it."

He moved his hand down over her belly and found her clitoris. The briefest skim of his finger set her core to a delicious clench. Being pregnant was awesome for her senses; everything was heightened, fine-tuned to catch the slightest touches, whispers, scents. She wondered if the babies could feel her orgasms, and then…let go, hoping her children would feel her pleasure and know it was their mother and father, hugging them.

The orgasm was soft, yet lingered, vibrating through her body, squeezing, shuddering her in the water against her husband's sure, strong frame. Eyes closed, her face bobbed in and out of the water. "Oh yeah." She slid her hand through his moist hair, drawing him forward until he lashed his tongue against her neck. The intrusion of his teeth gave her another orgasm.

Chapter Nine

Creed wrapped Blu's black wool coat about her shoulders and helped to button up the front over her belly where she couldn't reach. He tugged her wool cap over a spill of black hair and kissed her forehead. "Don't go too far."

"I always make a round or two of the property," she said. "Don't worry. It's daylight. The snow is coming down softly. You know how much I love the big flakes that look like goose down. I'll be back in an hour. Besides, maybe if I jog I'll loosen up the kids, eh?"

"No jogging," he admonished. "Take it easy."

"Spoilsport."

"Whale," he shot back.

"Longtooth."

"Oh, is it like that then?"

"Bring it," she said, then couldn't fight the grin any longer. "Sorry, lover. I didn't mean that. I'm going to blame that one on mood swings."

He kissed her mouth and tugged the fake fur lapels up close underneath her jaw. "I will serve you fitting punishment when you return."

Dashing her tongue in a sexy swish across her lips, she said, "I think I'm going to make this a quick walk. Love you."

And she waddled out through his office door and through the side fence. The world offered up a winter wonderland. No wolf would refuse this gorgeous day.

Creed watched Blu until she disappeared through the copse of birch behind the house. He wanted to rush out and walk alongside her to protect her, but she'd made it clear months ago she needed the time alone to walk. If she could not shift, she needed to commune with nature in some manner that was beyond his ken. She felt the trees and earth and air differently than he did. It was a wolf thing.

Well enough. He had plans.

Grabbing the battle sword Wolfsbane from his office wall, he stepped out into the backyard. Not far from his office door grew a massive willow tree that one could walk under and look up to admire the umbrella of sinewy branches falling toward the ground. It was coated with frost this morning and glittered in the pale winter sun.

Swinging the sword with both hands, he scythed the blade through the air while his thoughts called beyond this realm to Faery. Though he was using the same chant he'd gotten from Rhys Hawkes, he had no idea if his beckon would be effective now. But he had to try. He probably shouldn't greet any possible visitors with a sword in hand, but he didn't want to take chances.

Besides, he'd once solved all of his problems with the swing of this sword. Old habits died hard.

A gush of wind swept through the air, crushing the willow limbs and spilling frost crystals to the ground in a hail of glitter. Or…no. That sparkle was not because of the frost.

Creed stepped forward, his boots crunching against the snowy ground. He paused before the great tree, for within, near the trunk, materialized a man whose dark eyes formed before the rest of his body fluidly took shape. Hair pulled tightly from his narrow face revealed angled cheekbones and a severe brow. His body was lean and tight, and he shook his shoulders, which unfurled great, sweeping silver wings.

Shirtless and wearing little more than breeches, his exposed skin glistened with markings, ancient and powerful with Faery magic. Some faeries could work magic by touching the symbols. Wolfsbane would prove no match.

"Malrick?" Creed wondered. "King of the Unseelie?"

"Lord Edouard Credence Saint-Pierre. Battle warrior, bounty hunter, enslaver of witches. Well met."

"Well met." Creed bowed. "But your intel is ancient. I'm now husband, former tribe leader and father-to-be."

"Says the vampire holding the menacing sword."

"I, uh…" Okay, so it had been a bad call. But he was not a man to face a powerful foe unarmed. "I'm pleased you've answered my summons."

"I answered nothing. I do not come at your beckon, but merely wish to ensure this ridiculous quest you seek is set aside."

"I realize, my lord, my wife and I ask a great favor, and I've no intention of disregarding the bargain I have made, or the bargain my wife made. But we refuse to honor both bargains. We will not hand over both our children to Faery."

With a twitch of Malrick's finger, the frost on the branches crackled free from the limbs and swiftly swirled toward Creed. The ice crystals cut through his cheeks and forehead when he wasn't quick enough to block the attack. But he would not charge his opponent. This was but a show of power. And he respected the Faery king, because not to was unwise.

"I grant forgiveness for your outburst," Malrick said, wandering closer and parting the willow branches with but a breath.

Creed licked at the blood dotting his lip. "I don't ask your forgiveness, but rather, your understanding. Are you not a father?"

"I am. To many hundreds."

Whew. The guy had been at it for some time. "Could you fathom having to sacrifice one, let alone two of your children?"

"I could not. Yet I would never make such a hideous bargain. Apparently you and your wife have the lack of morals to do so. And now you've the audacity to beg for lenience? When once I would have stood beside you in battle, Saint-Pierre, I now look upon you with disdain."

Creed was startled by that revelation. He straightened his shoulders and lifted his sword to inspect it, then stabbed the tip into the snow, releasing the hilt. "I wish no war, only love."

"You've become soft. I do not admire you for that."

"It happens when a man learns to love. Of that, I know you can never relate." The sidhe could not love, or so he'd been told. "The love for a child, whether born or still gestating, is unfathomable. I was foolish to make the bargain, as was my wife. But had we not, we would have never the opportunity to know the joy of family."

"Faery has granted you a great boon, and in turn you sneer at me and make even more demands?"

"Just one," Creed said confidently. Every sinew of him wanted to lunge forward and rip the bastard's heart out, but it would serve him no purpose, and would further malign his standing with Faery. He gripped his hands in fists to keep from grabbing the sword. "That is all I ask. Let us keep one child."

"You know we favor half breeds."

"I do. But you've no promise either of our children will be so. They may be full-blood vampire or completely werewolf."

"Unlikely."

"But not impossible."

Malrick tilted his head. "Perhaps I might extend the handing over of your children until they reach puberty? If it is proven then one or the other are not half breeds, I will revisit your request then."

Creed's breaths quickened, but too soon, he cautioned himself against making another foolish bargain. The wait would only prolong the agony, and allow him and Blu to become more attached to their children. It would tear out his heart should he be forced to give up an adolescent child he and Blu had nurtured for years.

He shook his head. "Is there anything else? Some sacrifice or gift I might offer?"

"You think me cruel? I am not, only fair and abiding of the bargains made with my champion, Ooghna."

"I am aware of that. You must stand by your champion, despite her malicious trickery."

Malrick's eyes glinted. No faery minded being accused of trickery.

"If we could have another child..." Creed began.

Suddenly a wolf howl echoed across the back field. He recognized the howl as Blu's. But closely following the howl, a gunshot echoed across the snowy sky.

"No." Creed gripped the battle sword and dashed toward the fence. "Blu!"

He found them at the edge of Saint-Pierre property, where a creek intersected it from Schmidt's field. The old farmer knelt over a dark form. Creed smelled the blood and quickened his pace through the thick, loose snow, plunging to his wife's side. Seeing the blood at her shoulder, he shoved away the farmer and swore at him.

Schmidt veered from the sword Creed still clutched. "Watch it!"

Tossing Wolfsbane aside, Creed bent over Blu, whose eyelids fluttered. She clutched her belly and moaned.

"I didn't know it was her," the farmer claimed. "I heard the howl and saw the black fur…but it was her hair and that coat!"

The persuasion he'd used on Schmidt must have worn off. That it had lasted for months was remarkable. Damn!

"You idiot! You could have killed her and my unborn children."

"Coming…" Blu managed. A drop of blood spotted her lip. "Now!"

"What?" Creed ripped aside the coat from her shoulder to inspect the wound. For all the blood staining the snow, it looked like just an abrasion. "What's coming?"

"The babies!" A guttural groan preceded her clenching scream. "It doesn't feel right, Creed. It hurts so bad!"

Creed grabbed the farmer by the collar—beyond him he spied Malrick, walking the property line, the Faery king's head down yet his glowing violet eyes on the scene. He blended with the white snow and his wings were tucked out of sight.

"Call an ambulance!" Creed commanded the farmer. "No! Wait." An ambulance would take Blu to a human hospital. The midwife had arranged for them to deliver at a clinic dedicated to the paranormal breeds. "You're going to drive us to town. We go to a private clinic."

"Yes. I can do that." The farmer dashed off. "Hurry up, Saint-Pierre!"

Creed lifted Blu into his arms, and she cried out and clutched her stomach. Her legs were wet. Her water must have broken.

"Hurry," she gasped. "It's piercing, the pain. I don't think it's right." She gasped, then her head dropped back over his arm, and she passed out.

Chapter Ten

Blu reached for Creed's hand. She'd never been so frightened. Yet never had she felt so reassured simply by holding her husband's hand. Safe in his arms, no matter what the world threw her way.

After four brutal hours of labor, the midwife had performed a sonogram and announced a C-section was necessary. The doctor had arrived and was scrubbing up.

"Why the surgery?" Creed asked as they entered the OR.

The midwife handed Creed a set of teal scrubs. "The babies' umbilical cords are wrapped around each other's necks. They are..." She glanced to Blu, who winced and squeezed Creed's hand hard to counteract the pain. "...literally strangling one another. The doctor is waiting. You can stay in the room, Mr. Saint-Pierre."

"You'll have a time getting me to leave." He winked at Blu and gestured he was going to scrub up.

"Hurry!" she cried as the warm reassurance of his hand left hers.

The doctor explained they were giving her a spinal block.

She would be conscious during the surgery, but would not feel anything. "How you holding up, Mommy?"

She smiled weakly at the motherly title. Tears spilled over her cheeks. Her babies were coming into the world, mad at one another, each trying to end the other's life by strangulation. Was it because they somehow knew their fate?

"Still here," she managed to say. "Where's Creed?"

Her husband's breath hushed near her ear. A warm kiss melted against her eyelid. "I'm back. You're doing great, Blu. It'll all be over soon."

Yes. Soon enough her belly would be empty. As would her arms, when the babies were taken to Faery.

"Just—help me get through this," she cried.

"We're in," the doctor announced, and Blu realized she had felt but tugs in her stomach region. "Both babies look great. Suzanne, help me here."

"Can you see them?" she asked Creed. "Tell me. I need to know everything." Yes, grasp the few precious details she could, before she would never again have them in her life.

"The doctor is lifting them from your stomach," he said. "I see some toes…"

"They're out," the doctor said. "A boy and a girl!"

"Oh, Creed." After the adrenaline coursing like mad over the past hours, the announcement of their sexes worked like a soothing hot towel placed over Blu's body. Her muscles relaxed and she looked up into her husband's eyes. "Go look at them. Tell me what they look like." When he squeezed her hand, she gave him a nudge and he moved down beside the doctor.

"They're purple," he said in amazement.

"Lack of oxygen," the doctor explained. "We'll need to put them under lights for a few minutes to get their body temperatures where we need them. Would you like to cut the cords, Mr. Saint-Pierre?"

"Of course." He cast a beaming smile over his shoulder at Blu.

Lips trembling, she returned his smile, then closed her eyes. She couldn't watch his joy, knowing it would soon be extinguished by the most selfish wishes they had ever made.

"That's a lot of blood," she heard him say as the first cord was cut.

"Control yourself, vampire," she murmured.

"Don't worry, love. Oh, Blu, they're gorgeous," he said. "Both have dark hair. And they have all ten toes, and look at those tiny fingers! Can I hold them?"

"In a few minutes, Mr. Saint-Pierre. Be patient."

The warmth of her husband's hand returned to Blu's and she gave him a drowsy look. His kiss lingered on her mouth, and he closed his eyes. Together they said silent prayers that would never be answered.

"You did good, my werewolf princess," he whispered. "They are bright and beautiful."

"And purple?"

"Yes, purple, your favorite color. It's from the cords about their necks. The doctor said they'll be fine. The midwife is rubbing our son's chest right now, bringing his color back."

"Which was born first?"

Blu lifted her head at the question spoken by a woman standing in the doorway.

"And which second?" the warrior Ooghna said as she entered the OR. The room's temperature iced instantly. The crystal scimitar at her hip glistened under the bright lighting. "Not that it matters. I'll take them both."

Blu's fingernails dug into Creed's palm. "No," she gasped. "Not so soon. Stop her. Don't let her—"

"Neither was born first or second," the doctor replied firmly. She held a swaddled infant and walked over to Creed, who stood at Blu's side. "Here's your daughter, Mr. Saint-Pierre."

Creed took the babe, while his attention was fierce on the faery. "Can't you wait?"

"What do you mean?" Ooghna observed intently as the doctor received the second baby wrapped in a blue blanket. "Neither was first or second?"

The doctor helped Blu to cradle her son in her arms. Blu wanted to cry and bawl and scream for the faery to leave her with her children for a few moments, but what the doctor had said… "Yes, Doctor, what do you mean by that?"

The doctor stood between Creed and the faery and said, "I lifted both babies from Blu's womb at the same time. Had to. The cords wrapped so tightly about their necks made it necessary. So one is not older than the other. They were both born at the exact same time, and I'll mark it so in the records."

"Impossible!" the faery hissed. She clutched the crystal blade.

It was then Blu noted the man who appeared in the doorway. Another freakin' faery, to judge his sparkle.

"Those babies are mine!" the warrior howled.

"Ooghna." The male faery held her back, blade slashing and teeth gritted, from rushing Creed.

"Amazing," Creed said, and he sat on the bed beside Blu. "That's Malrick, the Unseelie king," he explained to her. "Born at the same time? It is our children's gift to us." The faeries struggled. "They belong to us. The bargain is forfeit."

"No!"

Malrick silenced the faery champion with a swipe of his hand before her mouth. "Born simultaneously? A clever means—"

"But an honest means," Creed interrupted. "It was not a trick by either my wife or me. The babies did this."

"Yes." Malrick tilted his head. "Most clever, indeed. The bargain is forfeit. We will leave you to celebrate your new family."

And like that, the faeries dematerialized, leaving the doctor and midwife bustling at the end of the operating table, and Creed standing with his mouth open, staring at the empty doorway. Warmth swept over the bed and swirled through Blu's hair like a summer breeze.

And Blu cried tears of joy that no one could stop, nor did they try.

An hour later, the happy family was snuggled in a private room. Blu breastfed her son while Creed held his daughter. Moonlight spilled over Creed's blue-black hair, his eyes on Kambriel's tiny fingers wrapped about his littlest finger.

"You can't stop looking at her," she said.

He shrugged. "I don't ever want to stop looking at them. They're so perfect. And they're ours." Now he did look up to meet her eyes, and his were watery with tears. "Forever."

The baby at her breast had fallen asleep and Blu tucked his tiny head against her chest. "Forever. That sounds so good. I can't believe it happened that way, but I'm not going to question it too much."

"They did it," Creed said. "You naughty things," he said to the babies, "trying to strangle one another. But you saved one another's lives in the process. I love you, Kambriel." He kissed the baby's head.

"And Malakai, too. Come here, lover. Snuggle up next to me, and let's have a family hug."

Creed slid onto the bed, careful with Kambriel. It amazed Blu how at ease he was with them both, when she felt as if she were handling delicate china. She moved slowly. Creed leaned in to kiss Malakai's soft tuft of black hair. "I think he looks like me."

"Kinda squishy and round? Yeah, I don't know about that. They look like gnomes. Put a pointy red hat on them, and—"

"Gnomes are related to the sidhe, dearest."

"Oh. Nix that. They are little pups, that's what they are."

Someone cleared their throat, and entered the room. Blu's heart stuttered, and she felt Creed's arm move across the babies in protection.

The Unseelie king remained by the door, presenting an unthreatening stance with his arms open and palms facing forward. "I hope you don't mind, but I wished to return to offer my regrets over the scene caused following their births. It was uncalled for."

"No apologies needed," Creed said. "We just hope to never see that faery again."

"I'll see to it. Though Ooghna must be granted the right to her anger."

"Of course."

Malrick opened his palms in offering. "May I have permission to bless the children?"

Blu met Creed's gaze and nodded. A faery blessing could harm nothing.

Creed nodded and sat up next to Blu. Malakai and Kambriel snuggled next to one another on her stomach, bellies up and faces tilted toward one another. Kambriel's lips moved in sucking motion and Malakai burped.

"Precious," Malrick offered with an unconvincing smirk. He moved a hand over the babies and faery dust twinkled down upon them. "I bless you with the goodness and charm of Faery. May you grow strong and hale, wise and calm, exuberant and bright." The faery king touched each on the fore-head, leaving behind a thumbprint glitter of dust.

"Thank you," Creed started, but with a gesture of Malrick's hand that he was not yet finished, the vampire waited.

"You have won your freedom, clever ones," Malrick cited, "yet should you ever dabble in Faery business, bring harm to the sidhe, or otherwise win the heart of any of my kind, you, the both of you, will suffer and Faery shall have its recompense as you must then ransom your very heart to Ooghna."

And the Faery king dematerialized in a wisp of shimmery dust, leaving Blu and Creed looking at one another, breaths heavy and eyes worried.

Finally, Creed spread his hand over Kambriel's head. "Don't worry. We'll keep them safe."

Blu nodded, and tentatively stroked Malakai's hair. "Yes."

She exhaled, and felt a clench in her belly that told her nothing would ever again be the same for the family Saint-Pierre.

* * * * *

WOLF MAGICK

CYNTHIA COOKE

Cynthia Cooke once lived a quiet, idyllic life caring for her beautiful eighteen-month-old daughter. Then peace gave way to chaos with the birth of her boy/girl twins. Hip-deep in nappies and baby food and living in a world of sleep deprivation, she kept her sanity by reading romance novels and dreaming of someday writing one. With the help of her local Romance Writers of America chapter, she was able to alter her life's path, give up her dull life of accounting and become a published romance author.

Cynthia and her family live in sunny California with her cat and two rat terriers. She counts her blessings every day as she fulfils her dreams with the love and support of good friends, her very own hunky hero and three boisterous children who constantly keep her laughing and her world spinning.

Cynthia loves to hear from her readers.

Chapter One

"Come to us, Rena. We're waiting for you."

The voice urged Rena onward while every instinct within her told her to turn back...to run. The moon cut through the trees, its icy-blue glow lighting the forest floor with a preternatural hue that made the shadows appear long and ominous. Rena pushed against a branch. The razor-sharp edge of a leaf sliced into her fingertip, drawing blood. She pressed her finger into her mouth, sucking until the sting disappeared.

She whimpered and she clung tight to her mother's strong hand. She didn't want to be here, would rather be anywhere but here. A wolf howled in the distance. The lonely baying skated down her nerves. "Mommy," she cried. "I want to go home."

"Shh, Rena," her mother whispered. "We're almost there."

"I'm scared. I don't like it here at night."

Her mother stopped and bent down to face her. "There is no reason to be afraid. Soon, I will be very powerful, and no one will ever be able to take you away from me. Okay?"

Rena nodded, blinking against the tears prickling her eyes.

"Good. Now be a brave little girl for mommy, okay? And help me find the lights."

Rena bit down on her lip and nodded.

Once more she moved forward, letting her senses guide her. Her heart danced, not in expectation, but in fear—a heady waltz that left her breathless as she moved farther along the path and deeper into the woods.

She found the clearing circled on all sides by towering trees. The wind howled in protest, beating the branches overhead until they thrashed against one another. It whipped Rena's hair into a fiery maelstrom around her head and still she moved forward, one tentative step after another.

She had to do this. For her mother. So she could get stronger and they could be together. Always.

In the middle of the circle, light pulsed out of the ground. Breathtaking colors that danced and shimmered. They approached the prisms of light bending back and forth, expanding and contracting, earth's altar to the gods, her mother had said.

"Rena, we've been waiting so long. It's almost time. Feel the magic. Feel the power. It's all for you." The voice whispered in her mind.

Rena looked up at Mommy to see if Mommy heard it, too. Mommy was smiling. She let go of Rena's hand and stepped into the lights.

Rena took a tentative step to follow but paused as she saw something hidden in the colors, a shadow peeking, peering, flickering into nothing.

"Mommy?"

Rena stretched her arm out, reaching her fingers toward the kaleidoscope before her, but hesitated as she heard a soft growl. The low rumble filled the air. She turned toward the menacing sound: her chest tightening, her heart racing.

Dark clouds at war with one another thundered across the sky. They rammed and converged, a bubbling molten stew that blocked out almost all the moon's rays, except for a sliver of arctic light that broke through to pierce the shimmering black eyes of the beast.

Fear grasped Rena by the throat and squeezed. She couldn't breathe, couldn't form the scream trapped in her throat. Her legs weakened, her bones turning watery.

The beast loomed over her. His elongated nose, dark and quivering, drew back revealing razor-sharp teeth glimmering to fine wet points. Doused in shock, her mind fractured, shuffling through broken images. Burnt umber, sienna, and kohl-black hair swept thick and full around the beast's face. Its breadth, its impossible height, its neck the size of a tree trunk, it was too much to absorb, to comprehend, as the beast towered over her.

Rena cried out and cowered beneath the outstretched claw. And then she was flying, tumbling through the air, falling into the thick grass, and lying alone in a still, dark meadow.

"Mommy!"

Tears seeped from her eyes, wetting her cheeks, the only indication that she was still alive. But where was Mommy?

She heard the snapping of the branches and felt the rumbling of the earth beneath her and knew it wasn't over.

She screamed. Calling, crying for her mommy to save her. But Mommy never came.

Rena gasped a deep breath then rolled over in bed, flicked on the light and wiped the back of her hand across her wet cheeks. She'd had the dream again. But this time she'd seen even more. She climbed out of bed, stretching as she walked into the outer room of her spacious suite at Vindecare—a school for people with special abilities. *A school for witches.*

She'd never considered herself a witch. She hadn't known her mother had been one, too, until after her grandmother had died and Rena had found her mother's journals detailing her years at Vindecare, and how they'd helped her. If Grandmother had had her way, Rena never would have discovered the truth about her mother, or herself. She'd done everything she could to make sure Rena knew witchcraft and the people who studied it were an abomination, were evil and belonged in hell.

Rena didn't know if there was such a place, but she did know growing up with grandmother had been real close to what she imagined hell to be. Before Rena had found that journal, she'd believed her grandmother was right and she, like her mother, was crazy and doomed to burn with the big man himself. Maybe she was crazy, but she had a gift. And hopefully, through her work at Vindecare, she'd be able to control it. To stop the voice from ruining her life.

And help her move past her nightmares. Obviously she still had a long way to go.

She filled the kettle with water and placed it to boil on the small stove in her corner kitchenette. In the living room, she pulled a sheet off an easel set up by a window revealing a large partially painted canvas.

The beast—all fangs and claws—stared back at her. This time she dreamed more than just a wet shine glinting off sharp pointy teeth. Her dream therapy instructor helped show her how to focus on different aspects of the dream. She hoped that by using her talents as an artist and facing the thing that scared her the most, she could excise the beast from her mind and get rid of the nightmare once and for all.

She squeezed paint from the tubes, mixing colors—vibrant greens, varying shades of browns and reds and cold white cast with a bluish tint. She set to work bringing life to the monster. The mixture of her colors coupled with the shallow quick strokes of her fan brush added depth and layers to the beast's fur and life to its eyes.

She didn't know how long she'd been standing there adding layer after layer when the doorbell rang. Surprised by the intrusive peal of the high-pitched chime, she looked around her, feeling slightly disoriented.

The sun's rays shone bright through the window and an empty mug sat on the table next to her. She couldn't recall making her tea let alone drinking it. The bell rang again. She dropped her brush and hurried to the door glancing down at her pajama shorts and T-shirt and wondered what time it was.

She glanced through the peephole. "Damn," she muttered and opened the door.

Kaydin stood in the hallway, surprise filling his forest-green eyes as they swept over her body. He looked impeccable, as usual. Strong and toned, his soft cotton polo stretched over his well-defined chest. He was one of those men who could almost be classified as pretty with his smooth skin and long lashes, except the width of his neck and the strength of his jaw was the very definition of masculinity.

"Kaydin," she said with a soft, embarrassed laugh and brushed her hands over her unruly hair, knowing with a moment of dread that not only had she not brushed her hair, chances were she hadn't brushed her teeth, either.

"Are you okay?" he asked. "I thought we had an appointment at ten."

Her eyes widened as alarm rushed through her. Of all the people to forget and she had to forget him. "I am so sorry," she blurted. And wondered with dismay what time it was. How could she explain why she missed their appointment? She wasn't sick, she hadn't overslept, she was just in one hell of a brain fog.

He stood expectantly in the hall, his dark eyebrows lifting.

"Oh! Please. Come in. Make yourself at home. I'll—uh…" She raked her fingers through her hair once more. "I'll be right back."

She bolted for her bedroom, pulled on a pair of jeans and a fresh T-shirt then ran into the bathroom where she scrubbed her face clean, ran a brush through her long dark hair before twisting it into a haphazard knot on the back of her head then quickly brushed her teeth.

She knew she shouldn't, but she took a moment to put on makeup. She liked Kaydin, and it wasn't just his incredible hotness or the way her insides quivered when their eyes met. He was everything she'd always dreamed she'd have for herself yet never believed she could actually get.

Because if someone like him spent too much time with someone like her, then he'd discover the truth about her.

And then he'd run.

"I'm sorry," she said again as she hurried back into the room. "Can I make you some coffee?"

She stopped as she saw him standing before the easel studying the painting she'd spent half the night and all morning working on. She gnawed on her bottom lip and wished he hadn't seen it. The beast was her nightmare and not something she wanted to share with anyone.

"This isn't part of the series," he said, his tone guarded, his hands clasped behind his back.

"No. This one is…" She searched for the word that would describe exactly what this was. This was her way of dealing with her nightmares. This was cathartic. This was an exorcism. "Personal," she said finally.

He turned toward her, his dark eyes narrowing into hard glittering stones. "Rena, your opening is a week from now.

You're still short one painting in the portal series. Why would you be working on a painting of a wolf?"

She stiffened, feeling the hairs stand on the back of her neck. "A wolf? Is that what you see?"

"Isn't that what it is?" Confusion played across his face. "What do you see?"

She hesitated as her tongue thickened. "A beast."

He was giving her that look. The one Grandma always gave her. The one the kids at school gave her. He thought she was crazy.

"Rena, I'm concerned about you."

Oh, no. This was how it always started. *"We're concerned about you Rena, worried you've lost your ever-loving-mind."* She stared at him, wide-eyed and unflinching.

"The gallery showing will mean a lot of press, a lot of attention. You will no longer be able to hide here in this castle."

"I'm not hiding. I enjoy my classes here. They are helping me. With my…art."

He looked at the painting of the wolf again. "Are you sure about that?"

"I will have the portal painting done in time, Kaydin. I promise. In fact, I'm going out to the last site this afternoon, getting a motel room nearby and staying all weekend. You can trust me. I want this. I need this." She stilled, waiting expectantly for his response. She didn't know if it was his height, a good six inches taller than her own, or his dark penetrating gaze that seemed to hook right into her soul and give a little tug. But something about this man grabbed her by the jugular and said—*sit up and pay attention. Don't screw up. There will be no second chances, no do-overs*.

Well, she was paying attention. Not only to the intensity of his gaze, his rock-hard chest and large arms, but to the voice inside her that wanted to please him, that wanted him to notice her as not just an artist who would fill his gallery, but as a woman. A desirable, fascinating woman who happened to have mind-wrenching, heart-stopping nightmares. And who heard voices. But no one was perfect, right?

Her lips parted as she blew out a heavy breath. She wished he would calm down and smile. Just a little. A small smile that would have her insides popping and fluttering, like pancake batter on a hot buttery griddle.

"I'm counting on you, Rena," he said, his voice deep and husky.

She cleared her throat. "I…I won't let you down. I promise. That—" she pointed to the beast on the canvas "—is just me working through some bad dreams."

He turned around and looked at the painting once more.

"Do you always paint your nightmares?"

Her gaze shifted back to the canvas. "Only the recurring kind."

"Trying to work it out of your system, eh?"

Her eyes locked onto his and something quivered inside her chest. "Some guys are just hard to get out of your mind."

"Do me a favor and forget about this one," he said. "Focus on your art. I'm counting on you. The gallery is counting on you. Don't let me down."

He didn't say the words that hung heavily in the air between them. *Let me down and you won't get another chance.* But she heard them loud and clear. Second chances were never an option. Not for her.

"I won't. I promise," she said and walked him to the door. As she closed it behind him, she leaned against the hard wood, took three deep breaths and tried to grab hold of herself. He was right. She was letting her nightmares take over her life. She had worked hard to get to this point, to get to Vindecare and she wasn't about to let some dark vision from her past destroy her future. What she had with Kaydin, an opening at a gallery, was an opportunity she couldn't pass up.

What's more, he saw her monster and he didn't turn away. He didn't think she was crazy. Because she wasn't crazy, those were the accusations, the ramblings of an old woman who was terrified of things she didn't understand. It was time to put the past behind her and move forward. She had to face the woods of her nightmare and prove to everyone that she wasn't insane.

She grabbed the bag she'd packed the night before and her satchel, placing her paints and brushes inside along with a sketchbook, her travel easel and a clean canvas then hurried out the door of her suite. She had one last place to visit for her final painting, the one spot she had never wanted to return to again. The one place her instructors at Vindecare had said she must go to, if she wanted to put the past behind her and move forward.

She knew the threat of having to face those cold woods again was the reason the beast was back haunting her dreams. The last time she'd been there she'd lost everything. She'd only been six. She'd gone in with her mother and had come out alone. No one could ever say definitively what had happened to her, but Rena knew.

She'd seen it. She'd seen *him*.

The beast.

For years just the thought of him had terrified and paralyzed her, but not anymore. She was taking back her life. She had a chance now. Kaydin, her art and Vindecare had given that to her. She wasn't going to be afraid anymore. Not of the voice. Not of the beast.

"Good for you, Rena. Stand strong. Come back to the woods. Come back to me."

She ignored the voice, pulled down the sheet covering the beast's face and walked out the door.

Chapter Two

Kaydin left Rena's apartment more determined than ever. She was finally beginning to remember. All the pieces of what had happened that night were falling into place. He had to hurry. If she knew what was waiting for her, he'd never get her back into the woods and to the portal. What surprised him was of all the horrible things that had happened that night, the only one she focused on was *his* face.

And yet, she promised she would go back to the site today. Did she still believe it was only a dream? She'd been so young when her mother had taken her to the demon. He'd made the mistake of saving her, and he'd had to live with ever since. It was time to put things right. He couldn't let his human attraction toward this woman get in the way of what needed to be done. He wasn't human, and he hadn't been for a very long time.

But even as he thought of Rena, her smile, her large trusting brown eyes, he was angered again at why her mother would have brought her young child to the portal in the first place. Was Rena supposed to be a sacrifice? A misguided way to increase her power?

Kaydin could only guess. All he knew for sure was that it was always a lonely witch who fell victim to a demon's seductive whispers. He only hoped Rena hadn't succumbed, too. The demon gate was still open, and no matter how many ways he'd tried, he hadn't been able to close it. Kaydin only hoped Rena wasn't following in her mother's footsteps and listening to the demon's voice.

He drove north out of the city toward the woods and the house he kept there. It looked as if he were finally reaching the end. All these years he'd watched the girl grow from a child to a beautiful woman, raised by her grandmother who had no clue who Rena was or what she could do. But then neither had Rena herself until she moved into Vindecare. All she knew was that she could see things others couldn't. Light. Colors. Shapes. Prisms.

Doorways to another world.

She must be a very powerful witch to be able to see the lights that highlighted the entrance to the demon realm. In years past, only shapeshifting portal guardians such as himself had been able to see them. But times were changing, everything was changing.

And somehow, someway, this particular doorway had been left open. And it fell to Rena to close it, to finish what her mother had started. Something had happened that night, something he missed that was keeping the gate open. He needed to discover what that something was. One way or another, he would rectify the mistake he made on that tragic night when he'd foolishly saved a little girl and left the portal to the demon world wide-open.

As Rena drove down the dirt road, she took a deep breath to ease the tightness squeezing her chest. Many times in the past few months she had driven out to this place, had sat in her car, staring at the trees only to be seized by terror. Even now, fear was nipping at her nape. She took a deep breath and focused on the relaxation techniques she had learned at Vindecare.

Doing the portal series for Kaydin's gallery was the best opportunity she'd ever had to showcase her work and make her mark. She couldn't turn back now. This place, this nightmare was her demon to slay and she would do it. She was tired of living in fear. Of *hiding*.

Kaydin's words came back to her. He was right, she thought with annoyance. She'd been so afraid of proving Grandma right, of being crazy, she had hidden herself away, had sabotaged her own dreams. Not anymore. She wasn't crazy. She had a gift and it was time she used it.

She grabbed her stuff and walked down the long path though the trees. She felt the wind's gentle breeze on her face and could almost hear her mother's voice whispering in her mind telling her about the woodland sprites and faeries, unicorns and imps. Her mom had made everything seem so magical. Rena had loved this place, until the darkness came.

One by one, the memories came to her, dissipating the tension, overshadowing the fading tendrils of her nightmares. Here, there were no monsters hiding in the thicket, only the heartfelt and happy memory of her mother. These woods had been her mother's favorite spot. She'd brought Rena here to pick wildflowers in the spring and blackberries in the summer. It was their special place.

And the last place Rena ever saw her.

Rena wanted her art to portray her mother's magic. This series of the forest's enchanting lights would be a tribute to her mom. To the woman she'd missed so much. Rena lugged her canvas and easel and large pack full of supplies down the path, breathing in the fresh summer air. And with each step deeper into the woods, happiness and a sense of well-being filled her. A sense of doing what was right.

Those feelings were something else she'd carried with her all her life, along with the nightmares and the voice, sometimes she just had a certainty of knowing when something was right. An instinct that had never steered her wrong. And as that instinct hit her once again, she felt even more certain that she was exactly where she was supposed to be.

After another half hour, she walked through a thick grove of poplar trees and saw the lights shimmering in front of her, every color in the rainbow bending and moving. Rena reached out her arm, stretching her long tapered fingers toward the magical light brought forth and worshipped by mere mortals such as herself for centuries.

She stood mesmerized. She didn't know what the lights meant or why she was the only one who was able to see them, she only knew that they called to her. She longed to take her shoes off and walk barefoot through the grass and into the center of the lights, to let them dance around her.

And she would.

When she was done. But now, she had to get started on this painting. Kaydin was right. She'd let her obsession with the beast get in the way of what was important. Her goals. Her future. She had a long week ahead of her before the opening and she had best get started.

She took a deep breath and circled the lights in the clearing, finding the spot that spoke the loudest to her then set up her easel, laid out her paints, a jar of water, turpentine and brushes on a large blanket. She stood before the blank canvas, brush and pallet in hand, staring once more at the lights and heard the voice again. It talked to her in soothing whispers, cajoling, bolstering her confidence, promising of rewards to come.

And it had always been correct.

She first heard the voice when she was young. And again after her mother died, when she'd had to go away and live with her grandmother. Even then, the voice promised she would be all right, that she was destined for great things.

At first she didn't believe. But then things started to happen. Good things. Competitions won. Hearts stolen. Wishes granted. As she mixed the paint, the soothing voice entered her mind once more, putting her fears to rest. She would finish this paining. She would be successful. She would impress Kaydin. All she had to do was focus.

She picked up her brush, dipped it in the turpentine then in the paint on her pallet, mixing the colors, sweeping red into white and yellow, mixing a large array of varying shades.

And she wondered, as she often had as a child, if somehow it was her mother whispering to her, helping her find her path. But then grandmother had found out, yelling she insisted that her mother was dead, that she must be left to rest in peace.

After that, Rena learned to keep the voice a secret. Not to talk about it or tell anyone. And she didn't. And after a while, she'd stopped listening. Until Grandma died, and the voice had become the only comfort she had. Even now, the whispers urged her to walk into the light. To feel it circling around her, to let the warmth and the colors cascade across her skin.

The wind picked up, sending the clouds racing across what had moments ago been a clear blue sky. She pushed her hat down onto her head and dipped her paintbrush into the vibrant red, swirling it around and pressing it against the paper. But was red the right color? Or was it more magenta? Purple?

As she mixed and swept the paint across the canvas, she frowned. She wasn't getting the exact hue right. She had to get closer. She had to see. She picked up her easel with the canvas held tight in her grasp and walked toward the lights, moving so close she could see them reflecting off the paper.

Better.

She started mixing again. Yes. So much better. She moved her arm up and down in long sweeping strokes, the bristle brush blending one color into the next. So intent on the images revealing themselves, she hadn't realized she had moved into the light until it was flashing across her skin.

She stared at it, mesmerized, hearing her mother's voice in her mind.

Look at it, Rena. Isn't it beautiful? Isn't it powerful? It's magical and it's going to make all of Mommy's dreams come true.

"Yes," she whispered.

Rena tingled everywhere as electricity fired her nerve endings. The small hairs on her arms stood upright. She knew this place was special. It was where she belonged. She set down her brush and walked deeper into the center of the lights. She saw what looked like a doorway and beyond the door—darkness. She focused, staring through the shimmering lights into the shadows beyond, her heart kicking up its beat.

The low menacing sound of a growl echoed around her. Fear froze the air in her lungs as a shadow filled the corner of her eye. She knew she should look, but she couldn't make her head turn. She didn't want to see. To know....

"*Rena. Help me,*" the voice from inside the doorway called to her.

Her mother's voice?

"*Help me, Rena. Call my name.*"

Horrified, she stepped forward, focusing on the darkness within the lights. "Mom?"

"*My name. The one She gave me.*"

Rena stared as confused horror seeped through her chest.

"You know it, Rena. You've heard it so many times before."

Panic filled her. It couldn't be possible. "Mom!" She reached for the darkness, for her mother.

"Remember, Rena! Remember the blood."

Images flashed through Rena's mind: Her mother dancing. Lights pulsing, glinting off the large gold locket hanging from her neck. There had been someone else, someone she was smiling at. A knife, long and sharp. Grabbing the blade, her mom pulled the sharp edge through her hand. Blood dripped. Her mouth slashed a bright smile against a pale face. Her fingers dripping crimson reaching....

Tears filled Rena's eyes. She cried out and stepped backward, brushing up against something behind her.

Something big. Something pliable.

This wasn't happening.

Not again!

It was only a dream. A nightmare.

Not a memory.

And still she wouldn't turn. Couldn't.

Thunder cracked across the sky.

The disappeared into a rush of ominous black clouds. She turned quickly looking behind her, but nothing was there. She turned back and a large black panther appeared before her, its yellow-green eyes gleaming, its ears standing straight up pointed toward the dark sky. It was snarling at her, baring its long sharp teeth. It was unlike any cat she'd ever seen. But she had seen it before. That night. Then she knew it wasn't a cat. It was a demon.

Rena...

She stared into its feline eyes and a deep feeling of calm washed over her. Would it hurt her? The cat looked up at her with wonder. Its big golden gaze locked onto hers, and she felt a whisper in her mind, an urge to move forward. To touch. To whisper the name—*Ubasti.*

Damn!

He was too late.

Kaydin stood off to the side watching Rena paint. She seemed focused on her work but then started walking toward the portal. A witch in direct contact with an open portal was all the invitation needed to set the demon loose.

He would not let that happen. Not again.

But it already had. Somehow she had pulled the light to her, without even moving. How was it possible? Unless she had already been in contact with the demon. The demon's familiar spoke to her now, beckoning her forward, enticing her with its words of seduction. Words that made so much sense. That spoke to a human heart telling it exactly what it wanted—no, what it *needed* to hear.

And the witches fell for it. Time and time again.

This was all happening much quicker than he'd expected. He stripped out of his clothes, calling on the ancient gods to help him. He stretched, reaching for the sky as he pulled the strength of Kratos into him, the fire from Hephaestus and begged protection in the pit from Hades. His limbs lengthened. His arms bulging. His neck thickened. Bones popped. Tendons tore. A roar of pain and triumph filled the air as he reshaped to his true self.

He could smell Rena's fear, her confusion, but most of all her special enticing scent that called to him like no other. The light swelled, encircling, moving around her, pulling her into its grasp as long tentacles of reds and purples reached for her grasping, soothing, caressing.

He extended his back, going up onto his hind legs. He roared; the sound echoing into the afternoon and bouncing off the trees. Forest animals scurried in fright running far and wide away from him. As if he was fire, as if he were the one bringing destruction to the land.

If she saw her mother behind the gate… If she muttered the demon's name then he'd have no choice. He'd have to do whatever it took to kill the demon, no matter who it was using as its vessel. He only hoped he could stop Rena before that happened.

Running into the lights, feeling the heat of the fire and the pull of the pit, he lunged. A roar bursting from deep inside him split the air.

Damn, he thought he'd have more time.

Chapter Three

Rena's fear crawled up her throat as the beast from her nightmares charged into the clearing and leaped on the panther, bouncing off its back and skidding to a stop beyond it. The panther snarled, baring its sharp teeth. Rena gasped a disbelieving breath, her eyes widening painfully as she stared at the large wolf. It was real!

Pierced with fright, she inched away from the animals and farther into the light. Dizziness swept through her. She faltered, stumbling, reaching out to steady herself as the two creatures, snarled, gnashed and thrashed one another.

She took another step then froze. Her hand fluttering to her mouth as she let out a small cry. A woman stood before her looking just like her mother had that summer day all those years ago when she'd walked into the lights and never came out.

Rena blinked, stunned and astonished.

Before she could step closer, could speak, the panther flew past her and smashed into a tree. The beast skulked, moving toward her. It was bigger than she remembered from her dream and Kaydin was right, it did look like a wolf. A very large, very dangerous wolf. She should run. She knew that, but she couldn't seem to make her legs move. Soft whimpering noises came from her throat as she lowered her head, letting the beast know she was not a threat.

And still it continued toward her.

Heart pounding, adrenaline surged through her. She screamed, long and loud, letting loose all her fear in one steady stream as she turned and ran away from the beast, away from the strange lights and straight into the cat. She skidded to a stop. It snarled, pushing her back toward the lights, toward the beast. She tried to move around it, but it came at her, swatting its paw, its outstretched claws swiping down her arm.

She screamed as fire burned through her body. The pain was excruciating. Blood flowed down her stinging arm. She grabbed the wound to staunch the flow, but it seeped between her fingers.

In a fury of horrific growls, the beast charged at the cat. Rena didn't wait to see what was happening, she turned to run but stopped.

She had to.

Her mother stood clear as day before her, beckoning, gesturing for Rena to come to her. "*Rena. Help me,*" she called from inside the doorway.

But how could it be her? It had to be a trick. An illusion.

"*Call my name, Rena. Please. Set me free.*"

Rena's insides twisted with anguish. Could it really be?

"Mom!" she cried, and hurried toward her into the lights. But as she neared the strange doorway, sounds intensified. Suddenly she could hear water rushing from a nearby river, wind moving through the trees and, above it all, the grunts and snarls of the two beasts posturing behind her.

But it wasn't just her hearing that was affected, suddenly

her vision was off, greens were more muted, looking almost yellow and the sky had become a kaleidoscope of various shades of blue and gray. She saw her mother clearly now, standing in the darkened doorway, her feet hovering just beyond the edge, inching forward as if she wanted to come out, but couldn't. As if she were...*trapped*.

"Oh my God, Mom!" Fear filled Rena to the bursting point. Had her mother been trapped here all these years? Horror saturated her brain at the thought. As she moved closer, she saw that the darkness behind her mother wasn't as dark as she'd originally thought. Flashes of light flickered within. What was that place?

"*Come, Rena.*" The words whispered through her mind, pulling, enticing....

She'd almost reached her mother when she heard the quick pants of the wolf behind her. She glanced over her shoulder. The beast was barreling toward her. The cat was nowhere to be seen. Rena knew she couldn't outrun a wolf, but there was no logic left inside her. Only fear. And the instinct to flee.

"*Rena....*"

She couldn't. Not now. She ran, feeling the power of the muscles in her legs as they carried her away from the clearing, away from her mother, away from the *beast*.

Once more, dizziness swam through her mind. Her strength left her and she fell to the forest floor. As she lay on her back, staring past the lush canopy of green at the bright blue sky, fatigue and sorrow washed over her. Her eyes drifted closed. Suddenly, she was so tired. She couldn't run anymore. Would the beast would find her? Would she die here all alone?

Rena woke to darkness but she was no longer lying on the ground. It was infinitely softer, warmer. A bed. She turned her head and saw a figure sitting in the shadows. He stood towering over her. She gasped and jerked back.

"It's okay," he said, softly. "You're safe."

She knew that voice. She stared into the gloom, her eyes trying to fill in the lines the dim light hid. "Kaydin?"

"You're going to be okay now."

"But how?" she asked, her head aching with confusion. She tried to sit up but pain fired through her shoulder. She winced and fell back into the soft pillows.

"Don't try to move," he said.

She looked at her arm and saw the oozing wounds. He leaned forward rubbing a thick oily salve across the deep gashes in her skin.

Immediately she felt better and as she watched his long fingers stroke across her arm, she realized she wasn't wearing anything but her panties under the sheets.

You undressed me?" she asked as heat flamed her cheeks.

"I had to. Your clothes were ruined."

"But how on earth did you find me? The last thing I remember…" She paused. How could she say what she'd last seen? What had happened to her? He'd think she was crazy. She *was* crazy. She had seen her *mother*.

He waited for her to continue, his gaze sharp with expectation.

"I'm not sure what I saw," she finally said.

"From your wounds it looks like you tangled with a raccoon."

She almost choked. "A raccoon?"

"Crazy, I know, but they can be ferocious little beasts."

She thought of the two animals—no, not animals—monsters fighting one another in the clearing and closed her eyes. Yes, it was crazy.

"Are you hungry?" he asked.

"Starved," she admitted, at once noticing the uncomfortable yearning in her stomach.

He picked up a bowl of strawberries off the nightstand, chose a berry and brought it to her lips. It looked wonderful. *He* looked wonderful. She took a bite, the juice spilling onto her lips. She slipped her tongue out of her mouth to lick it away then warmed as his eyes followed the movement.

How was it possible she was lying here naked in Kaydin's house and he was feeding her berries? She must be dreaming.

A clattering of rain beat the roof.

"Oh, no! My stuff!" she cried, and tried to sit up but stopped as pain arced through her shoulder.

"It's okay. I got it all," he said, and eased her back down with a firm hand.

"You did?" she asked, clearly surprised that he'd been able to find it. To find her.

"I did. And not a moment too soon. A storm hit not long after I got you into the car. It's been raging for hours."

She heard the wind whipping through the trees, the rain beating at the ground washing away all evidence that she'd ever been there. That the beast and strange cat had ever been there.

"Did you see anything?" she asked, hoping she hadn't imagined it all. Praying that she wasn't losing her mind. Though obviously she was.

"No, just you, lying on the ground, your stuff in shambles. I'm afraid you're going to have to get a rabies shot. We can't take any chances. Not with raccoons," he pushed.

"It wasn't a raccoon," she said softly.

"No?" He looked at her expectantly waiting for her to explain what had happened. But how could she tell the truth without taking the chance that he'd drive her straight to the nearest mental institution? "No."

He brought another berry to her lips. She took all of it in her mouth, the sweet flavor bursting on her tongue.

"Dinner will be ready soon, if you feel up to it," he said, his voice sounding strained as he leaned forward and wiped the excess juice off her lips with the tips of his fingers. She stilled as his skin touched hers, completely aware of how close he was and how nice he smelled. Strong. Spicy. Male.

"How did you find me?" she asked, and had trouble swallowing as her breath hitched. "Why were you even here? Were you checking up on me?"

"No. I—" He brought another berry to her mouth. She took a smaller bite this time, though she had to fight the urge to let her lips slip over his fingers. To taste his skin.

"I felt bad about the way we left things this morning." His eyes locked onto her hers. Her chest tightened. "When I saw your car parked along the road, I thought I would make sure you were all right and talk you into letting me take you out to dinner to make up for…everything."

She smiled, feeling slightly embarrassed. "There is nothing to make up for, but I am glad you found me."

"Me, too." He gave her another berry, his gaze focusing on her lips.

She knew she shouldn't. Knew it would muddy their relationship but when his fingertips brushed her lips once more, she opened her mouth around them, flicking her tongue across his warm skin.

An energy of expectation swirled around them. Desire curled in her stomach. "Oh, hell," she muttered and brought her good arm up around his neck and pulled him down to her. She tasted his lips, opening her mouth to him. He groaned and covered her mouth with his, pushing his tongue inside. Sweeping, tasting, kissing her with a passion that surprised and excited her.

She had imagined this moment, dreamed of this moment since the first time she had met Kaydin and yet, her thoughts, her expectations had never compared to this. Kissing him felt like she'd found a piece of herself that had been lost. His touch filled her with a rush of warmth, with a feeling of *rightness*. She wanted to burrow into him. To feel his arms wrapped around her, to feel his strength, his heat.

She tried to pull him closer, to lift herself higher. But as she did, pain shot through her and she let out a soft cry.

Kaydin pulled back, alarm on his face. "Did I hurt you?"

"No," she assured him, feeling slightly surprised and embarrassed by her ardor, though she didn't want him to stop.

But he did. He stood, stepping stiffly away from the bed. "I should check on dinner. I'll be right back," he said and hurried out the door.

What had just happened? Kaydin couldn't remember the last time he'd desired a woman. He'd spent the last few centuries keeping witches out of the portals, never quite understanding how they could fall victim to the seduction of a demon. And yet, he wanted Rena. Wanted to kiss her. Wanted.... It was just so...*human*.

Which he definitely wasn't. And hadn't been since his descent through the portal and into the pit where his transformation from mere man to shapeshifter and portal guardian had taken place. It had been an honor and one he welcomed. It had given him purpose.

And yet, he had once been a man. He remembered what it had felt like to want...and need...and desire.

But he couldn't let those baser emotions affect him now. Not at this critical point. Something about this witch and her mother was different. Somehow they were able to open that portal and keep it open. Why couldn't he close it? What was so different about this witch?

And why was she so closely connected to this demon? So many questions, and yet, he sensed Rena had no idea of what was happening. And if he spooked her, she'd run. He couldn't take that chance. He had to help her remember what happened that night. What had been different? The demon had her mother as a vessel. Why hadn't it come back out? Why was it still trapped?

The answers were locked inside Rena's head. Somehow he had to discover what they were. Together they had to finish what her mother started. They had to close that portal.

He only hoped he could do it without losing Rena, too.

But that shouldn't be a factor.

Why was he so drawn to this woman? What was it about her that made him forget everything but the touch of her skin, her delicate smell, her intoxicating taste?

His body pulled at him even now, even as he tasted her sweetness on his tongue. He couldn't let himself be distracted by it. Whatever *it* was. Whatever she was—a witch, a temptress, a demon—he wasn't sure. All he knew was that if she called the demon's name, if she invited it into her before they could get the portal closed, then he would have to kill her.

He would have no choice.

His only hope was to convince her of what was happening, what was at stake and hope she believed him.

He thought he'd have more time.

He was wrong.

Dead wrong.

Chapter Four

Rena kicked herself two ways from Sunday. What was she doing kissing Kaydin? What was she doing here? She looked around the well-kept room at the pine walls and rustic furniture. The rust colored curtains perfectly matched the bedspread and the pillows on the bed. But what drew her eye were the pictures on the walls, and the cast iron sculpture on the dresser all with the same motif—*wolves*.

Dread skittered up her spine.

"Where are we?" she asked, as Kaydin came back into the room.

"My house. Here, I found an extra pair of sweats." He held up an oversize black sweatshirt and sweatpants.

"Your house? You live out here in the woods?"

"Most of the time, though I do have a loft in the city. This place has been in my family for generations."

She took the sweats from him as her sense of foreboding grew. "What are the odds that you live in the same forest where I was painting?"

Where she saw the lights?

His eyes held hers. "I'm just glad I saw your car parked along the road."

What could she say to that? If he hadn't found her, would she still be lying out in the dark and the rain, miserable and lost deep in the forest?

"Kaydin," she called, stopping him as he turned to leave. "Would you mind helping me up?"

He hesitated. He was reluctant to come near her again. Why, because she kissed him? Or because he wanted to kiss her again? Her skin flushed with heat as she remembered the feel of his touch.

"Of course," he said and walked back to her. He helped her sit up. And even though her head was swimming, she gingerly lifted her arm and let him slide the oversize sweatshirt over her head. He helped her stand, holding her steady for a moment until the room stopped swaying and she found her footing. After a moment, she leaned against him and stepped into the sweatpants.

The feel of his warm touch around her waist along with his distinctive spicy scent and suddenly she was against him, unable to stop herself from putting her arm around him, from leaning her head against his shoulder, from inhaling his scent and nuzzling his neck.

She felt him stiffen. "I'm sorry," she said. "I don't know why I'm so weak. Every time I stand, I get dizzy."

"Let's get you something to eat. That should help."

He helped her out of the bedroom and into the great room. A fire was roaring in the stone fireplace and the delicious scent of garlic and onions filled her nose. Her stomach growled. "Smells wonderful."

"I figured you'd need a little more sustenance than strawberries."

"Very perceptive." A large painting of a wolf hanging

above the fireplace caught her eye. She shivered as she stared at it. "You like wolves, don't you?"

He followed her gaze. "My grandfather had that painting commissioned. He rescued that wolf as an orphaned pup in Canada and raised her. They were inseparable."

Nice story. Heartwarming even, so why did it leave her so cold? For years after her mother's disappearance, she'd been told she'd imagined the beast. But she had seen it again today. She hadn't imagined it. She wasn't crazy. And yet, she also thought she saw her mother looking exactly as she had fifteen years ago. If that wasn't crazy, she didn't know what was.

"After you get some food in your stomach and a good night's rest you'll feel better," Kaydin said, as if he could read her thoughts.

He helped her to a seat at the table then walked into the open kitchen. He came back carrying a large casserole dish. "I hope you like Italian."

"Love it," she said, and inhaled deeply as he filled her plate with a large serving of lasagna. "Looks great." She took a bite. "Tastes great, too." She marveled at the deep rich flavor of the sauce.

Attractive, sexy and a great cook. This man seemed too good to be true.

But one thing she learned today, nothing around here was as it seemed. As they ate in silence, she realized she wanted to trust him, to confide in him about what she'd seen. But would he believe her? Would he help her or would he look at her like her grandmother had.

"Kaydin, I know I said I would be able to finish the painting—"

"We're not going to worry about that right now."

She stilled, staring at him as she thought about how adamant he'd been earlier at Vindecare. "No?"

"No, but tomorrow I would like you to take me back to the clearing where you were painting."

If it were up to her, she'd never go near that place again. "Why?"

"I need you to remember everything that happened there. If there is a dangerous animal in these woods, I want to know about it."

"Can't we just call the wildlife department?"

"We could, but they'd take one look at your arm and tell you what I told you earlier.

She lifted her eyebrows.

"That you tangled with a raccoon and you're going to need a rabies shot."

She grimaced. "It wasn't a raccoon."

He waited for her to continue, to explain what she meant though she wasn't sure she wanted to. She wanted to go back to Vindecare and leave the forest, the lights and the beast behind her. If she could. But somehow she knew that running away wasn't the answer.

Her gaze swung to the painting above the fireplace. "It was a lot bigger than a raccoon. In fact, it looked like a wolf."

Kaydin stiffened. She thought *he'd* hurt her? He'd been waiting for her to open up to him, prompting her to tell him the truth. But this? Did she not even remember the demon's cat? How was he going to get her to understand what was happening if he couldn't get her to remember the truth?

"I know it sounds crazy," she said in a rush.

"No, it's just…well, those marks were made by sharp thin claws. And there haven't been wolves in New York in many years. What about a cat?"

"A cat?" Doubt crossed her face as she looked at her wounds once more.

What was she hiding? He could feel uncertainty and vulnerability rolling off her in waves. A part of him wanted to stop pushing. But he couldn't. Too much was at stake. He was going to have to try a different tactic. "Do you really see the lights you paint in your pictures?"

She looked up at him, indecision warring across her face.

"I only ask, because I've seen a painting a lot like yours before."

Disbelief widened her eyes. "You have?"

He nodded. "That's why I was so interested in contracting a series from you in the first place." Finished with his dinner, he stood and held his hand out to her. She took it, her soft small hand dwarfed within his.

He led her into his room. Above the bed was a large painting portraying a kaleidoscope of colors and within the colors, in the center of the geometric patterns was the subtle outline of a dark doorway. Beyond the rectangular darkness was a cluster of twinkling white lights.

Rena gasped as she stared at the painting.

And then he knew. She hadn't just seen the lights. She'd seen the gateway to hell.

Rena stared at the painting on the wall, her heart skipping and thumping in her chest. *The lights in the painting were exactly as she'd seen them. How was that possible?* She stepped as close to the painting as she could without climbing up on the bed and stared at the dark shadow in the middle. She hadn't seen it in the other places where she'd seen the lights. This one was different. This one looked like a *doorway.*

It *was* a doorway. Suddenly she was certain. She turned to Kaydin at once suspicious. "This isn't about a gallery exhibit, is it?"

"No," he admitted.

Wariness had her on edge. She was sore and scared and tired of feeling ambushed. "Then what is this about? Why am I here?"

"I need your help to close the portal," he said, stepping closer. The warm timbre of his voice echoed through her.

Portal? "What's a portal?" She didn't know where he was going with this, but she was beginning to feel itchy inside. "The lights are a doorway to the demon realm. And one your mother left wide-open when she walked through to the other side."

Demon realm? She shook her head. "No. That's crazy." But was it?

"You don't believe me?" he asked, surprise filling his voice.

"Would you?"

"You hear voices," He stated matter-of-factly. As if it were common knowledge. As if it were no big deal.

"No," she said, the denial automatically coming out of her mouth before she even had a chance to wonder—*how did he know*?

"Your mother brought you here as a child. She opened the gateway. She walked through. You were saved, but the gate was left open."

Rena shook her head. "No, not saved. Attacked."

"Attacked?"

"By the beast. It's all I can remember. It's what I dream about."

"You don't remember the demon's cat?"

He knew about the cat? But how? Was he there today? Did he see? "You said it was a raccoon?" she challenged.

"It was a cat from the other side. See, look." He pointed to a shadow in the lights. At first glance, the faint outline wasn't noticeable. But she'd seen that shape, that shadow. *The panther.*

Her stomach turned. Had the panther been there that night, too? Her head spun. She needed to sit down.

"Think of it like a doorway to the other side." He pointed to the darkness buried within the lights. "The lights you see are portal sites. Gateways. There are several of them around, but only a very few, very special people can see them. And only a witch calling upon a demon can open one."

This wasn't real. None of it was real. But she remembered golden eyes set deep into black fur. And she heard the name whispered through her mind...*Ubasti.*

"What happens if a witch calls the demon's name?"

"She becomes a vessel for a demon."

"A vessel," she repeated, her stomach turning sour. "Why would anyone do that?"

"Why does anyone do anything? For power."

"Are you saying that's what happened to my mother?"

"No. That's what almost happened to your mother. Except instead of the demon coming out and entering her, your mother went over to the other side."

"To the demon dimension," she said, trying to understand, but not really able to make sense of it all. It was crazy. He was crazy. But she'd seen her mother standing there...*waiting.*

"What about the beast?" she asked.

"He's a portal guardian."

"You mean he guards the gateway? From what?"

"From witches who let demons loose into the world."

"And my mother?"

"He saved you. He lost her."

She shook her head. "No. That's not how it was."

He rocked back on his heels, his jaw hardening. "Then how was it?"

"I wasn't saved."

"You are here today. Your mother isn't. Your mother

opened the gateway. It's still open and calling to you. You know it's true. You dream about it every night. Your paintings prove that much. You are responsible for fixing what your mother broke."

"My mother," she whispered. "I think I saw her today." Panic squeezed her heart as she tried to make sense of it all, tried to understand. "So you're saying my mother has been here all this time, trapped in some demon dimension?"

Antsy, she started pacing the room, rubbing her hands across the top of her head.

"Yes."

Sick dread filled her. It was too horrible to imagine. Too horrible to grasp. *So many years.* She thought about what that must have been like for her, how unbelievably mind-numbingly terrible. She tried to reject it, but as incredible as it sounded, she knew it was true. Every crazy thing he said.

"I have to help her," she whispered over the lump in her throat.

"The demon is inside her, but for some reason it can't get out of the portal. I think you were supposed to go in, too. I think she took some piece of you in there with her. That's why she can't come out and the doorway can't close. It's why you hear her so strongly, and why you were compelled to come back here."

"A piece of me?" Rena thought of her mother standing in the doorway beckoning to her, and then she remembered the large gold locket that had always hung from her neck. "She was wearing a locket with a cutting of my hair."

"That would do it."

"But how can I help her? If I go in, can she come out? Is that what's keeping her locked inside?"

He shook his head. "There is nothing you can do to save her. The demon wants you to call its name, to become its vessel so it can come out. If you do, you will be lost." His face hardened. "Somehow, we have to get that locket. Then we can close the portal. I will take care of it. It's important that you stay away from there and away from the cat. Do you understand?"

"I can't just leave my mother there." Her voice sounded shrill, but she didn't care.

"Do you really believe after fifteen years there is still a trace of your mother left? What you saw was a shell. A skin for a demon. Your mother is gone."

Horror-struck, Rena stared at him as his words barraged her. Before she could fully grasp the implication of what he said, a loud screeching howl lifted the hairs on the back of her neck.

"What was that?" she asked, turning toward the window, her voice shaky.

"The demon's cat. It's found you."

Chapter Five

The cat hit the window shaking the glass within its frame. Rena screamed.

Kaydin came to her and pulled her into his arms. "Shh. It's okay. It can't get in."

"Are you sure?"

"Positive."

"What does it want?"

"You. It won't stop until it has you." She shuddered. "How can this be happening?" She backed away from him. From the painting. From the glowing eyes of the cat at the window. "I don't understand."

"Rena, come to me. Come where you belong."

"I'm here to protect you. If you listen to me and trust what I say, I won't let anything happen to you. I promise," Kaydin said, his eyes softening. "I'll get the locket and close the portal. It's your only chance."

"Rena!"

He opened a panel in the wall and hit a button. Heavy shutters slid over the outside of the windows, blocking her sight of the cat.

And yet, she could still hear it. Calling to her. Begging. Pleading.

She pushed her hands against her head, trying to block out the voice, but knew it was no good. The voice came from within.

Kaydin placed his hands on her shoulders and looked down at her. "Are you all right?"

The voice stopped. She looked up at him. "I am now."

He dropped his hands and stepped away from her. She reached for him, pulling him back. "Please. When you're near, when you're touching me, I don't hear its voice."

He sat on the bed and took her hand in his, pulling her down next to him. "I want to help you. You have to trust me."

"I...it's just so hard to comprehend. You're talking about demons." She stared at his face, his lips. She wanted him to hold her, to make her feel like the world was normal like there wasn't a demon's panther waiting outside the window, that her mother wasn't stuck in some demon dimension, that everything was as it should be.

But the world wasn't normal. And she feared it never would be. Not for her.

Seeking his warmth, she leaned into him and he put his arms around her. She could hear the steady rhythm of his heartbeat and it comforted her. She'd thought about touching him, wishing she could hold him ever since she'd first met him. But did he want her the way she wanted him? She nuzzled closer, taking a deep breath, inhaling his masculine scent and wishing he would kiss her. She wanted to feel his lips against hers; she wanted to feel his passion for her.

She lifted her head and pressed her lips against his neck then moved them gently across his collarbone, kissing and tasting until she reached the hollow of his neck where she pulled the tender skin into her mouth.

He inhaled a quick breath. She looked up at him and hoped he wouldn't move away. His deep green eyes locked onto hers and she could see the indecision warring within him. He wanted her, she could feel it. But she could also feel him trying to fight it.

She moved closer to him, her breath running shallow as she felt his temperature rising, his muscles stiffening. Before he could pull away, she shifted over him, pressing her breasts flat against his chest, resting her hands on his shoulders, pushing her lips against his.

Slightly embarrassed by her wantonness, she held her breath as she waited for him to respond, to kiss her back. It was unlike her to be so brazen, but at this point she didn't care. She wanted to feel his arms around her. She wanted him to kiss her back.

"This…is not such a good idea," he said, pulling away, even as his hands moved over her shoulders and down her back. His words might be pushing her away, but he was drawing her closer.

"I need you," she said, and ran her hands up the side of his neck until her arms twined around his neck. Expectation thickened between them. "Please," she murmured, moving until she was only a breath away.

As if a dam broke, his mouth fell over hers, crushing her.

He kissed her long and hard, until finally she had to break free to breathe. Her heart fluttered erratically in her chest, and all she could think about, all she could feel was his touch on her skin and his taste lingering on her lips.

Which was exactly what she wanted. She didn't want to think about what he'd said or what any of it meant anymore. She didn't want to sleep or dream. She only wanted to lose herself within him.

"I won't let anything happen to you," he promised on a

heavy breath while he ran his lips down her neck, nibbling her tender skin, setting her nerve endings ablaze.

Heated, her body turned liquid beneath his strong touch. She swept her hands up his massive chest, feeling the swells beneath her fingertips, marveling at his perfection. His nipple peaked at her touch, and she played with it, pulling a deep gasp from within him.

"I…I haven't. It's been a while," he confessed.

She smiled. "How about if tonight, we take care of each other?" She lifted his shirt and clasped her lips around his stiff nub, flicking her tongue until it tightened in her mouth and his breath turned ragged.

She had to have him next to her. Touching her. She raked her nails down his back in her effort to remove his shirt, to feel his skin, now almost hot to the touch. Overheated, she struggled with one hand to take off her sweatshirt and almost cried out loud when he helped her out of it then took the tender skin of her breast into his mouth, sucking as if he couldn't get enough of her.

Fiery passion rose within her and she pulled him closer, her own breath coming in short heated gasps. She took off the rest of her clothes and within seconds was pressed against him. Mercy, he was beautiful. Large, strong, hard and so male. She clung to him as he shifted and in one deep, ragged breath, buried himself within her.

She held on tight and with each stroke, rode their passion as he went deeper and moved faster. Her temperature spiked. Her body quivered. Her lungs constricted, until she felt like she couldn't get enough air.

The room around her spun, as the hunger building within her tightened all her muscles until they were taut enough to snap. Unbelievingly, he moved even faster, harder, holding on to her as if she were a part of him, and he a part of her. The room darkened, but sounds intensified and all she could hear was the pounding of her blood rushing through her veins, all she could feel was the stretching of her skin as the tension within her reached the breaking point.

She screamed, her back arching as she pulled him deep within her and let loose a bellow that rattled the windows. Desire, hot and fluid, moved through her in wave after wave, stealing her breath and her strength as she fell in an exhausted heap against him. He grasped her tighter as he approached his own release, his already hard body stiffening. He gasped a deep breath, then threw back his head and roared.

The sound shot terror straight through her heart.

She looked up at him, fully expecting to see the beast. But it wasn't there. It was Kaydin she was clinging to, Kaydin who was still buried deep within her, Kaydin who sounded so much like the wolf from the clearing. Only his beautiful forest-green eyes were now jet-black.

Rena scampered off him, moving as far across the bed as she could.

He fell back against the pillows, his hand reaching for her. "Come back," he said, his voice gravelly.

Wide-eyed she stared at him, trying to comprehend what just happened.

He took a shaky breath then turned to her, his eyes once more deep forest-green speckled with amber flecks. "What's the matter?"

"Your eyes," she whispered and climbed off the bed. "They were black. They were different. They looked like..."

She couldn't say it. Couldn't think it.

"Like a wolf's?" he asked.

The cat was going crazy outside.

With one arm, Rena struggled back into her sweats,

then leaned against the wall, trying to still the trembling in her legs.

"Don't be afraid," he said.

Rena didn't say anything, but if there was any way she could push herself through the wall to get away from him, she would have done so.

"I'm not going to hurt you. I would never hurt you."

"What are you?" she asked, her voice trembling.

"I'm the portal guardian."

She started to shake her head. *The beast*? "No. Not possible." She slipped down the wall to the floor.

He got off the bed and walked slowly toward her. "It's all right."

"Stay away from me."

"I'm here to protect you. To help you."

"I don't want your help." She scrambled to her feet and backed away from him out of the room.

He followed. She had to get away from him. She didn't care if it was storming or pitch-black outside. She couldn't stay in here with him. Not a moment longer.

"Rena, you need my help. I know now why you can see the lights. And why the demon wants you so badly."

"What are you talking about?" she screamed, as she continued down the hall and into the guest room she'd slept in earlier. She grabbed her purse, checking to make sure her keys were inside.

"You aren't a witch," he said. "It's why they couldn't help you at Vindecare. Why you weren't making any progress."

"You don't know what you're talking about. I was making progress. I was remembering more and more of my dreams."

"But you couldn't stop the voice. It calls to you. It's why you are compelled to paint the portals, opened ones and closed. It's why you feel the need to come back here over and over again."

She narrowed her eyes as fury filled her. "The only reason I'm compelled to come back here is because this is where I lost my mother and faced a *beast*." She yelled the word so loud her voice broke into a high-pitched shriek.

"I am not a beast. I'm a shapeshifter. And I'm here to help you. If you'll let me."

"The only way you can help me is to leave me alone." She turned and ran from him, but hesitated at the front door, knowing the demon's cat was out there somewhere. But better she take her chances out there than trapped in this house with *him*. She ran then, out of the house and into the dark.

She had to get as far away from him as she could. How could he have fooled her so completely? She made love to him! She rushed around the front of the house but didn't see her car. Where could it be? Was it still on the main road? She hurried down the wet gravel drive, hoping her car wasn't too far. Luckily the rain had stopped and the moon had come out to guide her.

She ran until her sides ached, then stopped, bent over and took a deep breath. She started moving forward again, but froze when she heard the peeling cry of the panther.

Terrified, she stepped off the drive, crouched low into the bushes and held her breath.

Please don't let it find me.

She hid in the darkness, her tears mingling with the rain dropping from the leaves and dripping onto her face. How was it possible that Kaydin wasn't…human? A shapeshifter? A portal guardian. What was that anyway? And how was it that he could make her feel so safe? So wanted?

It doesn't matter. It had all been a lie.

She wiped the tears off her face and looked around her. She

had no idea where she was. As the rustling of the underbrush filled her ears and the dank smell of the damp earth filled her nose, she wished she was back at Vindecare. Wished she was anywhere but here.

When she could no longer hear the cat, she stood and started moving again. This time, staying in the trees. Before long, she was standing back in the clearing, looking at the lights, watching the demon's cat glide into the circle. The rectangular darkness in the center shimmered, opened, and her mother stepped into the doorway. Why did she always end up here?

Because this was where she was supposed to be.

"*Rena.*" Her mother gestured toward her.

Tears burned Rena's eyes as she walked toward her, remembering the sound of her laugh, the gentleness of her touch.

She didn't care what Kaydin said. How could she believe anything he said? It didn't matter how she felt when she was with him, or what it felt like when he touched her. He was the *beast*.

He was the cause of all her nightmares.

Rena had to help her. If there was even the smallest chance that Kaydin was wrong, that her mother was still in there, stuck inside that horrible place, then Rena would get her out. She wouldn't leave her there.

She remembered now why her mother had come here. Her grandmother had threatened to take Rena away from her. Grandmother was afraid of what her mother was. Afraid she would go to hell.

And maybe she'd been right. Maybe her mother was in hell. But if she was, she went in there to keep Rena, now Rena would bring her back.

Determined, she stepped into the lights and toward the

doorway. She heard the snarl of the panther behind her and thought that maybe she heard the low growl of the beast. But she knew now, it wasn't a beast. It was Kaydin.

The man who had saved her.

And let her mother walk into hell, leaving her daughter alone to be raised by a crazy woman.

How could she ever get over that?

"You came," her mother said, smiling.

"Yes. I've come to bring you home."

"I am home, Rena. Come, join me. As you were meant to do so many years ago." Her words touched an empty spot in Rena's heart and she realized that since her mother had left, Rena hadn't been anywhere that she'd felt wanted.

Could this place really be why? Was this what she'd been missing, what she'd been longing for all these years?

Her mother held out her hand and Rena took it. And the moment she did, the moment she felt her mom's warm, familiar touch, she knew she'd made the right decision.

She knew she'd finally found her home.

Chapter Six

Kaydin ran after her. She'd seen what he was and horri-fied, she'd run from him. He was what she'd always feared and what had haunted her nightmares since she was a child. As he ran into the clearing, he saw her reaching for the shell that was her mother, her hand outstretched.

"Rena," he called! "Don't!"

She turned back to him, her eyes gleaming with moisture, a small smile lifting her lips. He ran toward her but it was too late. She stepped through the doorway and the demon in her mother's skin stepped out.

"No!" he yelled. But it was no use. It was too late. Rena was gone.

The demon sauntered up to him, her red hair flowing around her shoulders, her green eyes gleaming with an oth-erworldly glow.

"Hello, Kaydin." She reached out her hand, running her fingers along his jaw, tempting him, like the wicked tempt-ress she was. But it wouldn't work on him. Not while he still had Rena's scent in his mind.

"So are you going rogue or going soft?" she taunted. "You

could have killed the girl and closed the portal years ago. Why didn't you?"

He snarled at her and she drew back, but she didn't lose that wicked smile.

"I know you'd like nothing more than to take me to the ground and have your wild, ferocious way with me. But that isn't going to happen. Not if you ever want to see your precious little Rena again."

"You got what you wanted. Leave her alone."

"Oh, I plan to. By the time you go in there and bring her out, I'll be long gone."

"And how do you know I won't kill you right now?"

"Because if you do, the portal will close and you will never see your sweet little Rena again. And you've already sacrificed so much for her. I know. I've watched you."

"You don't know what I'll do."

"Don't I? Happy hunting, Kaydin. I really hope it won't take you too many years to find her and then find your way back out. As you know, it's a maze down there."

She turned and walked away and he knew she was right. Knew he was making a critical mistake. Again. By letting her walk away, he was letting a temptress demon loose in the world to cause all kinds of hell on earth. It could take him years to track her down, years that this portal would stay open, unguarded and unprotected. It went against his creed, his honor, his principles.

And yet, he couldn't bring himself to kill her. If he did, the portal would close trapping Rena inside with no hope of rescue. She'd go mad within days. And she'd be lost to him forever.

He couldn't do it.

He couldn't let her die today any more than he could let her die fifteen years ago. Something about her had reached inside him, grabbed hold of his human heart and refused to let go.

He turned his back on the demon, stretched up on his hind legs and roared as he began his transformation. He only hoped he'd be able to find her. And soon.

Kaydin entered the portal lights and ran through the doorway. Immediately he was immersed in darkness, guided only by the lights twinkling far off in the darkness. He hadn't been inside the portal since his transformation, but he remembered his fear and confusion, he knew what Rena must be feeling.

He hurried forward, taking one turn after another, passing demon after demon, some who shied away, some who taunted and laughed. He caught a faint whiff of Rena's sweet scent and followed it, turning down one tunnel after another, chasing that scent, chasing her.

He knew she must be scared and confused. The demons would be taunting her, trying to drive her to madness. If she lost touch with reality then she'd never find her way back. She'd never be able to make the transformation to guardian.

He turned down another corridor and saw her crouched against the wall, her head buried in her knees. He hurried to her, and pushed his nose against her hair and whimpered. She looked up at him, her eyes the same golden amber he'd seen when they were making love.

It was then he knew the truth of why she could see the lights, why the demon wanted her so badly. She wasn't a witch. She was a shapeshifter. She was one of the few left who had a dormant gene passed down through the generations. It would have stayed that way had she never come near the portal or made the descent into the pit. Once they entered the gateway, they became what they were meant to be—guardians of the earth.

She wrapped her arms around his neck and cried into his fur. He whimpered and licked her cheek. This was why he was so drawn to her, why he couldn't let her die. She was meant to be with him. He was meant to help her.

And to do that, he needed to change. He needed to return to his human form and hope they could find their way out together. Hope she'd let him help her do what needed to be done. He took a deep breath and focused on his human form, the beat of his heart, the tenderness he felt for this woman clinging to him. And then he shifted once more, back into his body. And as he did, his senses became muted. He felt the demons circling, heard their taunts, their laughter and he knew he had to get her out of there. Now.

He lifted Rena into his arms.

"She wasn't there," she said into his ear. "My mother was gone."

"I'm sorry," he whispered, and held her close as she wept into his shoulder.

"I should have listened to you."

"It doesn't matter. We're going to get out. We're going to find her."

"No. *I'm* going to find her, Kaydin."

He looked down at her surprised by the steel in her voice.

"I'm going to find her, and then I'm going to kill her."

And he'd let her. But first, they had to make it out of the pit. The voices were overpowering now, whispering, pulling, pushing. He was going in circles and couldn't find his way. Finally, out of breath, he stopped and leaned against a wall and was stunned to discover it was the same wall he'd found Rena against earlier. All this time, and they were back where they'd started.

"Rena, we're not going to be able to find out way out of here. Not as we are."

She looked up at him. "What do you mean?"

"We've been wandering in circles. We're in the pit, which is nothing but a huge maze. It entices you one way, pushes you in another until you end up back where you started without knowing how you got there."

"We can do this, Kaydin. We have to."

"You need to embrace your path. You need to transform."

"What are you talking about?" Her eyes widened in the gloom.

"The reason you're here. The reason you hear the voices. It's because you're like me. You're a shapeshifter. You had to enter the pit to make the change. We all did, at one time or another. It's your rite of passage. It's how you'll find your true path."

She shook her head. "No. You're wrong. I'm not like you. I'm nothing like you. You're not even human!"

"You are. And you know it."

She pushed away from him as angry tears filled her eyes. "If you hadn't brought me here, if you hadn't commissioned me to paint those lights, I never would have come back here. I could have gone on living at Vindecare with my friends. Life could have been good. Life could have been normal."

"You always would have heard the voice of the demon calling you."

"So? I could have ignored it. Like always. You did this to me. You brought me here!"

He tried to grab her, to put his arms around her and pull her tight, but she beat him, her small fists flailing against his chest.

"You did this to me. I won't become like you. I won't."

"You have to. If you don't, we will never get out of here. Don't you understand, it's what you're meant to do. It's your journey. I can help you. I can guide you. But in the end, it's you who will have to make it back out of the pit. Only you can find the way."

"But I can't. I don't know how." She collapsed against his chest, her shoulders heaving with her grief. And his heart broke for her. For all she was about to lose, and for the incredible burden she was about to gain. He only hoped that she would find her way and that maybe, if the gods allowed, they could find happiness together.

"Think Rena. Think back to all the times you just knew. When you felt guided by something beyond yourself. Look inside and listen to the voice, not 'her' voice, but yours. You are the only one who can lead us out of here."

And then he changed, doing what he had to do. He transformed in front of her, turning into what she had always feared, yet what was buried deep within her. He turned into her beast.

Rena watched in morbid fascination as Kaydin left her. She knew she should be afraid, but she couldn't anymore. There was no fear left in her. Only anger and sadness. Everything she knew, everyone she loved was gone. Nothing mattered any longer. Not even her humanity.

And as Kaydin dropped to the ground at her feet, she yelled at him. "Go away. Go on. Get out of here. You don't belong here. I don't want you with me."

He just looked at her and whimpered, then laid his head on her feet.

"Damn you," she muttered.

She knew they had been going in circles, knew they would never find their way out. But he didn't need to stay in here with her. He could go back and do what he'd always done. Guard a doorway.

And not very well.

Otherwise, he wouldn't have let her mother go in all those years ago. And he would have killed her tonight when he had the chance. But he didn't. And now it was left to her. She would kill the demon who stole her life. That was her purpose now. Her only reason for getting out. For dragging him out.

She reached down deep inside herself and found the path he was talking about. She found the hard, dark fist of anger clenched around her heart, and she felt it squeeze.

And as she did, she lifted her head back and roared.

And then she was running, loping on all fours. It didn't matter that it was dark, because suddenly she could smell the forest, she could hear the water rushing in the nearby river. She could easily find her way out of the darkness and toward the demon that had brought her there.

She could smell the demon, too. Smell her evil. Hear her whispers. It fueled her fury, and she ran faster, not even sure if Kaydin was still behind her. She just kept running, until she saw the lights ahead, and then she extended her front legs and jumped, breaching the perimeter, bursting through the heavy darkness and into the night of the forest.

She ran into the dark, following the scent of the demon, determined to end this once and for all. She didn't know how far she'd run or for how long, but now she felt Kaydin on her heels behind her. She stopped in front of a small cabin. The woman was inside.

The woman who would be her mother.

But before she could step closer, she heard the growl of the panther. The hair rose on the back of her neck. Then Kaydin was flying through the air. And as the two beasts clawed and tore at one another, Rena moved closer to the cabin. She concentrated on her body—her legs, her arms and easily transformed into her human self once more.

She walked up to the cabin and knocked on the door.

"Rena," her mother said, and smiled as she opened the door. "It's good to see you."

"Is it?" Rena asked. She walked inside, grabbed a throw blanket off an easy chair and wrapped it around her, covering herself.

"Of course. I only needed you to go in long enough for me to get out. I didn't need you to stay in there. In fact, now that you're out, we can be together. The way it should have been. Could have been, if it wasn't for that damned wolf."

"He came after me."

"He must be very attached to you."

Rena stared at the woman who would be her mother, but she knew her mother was no longer there. Now it was so easy to smell the demon within.

"You killed my mother. You stole her from me," she accused. "Then you whispered to me for years, wanting me to call you. To say your name."

Surprised, the demon took a step back.

Rena stepped forward. "Ubasti," she whispered.

Her mother's face paled and her eyes widened as she shook her head.

"Ubasti," Rena said again then yanked the golden locket off her mother's neck. "I'm calling your name. I'm commanding you to enter me. Come to me, Ubasti. Come to me now."

In a flash of light the demon flowed from the form of her mother and filled Rena's body. Her mother dropped to the floor, and without the life force of the demon inside her, quickly decayed and turned to a pile of dust.

Rena walked out the door and as she did she pulled the strength of Kratos into her, the fire from Hephaestus, and the protection from Hades inside her. Then with a roar of sweet satisfaction she transformed into the wolf—into the guardian of the earth.

Ubasti screamed inside her.

"I am not like my mother, Ubasti. I am not a witch. And now that I've been inside the pit, I can never be host to a demon. Because I kill demons. It's what I'm meant to do."

Ubasti screamed again before disintegrating and pouring out of Rena in a powerful column of smoke and ash.

The next morning Rena woke in the tall grass with the sun shining in her eyes and the morning dew kissing her cheeks. She lifted her hands in front of her, stared up at her fingers and wiggled them. Had it all been a dream? Had she been lying here since yesterday afternoon?

She turned her head and saw Kaydin lying naked next to her. He had three long bloody gashes along his side. Claw marks. And then she knew it was all true.

She traced her fingers along the cuts knowing that by to-morrow, they'd be healed just as hers were now.

He opened his beautiful green eyes. "Are you okay?" he asked.

She nodded. "Better than okay."

He smiled then ran his fingers down her arm, gently caressing, sending shivers of heat along her skin. He kissed her, gently at first then harder and faster as his hunger rose. His taste filled her, heating her blood as he pulled her to him. Skin against skin, tongue against tongue.

She heard the thunder of his heartbeat as his blood pulsed within him and smelled the musty scent of their desire thickening in the air. She arched her back, pushing her breast into his cupped hand, letting loose a whimpering moan as he tweaked her hardened nipple.

She felt his need for her, hot and hard, pushing against her inner thigh. And she wanted him. Wanted him buried deep inside her. She rolled herself beneath him, thrusting up her hips and wrapping her legs around him, cradling his erection within her moist heat.

"Now Kaydin."

With one quick thrust he sheathed himself within her, moving fast, moving hard, until she couldn't think, couldn't breathe, could only feel the sensations shimmering through her. She clung to him, riding their primal movements, oblivious to everything but this man and his love. And when she finally reached her release, she leaned her head back and screamed, again and again, until the screams echoing back at her sounded almost like a howl.

After a few minutes of lying in the grass, trying to catch her breath and still her beating heart, Kaydin rose off her. He stood looking down and smiled.

She smiled back, not needing to say anything, to put words to how she felt. He held out a hand. "Let's go home."

She put her hand in his. He helped her up and they walked together through the woods toward the house with the painting of the wolf above the fireplace. Toward where she was meant to be. She knew it, just like she knew Kaydin was who she was meant to be with. She knew it with certainty.

* * * * *

PROTECTOR'S MATE

KATIE REUS

Katie Reus has been reading romance for as long as she can remember, but she didn't always know she wanted to be a writer. After graduating *summa cum laude* with a degree in psychology and working too many jobs she hated, she finally figured things out. She currently lives in the South with her own real-life hero. When she's not busy with her family, she spends her days writing dark paranormal romance and sexy romantic suspense.

Chapter One

Felicia Serna wasn't ready for the shock of cold air that hit her when she exited the sliding glass door of Huntsville International Airport. The chilly February air was a drastic change from the dry heat of Afghanistan.

The airport was bustling but no one would be there to pick her up. She'd kept her return home to Alabama a secret. Well, home was a relative word. After the way she'd left two years ago, she didn't think the Alpha of her pack would want to see her. And if he did, it would only be to punish her for defying him. As far as she was concerned, she didn't belong to his pack anymore and hadn't for a long time.

She was through with pack rules and through with being someone's doormat. If she had to live as a lone wolf, so be it. She could take care of herself. Hell, she'd been doing fine on her own for years. The only reason she'd returned was because she had a few human friends here and had shipped most of her belongings back.

As she started to wave down a taxi, a dark SUV with even darker tinted windows pulled up to the curb, blocking her view. She grasped the handle of her suitcase and walked down a few feet so the taxi could see her. It was late and she didn't want to risk having to wait an hour for another ride. Unlike in Kabul, at least here she didn't have to worry about safe transportation.

When she raised her hand again, the SUV pulled up farther, effectively blocking her again.

An icy fist clasped around her heart and she tried to shake off the dread that welled up inside her. The driver *couldn't* be following her. She was just being paranoid. No one knew she was back. How could they? Before she took another step, the driver's side door opened and out stepped over six feet of pure muscle and sex appeal and the only shifter who'd ever made her panties dampen with just one look. Her mouth went dry when they made eye contact. What was *he* doing here? His Alpha's territory didn't extend this far north so there was no reason for Alaric to be here unless he was specifically checking up on her. Because she knew for a fact his Alpha had a private plane and he would have no need to be at the airport.

When Alaric, the five-hundred year old shifter who starred in all her fantasies, walked around the front of the vehicle she automatically took a step back. She inwardly cursed the sign of wariness, but if any werewolf intimidated her, it was definitely this one.

Dark hair, dark eyes, generally dark disposition. She'd never seen him in shifted form but, even as a human, the man had a way of putting others on edge in his presence. It was no wonder he was second in command to one of the strongest packs in the United States.

His espresso-colored eyes assessed her from head to foot in a slow sweep. Though she was sure the perusal was cursory, her cheeks heated just the same. She'd forgotten what his mere presence did to her nerves. Okay, maybe not forgotten exactly. Just buried the memory.

Somehow she found her voice and was surprised when it came out strong. "How...why are you here?"

"I'm picking you up." He answered as if it should be obvious. The deep timbre of his gravelly voice sent a shock of awareness straight to her lower abdomen. She didn't want to admit that it affected her but just hearing him... She fought off a shiver.

She hadn't seen him in almost five years, then a few months ago he'd contacted her via email out of the blue. She'd been more shocked than anything that the sexy wolf even remembered her, since they'd only met once before that. When the last few emails had turned flirty, sexual even, it had freaked her out. At first she'd thought maybe she'd misread their tone, but then he'd gotten more blatant and she'd known there was no mistaking he was flirting with her. She'd begun to wonder if he'd maybe confused her with someone else from her old pack. It made no sense for Alaric to be interested in her. So she'd started limiting their contact.

How had he known I'd be at the airport? She wanted to ask but keeping her cool around this wolf was important. Bigger, stronger wolves pounced on any perceived weakness. She'd learned that lesson long ago. Even if Alaric seemed different, she wouldn't forget the lessons she'd learned as a cub. Some memories went bone deep.

"Knox recently expanded and took over all of northern Alabama. That includes your old pack's territory—now my Alpha's territory." There he went with that voice again.

How did he expect her to think when he talked like that? *Wait, what did he just say? His Alpha had taken over?* "What happened to Lamont?" Wilson Lamont. Her old Alpha. Even saying that wolf's name left a bitter taste in her mouth.

"Dead. From vampires."

He didn't sound too torn up about it either. Interesting.

Despite the acute relief that splintered through her at the news, she held back her frustration at his fairly vague answer. "When?"

He shrugged in a maddeningly pure male way. "A while ago."

She resisted the urge to growl. That was most definitely something he should have told her in their email correspondence. At the moment, she was so tired even her eyelids ached. All she wanted was a straight answer. "So your Alpha took over his territory? What about the old members of the pack? And I still don't understand why you're here to pick *me* up."

His dark gaze narrowed for a second. "Most shifters would say 'my' pack, not 'the' pack."

She looked away under his intense scrutiny. When Lamont had demanded she submit to him, in addition to his first mate—as if she were some whore—no one had stepped up to defend her. Screw them. They weren't her pack. They weren't her anything. "You didn't answer my question."

"No, I didn't."

Out of the corner of her eye she spotted a yellow cab pulling up to the curb. It didn't look like anyone had claimed it and she didn't want to miss her chance. She didn't know why Alaric was here but she wasn't going to put herself in a position to be at his mercy. "Thanks for coming to the airport, but I'm afraid you wasted your time."

She turned away from him, but before she'd taken a step he plucked her suitcase and her carry-on from her hands and shoved them in the backseat of the SUV. She blinked once. The man moved lightning fast. Faster than any shifter she'd ever seen.

"What are you doing?" Panic laced her voice and she was unable to mask it.

"You're coming with me, little wolf." His voice softened slightly.

Why had his voice gone all husky like that? And why do I like it? Maybe she really was more tired than she realized. She mentally shook herself. It didn't matter. "Why didn't you tell me your Alpha had taken over this territory, Alaric? You've had plenty of opportunities."

"Why didn't you tell me you were *leaving* Afghanistan?" Now there was no softness in his voice. Just anger and something that sounded a lot like…hurt.

She swallowed hard at the surge of guilt that erupted inside her. The thought of telling him had crossed her mind, but he'd have likely wanted to see her. And after those last few emails… She couldn't deal with that now. Didn't want to deal with *anything*. All she wanted to do was sleep in a soft bed. She shifted from foot to foot as she ran over her options. He had her bags and she certainly couldn't overpower him. Not to mention, making a scene at the airport was stupid. His reputation was fearsome, but she'd never heard that he hurt females. Not much to go on, but her inner wolf didn't fear him and that said a lot. She ignored his question and asked another one of her own. "Where are you taking me?"

"Where you belong," he growled softly. Possessively.

She frowned at the tone of his voice, then raked a hand through her hair. She'd been traveling for nearly thirty-six hours and didn't have the energy to figure out his riddles. Her entire body was tired. And she desperately needed to shift and run free for a while.

When an unbidden thought assaulted her mind, her eyes narrowed on his. "Is the reason you started emailing because of the way I left my old pack? Is this about punishment for my defiance? Your Alpha's angry with me so he sent you to deal with me?"

His jaw clenched tightly, but he didn't respond.

When his expression transformed to an unreadable mask, she rolled her eyes to cover her nervousness. That seemed to annoy him and for some reason she took perverse pleasure in the fact. "Fine, but if you're going to kill me or punish me make it quick."

He muttered something that sounded German but she couldn't be sure. Whatever he'd said, it wasn't endearing. He sounded pissed. At least he had the decency to open the passenger door for her. When she slid inside she was surprised to find they were alone. She'd assumed as second in command for a powerful pack, he'd travel with security. Of course someone like him likely didn't *need* security. He could probably kill ten wolves with his pinky toe. Or just stare them down with that penetrating gaze until they submitted.

As Alaric pulled away from the curb, he wanted to strangle and kiss the gorgeous she-wolf at the same time. *Kill her?* Not bloody likely. The slim, dark-haired, blue-eyed beauty brought out all his protective instincts. She always had. He'd wanted to claim her years ago but she'd been too young. Barely nineteen, she wouldn't have been ready for him then. And he'd wanted her to spread her wings and get an education before he made his move. By the time he'd heard what that bastard Lamont wanted from her, it had been too late.

She'd been on a plane to a war zone and had ignored all attempts her pack made to contact her. That's why he was surprised she'd returned his first attempt at contact all those months ago. A couple years had passed since she'd left the country and he'd gotten tired of waiting for her to come home. She was strong and old enough now and his inner wolf wanted her so bad he constantly ached for it. Given her distrust of her own kind, he needed to somehow convince her she was meant to be his. It surprised him she didn't feel the same pull he did for her, but persuading her wouldn't be a chore.

He glanced over at her and had started to ask a question when he realized she was asleep. Not a deep slumber, but her breathing was calm and her eyes had drifted shut. She really must be tired. Only a couple minutes had passed since he'd pulled away from the airport. Her head lolled back against the headrest and although her arms were crossed protectively against herself, her chest rose and fell in a steady rhythm. Even if she might not trust him, her inner wolf knew she was safe in his presence. That had to mean something.

He resisted the primal urge to reach out and trail a finger down her cheek. To run his hands through her slightly curly, chestnut-colored hair. She'd let it grow a few inches since he'd seen her last. Hell, she'd probably had a dozen different styles since then. Her café au lait skin was darker, more tanned than the last time he'd seen her. No doubt from the time she'd spent outdoors. As a nurse for an international health organization, she'd spent a lot of time in refugee camps, something he vastly admired about her even if every day he'd worried about her. He forced his gaze to the road in front of him. He'd been dreaming about this moment for years. He could wait a few more minutes. Too bad his inner wolf didn't want to listen.

As he cruised through the quiet night streets, he spotted the same green truck that had tailed him to the airport. At first he'd thought he was being paranoid, but this was too much of a coincidence. When he neared the upcoming yellow light, instead of slowing down, he flipped a sharp U-turn into the parallel two-lane road.

Felicia jerked awake with a gasp and grabbed her armrest. A few horns blared and the spike of adrenaline that rolled off her was sharp and acidic. Thanks to the close confines of the vehicle and his extrasensory abilities, he could hear the thump of her erratic heartbeat. "What's going on?"

"I think we're being followed."

She whipped her head around.

In the rearview mirror he watched the green truck jump the median and swerve into their lane. Lately both he and Knox suspected someone from the new pack they'd taken over was plotting to cause dissension among their ranks. Knox had recently mated with a vampire—something rare for a shifter to do, especially an Alpha—so all the warriors had been on edge lately. Especially since they'd had to kick out one of their own when he tried to attack Knox's new mate. While Alaric couldn't be sure this was related, he had no way of knowing that it wasn't. Hell, it could just be a rogue vampire or rogue werewolf out for blood, but he didn't think so. Alaric wasn't easy prey and the rogue beasts from both species liked easy hunts.

As the truck gained ground, he switched lanes and pulled down a side street.

"Why would someone be following us?" Despite the tension he scented rolling off her, her voice was calm.

Before he could answer, the back window exploded in a shower of raining glass. Metallic pings ricocheted off the inside of the vehicle.

"Get down!" he shouted.

A slight trail of fear trickled off her as she unstrapped her seat belt and scooted lower in her seat but she didn't panic. "Do you have any weapons?"

"Yes but they're in the back—"

Without pause, she dove into the second seat with a speed that impressed him. He tightened his grip on the steering wheel and swerved down another one-way side street. For a moment they lost their tail and the only sound was the whistling of the wind rushing through the blown-out window. He caught sight of her in the rearview mirror digging through his bag of weapons. "What the hell are you doing?"

"What does it look like? You want to let some crazy human hunters try to kill us? I'm going to blow out their tires."

As a shifter, from a young age she'd have been trained like all of their kind to use weapons, but he didn't like the thought of her hanging out the window making herself a target. "I don't think they're human, Felicia."

Understanding crossed her face as she met his gaze in the mirror. If it wasn't humans hunting them—and few even knew of their existence so he doubted it was them—it would be someone of the supernatural variety and they'd be more than capable of tracking and killing them. It was one of the reasons the tribe leaders from the six most powerful vampire covens and six of the strongest werewolf Alphas in North America would be gathering soon to discuss a treaty between their kinds. Too many rogue vampires and rogue shifters without tribe leaders or Alphas were wreaking havoc in the human world. Taking victims whenever they felt like it. Since there wasn't a formal organization to mete out justice to offenders, if paranormal beings didn't belong to a group and they hurt humans, there was no one to bring them to justice. If the shifters and vamps could come to an agreement and actually work together, everyone would be held accountable for their actions, especially loners.

But Alaric knew a few blown tires wouldn't slow down either shifters or vamps. It would only enrage them. Not to mention they'd be smart enough to be packing silver-lined bullets, which could be fatal to shifters.

Under normal circumstances he'd stay and fight but he couldn't risk it. Not with Felicia. Not when she was finally under his protection. As the headlights appeared in his mirror again, he did the only thing he could.

"Hold on," he said through gritted teeth.

The needle on the speedometer spiked sharply as he pressed on the gas. When he'd put enough distance between them, he took his foot off the accelerator, slightly depressed the brakes and yanked the wheel.

Everything in the vehicle shifted at once.

Felicia let out a startled cry as she slammed against the door, but he didn't glance back at her. He couldn't afford to be distracted. Mercifully, the SUV didn't flip when he pulled it into a one-eighty spin. The engine sputtered and growled as he hit the gas again.

"Are you playing chicken with them?" Now her voice rose, panic clear in every syllable.

He didn't answer. They'd survive a crash. Sure, they might suffer a few broken bones and internal injuries but they'd heal quickly. It was a calculated risk but he needed to slow down their pursuers and get her to safety. Racing all over Huntsville was a surefire way to get noticed by the human cops, something they couldn't afford.

Protect Felicia.

It was all that mattered.

The silhouettes of the driver and passenger were becoming more visible. Two males, and possibly a third person in the backseat. He couldn't be sure. Might be a shadow.

The truck wavered and jerked back and forth, but it didn't alter its path. Alaric braced himself for impact. If the other driver didn't back down, this was going to be painful. He'd broken more bones than he could remember over the past five centuries, but it still hurt every time.

As he increased his speed, the truck weaved erratically.

"Strap in, Felicia," he ground out. Hurting her was the last thing he wanted to do, but there was no other way.

All his muscles tensed. As he prepared for the impact, the truck swerved off the road at the last second. Glass and metal crunched behind them as the vehicle rammed into a telephone pole. With his extrasensory abilities he heard the pole creak dangerously as it cracked and fell onto the truck, but Alaric didn't pause in his escape.

"What the hell is going on?" Felicia demanded as he turned back onto a main street. At least she sounded more annoyed than scared.

Even though his Alpha had recently taken a vampire as a mate, he wasn't sure who would be coming after them right now. Some of the new pack members might not like their new female Alpha, but making a move like this against him made no sense. Alaric wasn't on pack business at the moment. And hurting him or Felicia wouldn't affect the upcoming formal treaty between vampires and shifters, which was barely a couple months away. It would only solidify the need for it. He didn't have time to go into all the possibilities though. "Grab what you need from your bag. *Necessities* only. I'm going to find a safe place to park then we're shifting." It would be harder to track them that way. He could go home to the protection of his pack, but he wanted Felicia to himself for a while. He'd already run it by Knox and his Alpha had given him the okay.

She'd left Huntsville because of her former Alpha and he planned to show her that his pack was different. That she could have a different kind of life than the one she'd run from. Her grace under fire tonight had only solidified how tough she was. She might have worked overseas in a war zone but it hadn't been in a military capacity. Her reactions tonight had been purely instinctive. Whether she realized it or not, her inner wolf had known they needed protecting and had taken over.

Unfortunately he couldn't get a read on her. She'd left Afghanistan without telling him, completely cutting him off as if he meant *nothing* to her. As if their friendship wasn't as important to her as it was to him. That cut bone deep. He might want her with a fierceness that stunned him, but it didn't mean she felt the same. A dull throb spread across his chest at the thought that she might never feel the pull that he did. If that was true…he shook his head. He couldn't even think about that possibility.

Chapter Two

Felicia's heart beat an erratic tattoo against her chest. She'd been under fire in Jalalabad more than a few times before, but she'd never imagined experiencing an attack on the streets of Huntsville. That was just too surreal. It didn't matter that she could survive almost anything— explosions and gunfire scared the crap out of her. Even though she had about a million questions for Alaric it was obvious he didn't plan to answer any of them at the moment. Stubborn male.

She'd love nothing more than to drag the answers out of him but now wasn't the time. She fished out her wallet, passport, a pair of pants, a sweater and one pair of sandals. Everything else was replaceable. She'd shipped most of her stuff back weeks ago to a human friend so she could travel light. At the moment she was thankful she'd made that decision.

Alaric steered into the dimly lit, nearly deserted parking lot of a closed supermarket and jumped from the vehicle. She followed him and watched as he grabbed a small backpack from the back—full of his weapons—then took her small bundle of clothes and shoved them inside. For a brief moment he trained that hot gaze on her and she could feel herself being swallowed up by his dark, soul-searching eyes. She knew his look didn't mean anything, that it was all in her head, but for a moment she imagined what it would be like to be on the receiving end of a heated glance from him.

He quickly looked away and scanned the area around them. "You need to stay close to me. We're going to have to run through a few residential neighborhoods, but it's late so we should be able to blend in." Despite his unreadable expression, his commanding voice had a soothing effect on her.

She nodded but her throat seized as he started stripping down in front of her. Just took off his clothes like it was no big deal. When he bared his taut, muscular chest, she averted her gaze. Most shifters didn't care about nudity but she was from a different generation. As far as she knew Alaric was almost five hundred years old and, well, he was a man. It didn't seem to matter what species they were, males didn't care about showing off their stuff.

But she did.

Turning her back to him, she slipped off her boots and then forced herself to undergo the change. She hated to ruin her clothes, but she was *not* stripping in front of him. Her cargo pants and T-shirt ripped as her bones broke and shifted. The pain rushed over her like she'd been flattened by a truck but, as always, it was fleeting. Once her ligaments and tendons realigned, the sudden euphoric charge nearly overwhelmed her. Everything was clearer. Smells and sounds were sharper. The night air rushed over her newly sprouted fur as she surveyed her surroundings.

A cold nose nudged her in the side. She turned to find herself looking at a hulking gray wolf. He was at least a hundred and thirty pounds of pure muscle. With strong back legs and a broad chest, she felt dwarfed next to him. She was already small for a shifter but next to him, she felt absolutely puny.

A weak mongrel. How many times had she been reminded of that growing up?

She shook away her insecurities and fell behind him as he darted down an alley toward a quiet neighborhood. Her muscles strained and stretched as they raced through the streets and darted in and out of backyards. She guessed that if any humans saw them he'd look pretty strange carrying a pack in his mouth. At least it was night and the asphalt wasn't hot against her paws. It seemed they ran forever, though she was sure barely an hour had passed by the time they stopped at the back door of a two-story brick house in a cozy middle-class neighborhood.

Before she had time to prepare herself, he shifted to his human form. Then he simply stood there in all his naked glory staring at her. *Waiting.* Lord, why did he have to look so good? There was no fat on the man. Taut skin stretched across his broad, muscular chest and shoulders. His arms looked like they were chiseled from stone, and she wanted to drool at the sight of what was between his massive legs.

She couldn't help it. She turned away from him as she underwent the change. Somehow she managed to stifle a cry as her bones shifted back into place. Her heart raced wildly and she could feel his gaze burning into her naked back. Staring at and assessing her. No doubt with a critical eye. Where he was built like a Greek god, she was way too skinny for a shifter. That's what the women of her pack had constantly told her growing up. She'd more or less grown into her body but her breasts were still pretty nonexistent. On more than one occasion Lamont had told her she was lucky he'd even offered for her. What wolf would want someone like her?

A shifter like Alaric could have any female he wanted. Hell, he probably had a new, stacked she-wolf in his bed every week. Something akin to jealousy jumped in her gut at the thought of him with a female, but she ignored it. She didn't care who he slept with, and it was none of her business anyway.

"Here." He reached over her shoulder and gave her one of his T-shirts.

She quickly tugged it over her head and was thankful when it fell to midthigh. His spicy scent enveloped her, all earthy and male and way too intoxicating. For the first time in years she felt like that awkward nineteen-year-old girl with a silly crush. How many nights had she lain awake thinking about him after their first meeting? His Alpha had sent Alaric to visit her pack for something since they were in neighboring territories at the time and she'd been absolutely smitten by the sexy wolf. It was embarrassing to even remember it.

Relief poured over her when she heard the door unlock then open. "This is it. We'll bunk down here for the night," he murmured, too close for comfort.

His deep voice rolled over her skin like a soft breeze. She turned and tried to brush past him, but he blocked her. Refusing to make eye contact, she glanced down but wished she hadn't. His erection stood tall, thick and proud against his abdomen.

An answering rush of need burned low inside her. She knew his reaction wasn't to her, but the result of the adrenaline rush they'd just experienced. After working in a war zone, she understood that it had that effect on some people, especially males.

One of his strong fingers lifted her chin, forcing her gaze upward. The concern she saw in his dark eyes surprised her. "I think we lost them, okay?"

She nodded mutely. If she spoke, her voice would shake and she couldn't afford to show any weakness.

He frowned and stroked her cheek with the rough pad of

his thumb. "You don't have to be afraid. I won't let anyone hurt you ever again."

When his voice softened like that, her stomach did annoying little flips. She swallowed hard and fought for control. "I'd like to take a shower, if that's all right."

More than anything she wanted to get out from under his watchful gaze. She suspected he could smell her desire and it was embarrassing. If she could get a few minutes to herself, she'd be able to gather her thoughts and contain her searing lust. The last time she'd reacted this badly to a man had been five years ago. Unfortunately, it had been to *Alaric*. But she'd been so young then and she'd never met any shifters outside her pack up until that point. It had been a silly crush. At least that's what she told herself. So why was she experiencing the same rush of uncontrollable desire again?

His dark eyes narrowed a fraction but he nodded. "Fine. The shower is upstairs. First door on the right. But when you're finished, we're going to talk."

Something about the way he said "talk" sent a shiver of something—fear maybe—rolling over her skin. When she'd run away she'd known there would be repercussions if she'd been caught, but no one had come after her. Maybe that's what was happening now. Since she hadn't officially declared her intent to leave her old pack she was still technically governed by whatever Alpha ruled her territory. A heavy knot twisted inside her and pulled tight. She'd run before and she'd do it again if she had to.

Chapter Three

Alaric waited until he heard the sound of running water upstairs before calling his Alpha.

Knox answered on the first ring. "Everything okay with Felicia?"

"Yeah, but she seems to think I plan to hurt or punish her or something." He dug his fingers into his palm at the thought of someone harming the petite she-wolf.

"Hurt her?" A sharp bark of laughter escaped Knox.

"Listen, that's not our only problem." He quickly filled his leader in on the attempted attack after he'd picked Felicia up from the airport.

When he was finished Knox was silent for a moment. "Vamps or shifters?"

"I don't know, but it's not a good thing whoever it was." Especially since the formal treaty between both species hadn't been signed. Neither side wanted any violent incidents before then. Even if it was a couple of rogue vamps who had tried to attack them, since there wasn't an official method of punishing rogues, it wouldn't do shifters as a whole any good if he meted out justice to vampires—even if his actions would be justified. Vamps could use his actions to try to gain leverage for the signing. Knox's sigh was heavy but he didn't respond. He didn't have to because they both knew how fragile the future was at the moment. "I'll send some of the men to check out the accident. See if they can pick up a scent. What about you? When are you bringing her in?"

Alaric had wanted a few days alone with her before bringing her to the compound and under the protection of her new pack, but his Alpha needed him and he couldn't shirk his duties. Since he was second in command, staying close to Knox right now was important. "I need a night alone with her, but we're at the safe house." Only Knox and Alaric's brothers knew about the place so unless someone managed to track them down—and considering how many side streets and detours he'd taken them on, he doubted it—he could keep Felicia safe for the night.

"It's up to you. If you want more time with her, you've got it."

"Thanks." When he heard the shower upstairs stop, he got off the phone and quickly pulled his clothes from his backpack.

He tugged on a pair of jeans but kept the top button undone. He preferred to walk around naked but it had obviously bothered Felicia. At least she'd *noticed* him. Not that he'd been trying to hide his reaction. He wanted to make it clear he was interested. She'd been ready to get the hell away from him though. It surprised him how deep her small rejection had cut him. Over the past few months they'd become friends—or he'd thought they had.

Thanks to his contacts overseas he knew she hadn't dated or been intimate with anyone in the past two years. If she'd shown a remote interest in *anyone* while overseas—human or shifter—he'd have been on the first plane to see her. His inner beast wouldn't have allowed him any other option. Hundreds of years ago he'd tamed and controlled his animal side, but the thought of Felicia with another male made something deep and dark inside him roar with anger and possessiveness.

A lot had changed since she'd been gone. Most of her old pack members had dispersed to various parts of the country, though a few had assimilated into Knox's pack. Felicia didn't seem to even care to meet the new pack. She'd come back to Huntsville and hadn't told a soul—including him—so he could only guess what her plans were. And she seemed intent to keep him at arm's length. That bothered him more than anything. He knew he should have mentioned his Alpha had taken over her old pack's territory in their email correspondence. Hell, he'd had plenty of opportunity but something had held him back. He hadn't wanted to spook her into cutting off all contact with him. He hadn't been willing to risk it. Not when she'd started opening up to him.

Before he heard her, he scented her descending the stairs. Something sweet, exotic and vanilla tickled his nose as she entered the brightly lit kitchen.

She'd twisted her damp hair into some sort of knot above her neck and her flawless skin glowed from being freshly scrubbed. Those electric blue eyes of hers regarded him carefully. Against her tanned skin they were piercing. His gaze trailed down to where she clutched her towel tighter against her chest and all he could think about was pulling it off her and seeing what he'd missed earlier. The thought of what color her nipples would be had kept him awake at night.

She loudly cleared her throat. "Can I have my clothes?"

Jerking his head to meet her gaze, he nodded at the backpack lying open on the kitchen island. "In the bag." He had to stop staring like a pervert if he didn't want to freak her out. Though he was tempted to hand them to her, he didn't trust himself to get so close to her when she was practically naked. The urge to touch her was overwhelming and his inner wolf was clawing at the surface. He turned toward the stainless steel refrigerator and pulled it open. "Are you hungry?"

"No, I ate on the plane, but a drink would be nice, thank you." He could hear her moving around behind him.

A gentleman would let her get dressed with some sense of privacy. He was barely civilized, however. As he turned around she was tugging on a slim-fitting pair of pants. Before she pulled them fully up, he got an eyeful of more than he bargained for.

She'd already put her sweater on so he missed seeing her breasts but he got the perfect view of her lower body. Her slim waist flared into surprisingly curvy hips. He barely bit back a growl as he watched the material slide up her legs. She'd been hiding a lot under those baggy cargo pants. And the soft thatch of perfectly trimmed dark hair covering her mound made him inwardly groan. Knowing she wouldn't be wearing anything underneath her clothes had him breaking out into a sweat. When his gaze finally trailed back up to her face, her cheeks were tinged crimson.

"Do you have no manners?" she snapped, but he didn't miss the burst of desire that rolled off her.

He fought a smile. "Not generally."

"Well...where's my drink?" The haughty way she asked sent a jolt of awareness to his cock.

He knew she was trying to cover her embarrassment. "We've got beer, wine, orange juice—"

"Wine is perfect," she muttered as she took a seat on one of the high-backed chairs at the center island.

"What made you decide to finally come back to Alabama?" He tried to keep his question casual.

She bit her bottom lip and he could tell she was weighing her answer. Finally she shrugged but he didn't miss the flash of pain in her eyes. "My contract was over so I had to go somewhere. It's the only home I've ever known and I still have a few human friends here from school. Mainly I…didn't know where else to go."

Her soft-spoken declaration touched something deep inside him. A place he'd forgotten existed. For the past three hundred years he'd been part of Knox's pack but even for the two hundred before that, he'd always had his brothers. After their parents had died, the four of them had stuck together until joining with Knox. They were all alpha in nature but none of them were true Alphas and they'd been lucky enough to find a good leader. Bottom line, they'd always belonged somewhere.

He knew enough about Felicia's history to understand that she didn't have anyone. Not truly. Lamont's pack had taken her in when she was a cub because she'd had nowhere to go. Didn't even know who her parents were. Finally he decided to ask the question that had been weighing on him for years. "Why didn't you call me two years ago instead of leaving the country?" His pack would have taken her in with no questions asked.

She raised her eyebrows. "Why would I have called *you?*" There was no malice in her voice, only utter confusion.

He placed her glass in front of her and sat. "Did Lamont never tell you…" Realization came in a swift punch to his stomach. Of course that sneaky bastard hadn't told Felicia that Alaric planned to claim her.

"Tell me what?" She eyed him warily as she took a small sip of her wine.

"Nothing." Now things made sense. If she had no idea of his intentions, she'd likely never given him a second thought after their first and only in-person meeting. His inner wolf had recognized her on a primal level and he'd wanted to claim her right then. He'd even contemplated asking her to join Knox's pack until she was older. But the beast in him had known he wouldn't have been able to wait to go after what he wanted. He hadn't been willing to doom their relationship before it even started. So he'd let her go. Going against all his primitive, dominant instincts had been the hardest thing he'd ever done.

"So who came after us tonight?" she asked.

He wanted to focus the conversation on her and their future, but she had a right to know, since she'd been caught in the crossfire. "About a month ago Knox mated with a vampire. Since then, we've had a few incidents in our territory. Nothing we can't handle. Usually young vampires or shifters who don't like mixing of the species or just don't want the treaty to move forward." He'd kept her informed on the details of the treaty in their emails, so when she finally returned she'd have an idea of how things were changing in North America.

She relaxed slightly at his answer. Just as quickly she frowned again, her pretty lips pulling into a thin line. "We've been emailing for *months,* but you failed to mention that your Alpha has taken over my old pack's territory. I want to know how you knew I'd be at the airport."

"I have friends in high places." Most humans might not know about their existence but a powerful few did. Alaric had been alive long enough that he'd made plenty of friends who owed him favors. And he'd been keeping tabs on Felicia from the moment she'd set foot on foreign soil. Something he wasn't sure she'd want to hear right now so he held back that bit of information.

Taking him by surprise, she slid off her seat and shoved it back. "Fine, don't give me a straight answer. I'm tired and cranky and unless you plan to hold me hostage, in the morning I'm leaving so—"

Before she could take another step, he was off his seat and had her pinned against the counter. His palms flattened against the flat surface on either side of her. The animal inside him demanded to take over. To claim her, *mark her.* He could feel his canines extending at the thought. Only the feel of her soft hand on his chest calmed him.

"Alaric?" Her voice was breathless and the pulse in her neck jumped with abandon. Lust, wariness and confusion twined off her in equal measures. The mixture of the sweet and sharp scents were an odd contrast.

"Why do you want to leave?" he asked quietly. He wanted to understand why she seemed to be afraid of him. After months of correspondence and getting to know each other—and his obvious physical reaction to her—how could she not know how much he wanted and cared for her? He thought he'd made himself pretty damn clear until he realized she was returning to Alabama without telling him.

"I...shouldn't have come back here. I have no reason to stay." Her blue eyes seemed to glow with intensity as she stared at him.

"Maybe I should give you a reason then."

She sucked in a deep breath but didn't look away. When her tongue darted out to moisten her pink lips, his entire body tensed as he imagined that tongue flicking over a certain part of his anatomy. Instinctively he rolled his hips against her. Letting her feel what she did to him.

She flushed a deep crimson when she felt the hard press of his erection but she didn't attempt to move away. A good sign.

"I want to kiss you." He wasn't asking but he also didn't make a move toward her. He wanted her willing and knew he had to play this right.

The hand she'd pressed against his chest suddenly flexed, her fingers digging into his skin. She wasn't pushing him away. It was almost as if she was trying to ground herself. Her other hand slid up his body and tentatively rested on his shoulder. When her eyes flared with unmasked hunger he took that as all the invitation he needed.

Covering her mouth with his, he barely restrained himself from growling. The slightly sweet taste of her wine mingled with the pureness of something that was all her. Something that made the most primitive part of him wake up and take notice. As her tongue tentatively danced with his, he had to rein in his animal side.

His inner wolf wanted out, to claim and mark her and take her right on the kitchen counter. But now wasn't the time. Now he needed to show her that not all wolves were like what she'd experienced in the past.

This was all about her and her pleasure.

Keeping his kisses light, he playfully tugged her bottom lip between his teeth. She let out a soft sigh and he could feel the residual tension in her slowly begin to leave her body. Unhurriedly, he ran his hands down her covered arms until he strayed to her waist. For a moment he had to force himself to keep still when all he wanted to do was pull her sweater up and off and feast on what he'd been fantasizing about.

Instead, he only pushed her top up a fraction and lightly stroked her bare stomach with the pads of his thumbs. Just the feel of her soft skin sent an electric shock through him.

He slowly stroked higher until he was almost cupping her breasts, but stopped just short. Instead he splayed his hands around her rib cage, savoring the feel of simply holding her. Her small build drove his protective instincts higher.

Her heart pounded a staccato thump under his hold, completely matching his own reaction. She was still slightly tense but her grip on him hadn't loosened. If anything it had tightened. The hand that had been on his shoulder now gripped the back of his neck and she was holding firm.

Giving in to his primitive side, he took a chance and started tugging her sweater up. Felicia pulled back slightly and though his lips ached to be on hers again, the payoff of seeing more of her skin was worth it. She lifted her arms and let him strip the top off her. Blindly he tossed it to the counter next to her. Her blue eyes practically sparked with electricity as she stared at him but he sensed the nervousness in her.

It was obvious she'd never learned to hide her emotions well. In a way it was nice that he didn't have to wonder what she was feeling, but at the same time he hated that she hadn't had someone looking out for her. Regardless of rank, pack is supposed to look after pack. Something she should have had growing up.

Her breathing was shallow and the lust she emanated was almost pure. But it comingled with something else, not fear exactly but…nervousness.

That was the last thing he ever wanted her to feel because of him. He braced his hands on the counter next to her and met her gaze. Keeping his eyes upward when all he wanted to do was drink in the sight of her breasts was damn hard. "You know what you smell like?" His question was a bare whisper.

Her blue eyes flared brighter for an instant, but then he could see her almost withdrawing into herself. Wariness crept over her features as if she didn't trust why he was asking her. "What?"

"Raspberries and champagne." He'd thought it from the first moment he'd met her. Fresh and sweet. "I want nothing more than to get drunk on you."

She blinked once. "Uh…oh."

He bit back a smile at the surprise in her voice and on her

face. When he'd started testing the waters during their emails with flirting, he'd known he had his work cut out for him when she didn't return his banter, but cut him off instead. Her inexperience was refreshing but he knew once they made it to the bedroom, they'd have fun together. Alaric leaned a little closer until he could feel her feather-soft breath brushing over his lips. "What about me?" he murmured.

She paused so long he wasn't sure she'd answer but finally she spoke, her voice a husky whisper. "You remind me of the forest, earthy and spicy and *very* male."

He smiled at her description. Closing the rest of the short distance between them, he swiped his tongue across the seam of her inviting lips, coaxing them open.

She quickly acquiesced, emitting a sigh of pure unadulterated pleasure as she let his tongue invade her mouth. While she might not have much experience, she gave as good as she got. As she explored his mouth, her hand slid up from his nape. She threaded her fingers through his hair and gripped him in a way he could only describe as proprietary. His inner wolf liked it. Even if her heart and head hadn't made up their mind about him, her inner wolf certainly had and it trusted and wanted him.

Slowly, he blazed a trail of kisses along her jaw, nipping and kissing and licking her soft skin. With each swipe of his tongue or teeth, she shuddered and held him even tighter.

Somehow he'd kept his hands firmly planted on the counter beside her but he needed more touch, more contact. He pulled his head back from where he'd been kissing the sensitive spot below her ear. As if drawn by a magnet, his gaze tracked down to her breasts.

Her brown nipples tightened and peaked under his appraisal. She sucked in a deep, shuddering breath, but he could tell she was about to say something. He thought about taking her mouth again but simply couldn't wait to taste more of her. When his head descended over her breast, she moaned out his name and both her hands grasped his head and held tight. Needing that contact, he reveled in the feel of her holding him as he tweaked and teased the hard bud between his teeth.

Felicia couldn't believe the way Alaric was touching and kissing her. The two strong hands that had taken off her sweater then grasped the counter next to her in barely concealed restraint now held firm against her waist as he flicked his tongue over one of her nipples. He held her as if he was afraid she'd take off. Not likely considering the way she was feeling. The way he was making her feel.

The erotic teasing of his tongue brought another rush of heat between her legs. She couldn't believe this sexy-as-sin alpha wolf wanted *her*. For the first time in ages she decided to stop being such a coward and enjoy herself. When he'd taken her sweater off, she hadn't even paused to think if she should let him. The action had somehow felt natural, even if she was nervous about being so vulnerable and exposed in front of him. It was obvious he didn't plan to punish her for leaving her old pack—and if this was his brand of punishment she'd gladly take it.

From the way he looked at her to the way he was currently teasing her body, it was obvious he wanted her as much as she wanted him. This was all about pleasure. For a wolf so old she thought he'd be better at keeping his lust at bay but he was letting everything out. She could scent his desire— it was so strong—and that turned her on even more. That someone like her could bring out such a reaction in him was a heady realization.

She might be inexperienced with the opposite sex but she obviously had something he liked and she planned to use that to her full advantage right now. When he switched breasts, she arched her back, giving him better access.

Lightly, he rubbed his tongue over her beaded nipple, then followed with his teeth. Just a gentle scraping that had her clutching him harder. Her skin felt too tight for her body, as if she could crawl right out of it to feel some sort of release.

She needed more but she wasn't exactly sure what that *more* was. It was as if there was an invisible string that linked her aching breasts to the juncture between her thighs and Alaric was tugging on it, bringing her right to the brink of release with each kiss. Right now the need for relief had her entire body heated to the point of combusting.

When one of Alaric's hands trailed down her stomach and played with the button of her pants, she tensed for all of a second before embracing what he was making her feel. Maybe it was exhaustion from traveling for thirty-six hours straight or maybe she just wanted to let go and enjoy herself. Whatever it was, she knew she could trust him. At least in this. With her body.

He drew his head back and watched her with those dark, dangerous eyes, as if asking for permission. Unable to find her voice, she simply smiled what she hoped was an invitation for him to continue.

He didn't make an attempt to strip her clothes completely off, and for that she was grateful. The thought of being totally bared to him, especially under the light of the kitchen was a little intimidating. Maybe he sensed that.

When he freed her pants and dipped his hand down to cup her mound she nearly came undone. Lightly—oh so lightly— he rubbed his middle finger over her pulsing clit. The bundle of nerves had never been so sensitive in her life.

She jerked against his hand and he increased his pressure. At the same time his mouth found hers again. His tongue played erotically against her own, matching the sweet tempo of his stroking finger. Soft and sweet, but she needed more. So much more.

Feeling uninhibited, she began grinding against his hand and body. Her primal side wanted to take over and it wanted release in the best possible way. For a brief moment she wondered if she should feel embarrassed by the way she was rubbing her breasts against his very muscular chest, but when he growled roughly into her mouth she let go of those thoughts.

As he rubbed her clit in a steady, rhythmic pattern, he began to trail kisses away from her mouth to the curve of her neck. He raked his teeth under the sensitive area below her earlobe just like he'd done earlier, but this time he practically purred in her ear. That sound made her absolutely crazy with need.

"Come for me." A demand.

Maybe she should have been startled by what he said but those three words lit her on fire. Holding his shoulders, she did exactly as he commanded because he'd perfectly primed her body for this moment.

She could barely catch her breath as the climax hit her with a sudden, unexpected intensity. He hadn't even penetrated her, just kept stroking her sensitive bundle of nerves with his finger in a steady rhythm. He seemed to know her body better than she knew it herself and that scared her.

As the orgasm rocked through her he pulled his head back from her neck and met her gaze. She desperately wanted to look away. Everything about this moment was so intimate. *Too intimate.*

But she couldn't tear herself away from those espresso-colored eyes. The dark depths of them seemed to suck her in and hold her tight.

Her lips parted slightly as pleasure continued to flow

through her veins in a rush of heat and raw need. She might not have much experience with the opposite sex but she had no doubt that Alaric definitely knew what he was doing.

If he could bring her such pleasure so quickly, she could only imagine what he could do if they were completely naked. As the wave of her orgasm crested and fell, she finally shut her eyes and let her head fall back.

A sudden thought hit her with surprising clarity. She had no control where this shifter was concerned, but it was hard to care when he made her feel this good. Tingles raced up and down her spine and to all her nerve endings. After what felt like an eternity she opened her eyes to find Alaric still staring at her.

His hand continued to cup her mound in that totally intimate way, but his finger had stopped moving. And he looked positively satisfied with himself. All male arrogance and it was completely justified. A small smile tugged at the corners of his mouth.

"You look beautiful when you come," he rasped out.

She blinked at the unexpected compliment. No one had ever called her beautiful before and it took her off guard. Instead of responding she bit her bottom lip. She wasn't sure if there was a response to that kind of statement.

Thankfully he didn't seem to expect anything. Leaning forward, he lightly tugged her bottom lip between his teeth before gently kissing her.

A new hunger swelled through her—the kind that made her want to strip off her clothes and then his. Her hands slightly shook with the unfamiliar urgency humming through her. She actually ached to feel his hands stroking over her entire body, and more than anything she wanted to do the same to him. To feel and kiss every dip and contour of his muscular body. He made her forget how tired she was. Who needed sleep? She wanted more of Alaric. Something primitive and needy inside her flared to life and she briefly wondered if this was the mating call she'd heard whispered about growing up. Just as quickly she dismissed that thought because it was impossible.

Jerking her out of her thoughts, Alaric pulled back as she started to slide her hands down his chest and stomach. When he picked up her sweater and handed it to her, she stared at him in confusion.

"What are you doing?" Disappointment surged through her.

"You need to get dressed." His breathing was harsh and uneven.

Clutching the sweater to her chest, she frowned at his darkening expression. She knew he wanted her. The sharp scent of his lust permeated the air, wrapping around both of them in a hot, almost physical embrace. "Why?"

"Because I want to take you on this counter hard and fast and you deserve better than that." His words were a soft growl.

They could go to the bedroom if he was concerned about the counter. "I don't care—"

"You've been traveling for days and I want you clearheaded when we take this next step. When I sink deep inside you, I don't want there to be any room for regret from you." It sounded as if he'd swallowed gravel and his dark eyes smoldered with something that put her on edge. The look he gave her was primitive and possessive and made the animal inside her slightly wary.

Felicia wasn't sure what surprised her more. The fact that he was so turned-on yet still willing to give her time or the fact that he'd was being so brutally honest. She wasn't sure what she'd been expecting from him but it hadn't been that.

Confused, she tugged on her sweater and slid off the counter when he stepped back. After what they'd just shared she wanted to say something flirty or witty but couldn't find the words. Instead she cleared her throat. "You want to show me where I'll be sleeping tonight?" Inwardly she groaned at herself. *Real smooth.*

He opened his mouth once and then closed it, growling something under his breath, and he motioned with his hand for her to follow him.

Chapter Four

Felicia jerked up in bed as she came fully awake. The unusual silence around her was deafening. She was so used to hearing explosions and gunfire in the distance, for a moment she forgot where she was. Until the past few hours crashed in on her like a tsunami. She was at a house with *Alaric*. And very recently he'd brought her to an intense climax with barely *any* stimulation. Her entire body still tingled from the memory. The thought was too surreal. *Too weird.*

Slivers of moonlight shone through the slat blinds and a glance at the clock told her only a few hours had passed. She should have passed out and slept for days but her mind was too wired. She kept reliving the way Alaric had kissed and stroked her to such exquisite release and wondering what it meant to him.

Now that her mind was clearer, panic started to set in. She wasn't afraid he'd punish her anymore, but she was afraid of what would happen if—*when,* he'd said—they took the next step. There had been no hesitation in his voice about them sleeping together. He'd been so sure about it and she hadn't said anything to contradict him. Why would she? She wanted him as much as he seemed to want her and a few hours ago she'd been ready to strip bare and let him inside her.

Her chest constricted as she thought about going to bed with him. She could only imagine how much experience he had with women. The way he'd played her body so expertly was all the proof she needed. Taking a deep breath, she fought the onslaught of dread coming on with the thought about how inadequate she must be in comparison to the woman he'd been with. Feelings she thought she'd buried two years ago when she'd moved away from her pack bubbled to the surface.

What if Alaric saw what everyone else in her old pack saw in her? A weak mongrel whose parents hadn't cared enough about her to stick around. They'd abandoned her at such a young age she didn't even remember them.

Alaric might view her as fine to warm his bed but in her heart she knew it would be a temporary arrangement. And she couldn't stand by only to be pushed to the side once he found someone better. She knew that was what would ultimately happen. It would be torture to live in the same pack and watch him mate with someone else, knowing he hadn't viewed her as good enough. Absently she rubbed the middle of her chest, hating the familiar ache of loneliness that began to spread.

Over the last couple years she'd made a decent amount of money so at least she could take care of herself. Living as a lone wolf with no pack protection would be hard but that's basically what she'd been doing her whole life anyway. Even if she joined this new pack, being around Alaric would cloud her judgment. *Clearly.* She'd been ready to let him take her on the kitchen counter barely hours before. Not exactly smart thinking. She needed to get away from him.

Fast.

Easing off the thick comforter , she cringed when the hardwood floor creaked beneath her feet. The next step she took was silent. So were the next and the next. The weight pressing on her chest lifted as she neared the door to her bedroom. Leaving with literally only the clothes on her back sucked, but she'd be able to go shopping soon enough. She just needed to find her wallet and passport and get out of there.

With a clammy hand, she turned the handle. She exhaled in relief when it opened soundlessly. Easing out of the room, she silently pulled it shut.

"Going somewhere?"

She stifled a scream at the deep voice behind her.

Swiveling around, she found Alaric sitting against the wall in the dimly lit hallway. His long legs were stretched out casually, but his gaze was sharp and knowing. She pressed a hand to her chest. Her heart pounded erratically. "Are you trying to give me a heart attack?"

"I asked you a question." In a swift, fluid movement, he stood and towered over her.

The man could move fast. Her throat seized for a moment. "I was thirsty."

"Don't lie to me, she-wolf." There was an edge to his voice that sent a shiver of alarm curling through her. His eyes smoldered in the muted light, reminding her that he was one hundred percent a predator.

She opened her mouth to lie again but he quickly silenced her with a finger over her lips. "For whatever reason you're feeling insecure right now, but that doesn't mean I'll let you lie to my face."

Felicia hated that he could sense her unease. Especially since she was trying so hard to hide what she was feeling. "I'm not afraid of you," she said against his finger. Nervously and out of instinct, she moistened her lips. When she did, her tongue flicked over him. His dark eyes flared with unbridled desire.

She shook her head when she realized he thought she meant it as an invitation, but he didn't give her time to protest before his mouth covered hers.

His kiss was demanding and raw and made her toes curl. This is exactly what she'd been worried about. All he had to do was kiss her and coherent thought fled. She wanted to let him strip her bare and take everything she had to offer regardless of the consequences. Regardless of the fact that in the end she'd be the one who ended up hurt and alone.

There was just something about him that made her aware of herself in the most feminine way. She'd felt it after their first meeting years ago, but had chalked it up to him being her first crush.

The need and draw she felt to him was exhilarating and strong but also terrifying. She didn't like the loss of control she experienced around him. Even so, her hands slid up his bare chest and her fingers dug into his shoulders. His muscles flexed under her touch.

As she savored the feel of all that strength under her fingertips his hands fisted tight around her hips and he hoisted her up against the wall.

Without pause she spread her legs and wrapped them around his waist. He growled low in his throat as their tongues intertwined and he pressed her against the wall with his hard body. His cock pressed insistently against her heat. They might have clothes on but she felt so exposed and open to him like this.

The way his tongue flicked and teased hers was almost frenzied. She could feel the intense energy rolling off him. It wrapped around her like a thick blanket, threatening to make her lose all common sense.

Somehow she tore her head back. Panting hard, she stared at him. In the dim light of the hallway everything about him seemed darker. Edgier. The heated look in his eyes was almost enough to make her lose what was left of her willpower.

But not quite. "We need to stop."

"Why?" he growled.

Since she wasn't going to admit all her insecurities she said, "Because we barely know each other."

"My inner wolf knows all it needs to know about you," he said softly.

Frowning, she started to ask what he meant but he continued. "I know your favorite color is purple and that you have a spine of steel for a shifter so young. Leaving the way you did a couple years ago took guts. I also know that you took a lot of risks while in Afghanistan. Risks you didn't have to. Going into certain territories and refugee camps when even members of your organization wouldn't." There was an underlying note of respect in his voice.

Wondering how he knew that, her scowl deepened but he kept going. "It only took you two and a half years to earn your degree because of how hard you pushed yourself. I also know you hate coffee but love tea. You're one of the most gifted healers I've ever met. It only makes sense you chose a field like nursing. You don't seem to realize the gift you've been given or how much I need you, but you're a very special wolf." His voice dropped a notch and her toes actually curled as he said, "I also know that your eyes glitter and your cheeks turn the sweetest shade of pink as you come."

When he stopped she could only stare at him for a moment. She understood how he knew some of the stuff, like the fact that she hated coffee. It had come up during one of their email conversations. Still, she was surprised he even remembered such an innocuous detail about her. But she didn't know how he was aware of the times she'd gone into danger-ous situations when none of her coworkers would. "How do you know all that?"

"I remember every email we've exchanged." He shifted slightly against her, pressing his erection even harder against her spread legs.

Wetness instantly flooded her core at the not so subtle movement. She fought for control of herself. "Not *that* stuff."

A wicked grin played across his face. "I know how you look when you come because—"

"Can you please be serious?" If he gave her a play-by-play of what he'd done to her body earlier she'd go up in flames. And something about the glint in his eyes told her he planned to do just that.

The humor left his face and his jaw clenched, but finally he spoke. "I kept tabs on you while you were overseas."

Her eyebrows rose at his admission. "How…why?"

"I have a lot of government contacts around the world so I called in a few favors and…I needed to know you were safe. It was the only way I could live with any sort of peace knowing you were over there without any pack protection. *My* protec-tion." His statement was so raw it tugged at her heartstrings.

As a shifter she would have lived through almost any kind of explosion or attack from gunfire but the fact that he'd watched out for her and remembered the small details from their correspondence touched her on a deep level. She re-membered all their letters too. The stories he'd told her about his brothers and their life growing up together had made her smile and had given her an insight into his personality. She'd read and reread those letters so many times it was embarrass-ing—and to know he also remembered what they'd talked about made her knees go weak.

If her legs weren't still wrapped around his waist, she

wasn't sure they'd have held her up. She wondered if she was all kinds of stupid for what she was about to do, but the insecure voice in her head that she usually listened to was silenced by the sincere, heated look on Alaric's face.

Felicia was so tired of not being able to trust anyone. Before she could question her decision she leaned forward, letting her lips mesh with his.

His tongue was hot and exploratory as he pushed them away from the wall. She was vaguely aware of him carrying her into the bedroom then just as quickly she was flat on her back and he was on top of her.

Splaying her hands across his chest, she allowed herself the freedom to explore everything she wanted. Digging her fingers into his muscular pecs, she savored the feel of him tensing under her touch. When he growled into her mouth she fought a smile. She loved that she could bring out such a primal reaction from him.

One of his hands cupped her cheek and the other trailed down to her waist until he held her hip in a firm grasp. His hold felt as if he was afraid she'd try to leave. Part of her wondered if she should but she knew deep down that she wasn't going anywhere. Not now. She was tired of running away from things and tired of not feeling good enough to take what she wanted in life.

Arching her back, she couldn't hold back a moan as her chest fully met his. The only problem was she had on too many clothes. As if he could read her mind, Alaric grasped the bottom of her sweater and practically tore it off.

Then it was skin on skin.

A shudder flooded through her at the intimate contact. Her nipples were rock hard and pressing against his chest only sensitized them even more. Feeling that strength against her own softness was nearly too much to handle. She felt as if she could literally combust at the hot sensations racing through her. Every single nerve ending tingled as she fantasized about what would happen next.

With the same quickness that he'd discarded her top, her pants seemed to disappear from her body with lightning speed.

Then Alaric was kneeling in front of her naked, splayed body and he was looking at her as if she were an offering for him and all his desires. Desires she had no problem fulfilling.

The dark look in his eyes stunned her. He stared at her with something that almost bordered on reverence. Like she was special and he wasn't sure if he wanted to kiss or devour her. She couldn't fully accept the way he looked at her because she wasn't sure if it was her imagination or if he really needed her that much.

Slowly, his eyes trailed from her face down to her breasts. Her already hard nipples tightened to almost painful points as his gaze lingered there. They were still tingling as he continued a searing path down her stomach until he stopped at the juncture between her spread legs.

No one had ever touched her so intimately until him and even though the thought might have horrified her at one time, she wanted him to kiss her *everywhere*. When he moistened his lips almost absently she knew she was going to get her wish.

Wordlessly, he pressed his large, callused palms to her inner thighs and spread them farther apart. A low rumble came up from somewhere deep inside of him as he bent his head and gently nipped her lower abdomen. Still too high up her body to give her exactly what she wanted. But just enough to drive her crazy. She had no doubt he knew he was torturing her.

Somehow she made herself relax as he began pressing

kisses along the top of her mound. When he expertly moved to her inner thighs she couldn't fight the shudders that racked her. His lips were so close to where she craved them but he was still teasing.

Though she was thankful for the foreplay, a primal part of her wanted him to just take her hard and uninhibited. Even if it was going to be her first time, her most primitive side needed to be able to let the animal inside her free.

And he was intent on taking his sweet time.

Shifting her hips slightly, she tried to force him to give her what she wanted.

His chuckle against the sensitive skin of her thigh sent another shiver through her. "I'll give you what you want, sweetheart." His words were whisper soft.

Slowly—so slowly—he dragged his tongue along the length of her wet slit. Unable to control herself, she jerked against his mouth. Her inner walls clenched with the need to be filled by him.

"You're so wet," he growled.

"So do something about it." She wasn't sure where those words came from but the rough sound he made let her know he was close to losing control.

His hands slightly shook against her thighs as he increased the pressure. Before she could suck in a deep breath and try to ground herself, he began a delicious teasing assault.

As he parted her folds with his tongue, he slowly inserted one finger inside her. The feel of his intrusion made her inner walls clench tight around him. When he began moving in and out in a slow, rhythmic pattern that matched the tempo of his tongue, she clutched the sheets beneath them.

It didn't do much to ground her but she was afraid to hold on to his head too tightly for fear her claws would extend. She definitely wanted what he was giving her but she needed some semblance of control. Unfortunately it was quickly slipping out of her grasp.

Her back arched off the bed as he narrowed in on her pulsing clit. He flicked and teased her most sensitive area with no reprieve. With each stroke of his tongue, his finger also slid in and out of her. He played her body so expertly she wasn't surprised when her climax hit fast and hard.

She felt as if she'd been tossed out of a plane with no parachute as the free fall of her orgasm swelled through her entire body to all her nerve endings.

It was all she could do to catch her breath as her fingers and toes tingled with the aftershocks. When she finally managed to open her eyes she found Alaric propped up over her, caging her body in with both his hands and simply staring at her face.

His dark eyes had a possessive glint that made her reach out and cup his cheek. He instantly turned his face in to her hold and gently kissed her palm. The action was sweet and unexpected. Something told her this wolf was about to break all her expectations in the best way.

For the first time in as long as she could remember she felt free of her insecurities and free to be herself. All because of him.

As he began a trail of kisses down her exposed wrist and inner arm she hooked her legs behind his back and pulled him tight against her. He tore his mouth from her arm and bent to cover her mouth again.

She went straight for the top of his jeans. The moment she grasped the button, he froze and pulled back.

His dark eyes were no longer filled with lust or...anything. The tender and attentive lover had all but disappeared behind a blank wall.

Chapter Five

"What is it?" That familiar insecurity rose inside Felicia's throat like bile.

Before she could speak or think about moving he was off her and the bed. "I can sense a shifter—maybe two—nearby. Stay in this room and lock the door until I come back."

Then he was gone. A second later she heard the sound of breaking glass downstairs.

Ignoring his order—because really, a locked door wouldn't keep a shifter out—she quickly dressed and then rushed to the other bedroom. She found his backpack lying on the end of the bed. She pulled out a black-and-silver handgun. Growing up, she'd learned to use all kinds of weapons and overseas she'd gotten in a lot of practice time with handguns. There hadn't been much else to do in her off time. Now she hoped that might pay off.

She quickly checked the chamber. It was loaded and by the extra weight she guessed it contained silver-injected bullets. Or she really hoped it did. They weren't visibly coated with the poisonous metal so she couldn't know for sure. But if shifters or even vampires were attacking, she wouldn't hesitate to use the gun.

She hurried back down the hallway, then descended the stairs. Listening carefully, she peeked around the corner when she reached the bottom. To the left, the front entryway was clear. To her right through the kitchen, she could see glass scattered by the open backdoor. *Had someone lured Alaric outside?* The house was eerily quiet and she fought the rising panic inside her. The thought of anything happening to him made her see red. Her heart pounded in her ears and she had to wipe one of her sweaty palms on her pants so she could grip the weapon.

Crouching low, she headed down the hallway and through the kitchen. Careful to avoid the glass pieces, she peered outside. Her heart caught in her throat at what she saw.

Two hulking wolves faced off with each other in the backyard. One of them was Alaric. She'd recognize his dark gray coat anywhere. His lips were pulled back, revealing razor-sharp fangs but he wasn't attacking.

Not yet.

The other wolf also bared his teeth as he darted back and forth, trying to find an opening to strike. Despite their similar size, Alaric looked more lethal because of his deliberate stillness. He wasn't hopping around. He slowly circled the other animal, taking his time. Looking for the perfect moment to attack.

When the brown wolf lunged wildly at Alaric her heart rate tripled. She shoved the door the rest of the way open and rushed onto the patio. She raised the gun but couldn't get a clear shot. At least her hand didn't shake.

The dark brown wolf lowered his head and tried to charge Alaric. But he dodged out of the way so quickly it looked as if he were floating. For such a large animal, Alaric moved with a fluid grace that shocked Felicia.

As Alaric easily escaped, he ripped fur and skin from the brown wolf's side with his teeth.

The unknown wolf let out an angry snarl and lunged at Alaric again. This time the other wolf didn't bother to protect his neck. As Alaric pinned him to the ground and went for his throat, another wolf appeared from behind one of the oak trees.

Felicia couldn't believe she hadn't scented it. The light gray animal was smaller than the other two but he was fast. He flanked Alaric from the back and effectively blocked himself from her line of fire.

Felicia leaped off the porch. "Alaric!"

He lifted his head. When their gazes collided, she realized her mistake. The brown wolf lurched upward and wiggled out from Alaric's hold.

The light gray wolf jumped at him from behind, displaying his chest and belly. She didn't think about anything other than saving Alaric. She lifted the weapon and aimed. Everything seemed to funnel out around her as she narrowed in on her target.

Pop. Pop. Pop.

She heard the shots but it was almost as if they came from a distance.

Her aim was true. She hit him directly in the chest. The gun kicked but she barely flinched as she watched him jerk back then fall to the ground. Blood poured out of the holes like small rivers. Her practice had paid off.

She couldn't believe he'd tried to attack Alaric with her a few feet away. The animal had been fast but maybe he hadn't seen her weapon. Or maybe he had underestimated her aim.

She stared as a lake of crimson spread across the animal's fur and leaked onto the earth beneath it.

She blinked and things weren't moving in slow motion anymore.

Before she could think about what she'd done, Alaric avoided the open jaw of the brown wolf, rolled over and jumped back up onto all fours. He bared his teeth and this time he didn't retreat or go on the defensive.

He used his steely muscle and sharp teeth to intimidate and push the other wolf back against the fence. Growling low in his throat, he took a small step back once he'd cornered him and gave the other wolf the chance to forfeit and submit. It was a common sign among their kind. Alaric was allowing him the chance to give up without further bloodshed.

Felicia gripped the weapon tight in her hand just the same. These two wolves had tried to launch a sneak attack without properly challenging Alaric. They obviously didn't care about fighting fair.

Her heart pounded wildly as she waited for the brown wolf to make a move.

Finally, it bowed its head in submission. But instead of giving up, it darted away toward the side of the house.

Instead of chasing after it, Alaric turned toward her and changed to his human form. He shifted faster than she'd ever seen another werewolf do. His bones cracked, broke and realigned with remarkable speed. All his fur receded until nothing but over six feet of taut lines, lean muscles and a lot of nakedness stood before her.

Fighting the blush she felt creeping up her cheeks, she hurried to his side. "Why didn't you go after him?"

He brushed a few flecks of dirt off his arm before taking her weapon. "My brother will stop him."

"What? How do you know?"

"He's waiting out front with a couple of other wolves."

"Oh." She still didn't understand how they knew about the attack, but she bit back the question.

He tapped his head once as if he'd read her thoughts. "My brothers and I communicate telepathically. After what happened earlier one of them has been nearby in case I needed him. I let all of them know we might have trouble."

She'd heard that some wolves with familial ties had that ability but she'd never met one who did. "That's a handy gift."

"Tell me about it." The corner of his mouth pulled into a slight grin. Just as quickly, that smile dropped. "Are you okay? Why didn't you stay put? You could have been hurt."

Ignoring his questions, she shot a nervous glance at the dead wolf then looked back at Alaric. "What happens now? I killed that wolf. What if his pack Alpha wants reparations or to punish me or—"

Alaric shook his head. "You killed him to protect me. I'll stand by your side and so will my Alpha. *Your* Alpha. I know you've only got Lamont's example, but Knox stands by his pack and we'll all protect you if it becomes necessary."

Relief forked through her. Before she could ask what the next move was, a man who looked vaguely familiar emerged from the direction of the front yard carrying a bundle of clothes. He had the same dark hair and dark eyes as Alaric but his features were softer. More boyish.

Alaric nodded once at him as he took the T-shirt and jeans, then looked back at her. "This is Rainer, my youngest brother. You need to go with him."

"What? Why?" Leaving Alaric right now made her feel strangely empty inside.

"I need to clean up this mess. If any of the neighbors heard the shots they might have already called the cops. We need to make sure this place is clean."

She didn't want to go, but she couldn't think of a reason to argue. The adrenaline high was wearing off and as the reality of what she'd just done set in, she started to shake. It wasn't from guilt either. That wolf had wanted to kill Alaric and something primal inside her had howled, demanding to be set free. It had been violent and angry and she didn't know what to do with those emotions.

Embarrassment joined in with her trembling. Alaric came at her fast. Just like in the house. Seemingly uncaring about his state of undress, he wrapped his arms around her in a tight embrace. He was so warm and comforting. She wanted to simply meld against him and let him hold her. Going against her normally immediate instinct to pull away from anyone, she slid her arms around him and held tight.

After what felt like forever, Alaric pulled back and gently cupped her face. His hand was as warm as the expression in his dark eyes. "I'll join you soon and we're going to finish what we started, I *promise*." He glanced at his brother and she was under the impression that they were communicating with each other.

When Rainer nodded at him, she knew she was right. Silently, she fell in step with his brother. There were two SUVs in front of the house. Two men had bound the wolf who'd tried to run and were putting him into the back of one of the vehicles. She fought off a shiver at the thought of riding in the same vehicle as him.

"We're not riding with them." Rainer answered her unspoken question.

She risked a quick glance at him as they neared the other SUV. "Where are you taking me?"

"Back to the compound."

Compound? Her heart started pounding a staccato beat again as she slid into the passenger seat.

Rainer chuckled under his breath and started the ignition. "It's not as ominous as it sounds."

"Are you a mind reader or something?" She gripped the armrest and resisted the urge to scoot away from him. If he and his brothers could communicate telepathically she wouldn't put anything past any of these shifters. The thought of someone being able to read her thoughts…she shuddered.

He shook his head. "No. You don't hide your emotions very well." Then he frowned. "Didn't anyone ever teach you how to mask your feelings?"

"No." The answer came out so quickly she didn't have time to censor herself. She swallowed hard and glanced out the window. She'd been given food and shelter growing up. Nothing more. Throughout her life she'd picked up on certain things but there was a lot she still didn't know. No matter how hard she'd tried to fit in with her old pack they'd always treated her like an outsider. It shouldn't affect her now, but if she allowed herself to dwell on the past, it cut deep.

Alaric scrubbed a hand over his face—though it did nothing to wipe away his growing impatience. He was beyond pissed at what he'd just learned.

"Calm down, brother." Rainer's voice did little to soothe him as they walked up the stone steps to the last house on the planet he wanted to visit.

He grunted a nonresponse. Nothing could calm him at this point. Not until he'd taken care of a certain problem. Someone had wanted to kill his future mate simply because of who she was. If he'd known Felicia would have become a target, he would have kept her return a secret from the pack—his Alpha and brothers excluded. According to the wolf he'd just interrogated, the attacks had nothing to do with the upcoming treaty. And Alaric was going to clean up this mess right now before it went any further.

Alaric knocked on the heavy oak door. Part of him wished *she* wouldn't answer, but he knew she would. He could sense the traitor inside.

After a long pause, the door swung open. Amanda Lamont—former mate to the now deceased Wilson Lamont—opened the door wearing tight, skimpy white shorts and an even tighter halter top despite the cool weather outside. The tall blonde looked him and his brother up and down like they were slabs of porterhouse steak then narrowed her gaze on his face with a slow smile he was sure she meant to be sexy. Even though she was ninety in shifter years, she appeared to be in her late twenties. "To what do I owe the pleasure?"

Alaric didn't waste any time. "Are you alone?"

Her smile faltered a fraction. "Yes."

"Good. We need to talk." He kept all inflection out of his voice. Keeping a tight control on his emotions was the only reason she was still breathing.

Now her smile fell. She *knew* why they were there. Standing to the side, she let them enter, but didn't invite them farther than the foyer. Crossing her arms over her chest, she stood motionless but he could see the wheels turning inside her manipulative head.

"Why did you send Jonathan and Alistair after me?" He wasn't going to make small talk when they both knew what he wanted to know.

It was slight, but her green eyes flashed with anger until her cool mask fell back into place. "Am I supposed to pretend to know what you're talking about?"

He ignored her question. "Jonathan is dead and Alistair is going to face punishment from his Alpha. He gave you up very easily. Do you really want to be judged for the attempted murder of your pack's second in command? Knox is ready to convict you tonight."

"I didn't want *you* dead," she snapped.

"No, just my mate." He pulled his lips into a thin line and it took all the control he had to rein his anger in. Even thinking Felicia could have been injured or worse because of this woman's pettiness made his inner wolf howl for blood.

"Felicia isn't your mate yet." Her voice dripped with loathing as she said Felicia's name. She also didn't deny her intent. When he didn't respond, she shifted her weight from one foot to the other. Finally she spoke. "What do you want? I didn't know those two idiots were going to go after you. If I had, I would have stopped them."

He still wasn't sure exactly how much guilt he could lay on her doorstep, but she'd put the idea in Jonathan and Alistair's heads to hurt Felicia in exchange for sexual favors and money. This woman deserved his wrath, but he kept control. "Since your mate recently died, you'll be given some leeway for your irrational actions. You admit your guilt to Knox and you have a week to gather what's yours and leave. There's a pack in New Mexico willing to take you in." If he'd been able to send her farther he would have, but no one else had wanted her.

She arched one perfect blonde brow. "And if I refuse?"

"Knox will banish you and you'll be on your own. I can't speak for the world, but no one in the Southeast will give you shelter. You'll be completely unprotected." He let his words sink in. If Felicia were to strike out on her own she'd survive and no doubt flourish, but someone like Amanda would have problems. In all the years since she'd mated, she'd never worked. Not because she wasn't capable, but out of sheer laziness and a sense of entitlement. She'd be easy prey.

Her eyes narrowed and he could practically hear her sarcastic comment so he cut her off. "You came after my intended *mate*. You're lucky you're still breathing. This is a onetime offer." The words were a soft growl and they got his point across.

Her face turned a putrid shade of gray as, no doubt, the reality of her situation crashed over her. "I'll be gone in a few days."

The predator inside him roared when a burst of fear rolled off her. He might be an animal but he didn't relish violence. Or he hadn't until today. When he learned the attacks had been directed at Felicia and not him, something inside him snapped. One of the wolves might be dead, but Alaric's inner wolf still wanted blood. Right now he was walking a razor-thin line of self-control. "What was the purpose of your attack anyway? Did you really think killing her would make me want *you?*" He couldn't keep the loathing out of his voice.

She gritted her teeth but didn't respond.

When he growled at her, she took a step back and held her palms up. "If she died I wouldn't have shed any tears but…I just wanted to scare her off, not kill her. She ran away once before so I didn't think it would be that hard to run her off again."

Alaric knew the only reason she was telling the truth was because she was well aware that he would sense if she lied. And she probably also knew he didn't need any excuse to take back the offer for banishment as opposed to her death. "Was anyone else working with the three of you?"

She shook her head. "There's no one else."

When she defensively crossed her arms over her chest, he knew he'd gotten everything he would from her. "Rainer will stay with you until you leave."

"Is that really necessary?" she snapped.

Of course it was. She didn't live at the compound, but in a house closer to town. He wasn't letting her out of anyone's sight until she was gone and someone else's problem. Ignoring her, he turned to his brother. "Call me if you have any problems."

Rainer nodded and as Alaric stepped out onto the front porch, a pressing weight lifted from his chest. Now that this mess was settled, he'd finally be able to ask Felicia to mate with him.

Felicia opened the French doors and stepped out onto Alaric's balcony. At least the "compound" had turned out to be the exact opposite of what she'd expected. Knox owned a huge mansion on a big spread of land in northern Alabama, and Alaric's room in the mansion was enormous. It was bigger than her old two-bedroom apartment. So far everything was much better than the apartment complex Lamont had kept his pack crammed into. Plenty of space to run free was a nice change of pace.

On the way in she'd hadn't seen any wolves she recognized so she figured most of her old pack really had dispersed. That was fine by her. Right now she just wished Alaric would hurry up and get back. Rainer had dropped her off, but he hadn't told her when anyone would be back to get her so she was making herself at home. So many hours had passed it was now sunny outside.

She still wore the same clothes she'd had on yesterday, but soon enough she'd go shopping and pick up the stuff she'd sent to her human friend. What she really cared about was seeing Alaric again. After this morning all she could think about was him. She'd kept herself closed off to other people for so long it was a unique feeling to finally drop her guard. When Alaric had held her after she'd killed the wolf, it had been so warm and real. She couldn't remember the last time she'd let a man—or really anyone—hold her like that.

Despite the cooler weather, she'd come out on to the balcony barefoot and the natural stone patio was warm under her feet. She sat on one of the lounge chairs and laid her head back, soaking up the warmth of the bright sun hanging overhead. As soon as she closed her eyes she was aware of another presence.

"Felicia? I heard you were back." She opened her eyes at the voice to find a familiar wolf perched on the edge of the balcony.

He must have jumped up from the first floor. Half-smiling, she stood as Chris Fleming stepped down from the stone balustrade. The wolf was a few years younger than her, but he'd been one of the few in Lamont's pack who'd been kind to her. "I didn't realize you'd joined Knox's pack."

Instead of responding, he pulled her into a tight hug. The blond, surfer-boy-looking wolf held her to the point that she started to feel uncomfortable. When she stiffened he let her go and chuckled. "Sorry, it's been so long since I've seen you. I thought about joining another pack but I like the weather here. Besides, Knox is a good Alpha and Alaric is a good second in command. This is a strong pack."

Holding her hand up to block the glaring sun, she tried to gauge his expression. "You really think so?"

"Yeah. He's a lot better than Lamont."

A demon would be better than the dead wolf. She didn't voice her thoughts and Chris continued. "Most of us work in one of Knox's hotels or other establishments and he's helping a lot of the younger she-wolves with college."

Felicia struggled to hide her surprise. She'd depended on scholarships and grants to get through school despite Lamont's objections. He hadn't thought she needed an education. He'd preferred his females to spend their time on their backs with their legs spread. "So Knox is…fair?" Despite her attempt to sound casual, the question came out strained. She knew what Alaric had told her but it wouldn't hurt to get another opinion.

"From what I can tell."

"What about Alaric?"

"He handles a lot of the day-to-day skirmishes and he's fair too. Everyone respects him. That's why I don't understand why he's taking Amanda as his mate."

She could feel the blood drain from her face and a low buzz started in her ears. "He's what?"

He glanced around then lowered his voice. "That's what I heard. Someone told me he was on his way to see her right now. That woman has been after him from practically the moment we assimilated into Knox's pack. She barely mourned her mate's death. It's shameful."

Felicia pressed an unsteady hand to her stomach as Chris's words sank in. She could think only about everything she'd shared with Alaric. And what she'd planned to happen between them once he got back. There was no way she'd imagined how much he wanted her. *I'm such an idiot.* Hating her stupidity, she bit back a curse. Alaric had never made any promises to her. Sure he'd told her how much he wanted her but that didn't mean anything. "Listen, it's great to see you but I'm not feeling well. Probably jet lag. Would you mind if we caught up later?"

He nodded enthusiastically. "Sure. I'm really glad you're back, Felicia. There were a few of us who hated the way Lamont treated you and…I'm sorry I never did anything."

Her throat tightened at his unexpected apology. "Thank you."

Once Chris was gone, she hurried back inside and fought to breathe steadily. Chris *had* to be wrong. She picked up the portable on Alaric's nightstand. She tried calling Rainer first but he didn't answer so she tried the next number on the list. Conrad. Another of Alaric's brothers.

"Hello?" a deep male voice answered.

Thankful he couldn't see her flushed face, she cleared her throat. "Um, you don't know me but—"

"I'm assuming this is Felicia, since you're calling from my brother's direct line."

"Oh, right." She'd forgotten about caller ID.

"Is everything okay?"

Knowing she was going to sound needy, she simply cringed and forged on. "I just wondered if you knew where Alaric was."

"Yeah, I think he's still at Amanda's but he should be heading back soon."

The low buzzing in her ears from earlier flared to life. "Thanks." Without bothering to respond further because she didn't trust her voice, she hung up the phone.

She didn't want to believe any of it but the proof was right in front of her face. The knowledge that Alaric was going to mate with Amanda rattled around inside her like hot, scorching lava. It burned up everything in its path with no mercy. She had no claim on Alaric but she'd thought he was different. The way he'd looked at her…a man couldn't fake that kind of need. So he wanted her—big deal—she still wasn't good enough to mate with. That burned a crater-size hole in her stomach. Tears pricked her eyes and she angrily brushed them away.

She was tired of everyone treating her as if she didn't matter and tired of having to feel grateful for scraps. Overseas she'd made a difference, had friends, and she'd even resigned herself to living as a lone wolf once she'd come home. But with Alaric, she'd thought things were finally going to be different. That Alaric was different and that maybe she'd found a place to fit in. She needed time to think and she couldn't do that here. Not in Alaric's room, where his scent completely surrounded her.

Chapter Six

Alaric raced up the stairs to the second floor of the mansion, his heart pounding wildly after the conversations he'd just had. First his brother had called him and told him about Felicia's phone call. Then he'd run into Chris on the way in and the young pup had asked him about his impending mating to Amanda. Apparently the rumor mill was out of control. And when Chris had let it slip he'd mentioned the same thing to *Felicia*—Alaric growled as his fists clenched into tight balls.

It had taken every bit of his self-control not to pummel the young wolf. If his intentions had been malicious in telling Felicia, Alaric would have done worse than that. Now he was focused on finding the woman who owned his heart. The intoxicating smell she exuded of raspberries and champagne was strong as he headed up the stairs to his room, but he feared it was an old trail.

The second he stepped inside his room, he froze. She wasn't there. If she had run, he would find her. Of that he had no doubt.

Turning on his heel, he froze again.

Felicia stood in his doorway, her blue eyes darkened with smoldering, undeniable anger. But at least she was there.

"You're here," he said, needing it to be true.

Unfortunately, it seemed to piss her off. Her eyes narrowed to slits. "Would you rather I ran away with my tail tucked between my legs?"

"No, I—"

"I get to talk right now. Not you. You…you…" Her face flushed crimson as she faced off with him.

"I what?" he murmured, wary.

After the walk she'd taken to clear her head, Felicia thought she would be able to talk to him in a civil tone, but the emotion she'd kept bottled up for years suddenly exploded. "You're a lying bastard! I can't believe you're going to mate with Amanda. You make me feel all these things and acted all possessive and caring. It's bad enough that it's her, of all she-wolves, but I wouldn't care who it was. What kind of wolf are you that you could be so intimate with me knowing you planned to take another mate?" Pain laced her words and for the first time in as long as she could remember, she didn't bother trying to keep up an emotional shield. She didn't care if he knew how much he'd hurt her.

"I'm not mating with her." His expression and his voice softened a fraction.

She paused. The statement took some of the steam out of her but… "What? Chris told me—"

"I've already spoken to him and he was misinformed."

"But I called your brother and he said you were at her house."

"I was." She narrowed her gaze at his admission, but he continued. "I had some things to clear up with her."

Felicia's temper sparked as she thought about what "things" he might mean. "Have you ever slept with her?"

He snorted softly. "Never. Not that she didn't try."

A low growl filled the room and it took a moment for Felicia to realize it came from her. Surprised at the raw animal possessiveness that surged through her, she clamped her jaw shut for a moment, then frowned at him. "Why were you at her place?"

"She sent those wolves after you." His voice had a deadly razor's edge to it.

Felicia's eyes widened at the sharp burst of uncontained rage that sparked off Alaric. "Did you...kill her?"

"Do you want me to?"

She paused for a moment and started to ask him why the she-wolf had sent anyone after her, but changed her mind. Some things could wait. "No, but what *did* you do to her?"

"She's been kicked out of our pack and sent somewhere out west. My Alpha's mate and most of the females of the pack couldn't stand her so don't worry about anyone holding a grudge."

She was surprised he hadn't done more to Amanda, but at the moment Felicia was more concerned about her own relationship with Alaric.

Before she could question him he closed the distance between them until he stood inches in front of her. "I've wanted you from the moment we met. I told Lamont that I planned to take you as my mate years ago, but at the time you were too young. He promised he'd keep an eye on you and inform you of my plans when you were older. I never thought he'd..." He shook his head. "If I'd known he wanted you for himself I'd have claimed you long ago. Or at least asked you to join our pack."

"Why didn't you ask me to join your pack anyway?" She couldn't help the hurt in her voice.

His expression softened. "I didn't trust myself around you,

but if I'd known what his pack treated you like, I swear I would have brought you in to our pack." Before she could respond, he continued. "For about a year I started that first letter a hundred times. I knew you were ignoring your pack's attempts to contact you and I wasn't sure I'd be any different."

She remembered that first letter. Just a quick hello and he'd asked her if she needed any care packages. He'd also told her he was worried about her. It had taken him a year to work up the courage to write that? The pressure in her chest lifted at his small confession.

She started to respond but he wasn't finished. "I'm telling you right now that I want you as my mate. I guess I didn't make that clear this morning, but I promise no one will ever hurt you again as long as I'm still breathing."

As she digested his words, shock rippled through her. It stunned her that he'd wanted her for so long. "And if I say no to mating?" She didn't plan to but wanted to hear his response.

"Then I'll just have to convince you otherwise." He reached out and cupped her cheek.

Raw, hot desire flared inside her. To go from anger to this intense feeling of need was insane. But this was exactly what she'd wanted, wasn't it? To feel such intense sexual hunger for someone who wanted her right back. When she'd thought Alaric was mating with another female, it had felt as if someone had hit her in the stomach with a two-by-four. She still needed to clear something up with him though. "I'm sorry I assumed the worst about you and Amanda."

He was silent for a long moment, as if considering his next words. "You've gotten a raw deal from your own kind. If I could rewrite history I would, but from this point forward you've got to know I'll always have your back. *Always*."

She nodded, knowing bone deep that it was true. They

might still have a lot to learn about each other, but the man she'd been exchanging emails with the past few months before she'd cut off contact—the man who'd basically just offered to kill someone for her—was telling her everything she'd wanted to hear. If she didn't take a chance now, she'd never be able to look at herself in the mirror. She couldn't keep expecting people to disappoint her or turn on her.

Before she could change her mind, she stripped her sweater off and then her pants, letting them silently fall to the floor. Her hands shook the entire time and all she could hear was the blood rushing in her ears. When Alaric raked her from head to toe with a scorching gaze, some of her nervousness faded. She was putting herself out there the best way she knew how.

Alaric's entire body heated up as he stared at the she-wolf in front of him. The thought of her leaving again had shaken him bone deep. It still did.

His inner wolf had howled in pain and frustration and he was having a hell of a time convincing himself she was standing right in front of him. Naked and beautiful.

As she started to cover her breasts, he grasped her wrists and pulled her tight against him, savoring the feel of her lush body. "Don't ever cover yourself in front of me. You're beautiful."

Her cheeks flushed at his words.

"Has no one ever told you how beautiful you are?" he murmured, unable to tear his gaze from the fullness of her lips.

A slight shake of her head. "Just you."

"Get used to hearing it." Her mouth curved up and it soothed his inner wolf to please her. Though he wanted to pounce and take what was his, he knew he had to play it smoother than that. Especially now. Rubbing his thumbs over the pulse points in her wrists, he was entranced as he watched her lips part seductively. An invitation.

"It's not fair that you're still dressed," she finally said, breaking the silence.

He didn't plan to stay that way for long. Not with Felicia pressed up against him like this, lust rolling off her in potent waves. And not with his own just as strong.

Knowing how much it had taken her to bare herself to him in this way—literally—he felt awed she was putting her trust in him. He wasn't going to screw things up either. He couldn't afford to.

He scooped her up and headed for his bed. With shaking hands, he placed her at the foot of it and stripped off his clothes in seconds. Later, when they had time and he had the patience, he wanted her to take his clothes off piece by piece. So he could feel her hands stroking over his entire body.

It was hard to think straight with her so very naked in front of him. Especially since he'd already seen what she looked like when she climaxed, had tasted her... That was a memory he wouldn't soon forget. And planned to repeat very soon.

When she placed a gentle hand in the middle of his chest, he tensed. *Did she want to stop?*

"I've never done this before," she said quietly.

A startling protectiveness completely filled him at her admission. The most primitive part of him was glad he'd be the first and only man to touch her. Because after this there would be no one else. Feeling humbled, he placed his hand over hers and squeezed gently. He planned to make this special for her and take care of her and the fact that she trusted him with this. It made his throat clench tight with emotions. Emotions he didn't even know how to voice to her. "I'd kind of guessed" he rasped out.

At his words a trail of unease wove its way off of her, bitter and slightly acidic. It was a thin thread but he sensed it just the same. He guessed she was uneasy for a multitude of reasons, the main one being he was a big guy and this was going to be her first time. More than anything he wanted to soothe her. He'd never been good with words but knew he had to try. "I haven't been with anyone since I met you."

Her blue eyes widened and for a split second, disbelief flared there. "Really? Why not?"

A bark of laughter escaped at her bluntness. "My inner wolf recognized you on a basic level. I knew you were my mate the moment we met and I didn't *want* anyone else. Letting you go…let's just say I almost didn't, but I knew it would be selfish to take you when you weren't ready." Slowly, he stroked his hands down her sides until he settled at her hips. His fingers tightened around her. She was lean but soft everywhere and he loved trailing his fingers over her body. Pulling her close, he let her feel his erection—not that there was any chance she'd missed it.

She linked her fingers around his neck. "How did you know I wasn't ready?" Her voice was unsteady.

"Because of what I wanted from you."

"And that is?" Now her voice was barely a whisper.

He dipped his head until their lips grazed each others. "Everything."

Her breathing was uneven and shallow, the same as his. Without giving her a chance to respond, he pressed his lips to hers, tasting and devouring her.

He'd wanted everything from her years ago and it was even truer now. While his wolf might have recognized that they were intended mates, his human side now knew without a doubt that he wanted Felicia to be his forever.

Not just wanted—needed.

They might not know everything about one another but

he knew the important stuff. She had the kindest spirit of any person he'd met and he planned to spend the rest of their lives making sure she was protected and taken care of. She'd have no doubt of her place in his heart and the pack. To him, she'd always come first. He would do *anything* for her. Even defy his Alpha if he had to. That knowledge jarred him, even while it awed him. He wanted to tell her he loved her, but the words caught in his throat. Talking was overrated anyway, especially when he could show her what she meant to him without words.

When her fingers threaded through his hair and cupped the back of his head in that proprietary hold he found he was coming to crave, he shuddered, knowing this was *her* touching him. He slid his hands around her body until he grasped her from behind.

Hoisting her up, he lifted until she wrapped her slim legs around him. He might have already seen her naked and even tasted her, but it did nothing to alleviate the tension and desire humming through him.

He wouldn't be sated until he sank deep inside her and marked her. The world needed to know she belonged to him. His canines ached as he thought about it.

As he stretched out on the bed with her underneath him—her legs still firmly tangled around him—it took all his control not to plunge deep inside her. But he knew he couldn't do that. No matter how much his primal side wanted it.

Surprising him, she reached between them and grasped his cock. It pulsed in her hand and the sheer pleasure of her soft fingers wrapped tightly around him was almost too much for his control. But he refused to lose it this way. When he came it would be deep inside her.

She pulled her head back from his, breaking their kiss, and stared at him. Her blue eyes lit up with a deep-seated longing as she watched him. When she lightly squeezed his shaft he nearly came undone.

"I feel I've been waiting forever to have you inside me," Felicia murmured.

He could barely think after that blunt honesty, let alone manage a response. There was nothing coy about her. Everything she said she meant and he loved that she was about to belong to him. When she began to lightly stroke him, he grasped both her wrists and held them above her head. He couldn't take her touching him like that. Not yet.

She didn't struggle against him, but simply arched her back, rubbing her breasts against his chest. The feel of those perfect, rock-hard nipples against him made him shudder. She was soft in all the right places and the contrast of her body to his was wildly erotic.

Holding her wrists with one hand, he slid his other down the flat plane of her stomach until he cupped her mound. She rolled her hips against his hand as he teased her with his fingers.

Gently he stroked between the lips of her wet slit, barely penetrating her. She let out a frustrated moan when he slowly inserted one finger. She was wet but he needed her to climax before he took her the way his body demanded.

As mates he didn't have any doubt she could take him, but she was still inexperienced and he didn't want to hurt her.

When she let out another agitated sound, he bit back a chuckle and increased his stroking. As he did, she kissed and teased his neck, intermittently raking her teeth and lips across his skin. The feel of her stretched out beneath him and kissing him was almost too much for his control. All he wanted to do was sink deep into her until they were both sated.

Moving his finger in and out of her, he paused only to add another, gently stretching her body. The moment he did, the pressure of her teeth on his neck increased and she let out what he could only describe as a purr. Satisfaction surged through him, knowing he'd elicited that reaction. But he wanted to do more than just make her purr. He wanted her to moan and shout his name.

"I need more." Her voice was ragged.

That he could do. Burying his two fingers inside her, he kept them still as he began circling her clit with his thumb. The moment he started teasing her, she writhed under him. Her heels dug into his ass and she actually bit his shoulder the faster he moved. Not hard enough to draw blood but enough that he noticed. And liked it.

Felicia felt as if she might combust if Alaric didn't give her what she wanted. It was as if she was riding a wave and had reached the crest but it wouldn't break for her. She was just hanging on, waiting desperately for relief.

Her entire body was strung tight. The way Alaric held her wrists above her head, keeping her lightly restrained, only turned her on that much more. Now if he would just give her that release she craved.

As if he read her mind, he increased his pressure against her sensitive, pulsing bud and began moving his fingers inside her once again. Her inner walls clenched around him the faster he moved. It was hard to breathe or focus on anything other than the toe-numbing pleasure she was experiencing.

When he raked his canines against her throat, it was exactly what she needed. The feel of his teeth against her neck—knowing they'd soon be mates, knowing she finally belonged somewhere, to Alaric—was like an erotic drug.

Arching her back, she let the release flow through her. She was vaguely aware Alaric had released her wrists only because she found herself clutching his back for dear life as her climax hit.

It was more intense than the first two he'd given her. Maybe because she finally felt completely connected to him. Whatever the reason it was hard to care why when she felt so good. Waves of pleasure rocked through her, hitting all her nerve endings until she was panting and murmuring Alaric's name over and over. After what felt like an eternity, the lust-induced haze cleared from her vision.

Alaric still had his head buried against her neck but as she loosened her fingers from the death grip she had on his back he finally lifted it. The look in his dark eyes was pure male satisfaction.

Not that she blamed him. Right now he could be as proud of himself as he wanted.

While her body was limp and sated, she still needed more. Her inner wolf felt incomplete somehow and she knew it was because he still needed to mate with her. To take her from behind and mark her.

"Are you sure you want this?" Alaric asked quietly even as his hard length pressed insistently against her bare stomach.

She didn't pretend not to understand. She knew what he was asking and she did want it. While her feelings for him at nineteen had started as a crush, they'd developed into something more the past few months. Something real. She hadn't even been willing to admit it to herself but on the days she'd had a chance to check her email she'd hoped for word from him. More than hoped. *Craved.* Each time she'd opened one of his emails she'd felt a ridiculous thrill. She couldn't stomach the thought of him mating with anyone else and she knew there wasn't anyone else for her. She loved him. It was as simple as that. Even if he hadn't said the words, she knew it without a doubt. So was she sure she wanted to mate with him? Hell, yeah.

She pushed lightly against his chest. If he hadn't wanted

to move he wouldn't have had to, but he sat back until he was kneeling in front of her, his big, powerful body exposed to her rapt gaze. Waiting for her decision.

"I know exactly what I want, Alaric." Without another word she rolled over and lifted up on her knees. When she glanced over her shoulder to look at him, the almost worshipful look in his eyes floored her. There was nothing soft in his expression.

Which was good, because she didn't want that tonight. A foreign hunger raced through her and she wanted him to sate it.

Alaric's inner wolf craved Felicia's submission during their mating and he felt humbled she was giving him this freely. Humbled because he loved her. Part of him wanted to tell her now, but he couldn't find the words. They caught in his throat because he was afraid talking would screw this up. He just wanted to show her how he felt and for once his animal and human side were in agreement. Words weren't what Felicia needed, actions were.

He ran his hand down her delicate back until he reached the base of her spine. As he leaned forward to kiss her there, he caught her gaze on him. Bright and hot. The blatant need in her eyes was as clear as if she'd told him exactly what she wanted out loud. He feathered a few light kisses along her back before grasping her hips.

The time for foreplay was over. For so many years he'd been waiting for her. For this bonding. He already knew she was wet, even more so after her orgasm, so he didn't test her slickness with his fingers. He didn't need his hand to guide his cock to her tight opening, but mainly he didn't want his callused hand on himself. He only wanted to feel Felicia wrapped around him.

His cock knew exactly where it wanted to go. Despite the

searing need inside him, he slowly eased into her tight sheath, careful to let her body adjust to his width.

She pushed out a long breath as he buried himself inside her. A long growl escaped him. He couldn't have held it back if he'd wanted it to. The feel of her soft folds holding him captive was almost too much. She was so damn tight.

That was the only thing that kept him still instead of pounding into her like his inner animal demanded. "Are you okay?" he managed to rasp out.

Her inner walls clenched around him and when she looked at him over her shoulder, he saw the raw hunger in her eyes. "I won't break and I don't need you to be gentle. Not right now."

That was the only answer he needed. Drawing back, he began rhythmically thrusting into her over and over, feeling her clamp around him tighter with each movement. Her inner walls convulsed in quicker successions the faster he moved.

She was tight but her body molded to him perfectly. As if they were made for each other. "I've fantasized about this for years," he murmured, barely getting the words out.

As soon as he said it, her back arched and she grasped the sheets beneath her in a death grip. The way her inner walls convulsed tighter and tighter told him that she was close to climaxing again. He planned to make sure she did. One of his hands tightened on her hip and he reached around with the other and palmed one of her breasts.

In this position it felt heavy in his grasp. He tweaked her already hard nipple, fascinated by how she clenched harder around him each time he teased her breast.

When she moaned and began milking him even faster, he let go of his control. His canines instinctively lengthened with the need to mark her. Palming her stomach, he pulled her until her back was tight against his chest.

Her climax flowed through her trembling body as he fastened his teeth onto her neck. As he broke the skin—claiming her—her entire body jerked under his hold. She cried out his name but he barely heard it as he let out his own shout.

With a sharp jolt, he came inside her in long, hot thrusts as she wrung everything from him. His growl was primal and probably heard by everyone in the house, but he didn't care. He wanted everyone to know Felicia was his.

As his climax subsided, he wrapped his arm around her stomach and slowly withdrew from her. Lowering them both to the bed, his eyes widened when he saw a small bonding symbol that had formed directly below her upper shoulder. It was an infinity symbol.

His chest tightened as he traced the slightly raised character with his finger. He'd never believed in any sort of destiny bullshit until he'd met Felicia. Seeing this was more irrefutable evidence they were meant to be together. Tattoo-like symbols always appeared somewhere on the body of true mates after they bonded. The symbol often related to the owners' heritage, so his would likely be something ancient Germanic. Right now he didn't care where it was on his body or what it looked like; he knew he'd have one if she did. He just wanted to hold his mate.

Before he could move, she turned to face him and curled her entire body around him like a silky ribbon. Her soft curves melded to him as her dark hair spilled seductively over his chest.

His breathing was still shallow, matching hers as they lay there. He didn't sense any discomfort from her but still… "Did I hurt you?" The thought of doing so tore a hole inside him.

He could feel her smile against his chest as she shook her head. "That was amazing. I didn't think the first time would be like that, but…wow."

Alaric pushed out a breath he hadn't realized he'd been holding. Even though they'd mated there was one more thing he needed to tell her. With a finger, he lifted her chin from his chest so she had to look at him. "I should have said this before, but I love you Felicia, and it has nothing to do with being mates. Even if my wolf hadn't chosen you, I would have."

Her blue eyes darkened as he'd come to learn they often did when her emotions changed. "I feel the same way. I was half in love with you a month into our correspondence—even though I wouldn't admit it to myself. When I thought you were going to mate with someone else, I knew I loved you. I..." She shook her head and swallowed hard.

Unable to stop himself, he kissed her. Her tongue met his in an erotic dance he knew he'd never tire of. As she slid her hands up his chest and around his neck, he fisted her hips and moved her so that she straddled him. He knew she'd be too sore to make love again but for now he simply wanted to hold her. They had the rest of their lives together to pleasure each other.

* * * * *

FIRST HEAT
JENNA KERNAN

Award-winning author **Jenna Kernan** writes fast-paced romantic adventures for two different lines—Mills & Boon® Historical and Mills & Boon® Nocturne™.

Jenna has twice been nominated for the RITA® Award and her debut paranormal, *Dream Stalker*, won the Book Buyers Best Award for paranormal romance in 2010.

Jenna Kernan is every bit as adventurous as her heroines. Her hobbies include recreational gold prospecting, scuba diving and gem hunting. Her adventures have taken her above the Arctic Circle in Alaska in search of gold nuggets and most recently to Maine for tourmaline. Jenna loves to walk and hike, whether through the urban jungle or in crisp mountain air. When not adventuring, Jenna enjoys time in her garden, jewellery making and reading a great romance, of course.

Jenna grew up in the Catskills, where she spent much of her time out of doors. This gave her a love and respect for nature that are strong themes throughout her stories.

Jenna currently lives in the Hudson Valley of New York State with her husband. Visit Jenna at her website, www.jennakernan.com for news, excerpts of her latest release and giveaways.

Chapter One

Someone was watching her.

Evalena Coble set her grande coffee on the condiment station as she scanned the customers of the University Café, where she worked, for the threat she sensed. And saw *him* again. Damn, her neck was prickling.

Outside the picture window stood that same guy, the big, intimidating one she'd seen uptown. He stared at her with his dark brows drawn low over his crystal blue eyes. His intent focus made her stomach flip. Had he followed her all the way down here from CCNY?

His hands were thrust in the pockets of his green army fatigue jacket, hunched as if against the cold, but it didn't disguise the breadth of his shoulders or the lean musculature of his frame. Suddenly, Evalena had trouble catching her breath. Was he stalking her?

She noticed that everyone on the busy sidewalk beyond the plate glass gave him a wide berth. She had done the same thing earlier, yet here he was tracking her like some damned bloodhound.

She didn't think he was a cop, not with such a lean face

and shaggy black hair. Cops usually looked well groomed and well fed, while this one had a hunger in his eyes that she recognized. He appeared as ready to bite your hand off as let you pet him.

Beside her, a perky coed stood holding the cinnamon shaker poised motionless above her latte.

"That hot guy is staring at you," she said.

At these words, Lena's familiar surroundings no longer seemed safe. Every nerve ending stood on alert. She glanced at her manager and wondered if she'd find safety behind the counter. Then her eye shifted toward the door, only a few feet to his right. Her instinct was to run.

"Don't come in," Lena breathed to herself.

But he did, jerking the door open with unnecessary force. Damn, he was heading straight for her. The smell of coffee, cinnamon and nutmeg was overshadowed by his scent —one that seemed familiar and yet new.

The prickling at her neck snaked down her spine.

Lena didn't know why, but this guy made her insides ring like a firehouse during a five-alarm blaze.

Their eyes met. His were framed with spiky black lashes, set below a prominent brow. The guy's skin had a golden-brown glow that said he liked tanning or was of mixed race, just like her. He looked young, focused and dangerous.

Lena followed her instincts and headed the other way, removing her apron and dropping it on an open seat.

She needed to ditch her pursuer. The guy was as persistent as a bedbug and just as unwelcome. Lena wanted to belong, just not to a man. She knew too many girls who got tangled up with the wrong guy, and she planned to stay clear of such relationships.

Why couldn't she be like the self-absorbed coeds around her who had nothing more to do than study and drink beer?

But she knew why. She didn't have the safety net that parents provided. Since she'd turned eighteen and was declared an adult by the state of New York, she didn't even have the group home. Aging out of the foster care system had thrown Lena out on her own. It wasn't going well. This job kept her fed, two meals a day, mostly carbs, when combined with her job as a cashier at the drug store on 14th Street, she paid most of her expenses but she didn't have much time to study and the classes were way harder than she'd anticipated. If she failed out, she'd loose her housing, bus card and Medicaid.

She'd be on the street.

Later, her mind whispered. Right now she faced a whole week ahead of her with the residence hall locked up tight. Looked like she'd have to try to plead with her fellow employees for help. It was so hard not having a family, parents…a home.

Lena abandoned her coffee, heading in the opposite direction, retrieving the backpack that contained all the possessions she had until the residence hall reopened next Sunday. Then she skirted the western edge of the park, watching as the crisp autumn day receded to evening. For safety, she stayed close to the waist-high, wrought-iron fence that enclosed the neat three-story brick buildings. The streetlights already hummed a warning of impending darkness, yet she could see everything. At night, objects lost color, but she could make them out in nearly perfect clarity.

Lena glanced at the wide marble banisters sweeping up elegant staircases, leading to doorways flanked with pillars; the kind of doors that were not opened to the likes of her. One of the little wrought-iron gates was ajar. Her pursuer intercepted her there.

How had he gotten ahead of her?

He dragged Lena back behind the tree and shrubs, and pushed her up against the wall.

"You've been avoiding me," he said. His mouth turned up as if this were all some thrilling game instead of her life. His grip was strong, too strong for her to break unless she landed a lucky blow. The triumph in his eyes pissed her off.

"I'll scream," she promised.

His brow knit. "Don't you remember me, Lena?"

He knew her name. How did he know her name?

"Hunter Ortiz," he whispered.

Lena knew him, or had known him, back in the group home when she was thirteen and he was fifteen. Five years... and a lifetime ago. He was so change she hadn't recognized him, a man now, with lean angular features and a big, muscular body. She looked at his eyes, still familiar, still haunting. Was the boy she had once trusted still there inside this stranger?

Back then she had wanted out of school and foster care, but not badly enough to follow a half-wild boy, even if she had loved him wholly and foolishly. Had he, too, spent nights sleeping in cardboard boxes and on doorsteps? After her last court appearance, the one where the State of New York declared her an emancipated adult, she'd secured an independent living counselor, but it was two long summer months before she qualified for housing at CCNY and entered the program that might sustain her until she hit twenty-one, if she didn't fail out.

What had he been through? Hunter certainly had a hungry look about him.

Had he found them?

He'd been so sure that both of their parents had just made a mistake and couldn't find them. She'd so wanted to believe him, but she knew the truth, even then.

Her parents weren't searching for her.

She still wanted a family, but not with her parents. She'd given up on them because they'd given up on her. Now she planned to make her own goddamn family. But first she needed a home and a job, because she wasn't bringing a child into this world until she could take care of herself.

She scrutinized the man's angular features and intent eyes, searching for the boy she'd once known. Could it really be him?

His nod was almost imperceptible. She inhaled his scent and found traces of the familiar. For eight months of her life, she'd had someone she cared about and someone who cared for her.

"You," she breathed, feeling again the knife-blade of pain, reliving the hurt of Hunter abandoning her just like everyone else.

He'd been one of the few people she let get close. She hadn't expected him to return, just one more promise broken. Her life was littered with them.

She stared up into his eyes, the boy she once knew, the stranger he had become. Before leaving, he'd asked her to join him. Lena almost had, but she'd been too scared. Then he was gone and she was alone again. She'd missed him ever since. Served her right for letting him in. Well, she wouldn't make the same mistake twice. He couldn't just pop back into her life and expect her to throw a party.

He captured her upper arm. "Come with me."

She pulled back, refusing to let him hurt her again. She had her life, he had his. No men until she could take care of herself. That included Hunter Ortiz.

"No."

"Lena." His voice chastened.

She stiffened her spine. "I have a place to sleep."

His forehead wrinkled and he frowned, looking as if she'd hurt him somehow. Then he rallied, setting his mouth in a stubborn line that she recalled was an indication of his fathomless determination. He stroked her jaw with the backs of his index and middle fingers and then captured her neck in a move so quick she didn't have time to evade. He leaned in, his warm breath fanning her cheek.

"Choose me," he said.

"What? Let go."

He didn't. His mouth turned and grim. "You prefer one of the others?"

"Prefer? What others? Let go, Hunter. I've got to get to class."

His laugh was resonant and made her stomach quiver.

"School's closed this week. There's no class. Besides, they can still sense something is wrong with you even without knowing exactly what it is. You belong with your own kind."

He was freaking her out. This was definitely not the boy she remembered. He had a raw hunger and dangerous sexuality that sent a shiver skittering up her spine. She tried to jerk away and he didn't move a millimeter. Once she realized she was his prisoner, he let her go.

"You want me to challenge them, is that it?" He moved so fast his action seemed a blur. An eye blink later he clasped the hair on the back of her head, controlling her. He leaned close as if he meant to kiss her. When his lips were a mere breath from hers, he whispered to her. "I'll win. I always win."

He released her again and she staggered back.

"The others are near." He turned his head and glanced about. "Soon."

With those cryptic words he backed up, leaning against the wide marble banister.

"I'll be close." Then he winked.

Lena stepped forward to watch him cross the street and melt into the park. She knew he was only twenty, yet something about him made him seem much older.

She tried and failed to shake off the chill brought on by Hunter Ortiz as much as the autumn breeze. She was too unsettled to return to work, so she made her way to the dorm where a coworker lived. These residences didn't close down like hers. Security called her friend who consented to come escort her in. She planned to sleep in the lounge , but as luck would have it, her friend said she could flop in the bed vacated by her carousing roommate.

By eleven she was tucked in with a clean foam pillow and a down comforter that smelled of fabric softener and the home Lena had never had.

But sleep brought her that same damned dream. Now there were six men pursuing her, each one with the same crystal blue eyes. They chased, she ran, until she was chasing as well, running with the pack, taking down the elk, shredding its hamstring and tearing into warm red meat as the elk screamed.

An echoing scream startled her awake. An unfamiliar woman stood in the open doorway, shrieking and pointing at Lena.

Behind her, her coworker scrambled to her feet on her twin bed, dragging the blankets with her.

"Who let that dog in here?" she screeched.

"That's no dog," said the other woman. "It's a damned wolf."

"Get it out!"

Lena reached for her backpack and saw her furred front paw. She yelped and ran, her toenails clicking on the tile of the hallway, her long white T-shirt flapping about her like a shroud. She reached the open elevator and swept in as a young man in a hooded sweatshirt backed up to admit her.

He hit the button for the lobby, but did not leave the car.

"I'm Tyler," he said. He lowered his hood, revealing chestnut hair and a lean face, punctuated with those clear blue eyes. "I've been looking for you."

Lena paced like a caged animal.

"First time?"

Was this still her nightmare or could this really be happening?

"Never smelled one so strong. I'm not the first here am I?" He hit the stop button then raised his voice to be heard over the alarm. "Why don't you shift back so we can take care of business right here?"

He squatted before her, holding a hand out, and then made a lunge for her. Lena bit his forearm, sinking her long white teeth deep, tasting blood.

She rose on her hind legs, her forepaws hitting the red button. The alarm ceased and the elevator descended. Tyler slumped in the corner below the hand rail, clutching his bleeding arm to his stomach.

"Bitch. I'll see you pay for this. Not going to take you easy." He pushed himself up and staggered after her like a zombie. Lena pressed back until her tail hit the stainless steel wall.

Wake up! Wake up!

The door dinged open and Lena ran. Tyler followed. She skidded to a stop by the revolving doors.

"No animals in here," called the security officer at the desk.

"Fuck off," called Tyler as he made a grab for her, missed and fell against the panic bar of the emergency exit.

Outside she could see clearly, well beyond the circular

pools cast by streetlights all the way into the dark corners. That's when she saw two more men, waiting.

"Back off, fellas," said Tyler. "I got here first."

Lena ran, darting down Third Avenue, past a woman walking a shaggy mop of a dog that leapt from her as if she meant to kill it. She ran on all-fours, low to the ground, fast, terrified. Behind her the men pursued, shouting as they came. She bolted down Sullivan and into an alley, hoping to hide from them.

What's happening to me?

A delivery van blocked her way, filling the narrow gap, the mirrors practically brushing the brickwork on each side. Lena dove under the truck, emerging beneath the front bumper and then slid to a halt. A chain fence thwarted her escape.

To her right was a battered dumpster. To the left stood Hunter Ortiz, eyes glowing an inhuman reflective green in the shadowy passage.

The others entered from the street.

"Looks like you got what you wanted. It's going to be a flat-out brawl for rights to you. You'll get the strongest among us. And that will be me." Hunter stepped past her, his voice low and dangerous. "If someone gets killed, it's on you."

Chapter Two

Hunter Ortiz stepped out to meet the other males, placing himself between them and the female in heat. There would be no stopping them unless he won. Lena had gone too far. The question now was not if, but who and how.

One of them would have her, maybe more than one. He prayed to the Great Spirit that it would be him. He'd never before been bested in such a contest. But he'd never taken on five at once, either.

Since leaving Manhattan, Hunter had stayed out of cities, away from humans and away from she-wolf Skinwalkers when possible. But he knew Lena's age, knew she'd becoming into her first heat and that this was his last, best chance to find her. So he'd come back, praying to the Great Spirit that she had stayed in the Metro area and not gotten on a bus to somewhere, as so many foster children did. When he'd first scented her the relief had been so deep it had buckled his knees. Lena was here. He had found her, the only girl he'd ever connected with or trusted, the girl from the group home, Starr Otis House, in the Bronx where he had spent the last four hellish years before running, the girl who he had known, even then, was just like him. This was Evalena, the only female he ever wanted, lost and now found. But, to his misery, she did not even remember him.

He told himself it did not matter. It was his need to mate had brought him to her. But now that he'd seen her, he knew he had deluded himself. It did matter because all this time he had been waiting for this one's call.

He advanced, facing the others as they stalked forward, still in their human forms.

Why hadn't she accepted him when he had offered? Did she need to see their blood? Did it arouse her to know they would all fight to the death for the chance to have her? It was her right to take only the strongest.

So be it.

The five glanced from one to the next. If they were wise they'd come at him all at once and then deal with each other afterward. He knew there would be no sharing. No male would tolerate another near her. Hadn't his own father chased Hunter from his pack the very day his sire perceived his son as a threat? That humiliating defeat had been his last.

The tallest stepped before him. "Stand aside or die."

Short and sweet. Hunter liked that. The others hung back, hopeful that the two of them would kill each other and leave the female to them, or be so injured as to be forced to withdraw.

In answer to the challenge he motioned with his fingers.

Did she watch him, judge him? Here was her own private coliseum with him and his fellows serving as her personal gladiators.

He'd known other she-wolves who became aroused by the spectacle of their male counterparts battling to win them.

We who are about to die salute you.

Ah, now that was the trick, to win and still be whole

enough to take her. Would Lena bear him a child, or was it true that he was sterile because of his refusal to take women who were not in heat?

Unnatural, they had called him. Were he able to deny a female's first heat, he would have walked away from all of them. Except Lena. He couldn't resist her, could never resist her, even as a boy, damn her to the Circle of Ghosts.

Were it up to him, he'd not have a child, for he could not face chasing off his son one day, scaring him, hurting him. It was a betrayal so deep, it made him sick. Yet his father had done so, as if Hunter could ever have been so twisted as to seek out his mother.

His opponent was strong, but slow. Hunter took him to his back. When the challenger reached for his knife, Hunter held his foe's head between his hands like a coconut and pounded it once on the concrete. He had not even straightened when the next one leaped onto his back. This one tore a hank of hair from Hunter's head before Hunter threw him onto the roof of the van. His rival was too stunned to keep from falling hard to the ground. The pop of his shoulder dislocating made Hunter smile.

Two down.

The others hesitated, seeming to have lost their libido amid the carnage. One attacked, clumsy as a freshman football player hitting the blocking sled for the first time. Hunter punched him in the nose. He didn't wait for the next one but used the heel of his boot to break a deck board from a wooden pallet and went at him swinging. One of the two remaining challengers ducked, while the other tried to use his forearm to block. The bones gave way, cracking like a stick breaking.

His final contender transformed to his wolf self and ran.

Hunter turned back to the van to see Lena lying beneath the back bumper, in human form, her forearms pressed to the dirty concrete while her mane of dark hair fell over her shoulders and out onto the ground. Lena did everything she could to be less desirable and still he wanted her. No, he needed her. He'd followed her all day, reacquainting himself with her, and had shown himself three times, yet she had still refused him. Well he'd won the right; she could not deny him now.

"Come out."

She flinched and crept farther beneath the battered delivery van. Was he so repugnant in her eyes?

"Come out or I will drag you out."

Lena inched forward like a marine in an obstacle course and drew to her feet, wearing nothing but a wet, stained white T-shirt, which clung to her curves and showed the hard, beaded outlines of her dark nipples. For reasons he did not understand, she did not wear her wolf skin, but left the unusual inky-colored fur on the ground as if it were trash.

When changing from animal to human, Skinwalkers first appeared in their animal skin. Most quickly altered their coat into some desirable attire. Her behavior puzzled him and he had the first inkling of doubt. Something about her was not right.

She stood before him, her keen eyes sweeping the scene. All remaining challengers lay bleeding, broken or unconscious.

"I didn't kill them. Do you require it to accept me?"

Lena stood trembling from a potent cocktail of cold and terror. Her bad dream had become a waking nightmare.

What was happening to her?

She folded her arms over her wet shirt as she looked from one injured man to the next. Lena turned her bewildered eyes on the one who had defeated them all. He stood with his jaw set in an expression of determination, his eyes burning with the hot blue flames of rage. Sweat and blood stained his T-shirt.

Who was this stranger?

"You could have prevented this had you accepted me earlier."

"I think you're all mad." She backed away and bumped into the grill of the van. The cold metal contacting her bare thighs caused her to jump forward. "You might have killed them."

He lowered his chin, now looking more dangerous than before. "Was that your wish?"

"What? No!"

"Then come here."

She didn't. In fact she crept along the bumper, considering her options and finding them all bad.

"You wish to be taken by force, then?" The downturn of his mouth and the pressing of his lips showed this was an option he didn't relish.

"No." Did he hear her voice squeak?

Her eyes widened as every nerve ending sprang to life. Blood coursed through her, making her eardrums pound. She rested her trembling hands on the hood, preparing to push off and make a useless run for the street, knowing she'd never make it past him.

He stalked forward, hands stretched wide to take her if she ran.

"I gave you the chance to come to me, but you wanted this, as is your right."

"I didn't! I just want you to go. To leave me alone."

"Not possible. So come with me or choose another." His arm swept the carnage he had caused.

She ran.

He captured her easily, dragging her back against him.

Then he stooped, scooped up the dirty hide from beneath the van and fastened it about her neck. The cloak, she realized. The one she'd found months ago and carried in her pack ever since. How had it gotten here?

"Let me go," she said, trying unsuccessfully to wrench her arm free.

"Soon," he promised. "I'm not one to linger. Once we've concluded our business, I will leave you as I found you, trying to con coeds into having a sleepover with the big bad wolf."

He dragged her past the men who had challenged him. What chance did she have when each of them had failed?

At the mouth of the alley he stopped to pull her full against him. Her head swam as his arms enfolded her. Instead of escape, she leaned in, pressing her breasts against the stellar musculature of his torso.

He gave her a knowing grin that was all lust and promise. Then he captured her hair in his fist and dragged her head back. He kissed her throat, first, licking the throbbing vessel at her neck, and then pressed his mouth to hers. A tiny sliver of heat sparked in her belly and caught. In an instant she burned, blazed, quivered with need for him. What was happening to her?

His tongue was hot and wet as it slipped into her mouth. A cry of hunger escaped her. What was she doing? She should be horrified. Instead, her body pulsed with a throbbing need for his touch, the longing for what was still familiar. Hunter Ortiz, her first love, now a living nightmare. She didn't understand it, but Lena closed her eyes and gave herself over to his kiss.

When she clung to him, he drew back, looking smug and also impatient.

"Here?" he asked.

Her eyes widened as she recognized what he meant. He

was suggesting they do it right here in the alley, surrounded by these other men. She shook her head.

"Privacy then." He nodded. "I have a place. Change your clothing."

She blinked at him. He gave a frustrated growl and swept a hand over his bloody T-shirt. When had he lost his coat?

"I left my backpack at the dorm."

He cocked his head, casting her a puzzled look and then rested a hand over his chest. Instantly, his shirt disappeared beneath a calf-length black leather duster.

"Hides the blood. Now you."

Her nostrils flared as she sucked in a breath. What was he? She backed away as far as she could with him securing each elbow.

"Lena, don't you know how to shift?"

She stared up at him, knowing she didn't want this, didn't want to hear what he was about to tell her. "I can't do that. I'm not like you. I—I just want to be normal."

He gave a snort of disgust. "This is normal for a Skin-walker. Now change your clothes or I'll do it for you."

She dropped her chin to her chest. "I don't know how."

He grasped her jaw and he lifted it until her eyes met his penetrating gaze.

"Who was your mentor?"

"What?"

"Lena, don't you know what you are?"

Chapter Three

Hunter stared at Lena. She was eighteen, ripe and in her first
heat and she didn't even know it. Hadn't understood it. All
the anger washed from him like a retreating wave, replaced
with a rising groundswell of compassion. She had not been
trying to force a battle, but had been trying to escape from
the men who pursued her. Lena didn't understand why they
followed, why they fought or that they would not stop until
one of them was the victor.

She stood before him, confused, frightened and trembling.

He wanted to gather her up in his arms and rescue her,
save her from what would come next. But he couldn't. No
one could. The best he could do was make sure that he was
the one who took her, *the only one*, and then try to control
himself as best he could.

Why was she so ill-prepared? How could she be full grown
and not have been told what she was?

"Didn't they come for you?" he asked.

"Who?"

"Your mother or your father."

She glared at him. "Hunter, you know my mom died in

jail and that I never met my father. I told you all that back…
before."

Before, when they were friends, confidants and so much
more.

"Your father must have been the Skinwalker, for none of
our kind could be held by a human jail."

"Human…jail. What do you mean, human?"

"Why didn't your mentor come for you?"

"Mentor? What are you talking about? I'm on my own.
Always have been."

Hunter did not understand it, but he knew they had to get
moving or risk the appearance of more challengers.

He took hold of her, his fingers sinking deep into the thick,
beautiful black coat that encircled her shoulders as he concentrated his energy. Some things were easier to believe if wit-
nessed, and this small thing he could do to see to her comfort.

There was a crackle and then a pop as her cape shifted. She
now stood in calf-high boots, a pair of skinny blue jeans and
a flowing blouse in a swirling flower pattern. This was the
outfit that Hunter had seen her admiring in a boutique window this afternoon. He'd only meant to please her. But judg-
ing by the look of terror on her face, he'd frightened her again.

"Wait, how?"

Police sirens squealed from a few blocks off.

"Later," he said.

He took her hand and pulled her from the alley, down Sullivan and then to Bleecker. They crossed Sixth and headed
down the alley beside a theater to the place he'd prepared
for her, his den.

He stayed behind Lena as she climbed the fire escape,
watching her back and checking for any sign of pursuit.
Finally, on the fourth floor he paused to push up the sash of
a half-opened window.

"This your place?" she asked, peering into the darkness beyond the sill.

"Yeah, for now." He never stayed anywhere very long.

Hunter extended his hand. She took it, pressing her warm, damp palm to his cool dry one as he assisted her inside.

"I can see everything, even without the light," she said, looking to him for some explanation.

"Because you're a wolf, Lena. We have excellent vision and no other Skinwalker has the sense of smell we have. Unparalleled."

She started to cry. "I knew something was wrong with me. I knew it."

He scooped her off her feet and carried her into the loft he'd rented for this purpose. He'd prayed Lena was still here in this morass of mortality, here among the millions and so he had come at the appropriate time, rented a loft for her comfort. He'd done well since running from the system. Once he'd discovered who and what he was, he'd used his tracking skills to find missing persons: runaways, wayward wives, absent ex's who neglected their child support. All easily found with his acute sense of smell. As long as he had something that held their scent, he could track them no matter where they ran.

Would Lena be satisfied with the den he had created? He'd never secured living quarters for a female before. But he knew Lena or he had known her. A bed of her own, a place where she felt safe meant everything to her. The loft was dry and warm and well supplied with food. She could stay with him through her time and he'd see she lacked for nothing. Or she could go and take another.

He would leave her when her body no longer hummed with need for him for that was the way of his kind.

He resented all females for calling him, using him, taking

control of him so that he had no choice but to do as his body
bid. Lena's call was strongest, for she called not only to his
body, but also to his heart.

He flicked on the overhead lights to let her see more clearly
what he had prepared. The room was spacious for New York
and had an industrial design, with walls of brickwork and
exposed piping. The kitchen flanked one wall beyond a large
dinette. In the center, a multicolored area rug lay before a red
sofa and two cushiony brown leather armchairs, flanked by
end tables set with vintage lamps. He tried to see the room
through her eyes and just now noticed that the Spartan utility
of the space seemed inadequate. The opposite wall was dom-
inated by an enormous bed made with fresh linens, covered
with many pillows and white down comforters. He would
have her in a proper bed, not up against the wall in an alley
that smelled of urine and sweat. Would it please her?

She still cried, and he stroked her thick hair, wondering
why she saw the need to dye a bit of her forelock a bright
royal blue.

"I just want to be like the rest of them. I'm not a wolf. I'm
not like you."

He couldn't let that pass. Hunter lifted her chin, bringing her face up until he could look into her golden eyes. He
raised his brow and pressed his lips together, letting her feel
his disapproval. Her denial did not ring true. Even without
mentoring, there would have been signs that she was more
than human, signs that even an inexperienced young woman
could not fail to recognize.

She exhaled through clenched teeth. "All right! I knew
there was something wrong with me, but I hoped it would
pass."

"In other words, you were in denial."

"I hate it!" she said, snapping with a ferocity that made

him draw his hand back. She was strong. He knew it, had recognized it long ago. Lena had the mental toughness required to survive the system that broke so many.

The look she gave him was haunting and familiar, the same look she'd given him when he'd come to say goodbye. When he felt his own change nearing, he'd naturally sought the wild places, but she would not come with him.

"I shouldn't have left you behind."

She lifted her trembling chin. Her misery knifed through him like a razor blade as she shrugged one shoulder.

"Everyone does." She said in a whisper so low he couldn't have heard her if not for his acute hearing. "What's wrong with me?"

"Nothing. You are as the Great Spirit made you."

That made her cry harder. He wished the heat didn't burn so fervently in him. God, the scent of her drove him to madness. He'd waited years for the right to win her, touch her, take her for his own. He could not wait much longer. Already he was half blind with need. She was so warm, so near.

He opened his arms and she leapt, colliding into him, her fingers knotted in his shirt as she clung fiercely to him. He enfolded her, aligning their bodies, praying she also experienced the electric zip of contact that stung his flesh. She stilled.

Thank God, he thought. Lena stood motionless against him, silent, her breathing altering from the rasp of tears to a heavy draw born of longing. Her scent changed, growing more heady, alluring. She rocked on the balls of her feet, side to side, her breasts brushing over his chest, veiled only by the thin gauzy blouse. He sucked in air through his teeth then stepped quickly away. She looked up at him, her face still wet with tears, but her eyes now glittered with want.

He drew her along, hurrying, racing his control. Trying

to see to her comfort, to show her that he wanted more than just the sex. Trying to prove he was different than the pack outside. And failing.

He felt it—his control dissolving like a sugar cube in hot water. It was only a matter of minutes now. He clenched his teeth against the terrible ache of yearning as they reached the master bath. He left the light off, needing none to see in the shades of gray that were his night world, knowing she could see just as clearly. He released her only long enough to open the huge glass door to the modern shower, so out of place in these industrial surroundings. Her eyes never left him as he turned on the water, adjusting the temperature and using his open hand to check the stinging spray. Various showerheads surrounded him on three sides, with the largest above them in a human interpretation of rainfall. Behind them a marble bench stretched the length of the back half of the chamber.

Steam billowed into the room.

He touched her shoulder, changing the outfit he had created to a gold necklace with a gleaming wolf-tooth pendant at the center of her throat. Her body gleamed pale and opalescent as the inner shell of an oyster, thin wasp waist, full hips, a concave belly that needed filling. His gaze slipped to the triangular thatch of black hair that pointed to his purpose.

He was here, she was here only to mate.

"I'll bathe you first." He drew back to allow her to enter the shower, afraid he could no longer control himself if he touched her. "You're in heat, Lena. Your first. That's why I've come, why we've all come. We answer your call. The scent is irresistible to male wolves."

"Male wolves," she echoed, her voice low and hushed.

"As long as we stay together, as long as we are coupling they will not interfere, but if you leave me or I leave you, they will pursue you once more."

She shivered at this, her eyes wide with astonishment.

"So, you're like me." Her voice held resignation and a note of desperation.

"The same," he assured.

Her eyes sparkled. "Let me see."

He nodded, then stepped back, calling the energy to change. The power sizzled through him, making his body hum like a high voltage wire as he transformed into his other form. He sat upon the plush bath mat before her, a large gray timber wolf, his long tongue lolling, as he stared up at her with hungry eyes.

Lena stepped toward him, her eyes unnaturally wide as she extended her hand. He licked it, tasting the salt on her skin. She shivered, her hand trembling as he nuzzled her, rubbing first against her fingers and then the silk of her bare thigh. She rested her hand on his head, her fingers delving deep into his thick fur. He closed his eyes to savor her touch as he called on his power to shift again, rising, capturing her hand, bringing it to his cheek.

"It's true, then," she whispered.

"True." He was drowning in her scent, the hot draw of her breath, the rise and fall of her full breasts. "The craving will not leave you until you take one of us. I want you. Choose me."

She knew what he said was true, felt the beating drum of blood in her veins, the prickling of each raw nerve and the ache of rising desire. Still, she hesitated.

"Lena, you know me. I'll take care of you, protect you from them."

He left the rest unspoken. The others wanted only her body and the chance to pass on their genes. It was natural, logical, terrifying. Lena shivered at the horror.

She did not want this, but wanted Hunter. Had wanted him

then, still wanted him, would want him after her time was past and he was gone again. Her birth control would keep her from an unwelcome pregnancy. But that was just one of the dangers here.

"Did you bring a condom?"

He smiled. "That defeats the purpose. Doesn't it?"

So, she'd not mention the birth control pill she was on.

"How do I know you aren't carrying something?"

"Lena, have you ever been sick?" His voice held a note of indulgence.

She felt uncertainty inching up her neck like a wet slug. "I'm a very healthy person."

He shook his head. "You're immune to the human diseases. Flu, food poisoning, polio, plagues. None of it affects us."

She stared up wide-eyed.

His mouth went grim. "Will you accept me?"

She stepped toward Hunter, drawn as much by his promise as the raw sexuality that oozed from him with the heady scent she could no longer ignore. He held himself back, still as any predator the instant before the chase.

She held her breath and nodded. He brought her to him, pressing her to his suddenly naked body, drawing her into the warm spray of water and closing them into this private retreat from the waking nightmare that was her life.

His voice caressed her. "I'm yours."

Hunter offered himself to her wholly.

"Yours, for as long as you need me."

She closed her eyes. If only he had not said that last part, she might have been able to pretend he wanted more than exclusivity.

If only he would stay. But she knew what he meant, the logical part of her brain did. He meant he'd stay with her, protect her and make love to her only for as long as she was in heat, and then he'd go.

Lena was a child of practicality. So she'd take what she could get. A few days with Hunter might just be enough to last a lifetime. It had to be, for it was all she'd have. What would he do if, this time, she followed him?

Why hadn't she followed him when he'd asked her all those years ago?

"I'm going to take you, Lena. I have to. If I don't, the others will come back."

Was that true? Were they waiting outside for her even now? Her stomach lurched at the possibility as she clung to the one person who had never lied to her. Hunter. Could she still trust him?

He turned her toward the spray and jets of hot water tingling over her sensitive skin, bringing her nipples to hard, tight knots of need as his erection pressed against her bottom. Their bodies aligned, soft curves to taut muscle. But he did not bend her over or grasp at her as she'd expected. Instead, he pressed tender kisses along her neck as he reached for a bar of soap. If she had ever been washed, she did not recall it, but what Hunter did, she would never forget. Hot water, steam, slippery bubbles of soap and his big, practiced hands caressing her in a slow dance that seemed designed to pay her homage as much as to drive her mad. He dipped his head and sucked the lobe of her ear, licked the shell and nuzzled the erogenous zone just behind. She began to rock against him, working his erection between her legs, sliding along the smooth, velvety length of his shaft, showing him wordlessly that she was wet and ready for him.

But still, he did not enter her. When she leaned forward and thrust her bottom back, he continued the slow erotic soaping of her back, shoulders and arms, cleansing her, caressing her with slow erotic strokes. By the time he reached around her torso to her ribs, she was trembling with yearning. She arched as he lathered her breasts, his hands swirling over the heavy, aching flesh, fingers spiraling around the plump curves and then pinching her nipples until she shivered with need.

The hot steam enveloped them as torrents of water poured over her skin. She was drowning in desire.

She splayed her hands against the hard tile, opening her legs and pressing back. Her need shattered her reason, begged her to surrender all she had to him. She rubbed herself against him with restless, urgent thrusts, becoming the animal she now accepted she was. His hands left her breasts and slid down, sliding between her open legs, his fingers danced over her soft folds, as he pressed his chest to her back. His fingers impaled her but it wasn't enough. She wanted him inside her, stroking the aching hunger he stirred.

He brought her to the edge of sanity. She surrendered to the need, to the wild calling of his body to hers, accepting him.

"Take me," she begged.

Chapter Four

Lena felt the low growl rumbling from deep inside Hunter's chest, rippling out to her as he bent his knees, aligning them and then he was there, pressing against her pliant needy flesh, the tip of him poised, ready. She rocked her hips, offering her cleft to him. He gripped her rump between his two strong hands. She locked her arms and waited.

In that moment of anticipation, Lena recognized that she could manage without everyone else in the world if only she had Hunter.

"Please." She breathed the word, a gasp, a sigh. Lena wanted Hunter, had wanted him, always and only.

He impaled her in one swift, hard stroke, locking them together, stretching her, filling her. She closed her eyes to savor the pleasure. He was huge and she was so ready.

Hunter withdrew with deliberate slowness until she feared she would lose him, but then he drew her back and she shattered, her knees giving way. He held her, his hips locked against her as the rolling contractions corkscrewed through her quaking body.

He paused then, as if savoring her release. The low, feral

growl came again from behind her, vibrating and merging with her own. An instant later Hunter rolled into violent, sensual, delicious motion.

He plunged. She braced, taking all of him again and again.

Hunter moved with barely controlled power, savoring the tightness of her sheath and the slick, wet slide of his penetration into her supple flesh. Oh, he'd had others, won by combat, but Lena, was so wild, so scorching hot. How many times had he dreamed of taking her? And yet he had still not come close to imagining the perfection of this union. Every single time his body had betrayed him, forced him to take some stranger, he had pictured Lena, the only one he ever wanted.

She was strong. She nearly pushed him off his feet with her mad bucking. He was close, yet he wanted it to last.

"Deeper," she commanded

He didn't think it was possible, but she lifted up on her toes and rolled her lovely hips and he sunk farther into her hot, wet body. It was his undoing.

"Sweet mother of us all," he groaned as the orgasm fired within him like a jet engine.

He arched at the rush of pleasure and groaned as he felt her come again, her body's rippling contraction gripping him, milking him.

Please, Great Spirit, let Lena accept him. Let her take this small offering into her lovely body and bring them a child.

They were falling. He controlled their descent as they tumbled out of the shower door and onto the plush mat spread upon the floor.

She sprawled across his chest, gasping too as he gobbled up the air into his oxygen-starved lungs.

After a moment he lifted his head, captured her by the hair and kissed her with all the passion and tenderness in his soul. He savored the taste of her, the soft pliancy of her lips and the greedy glide of her tongue on his.

When he released her, it was only to cradle her head against his chest and hold her in the place next to his heart that he had kept for her all this time. He rested his cheek on the top of her wet head. How he had longed for her during all the days of their separation, but his conjuring did not include this unexpected knot in his throat or the heavy ache in his chest. What had she done to him?

Lena shivered. He released her to capture one of the fluffy towels, enfolding her in the thick terry cloth.

"Are you all right?" he asked, suddenly unsure, worrying that he had been too rough.

She clung to the edges of her towel. Her wet hair hung about her pretty face. Beads of moisture clung to her skin, making her look wilder and more feral than before. She lifted her gaze and showed him a new light in her eyes, a kind of dangerous glint that told him she wasn't done with him yet. His nostrils flared, bringing him the scent of sex, laced with a female in heat. So soon. She wanted him again.

She licked her full lower lip, sending a shot of need right to his hardening cock.

She was on her hands and knees now, stalking forward, pushing him to the floor, her hair dripping puddles on his chest that ran in rivulets down his torso.

Lena kissed him hard on the mouth, then left him to lick, kiss and nip her way down his neck. When her teeth scored over his nipple, Hunter dragged her away and pulled them to their feet.

"I've got a perfectly good bed out there," he said thumbing over his shoulder. "We don't need to lie on the floor."

Lena quirked a brow and then dragged her gaze slowly over him. His skin caught fire beneath her perusal. He offered her another towel and she used it on her hair as he wrapped one about his middle. When she had finished, she stared at the place where the towel jutted out over his erection and then met his gaze and licked her full lips.

Lena on the prowl. His breath caught.

Hunter looked at the woman he had captured and feared that perhaps she had also captured him.

He provided a comb and then wrapped his hand about his cuff bracelet, feeling the pop of energy as his coat shifted to a pair of faded jeans.

"I need to learn to do that." She placed a hand possessively on his hips. "Or how to undo it."

He grinned and then helped her, placing her fingers over the tooth necklace and pressing it down. "Just picture what you want it to do. Picture it clearly."

He stepped back and her eyes fluttered closed. He heard the sizzle and Lena straightened as a pale, satiny, thigh-length robe swathed her.

She grinned up at him and he beamed his pride back to her. Then offered his hand, leading them out, their bare feet padding soundlessly on the hardwood floor to the main room where the electric lights blazed from the ceiling fixtures. His eyes adjusted instantly.

Beside him, Lena slowed, releasing his hand and glancing toward the living room window, which led to the fire escape. He sensed the new tension in her.

She gazed up at him. "Will the others go now?"

He shook his head. "But they'll know we've mated. That will buy us some time."

"Are we safe?"

He nodded. "For now. I can protect you, Lena, and I can provide for you as well." He motioned toward the kitchen. "Are you hungry? Would you eat first?"

He knew a she-wolf was ravenous in all things and had prepared accordingly.

She nodded. "I don't get to eat regularly."

Knowing how she had suffered hurt him. The ache was back and the urge to keep her safe thrummed through him with each beat of his heart. Would she allow him to stay after her time had passed? It was unlikely. Females of his kind did not often choose a permanent mate, preferring to take one only when necessary.

He led her to the kitchen table and held out a chair for her.

She gave him a pleased smile and sat, adjusting the edges of her pink satin robe and cinching the sash. He thought the contrast of her cinnamon skin and the shiny pink robe was the prettiest thing he'd ever seen. He turned to the kitchen area.

Lena watched him, weighing her need for food against her need for sex. She'd been with a few boys, even spent the night with one. But this was different because this was Hunter.

His biceps flexed and his back corded as he opened the refrigerator. She gobbled up the sight of him. She smelled food, lots of food. Lena's mouth watered.

A sound from the alley reached her, a shuffling and scratching. She swallowed back her dread. They were out there in the darkness. Lena shifted her gaze back to Hunter.

As long as she held him, as long as he loved her, they'd be safe. Her instincts told her this was true. The knowledge seemed as deep and ancient as her survival instinct, only stronger, far stronger even than her need to protect herself from danger.

Another thought struck her. He would protect her with his life. She knew it, but she also discovered that she wanted to protect him. He wouldn't leave her while she burned. So for the time she was in heat, he was in danger. She realized that winning her was no prize. It was a huge frickin' target on his back.

How long would he want her? How long would he let her stay?

She never stayed anywhere very long any more. Most of the places she slept this summer had been horrible. She glanced at Hunter. Lena trusted him and that made her feel safe.

Lena glanced about at the apartment. If she let her mind wander she could imagine that this was their place, that he was really hers, not just for tonight, but for a lifetime. She could love him and he would feed her and keep her from the streets. Safe from the others who prowled the night.

Wasn't that a pretty picture? So pretty, in fact, that she cast the fantasy immediately aside. It would be hard enough when he put her back out there. And he would, she sensed that, too. He'd left her before and he'd do it again. She didn't need to make it worse by pretending this was more than the coupling of near strangers.

He was not the boy she remembered. He was here to satisfy her need and his. Once done, he'd go. She needed her wits more than she needed pretty pictures of things that would never be.

Would it make any difference to him if she told him that she didn't want him to leave?

Lena was no child. She'd been through enough to understand that she rarely got what she wanted and when she did, she couldn't keep it. Then why not just enjoy their time while it lasted?

Because, after this, it would make being alone and unprotected even more miserable.

Chapter Five

Hunter set a huge platter of bread, cheese and fruit before her, like an offering. A grape rolled from the bunch and onto the table. He lifted it to her lips. She bit it in half. He popped the other half into his mouth, then returned to the refrigerator.

Wine, sparkling water, a spiral-cut ham, thinly sliced roast beef and an entire cheesecake covered with gooey red strawberries appeared from the enormous refrigerator. She ate more than she should have, wishing she could stuff some of the bounty into her backpack, but then recalled that she had left that in the dorm room. She'd lost all she'd packed and everything else she owned was locked up tight in the dorm until Sunday night.

He held tempting morsels to her lips and she licked the juices from his fingers. She'd never thought of eating as a sensual experience until she did it with Hunter.

"Is everything about sex with you?" she asked.

"Can't really think about anything else when I'm around you, Lena."

Her smile dimmed when she recognized that he was not really attracted to her. It was her heat. Not her, but his body's response to a female who was ready to mate. She could be any female in this condition and he would have fought—no, killed—to have her.

"How long does it last?"

"Hmm?" He lowered the morsel of ham from her lips, the smile receding by slow degrees as he met her gaze with troubled eyes. "Three days, four maybe."

So little time. Her stomach ached in anticipation of their parting. She fidgeted with the collar of her robe.

Hunter drew his chair closer, lifting a hand to stroke her cheek.

"I'm glad I won. Honored to be your first."

She blinked in confusion. "You aren't my first."

"Humans don't count with us. Their just entertainment."

She refused to acknowledge the increase in her heart rate. Did she count? She just wanted to be normal, but that would never happen now. Perhaps she could, at least, be a part of his kind. Lena held her breath as the possibility of being one of a family of Skinwalkers flickered inside her, fragile as a candle flame. She pressed her hand over her mouth as she clutched her hopes.

"What happens afterwards?" she asked.

She saw the answer before he spoke. His eyes narrowed and his lips grew thin and bloodless. He would not be taking her with him.

"I'm a lone wolf."

"Don't wolves run in packs?"

His laugh grated, harsh, mirthless. "Some. And others of our kind create a pair bond. The alphas. They have exclusivity to each other, some raise young."

He raked his hands through the thick hair at his temples. She watched his shoulders bunch, trying not to be distracted by his physicality. Right now she longed to know more of him than that, to reacquaint herself with him, to share their secrets as they had once done.

Lena inched closer, drawn by forces she could only just control.

"Have you ever been a member of such a pack?"

After a long silence, he slouched, dropping his elbows to his thighs.

His eyes met hers and she recognized the haunted expression. "After I left the group home, it was hard. I knew something was happening to me, something dangerous. It's why I left. Then my mentor came for me."

He hadn't told her about his mentor. There was so much about him she didn't know. "When I finished my training, he took me to my sires. My parents were an alpha pair."

He'd found his family. She tried not to let the envy poison her. His luck was not the reason for her misfortune. But, according to what Hunter had just said, her human mother had been no more than entertainment to her Skinwalker father and he had quickly moved on. What did that make her, just another mistake?

"I hunted with them for a time. But when I grew strong and fast, my father turned on me. Nearly killed me. And my mother did nothing to stop him."

"Why would he attack his own son?"

"No pack can have two male alphas. My strength threatened him. So he drove me away."

"But how could they do that to their own child?"

"Is it so hard to believe?" His voice was hoarse when he spoke again. "It doesn't matter. I don't want what they had. I don't want to raise a family only to have to chase them away when they grow strong enough to defend themselves."

She turned to him. "Why would you have to?"

"It's our way."

"Is it, or was it only your father's way?"

One of his elbows slipped from his knee and he straightened. Was that shock or confusion she read on his face? He stood abruptly and stalked across the room, then returned, settling beside her again, his expression looked pained now, as if she had hurt him.

"Could that be possible?"

She inched closer.

"Did my mentor ever say that this was a requirement?" he whispered to himself.

"It was wrong."

Hunter lifted his head. For the first time she saw vulnerability in his expression, doubt and indecision. He shook his head in denial, his expression dark. "No. I do not think this is possible. I do not think…"

Hunter stared at her with a look of speculation. His brow furrowed and his mouth pressed tight.

She dropped her gaze and spoke as much to herself as to him. "I'd never abandon my child and I wouldn't let his father hurt him. I'd kill him first."

He gripped her about the waist and tugged her onto his lap. Hunter looped his hands casually about her waist, but she felt a new tension rippling in his muscles and saw it flashing in his cold blue eyes.

"You'd place your child above your mate?"

The gruff tone and the astonishment in his voice made her realize this was a question of grave importance. But what was the right answer? Suddenly she didn't care if she was a wolf and she didn't care if he liked what she had to say because she'd guard her babies from anyone, even him.

"Yes. Children need protection. Sometimes that includes protection from bad parents." If she'd learned anything in foster care, it was this.

She didn't understand the smile that curled his lips. Did he agree or just find her naive?

"My mother bore other children and abandoned them as well."

"You have siblings?" she asked.

"Yes, but they're much older."

"How much?"

"One hundred years, maybe."

She gasped. "How is that possible?"

"We live long lives. Four hundred years, I'm told. You and I are still young."

She inched away and he laughed, grasping her and dragging her closer.

"We'll need to find your mentor. I've never met a Skinwalker who was not mentored. It is our way. Perhaps your father did not know of your existence, for it was his duty to return for you or send a representative, as mine did."

"Well, he didn't."

"I understand, and that is why you did not know what to expect when your time came. But you must have shifted form before now."

"Until tonight, only in my dreams. I thought I was sleepwalking. I'd wake up naked and…" She let her chin drop to her chest at the lie. There was the cloak and her instinctual need to keep it with her. And there had been other signs. "Once, at a group home, one of the counselors attacked me and the next thing I know he was bleeding and I was running. I don't know how I got out. I don't remember, but maybe I didn't want to."

"I'll teach you to shift your cloak and your form."

Would he be staying to mentor her? She tried not to let the hope creep back into her heart. "Then when we find your mentor you can go with her."

"Her?"

"Mentors are usually of the same sex."

"Not you?"

"Not me."

Lena left his lap, walking to the large industrial windows. Hunter would leave her, just like all the others. She'd be abandoned all over again. She'd never be a part of his family, never be his alpha female.

Behind her the lights clicked off. Her vision shifted as she glanced back, seeing him clearly as he left the wall, and the light switch there, and strode over to her, clasping her shoulders and drawing her into his strong arms. She allowed herself a moment's comfort, even knowing it was an illusion.

"What else troubles you?" he asked.

She turned to face him. "Hunter, how many times have you done this?"

"What?"

"How many women have you won in this way?"

His arms fell away and he stared down at her, his heavy brows setting low over his pale eyes like two dark storm clouds. She'd stolen some of his pleasure. She didn't care. She had to know.

"Lena, listen..."

"How many?"

"Five. Six, maybe."

She reached back for the wall, needing to steady herself as a wave of nausea rolled in her belly. Her fingertips scraped across the rough surface of the brick.

"What does it matter?"

"It matters because I don't want to be just another itch, just some need that you have to satisfy, like filling your belly."

"An itch...Lena, I need you. I thought I explained."

"Yes. You've explained."

They glared at each other.

"And how do you think I feel?" he asked. "Called by this craving I can't control, drawn to any stranger who needs a quick fuck? I hate it, hate being used as a tool and then discarded like a used tube of toothpaste."

Her shock overcame her anger. He had no control either. They were both pawns. Her throat prickled and her eyes began to burn. She sniffed, holding back the tears that threatened.

Her voice dropped to a whisper. "So what happens afterwards? Will you give me to the others?"

His answer was a feral growl. "No!"

"Then tell me what *will* happen?"

"I'll fight again and win. Then, when you no longer have need of me, I'll go."

"What if I don't want you to go, what if I want to stay here?"

He blinked at her, as if her question made no sense.

"Lena, I don't live here. I created this place for us, for you in your time."

"It's all just a fantasy, then, like make-believe."

"No. This is real."

She threw up her hands as she backed away. "I don't even know what I'm doing here."

He stalked towards her, chin lowered, looking dangerous again. "You know."

She pushed off the wall and managed to bound in the opposite direction, fleeing from her confusion and from him. He beat her across the room, blocking her escape.

"You're not going," he said. "Not yet."

She was his prisoner here. She understood it. He wouldn't let her go until both their needs were satisfied, burned to ash like charcoal soaked in lighter fluid. He wouldn't let another male near her until she was past wanting any other, and then he'd cast her off.

Even knowing all that, she could still feel the desire for him stirring, gathering and pooling like warm honey in her middle. And she could see the hunger glowing, like green fire, deep in his pale eyes.

"Have you ever wanted to stay with one of them?" she asked.

He shook his head. She felt reality slap her in the face again.

Why couldn't she find one single place or one single person who made her feel as if she belonged? But someone *had* made her belong. Hunter had, once.

"At least I can't get pregnant," she muttered.

He glowered, obviously displeased. Did he want her pregnant and alone?

"Why's that?"

"Birth control," she admitted, feeling her cheeks heat at keeping this from him.

His slow smile chilled her to the spine.

"Human birth control?"

She couldn't speak, but managed a nod.

He shook his head and her stomach dropped. "Won't work," he said.

Her shock solidified into fury. She had sworn she'd not go there, yet here she was making the same stupid mistake she'd watched the girls all around her make over and over again. Damn him and damn her raging hormones.

Single mother, welfare, foster care, the circle spinning back over her again.

"If you want a child, then why walk away?" she asked.

He stepped forward, she inched back. Hunter lifted a hand and stroked her cheek. She allowed it.

His voice was a whispered caress. "I'm not walking away, Lena. But you will. They all do." He captured her hand, laced her numb fingers with his, then lifted the entwined knot to his lips and kissed her icy knuckles.

He had rescued her, saved her and damned her all in one night.

"Come to bed," he murmured.

Evalena shook her head.

Her heart ached for him even as she stepped away.

It would be hard to forget him—so hard, and even harder to forgive him for what he had done.

His voice held a hard edge. "I can't protect you if you don't come to bed."

Lena bumped against the wall beside the window, gazing down into the dark alley, seeing them there waiting. She glanced back to Hunter. "You aren't protecting me. You're just like them." She motioned with her head to the window as she faced him, her skin tingling and her pulse pounding. Acidity burned her stomach and she felt ill. "You left me five years ago and you only came back for this." She opened her robe, revealing herself to him.

His eyes flashed hot. She drew the edges closed as he reached, evading his grasp.

She leveled him with a cold stare. "But you won't touch me again."

She knew he could take her by force, had earned the right through combat. Still she laid down the challenge and waited, every hair now standing on end as she waited to see if he would destroy all they had once been.

He glowered. But he did not move toward her.

Hunter held her gaze a moment longer, his jaw muscle ticking his displeasure. Then his shoulders sagged in defeat. His voice was a mere whispered breath.

"I wish it could be different."

She squeezed her eyes closed at the lie.

"But if you will not accept me, I must fight to keep you."

Fear for his safety flooded through her, drowning her pain and anguish.

"No!"

She grabbed him, pulling them away from the window, from the alley where the others waited. If she could see in the dark, so could they.

Her focus now turned from her own safety to Hunter's.

"Can't you just tell them I'm with you?"

He snorted. "You don't understand. It doesn't work that way. *I* don't choose. *You* do. The female chooses her mate. Not the other way around. The only way for a male to stay is for the female to claim him."

She would, if she were not certain that by doing so she would only make a bigger fool of herself. He'd just told her he was a loner. That he didn't want a woman or a family. And he'd left her once already, not to mention the betrayal of neglecting to tell her she might get pregnant. She stared up at him, wanting to plead with him, but her pride prevented her.

For an instant she thought he was waiting for her to speak. The moment passed. Hunter gave a nod of his head.

"Right. I thought not."

Hunter swept a hand over his naked chest and he stood fully dressed.

"Stay with me," she urged.

"I can't, unless you claim me."

"I do."

He shook his head. "No Lena. You do not. To choose is a matter of the heart, not the mind. It changes you and I could scent the difference." He motioned toward the window. "They could as well."

"I don't understand."

"You want only my protection. That is not a pair bond. Mated pairs will have no other and will fight to the death to defend their mate. I would protect you, but you would also protect me. Are you prepared for that?"

She backed away.

His smile was sad. He took her hand and held it over her necklace. "Just concentrate on energy. Call it and the change will come. Once in wolf form you need only to picture your human shape to turn back." He drew away. "And guard your cloak. Never leave it unprotected for you cannot transform without it."

He lifted the window sash and then hesitated, glancing at her.

"If I win, I will return. If not, then I will miss you, Evalena. You have grown into a most unusual wolf."

It was on her lips to call him back, to beg him not to go. But she did not want him to remember her whining and crawling on her belly like a dog. After all, she was a wolf now.

He threw a leg over the ledge, straddling the sill. "I can hold them. Give you time to run, if it is your wish. But you will have to go far and fast, for they will follow until your time is done."

"Wait!" She clasped her hands together to keep herself from reaching out for him. He turned back, giving her a long steady stare. "Why didn't you come back for me, as you promised?"

"Why didn't you wait for me to come?"

She blinked at him, as a tiny possibility grew inside her like a seedling.

"What do you mean?" She held her breath, waiting for the answer.

He stepped out onto the fire escape, then glanced at her. "Oh, Lena. I did come back. But too late. You'd gone and they had no record of your location. I had nothing to track you with, so I waited, knowing that when your time came I could find you."

Chapter Six

Hunter landed lightly on the concrete. The day had broken but here in the alley behind the theater it was gray. He smelled stale bread and rotting lettuce from the dumpster behind the bakery. And he smelled wolf. They'd begun to gather here, none aggressive enough to face him alone.

He crouched, changing into his animal form in a burst of brilliant white light. Energy zipped and crackled through his system and he stood on all fours, back to the wall as they came, a pack of young males, all after Evalena—and the only thing between her and gang rape was him.

One, two, three...the final male stepped from cover and Hunter faced eight. He was good, but eight to one was terrible odds. He determined to hold them long enough for her to escape. That much he could do.

He scanned the group searching for their leader and found him easily. He was no larger, yet stood just ahead of the others, eyes pinned on Hunter, while the pack looked to him for the signal to attack. An instant later Hunter bared his canines and crouched.

The others launched themselves at him. Hunter bit and

snapped. He tore open a shoulder and heard the cry of his opponent. One down.

But another took his place, and another. They surrounded him. It was just a matter of time before one got behind him and tore open his hamstring. Then he'd be finished. Once down they'd rip open his stomach and leave him to bleed to death.

Evalena. Had she gotten away?

Suddenly the snarling and snapping grew louder. He heard another wolf cry and saw another attacker limp from the fight. But he had not caused the injury.

His sense of smell told him first what had happened. Evalena had not run as he had instructed. Instead, she had come to fight at his side. Hunter fought harder. Trying to protect her and disable the others. But he quickly saw that she was fearless and fearsome.

Evalena, the black wolf, was a devil to face.

The remaining six suffered injuries. Their leader withdrew and the others followed. They had won.

The pack leader turned, transforming into his human form, and Hunter saw he was one of the men that he had faced on Sullivan Street. The others shifted as well, bleeding, clutching their wounds.

"So, she has claimed you," said his rival.

Evalena turned first, appearing in her black fur cape and then a moment later in the outfit he had created for her.

"This one is mine and I'll kill anyone who threatens him."

Hunter was standing at her side an instant later. By choosing to stand with him against the others, she'd claimed him. He knew instantly. She was still in heat but the scent was laced with a metallic fragrance of blood and the sweetness of fresh grass.

He offered his hand and she took it. Only then did he recognize her fear, from the dampness of her palm.

The pack dispersed, leaving only their leader.

"You are a lucky man, for she is an alpha unlike any I have ever seen. Walk in beauty," he said, giving the customary farewell and blessing.

"Walk in beauty," said Hunter.

Only after they were alone did Evalena's shoulders sag. She bent to place her hands on her knees as if she were suddenly taken ill.

He wrapped an arm about her narrow shoulders, the fear blasting him like a cold wind. "Are you hurt?"

"I think I'm going to puke. Oh, I'm dizzy."

He guided her to the plastic chair someone had set beside the back door of the bakery.

"It's the adrenalin. It just abandons you after a fight."

She sank to the chair and cradled her forehead in her hands.

He crouched beside her, rubbing her back. At last she lifted her head and tucked her inky hair behind her ears. She grinned at him.

"That was something," she said.

"You defended me." He could not keep the awe from his voice.

The grin grew wider. "Sure did."

"No one's ever done that before."

Her smile receded. "I know you told me to run, and I tried, but I couldn't leave you."

"Do you know what you did, Evalena? You've claimed me."

She swallowed, a bitter taste now in her mouth. She'd let him see her commitment, smell it on her skin. But it wouldn't matter.

"Listen," she said. "I understand if you don't want to accept me. I just, I couldn't stand by and watch them hurt you."

He took her hands in his. "Why?"

She felt herself shrinking. He was going to make her say it aloud, make her admit that he had shown her a new way to be normal and given her a chance to belong.

"You're a wolf, Lena, and a damned brave one. Don't turn coward now. Tell me. Why couldn't you watch me be defeated?"

She knew she'd be humiliated by her admission. Why couldn't she just watch him go like all the others? But she knew why. This was Hunter and she loved him.

But saying so was harder than the battle, because she could bear the physical pain of that. But his rejection, oh, now that was an anguish that might kill her. She drew a heavy breath and fixed her eyes upon him, letting him see the fierce possession there.

"No matter how hard I tried to fit in, I never felt like I belonged before and now I understand why. I couldn't belong anywhere, because I lost my place in this world when I lost you. I should have come with you, Hunter. But I was just too scared. I'm not afraid anymore. I'll follow you wherever you go. Because I love you and because you're mine." She held a hand to her mouth, aghast at her own audacity.

He smiled his approval, a baring of white teeth. "A pairbond then. Is that what you want?"

She nodded.

"I've never been asked and never thought to be asked to join with an alpha female. You honor me."

"Does that mean yes?"

He drew her to him. "Yes, Lena. Oh, yes, because I love you, too."

Hunter pulled her into his strong arms and rocked her tenderly. Lena held him, resting her head upon his chest, listening to the strong, reassuring stroke of his heartbeat.

"I thought I had lost you," she whispered.

"Never again, Lena. We belong together——now and always."

She knew that, but there were still so many uncertainties. She pulled back staring up at him as roiling questions kept her from savoring the sweetness of this moment.

"But what will happen now? What about my school and you? I don't even know where you've been or..or anything."

His smile reassured her before he even spoke. "I work as a P.I., specializing in finding missing persons. Our tracking ability makes us naturals. I can teach you. You'll be excellent at recovery, too. I do very well, more business than I can handle, and I can set up anywhere, so you can stay in school if you like, go full-time or join me as a tracker. Either way, we'll be together." He took hold of her shoulders and gave her a little squeeze. "Do you understand what I'm saying, Lena? We can finally build a home of our own."

"A home?" she whispered, breathing the word that was as sacred to her as holy ground.

A home, with Hunter, together. Their home. The dream she'd feared would never become reality was now within her reach.

Tears filled her eyes.

"Lena? Say something."

She threw herself into his arms, hugging him fiercely. "Oh, Hunter. Is it true?"

He enfolded her in his strong arms. "Yes, Lena. We'll make a home together."

He cradled her head against him, holding her, protecting her, and she knew in her heart that he always would.

* * * * *

DEMON'S EMBRACE

ELLE JAMES

Award-winning author **Elle James** grew up as an air force military brat. She received her work ethic from her rock-solid father, her creative streak from her artistic mother and inspiration from her writing partner and sister, Delilah Devlin.

As a former member of the army reserves and a current member of the air force reserves, she's travelled across the United States and to Germany, managed a full-time job and raised three wonderful children. She and her husband have even tried their hands at ranching exotic birds (ostriches, emus and rheas) in the Texas hill country. Ask her, and she'll tell you what it's like to go toe-to-toe with an angry three-hundred-and-fifty-pound bird and live to tell about it!

Her adventures in the army and air force reserves and the wild antics of her life on a small ranch in Texas give her fodder for mystery, suspense and humour in her writing. A former manager of computer programming and project management professionals, Elle is happy she now has the opportunity to pursue her writing full time. Elle's paranormal romantic comedy, *To Kiss a Frog*, won the Romance Writers of America's 2004 Golden Heart for Best Paranormal Romance.

You can reach Elle by e-mail at ellejames@ellejames.com.

Chapter One

I struggled through a haze of cool fog, pushing my way out to emerge naked on an empty city street where a solitary streetlamp lit the corner of the next block. Drawn to its un-earthly glow, I floated along on silent feet, my focus forward, the warmth it promised tugging at me like an invisible string, guiding me, beckoning, pulling me.

As I neared, a shadow broke away from the lamp pole.

A flash of fear brought me to a momentary halt, my pulse leaping, flight instinct warring against the lure that urged me forward.

The shadow's soft chuckle heated the night air. Warm hands reached out to grab me, wrapping me in a cocoon of naked, muscular male.

My fear evaporated and I sighed, burying my face against his chest. "Blaise."

"Yes, sweet Katya, it's me."

My fingers curled into the hair at the nape of his neck, tilting his head toward mine, my lips longing for the caress of his. I hated that I needed him, like a body needs liquid to quench its thirst. "Where have you been?"

"Out." He brushed his mouth across mine with the light-ness of butterfly wings.

I wanted more, pressing into him, lifting my head, impatient, my nerves tingling in anticipation.

His lips met mine, crushing, invading, his tongue edging past my teeth. He pushed me backward until my shoulders connected with the solid brick wall of a building. Then he pressed a knee between my thighs to part them and lifted my legs to wrap around his waist.

The brick fell away, replaced by the soft, billowy bed of cottony clouds. I sank into the comfort, taking him with me, my ankles locking behind his back.

His cock pressed into me, thrusting into the slickness of my channel, stretching me with his thick, hard girth.

I moaned, my tongue twisting around his, thrusting in rhythm with his hips, his cock, the way he moved over my body.

Ripples of release pulsed across my nerves, building in cascading explosions until my back arched off the clouds.

His cock thrust one last time and we ignited in a simulta-neous release of the purest sunburst of energy.

My breath held as I rode the waves of ecstasy to shore, the ebb and flow of sensation drawing me back in and out until I fell back to earth, my descent cushioned by the grasp of his hands on my hips.

When at last I could breathe on my own, I lay limp, my muscles and bones liquefied under Blaise's intense assault.

"Open your eyes," he whispered, pressing his lips to each eyelid, coaxing me to comply.

"Not yet," I mumbled, my legs tightening around him, refusing to let go, refusing to awaken from whatever dream I was in.

An annoying buzzing blasted through my refuge of half-sleep, half-dream, shooting through my ear, straight into my head. "What the hell?" My eyes popped open, my ankles released, my heels falling to the mattress of my bed. The incessant buzzing continued, complete with a clatter of plastic on the wooden surface of my nightstand, effectively ending my sensual dream.

Blaise rolled off me, collapsing against the pillows.

I snatched my cell phone up, punching the talk button. "Danske."

"Meeting at the precinct in fifteen."

My boss's words cut through the remaining haze of sleep, chasing back the lingering fluffs of fog, returning me to earth with a resounding thud.

"Fifteen?" I glanced at the clock and groaned. I wasn't due on duty for another hour and a half. "I need a shower."

"I don't care what you smell like. Be here in fifteen." Lieutenant Thomas, the detective assigned the illustrious duty of managing Manhattan's Paranormal Investigative Team, had spoken. "And bring Blaise with you."

"What if I don't know where he is.'"

"Cut the crap, Agent Danske. Where you are, he is. Both of you, in the War Room in fifteen." The line cut off.

I glanced at my partner, Blaise Michaels, the demon who'd taken up residence in my life. "You hear that?"

He nodded.

"Does he think you live here?" I tossed back the blankets, strode naked to the scuffed dresser I'd purchased from a secondhand store and yanked open the top drawer, digging around for a bra and panties.

"How will anyone take me seriously, if they think you're living with me?" I flung a narrow-eyed glare at him. "And how the hell did you get in? I locked the double bolts and windows before I hit the sack."

He shrugged. "I have ways."

"Don't tell me another one of your *talents* is to walk through walls." I shoved a foot into the leg of my panties and then another, drawing them up my thighs, completely aware of the demon eyeing my every move.

And damned if my body didn't play traitor on me and burst into red-hot flaming desire. "You—" With my underwear firmly in place around my hips, I poked a finger at him. "—are not invited into my apartment without my explicit consent. Do you hear me?"

His grin infuriated me, at the same time it flicked all my damned "on" switches, sending a wash of purely decadent juices to my pussy.

"I mean it." Ah hell, who was I kidding? "No one will take a female on the force seriously if she's sleeping with a team member. We can't see each other anymore."

His smile broadened. "Okay."

I turned my back so that I wouldn't have to look at his mocking face and slipped into a pair of black jeans, yanking the zipper up before I could get further sidetracked. The patronizing look he'd given me only made my gut tighten along with my resolve. As I clipped on my bra and twisted it around my ribs, I prepared a scathing retort.

Before I could slip the straps up my arm and deliver a suitable comeback, warm hands reached around from behind me to cup my breasts.

"Tell me you want me to stop, and I will." He kissed the sensitive area below the back of my right ear, his breath stirring tendrils of hair, tickling my skin and sending shivers down the length of my spine.

Oh, sweet Jesus. How was I supposed to resist him when he was a damned demon with the ability to throw my hormones into hyper-drive with a single touch?

I dragged in a shaky breath, reveling in the heat he generated, his naked body aligned with my backside, his cock nudging at my bottom. With the strength of a saint, I shoved his hands from my breasts and leaped out of reach before I faced him.

"We can't do this anymore," I said. "I want my employer to respect me for my skills as an officer of the law, not for my skills at pleasing our token demon."

He nodded, the smile disappearing from his too-handsome face, his ice-blue eyes boring into mine. "As you wish."

In the time it took me to complete dressing and brush my hair into a ponytail, he was dressed and waiting by the door to my apartment.

Together, we walked the couple blocks to the station. When we were within a stone's throw of our destination, I paused at a newsstand. "You go ahead. I want to get a pack of gum."

Blaise stopped. "I'll wait."

"Not only are you arrogant, you're thickheaded. I don't want to arrive at the same time as you. Now, go." I shoved him toward the station and turned my back on him. When I'd paid for the pack of gum, I resumed my trek, a good fifty yards behind the demon.

Take that, Lieutenant Thomas. We're not together.

Yeah, yeah. The only person I was fooling was myself.

In the War Room, Lieutenant Thomas paced the floor in front of the huge whiteboard, deep lines furrowing his brow. "About time you got here, Agent Danske. Now we can begin."

I glanced around at the empty chairs. "Where's the rest of the team?"

The lieutenant's lips thinned. "Out patrolling the streets where you and Michaels should be."

"I wasn't due on duty for another hour. If you'd wanted me earlier, you could have called earlier."

"I did. No answer."

I pulled my phone from my pocket and scanned the recent calls. Just as the detective stated, there were three unanswered calls from Lieutenant Thomas. "I don't understand. I didn't hear it ring." I glanced across at Blaise.

His gaze didn't meet mine.

Irritation flared, pushing heat into my cheeks. "Perhaps my phone was mysteriously off at that time."

"I suggest you talk to the technical personnel and get that fixed. I have to be able to contact you at a moment's notice. Paranorms can't be trusted to stay on a set schedule."

"You were right when you said paranorms can't be trusted." I glared at my partner, the only paranorm in the room.

Lieutenant Thomas calmed. "You're assigned to follow Jimmy Raggio tonight. He's a small-time werewolf druggie. I have it from a good source that he'll be making a purchase to stock up on drugs to push to the local lupine teens. I want his contact. Teens and drugs are a bad combination to begin with. Werewolf teens and drugs can get downright dangerous."

"Got it." I gathered the street address of one Jimmy Raggio and the keys to one of the unmarked vehicles at our disposal. Without waiting for my partner, I headed for the door.

Blaise caught up with me as I reached the elevator. "I'm sorry. I shouldn't have set your phone to silent, while we were…"

I jabbed the down arrow. "Damn right you shouldn't have."

"I promise I won't do it again." He gave me that dark-eyed, heart-stopping, sad-demon look that always made my knees go weak.

Not this time.

The door dinged and slid open. "Damn right you won't." I stepped in and hit the button for the garage level and the button to close the elevator door. "You're not ever going to come into my apartment again."

Blaise jumped in before the doors closed. "You don't mean that."

"The hell I don't." I faced him, all the anger I'd contained while in the same room with my boss bubbling up. "You have no right to interfere with me or my job, and today you crossed the line." I turned away. "Don't show up at my apartment, uninvited."

"What if I need to get a hold of you?"

"You can call my cell phone. I'll leave it on, unlike you."

Blaise stood beside me, his height and broad shoulders filling the tight confines of the elevator car.

Before he or I could utter another word, the bell dinged and the doors slid open into the garage. I found the car and slid behind the wheel, turning the key in the ignition as Blaise dropped into the passenger seat. With more force than necessary, I whipped the shift into reverse and backed out of the parking space, laying a strip of rubber on the pavement when I gave it more gas than necessary.

We drove to an area in Brooklyn that had seen better days and bordered on a warehouse district. Some of the buildings were being renovated, others stood dull and poorly maintained, dusk adding to the air of gloom. Warehouses built in the 1940s stood empty, broken windows like so many sad eyes staring down at them as they passed.

I parked in an alley a couple blocks away from our designated pick up point, picking a spot behind a stack of broken pallets and trash. Jimmy was due to leave his apartment building around nine o'clock. I sat for a few minutes, taking the time to check my Glock and flipped the safety switch on.

Blaise and I hadn't spoken two words since we'd gotten

into the car. It suited me just fine. And the demon hadn't pushed any words into my thoughts. Even better.

Beside me, his lips twitched. *I was afraid you'd shoot me.*

I'd spoken too soon. "I'd appreciate it if you'd stay the hell out of my head." Infuriating demon.

With more force than accuracy, I jammed my radio head-set into my ear and handed one to Blaise.

He shook his head. "We're going together on this."

"I want you a block over. We don't want him to catch our scents and make a run for it."

With a heavy frown, Blaise plugged the miniature radio into his ear and tested it. "I don't know why I can't just push thoughts."

"I like having a back up." I got out and stretched, checked my watch and nodded. "It's time."

Before we reached Jimmy's apartment, I spotted a man fitting his description on the other side of the street, heading away from where we were standing. He disappeared around a corner.

"You take the next street over. Don't lose him." I took off at a controlled jog, eager to close the distance before I lost the werewolf.

I slipped through the streets, dodging yellowed streetlights and hugging the shadows of buildings as I ran a parallel course from my target, one street over. "You have Jimmy?" I whispered into my headset.

Yeah. Blaise's warm tones invaded my head sans the head-set, sending shivers of awareness across my skin. *Twenty yards ahead, moving slowly.*

Pushing aside the toe-curling lust his voice induced, I focused on the task at hand. "Stay far enough back he doesn't get wind of you."

One of Manhattan's young werewolves, Jimmy Raggio, had better olfactory nerves than I did and could smell a demon within a fifty-foot radius. Farther, if the wind was blowing his way. Although, this kid's senses might be dulled by the amount of drugs he'd been snorting or shooting. His habit had pushed him over the line into selling to support his drug needs.

That's where Blaise and I came in. When otherkin ran amuck, we were called in to clean up the mess. Tracking Jimmy to his source should be a slam dunk. Nab Jimmy, nab his contact and we'd have two less scumbags trashing the New York City underworld.

A month ago, I'd have laughed in anyone's face who tried to tell me creatures that weren't human roamed our city streets.

All that had changed in a matter of days, when NYPD recruited me to their special taskforce—the Paranormal Investigative Team—lovingly referred to as the PIT crew.

He just turned into an alley, headed back your way. Blaise's thoughts cut through my musings.

The alley I assumed he was referring to loomed half a block ahead of me like a dark maw, the streetlights barely penetrating the entrance. I held back, ducked behind a huge trash bin and waited, giving the young werewolf time to emerge. As I crouched there, the stench from the trash overpowered my senses.

A really long minute went by.

"See him?" Blaise asked.

"No." I gave it another half of a minute and left my hiding place and the smell, moving toward the alley entrance. I eased the night vision goggles over my eyes, careful not to look back and be blinded by the streetlight a block behind me. Werewolves and some demons, like my partner, could see at night. Humans, not so much.

I paused at the corner of the building, my Glock drawn, thumbing off the safety switch.

Voices echoed off the brick walls, the actual words garbled by distance.

Squatting low, I peeked around the corner. Through my night vision goggles, three figures appeared in the alley, two standing, one carrying a limp form, glowing just as green as the others. A warm body, possibly alive for now.

Damn. A simple drug run was turning into more.

The green glowing figures stepped toward her, their voices low, intense, as if they were arguing in whispers.

Don't move on them until I get around to where you are, Blaise warned me.

I slipped back around the side of the building, pushing the goggles to the top of my head. "They're heading my way. Don't try to come up behind them. The wind's coming from that direction."

"Hide and wait."

As quickly as I could, I moved half a block back to the trash bin, sliding between it and the building.

As footsteps clumped toward the alley entrance, I could make out their words.

"If ya know what's good for ya, you'll ditch the bitch."

"Can't. She's my cousin. My ma'll kill me if I leave her there."

"When Nic finds out you took her, he'll do the job and make it hurt as you go down. He likes to make examples of anyone else who takes what's his."

"He wasn't there when I took her."

"That demon has eyes and ears everywhere. He'll know."

"Look, Jimmy, I can't leave her."

"You're on your own, Mario." Jimmy emerged from the

alley, leading the way. He glanced right and left before cutting across the street.

"He's on the move," I said into my microphone. Before Blaise could respond, a hand clamped over my mouth, another around my waist pinning one of my arms to my side. I was hauled up against a solid wall of muscle.

Chapter Two

My heartbeat stuttered then raced. Instinct kicked in and I jabbed my free elbow into my attacker's gut.

A muffled *oomph* sounded behind me, but the hand over my mouth didn't loosen. Then a voice whispered, "Katya, it's me."

My pulse slowed and I dragged in a deep breath.

Blaise's hand dropped from my mouth to my shoulder.

"Damn it, Blaise. You could warn me next time." His fingers warmed me, even through the fabric of my black leather jacket.

"I will, next time." He nodded toward the young thugs. "I'll take Jimmy. You go after the guy carrying the girl."

"Why don't I go after Jimmy and you take the others?" I pushed away from the brick wall and crept to the corner of the trash bin.

"You know I can move faster, and Jimmy's on the run now."

The sound of footsteps pounding through the alley reached me. "Fine. But don't do anything until you see him make the sell."

Blaise saluted me. "Be careful. Just because he's carrying someone doesn't mean he's not dangerous."

I nodded. "Same to ya. I don't want to train a new partner."

He chuckled softly, pressed a kiss to my lips and disappeared, moving so fast, he'd crossed the street before I could tell him how unprofessional it was to kiss your partner on duty.

Instead I shook my head. I couldn't tell that demon anything.

Blaise did whatever the hell he wanted. Though he worked with the PIT crew, he wasn't on the payroll and he came and went as he pleased.

I was glad he was on our side—not that I'd tell him that. The demon had a big head to begin with, thinking he was better than anybody else.

He had reason to think that. I'd seen him practically rip a man apart, limb for limb. The guy deserved it, but the incident reminded me that my partner had superhuman strength and speed.

Must be nice.

I was stuck with being a five-feet-two-inch female cop with big boobs and no respect. Well, at least no respect until I flattened a guy on the way to the locker room for pinching my ass. Since then, all of the cops of the Fifth Precinct had steered clear of me. Had I known that was all it took, I would have decked someone earlier.

I didn't have time to put up with dumbass men who thought small meant weak. I'd been a cop a lot longer than some of them and didn't put up with much. I could drop a perp with a bullet or tackle them and put the fear of God in them with hand-to-hand combat. Mostly because they didn't expect a *girl* to be tough.

I'd learned to stick up for myself the day my dad walked

off and left me, my brother and mother to fend for ourselves in the not-so-great neighborhoods of Chicago.

Manhattan was a cakewalk compared to some of the places I'd cut my teeth on. Or so I thought, until I discovered people I thought were human…well…weren't.

Mario had turned to the right and headed the opposite direction from me, stooped under the weight of the body he carried.

I followed at a safe distance, wondering where he'd take the woman, knowing I wouldn't let them get far. If he was involved in drug trafficking with Jimmy, I needed to question him, put the screws to him and see if he knew who was supplying his partner.

As I moved closer to Mario, my nostrils picked up a canine and cologne combination that confirmed my suspicion. Mario, like Jimmy, was a werewolf. Even the girl he carried put off the same kind of odor.

Gun drawn, I closed the distance, running lightly across the uneven sidewalk.

"Look, if you're gonna shoot, pull the damned trigger." Mario ground to a halt, his back to me.

"Don't tempt me." I trained the weapon, loaded with silver bullets, on the werewolf, having been warned of their strength when in wolf form. "I have a gun pointed at you. Turn around slowly." For all I knew Mario could be calling on his inner beast, or whatever werewolves did to go from human to wolf.

Mario turned, his young face haggard, dark circles beneath his eyes. "I'm too tired to fight. You want my wallet. It's in my back pocket. Although there isn't much in it."

"I don't want your wallet or your money."

His arms tightened around the woman. "If Nicolae sent you, you can't have her. She's family."

"I'm not with Nicolae. I'm with the NYPD. I want some answers."

His eyes narrowed. "Sorry. Unless you got a reason to arrest me, I have nothing to say." Mario nodded toward the gun. "And I'm guessing you won't shoot someone you only wanted to question." He spun and walked away.

Damn.

I hurried to keep up, but he made it to the next corner before I did and disappeared.

I hesitated. If the man didn't want to talk, I had nothing on him that I could hold over his head. I had to let him go. Question was, whether to follow or go back and see if Blaise needed help with our real target, Jimmy.

I'd turned back and had taken all of two steps when the blast of gunfire ricocheted off the walls of the street Mario had turned onto.

Adrenaline spiked in my system and I raced to the end of the building.

Mario lay on the ground, light glinting off the circle of blood spreading from the hole in the side of his head. Several men, make that werewolves—by the smell of them—stood in a semicircle around the downed man. One of them waved another forward. "Get the girl. Nicolae will want his property returned."

The man's words made my blood boil. Before I could think through the odds, I stepped forward.

One five-feet-two-inch female cop against seven burly male werewolves.

Yeah. I could be stupid when passion kicked in.

A woman in jeopardy —human or werewolf—got my ire up and I didn't back down. I held my weapon steady, aimed at the man who'd given the orders. With my finger, I pointed at the man hefting the woman onto his shoulder like she was an insignificant bag of potatoes."Put the girl down."

"You gonna make me?"

"NYPD." I dug my credentials out of my breast pocket and flipped them open with my empty hand, my gun-bearing hand steady on the leader. "You are all under arrest for the murder of this man."

The man carrying the woman sneered. "You're gonna arrest all of us?" He laughed out loud.

I fired at his feet.

The man jumped, a scowl bearing down on his forehead.

The leader stepped forward. "You got enough bullets to take us all out?"

"I have plenty, they're silver, and I'm starting with you." I held my position. "Put the woman down."

Their leader jerked his head to his partner. "Put her down, like the she-cop said."

"You're kidding right?"

"On the contrary. I see this as an opportunity we can't resist." The leader's hand went to the front of his jeans and he cupped his package. "We can all have a little fun with the little she-cop before we deliver the goods to the boss."

"He said get the job done and get back."

"Think, dumbass. How will he know how long it took us?" The leader's mouth pulled up in a sneer. "In the meantime. I get her first."

"Did you miss the fact I'm holding a gun?" I pointed the weapon at his chest.

"Nah, but I'm banking on you shooting him first." He thrust the man standing next to him in between him and me. I shot the man in the knee, he went down. Without blinking, I took the leader out with a shot in the knee as well.

"Did I mention, I was top of my class on the firing range?"

I pointed at the man carrying the woman. "Now put her down and leave before I take you out as well."

The werewolf slid the woman to the ground and ran, taking the other four weres with him, abandoning the two with the injured knees.

As they clutched at their wounds, cursing me, I divested them of their weapons and crouched beside the woman.

She moaned and stared up at me, her eyes glazed, but open.

"Nicolae will kill you."

"Not today, honey. Not today." I tapped on my headset. "Blaise, you out there?"

Static rumbled in my ear. Not good. I'd have to find a phone or get back to our vehicle to call this one in.

The woman gripped my arm, her fingernails digging into my skin.

"Hey, lighten up. You're safe." I patted her shoulder, awkwardly. Give me a gun and I'm all over it. Nurturing wasn't in my nature.

She shook her head, her eyes round, staring over my shoulder at whatever was standing behind me. "Nicolae."

Too late, my sense of smell kicked in with a sickly sweet aroma, similar, but not the same as what I sensed around Blaise.

Demon.

Instinctively, I spun, swinging my leg out, while still in a crouch.

I caught the demon's legs at the shin, knocking him off his feet.

The woman on the ground pushed to a sitting position and swayed. "Get the amulet. The necklace. It's the key. Get it."

I only half-heard her as the demon staggered to his feet, eyes gleaming red, his hands rising, fingers curling.

My throat tightened. No air made it through to my starving lungs. I clawed at the invisible fingers that squeezed the breath out of me.

The demon the woman had referred to as Nicolae lifted his arms into the air.

As if a noose tightened around my neck, my body rose from the crouched position, my feet left the ground.

For a moment, I dangled in the air.

In the next second, I was flung twenty feet, hitting a brick wall, my weapon knocked from my grasp, skittering across the pavement, out of reach.

My head bounced against the hard surface, and I slid to the ground, gray fog engulfing me. Not the pleasant cloud of my earlier dream, but the encroaching pall of a nightmare unfolding before me.

Nicolae gathered the woman in his arms and turned to leave.

"Help me." Her bleating cry for help jumpstarted my lungs.

I sucked in a breath, pushing back the darkness, and lurched to my feet. The demon would not get away with the woman.

"Not on my watch, you don't," I muttered as my feet churned beneath me and I threw myself at the demon's back.

Caught off guard, he dropped the woman to the ground and spun.

I clung to his back, my arm hooked around his throat, hanging on for dear life. I hadn't gotten around to clarifying how to kill a demon with my partner, no matter how many times I'd wanted to kill him for one infraction or another.

The demon reached over his shoulder and grabbed my jacket, his fingernails lengthening, tearing into the leather, slicing through my shirt and ripping into my flesh.

Pain ricocheted throughout my body, the affected area

burning as if he'd poured battery acid directly onto the wound.

I bit down hard on my lower lip to keep from crying out and tightened my hold, one finger wrapping around a leather strap hanging around his neck.

The woman on the ground reached up. "The amulet. Take it," she cried.

Flipping my wrist, I twisted the leather around all the fingers on that hand.

Then as if shot from a cannon, my body was blasted away from the demon. The force sent me flying. Since I had the leather strap wrapped firmly around my wrist and fingers, the leather tie snapped and the necklace came with me.

Again, I hit the wall, my head slamming against brick for the second time in as many minutes. My vision blurred. I blinked to clear it, but it remained blurred. I couldn't breathe and my insides boiled, as if each cell was on fire. Had his talons injected me with poison? Was this to be the end of my career as a cop?

As quickly as it blurred, my vision cleared and I blinked up at the oncoming demon, as he ducked low and charged toward me.

I rolled to the side and shot to my feet.

He had me by the throat before I could call out.

"Give it to me."

"To hell with you," I squeaked with my last breath.

"You have no idea what hell is." The man snarled, leaning his face so close to mine I could see the blood in his eyes. "Give it to me or you'll soon know hell, firsthand."

I fought to inhale, my feet flailing out.

Then a surge of electricity powered through me. Lightning shot from my fingertips and bounced off the brick with a loud crack.

The demon cried out, releasing me, holding his hands out as if they'd been burned.

As I dropped to my feet, the acrid scent of burning flesh filled my nostrils. The sting in my back where the demon had pierced me with his fingernails eased up until all pain melted away.

"Give it to me." Nicolae stepped forward, his charred hands reaching for the necklace.

"No way." I slipped the necklace inside my shirt, tucking it into my bra. "You're under arrest for assault."

He turned as if to leave.

I stepped forward.

Before I could think, he backhanded me, his wrist catching me across my cheek, sending me flying backward, once again hitting a brick wall.

For precious seconds I lay dazed, the wind knocked from my lungs, my head spinning.

Nicolae loomed over me and tore at my jacket and shirt.

I fought him, my head reeling. "Isn't this a bit...much... for a...first date?" I gasped.

Then the demon jerked away from me, and bounced against one of the walls he'd thrown me against.

My partner stood over Nicolae, his chest heaving, his pitch-black gaze boring into the demon's. "Don't ever touch her again."

Nicolae snorted, dragging himself to his feet. "She stole something from me, and I want it back."

"You'll have to take it up with the Tribunal." Blaise held out his hand to me. "Give me your cuffs."

I stood, brushing the dirt off my jeans, reaching into my back pocket for the handcuffs. "I didn't bring cuffs. Will this do?" I handed over the zip tie from my back pocket.

"It'll work." He grabbed Nicolae's hand and twisted it up

behind the demon's back and yanked the other over it, pulling the zip tie together until it was snug. "Go get the car. And hurry, before his minions come calling." Blaise gazed at me, a smile quirking his lips. "And ignore the pounding on the trunk."

"Jimmy?"

He nodded. "I used some of your duct tape to gag him, or he'd be howling his head off."

Though I didn't appreciate being ordered around by man or demon, my knowledge of what demons were capable of was minimal. Blaise knew all the tricks. I took off at a run, working my way back to where I'd stashed the car.

I could hear the noise before I reached the vehicle. Ignoring the pounding, I slid into the driver's seat and pulled out onto the practically deserted street, while checking in with Detective Thomas. A nearby containment wagon and an ambulance were in route, and Detective Thomas would meet us to debrief on location. I hoped all the paranorms would still be there when the powers-that-be converged.

Half expecting the injured werewolves and the red-eyed demon to be gone when I returned, I was pleasantly surprised to find that Blaise had them all under control.

I went to the female first, checking her over to make sure the demon hadn't injured her further. "Hey, can you stand?"

She clutched my hand, her grip weak, listless, like she could barely hold her arm up. "The others."

"What others?"

"Shut up," Nicolae snarled.

The female werewolf's head lolled back. "He has others like me. Prisoners."

"Where?"

The female's eyes closed, her breathing shallow and

growing more shallow by the moment, her hand rising to her throat.

My gaze captured Blaise's. "She's choking."

Blaise's eyes narrowed and he jerked Nicolae's arms up behind his back. "Let go of her."

The demon laughed. "I don't know what you're talking about."

Blaise slammed the demon into the brick wall and pushed him up off his feet, until he dangled like I had.

The female gasped, dragging in a gulp of air. Then she sagged against me. "Please. Help them."

Sirens wailed, echoing in the night, growing closer.

"What do you mean?" I hesitated, then brushed the hair for her face. "What others?"

"Women. Help them." Her eyes closed and she passed out.

I stood and walked over to where Blaise held the demon pinned to the wall. "What women?" I demanded.

The creep laughed.

My fists clenched. "If you're holding women captive, we'll find them."

He laughed again.

A surge of anger roared through me. I counted ten in my head, only it made me even angrier that this demon had information I needed and he refused to give it to me. The anger intensified, building. A gust of heated air lifted the stray tendrils of hair from my neck and wafted across my face.

"Tell me where you keep the women." My voice boomed, echoing off the brick walls.

The demon's eyes narrowed.

I touched a hand to my chest where the amulet nestled inside my bra. For a second, I could see a large room divided by curtains. Inside each room a woman lay on a pallet on the floor. The image appeared so vivid I could feel the pain, sadness and hopelessness of each woman's thoughts. "You've got those women drugged." I grabbed the front of his shirt and planted my nose to his. Where are they, damn it?"

"You have no idea what you have or how to use it." He spoke in a low, steely tone that sent shivers coursing down my spine.

"You're stalling." I shoved him away. "We'll see what the Tribunal has to say when we find them. Trafficking people for sex is illegal, immoral and just wrong now matter what kind of creature they are. I wish I'd killed you while I had the chance."

"Killing him out of anger would only make you as bad as he is." Blaise shook his head. "The Tribunal will punish him."

Nicolae growled like a cornered dog. "You have something that belongs to me. I will get it back. When I do, I'll kill you."

Chapter Three

A chill slithered across my skin, raising gooseflesh. I forced a laugh. "Seems you're not in a position to do much of anything."

He didn't respond, just stared at me, his gaze like daggers.

I turned away. I didn't want him to know that his threat had made me more afraid than even the zombie attack during my first case.

Before long, the deserted street filled with ambulances, police cars and the transport vehicles specially designed to haul paranorms to the containment cell in the basement of the warehouse where the Paranormal Tribunal held council to decide the fate of rogue paranorms.

The containment team loaded Nicolae into the wagon and left the scene.

Blaise dragged Jimmy from the trunk of our vehicle and set him on his feet. His face was bruised and blood dripped from his nose.

"You don't have anything on me."

"What do you call drug trafficking?" Blaise shook his head. "I saw you pay Lenny Baecowski for a bag of cocaine."

He pulled the bag from his back pocket and dangled it from his fingers. "I don't think this is powdered sugar."

Detective Thomas slipped the plastic bag into a brown evidence bag.

EMT personnel loaded the female werewolf onto a gurney. I walked alongside her until they reached the ambulance.

Her eyes fluttered open and her fingers squeezed mine. "Promise me you'll find them."

"I'll do my best." I tried to pry my hand loose. "Do you know where he kept you? Where he has the other women?"

She shook her head, her eyelids closing.

"We need to get her to the hospital." The EMT pushed past me and shoved the gurney and patient into the waiting ambulance, closed the door and left.

I returned to where Blaise and Detective Thomas were grilling Jimmy about the other women Nicolae held hostage.

"Look, we'll cut a deal with you," Detective Thomas was saying. "Tell us where your buddy Mario found his cousin and we'll let you off."

"You don't understand. Nicolae will kill me if I tell you anything, just like he killed Mario."

"That's right." Blaise crossed his arms over his chest. "You were still in the trunk when they hauled Nicolae off to jail."

"You think you can hold him?' Jimmy snorted. "I've seen Nic get out of even tighter spots." The young punk's lips curled into a snarl. "And I've seen Nic rip people apart for crossing him. If he's got it in for you, there's nowhere safe to hide."

I laid a hand on Blaise's arm. "You're wasting time. I think I know where they are."

Jimmy was cuffed, shoved into the backseat of a squad car and whisked away for his day in front of the Tribunal.

"Come on, we need to get there before someone decides to move the women." I turned toward our vehicle.

Detective Thomas grabbed my arm. "How do you know where they are?"

I shrugged. "I just do. I figure they couldn't be far from where Jimmy met Mario in the alley."

"We have about eight men who can provide back up." Detective Thomas nodded. "Lead the way."

I climbed into the driver's seat.

Blaise settled into the passenger seat, unusually quiet and particularly interested in staring at me while I maneuvered through the streets.

"Keep your eyes peeled for Nicolae's men as we get closer." I pulled into an alley a couple blocks short of the area I figured we'd find Nicolae's stash.

The detective and the others turned down nearby streets and parked illegally, then climbing out, weapons ready.

I tucked my Glock into my shoulder holster underneath my torn leather jacket and stepped out onto the street.

The area had more traffic. A neon sign glowed pink over the entrance to a gentlemen's club, advertising naked strippers. Men entered, drunk and sober, and a few prostitutes lingered on the street corners, leaning into cars that came to a stop at the curb.

Lovely. How was I supposed to get inside a gentlemen's club?

Backtracking, I ducked behind a building and briefed the Detective Thomas. "They're somewhere inside that club. The basement, I think."

Detective Thomas pointed at me. "You need to stay back."

"Sir, I can find them."

"You'll never sneak through the front door of that club. Not a female dressed like you are."

"Then I'll get in through the back." I hooked a thumb at Blaise. "I'll take tall, dark and demon with me for backup."

Detective Thomas frowned. "He'll have plenty of men guarding the entrances."

"Fine, I'll take two of the others with us." I planted fists on my hips. "I can do this. And for some reason, I can see just where I need to go."

"I don't like it."

"You provide a distraction. We'll get in and find the girls."

Detective Thomas glanced at his watch. "Give us five minutes, then head in through the back."

I smiled. "You got it." When I turned, a hand on my arm pulled me back.

Detective Thomas stared into my eyes. "We don't need any dead heroes on our team."

I saluted. "Trust me. I don't plan on dying anytime soon."

The lieutenant let go, muttering, "That's what they all say."

Behind the building, we found two doors. I positioned two men at the first. Blaise and I would enter the second. The images of the women and their anguish grew stronger inside my head. "They're in there. I can feel them."

Blaise glanced at me, his eyes narrowed. "How?"

"I don't know, but I can't get them out of my head." I grabbed the door handle and tested it. Locked. "We need to get inside."

"Two more minutes by the detective's clock." Blaise pulled me into his arms. "You can wait two more minutes." His lips nuzzled my neck, his hands tugging me to lean my back against his chest.

For a brief moment I let him hold me, counting the seconds until I could storm into the complex and find those poor souls.

His fingers slid down over my hips, warming my skin through the denim of my jeans.

The closer his hands moved toward the apex of my things, the hotter my blood burned. Adrenaline and sex. Nothing made me hornier. I groaned. "I should have sent you to the front. You're too much of a distraction."

"That's the idea." His hands stilled. "Five minutes are up."

An explosion erupted on the other side of the building.

"That's our cue." I jerked my Glock from my shoulder holster, grasped the handle of the doorknob and twisted hard, all my concentration centering on the locking mechanism.

The lock broke and the door swung inward.

Two brawny men, werewolves by the smell of them, were halfway down the hall headed toward the front of the building when the door crashed open.

They spun and drew guns.

I dove inside and to the right, somersaulted and sprang to my feet, aiming at the chest of the guy closest to me.

He pulled the trigger, the shot blasting a loud report in the narrow hallway. The bullet skimmed past my ear and splintered the wooden doorframe behind me. I squeezed off a round, hitting the werewolf in the side of his head as he dove for the floor.

Blaise charged at the other man, blocking my shot.

"No!" Fear blew through me and I leaped to my feet, my free hand rising. "Get out of the way!" I yelled.

Blaise's body jerked to the side as if an invisible hand pushed him that way, leaving my lane of fire open.

I discharged my weapon, hitting the werewolf square in the chest, not once but twice.

Had Blaise not fallen to the side, he'd have been killed or seriously injured.

Blaise lurched to his feet. "How did you–"

A strong sense of urgency pushed me forward. "No time to explain. They're moving the women." I raced to the end of the hallway to a staircase. Holding on to the railing, I ran down two flights before I stopped at a door and tried to open it. It wouldn't budge.

"They're in there. We have to get to them." I leaned my ear to the door.

Muffled screams and men yelling echoed in the images in my head.

"They're getting away." Fear, anger and desperation blasted up from somewhere deep inside. I gripped the door handle and a surge of energy ripped through my body and out through my fingertips. I flew backward, slamming into Blaise's chest.

The door hung open, the lock charred black and the metal doorjamb bent.

Blaise set me on my feet and I took off, charging into the chaos of a dark and hopeless place, where women had been drugged and forced into prostitution.

Werewolf men dragged women out of the makeshift rooms, hurrying them toward another staircase.

"Stop!" I yelled. "Police!" I aimed my weapon at the werewolf closest to me.

He spun, his eyes wide. When his gaze found me in the dim lighting, his face relaxed into a sneer. "You're a cop?" He laughed, his eyes narrowing. "Guess you'll have to shoot me." He flung a woman over his shoulder.

If I pulled the trigger, I might hit his captive. I was a good shot, but I wasn't willing to risk an innocent's life to prove it.

"We didn't come alone. There are more cops where you're headed."

Blaise stepped up beside me. "This place will be surrounded. If you know what's good for you, you'll leave the women alone."

The werewolf's sneer deepened into a growl. "So now demons are playing both sides of the law?" He snorted. "You can have her." He flung the woman to the ground and dropped to all fours, morphing into a wolf before my eyes.

Hair sprouted from his hands and face and he ripped his shirt from his body as his shoulders broadened. The animal pointed his snout in the air and howled, then he leaped at me.

Out of instinct, I flung out my arm to block the attack.

Before I touched him, his body jerked sideways and slammed into a wall with enough force I heard the snap of bones breaking.

The werewolf slid to the ground and lay still.

The rest of the male werewolves laid down the women they carried and edged toward the stairwell.

"Stay where you are." The air crackled with an electrical charge, like threads of lightning shooting through the huge room. The tiny hairs on my arms stood at attention and my blood sizzled in my veins.

Each werewolf froze in position.

Detective Thomas and the other PIT crew members converged on the warehouse basement. Additional backup had arrived and before long at least twenty uniforms appeared along with a dozen emergency medical technicians.

Once the women had been loaded into ambulances and taken to the hospital, I could barely stand. All the energy completely drained from my body. When I stumbled, Blaise reached out and steadied me.

"I think we need to get you home." Blaise guided me toward Detective Thomas. "Are we through here?" he asked the Lieutenant.

Detective Thomas nodded, his lips twisting into a grin.

"Good work. I sent you out to track a drug dealer and you bagged a prostitution ring. The city will be a safer place, thanks to you."

"Just doing my job, sir." I dragged in a deep breath and let it out. "If it's all the same to you, I could use some rest."

"You earned it. We can debrief later this afternoon, after you've had time to catch some zs." Thomas patted my back. "Thanks, Detective Danske."

"My pleasure." I leaned into Blaise as we exited the back door.

Blaise hailed a cab.

"What about the car?"

"I'll send someone over to collect it. We need to get you home."

When the cab slid up to the curb, I fell onto the backseat and lay still all the way back to my building, incapable of moving. The thought of climbing the stairs to my apartment made me cringe. Bless the demon, he carried me up the flights of stairs.

Inside my apartment, I fished my phone from my pocket, stripped my jacket, my holster, boots and jeans and dropped onto my bed, face-first, wearing nothing but panties and a bra. "What's wrong with me?" I moaned. "I'm exhausted." I turned my head and stared across at the gorgeous demon, too tired to work up an orgasm.

Blaise stood in the doorway, his arms folded. "You had a rough night. Don't worry, I'm leaving. I'll see you this afternoon at the precinct."

"Good. I didn't want you to stay anyway."

Before the demon made it to the door, the phone on my nightstand buzzed.

With every ounce of strength I had left, I lifted the phone and punched the talk button. "Danske."

"You have something of mine, and I want it back." The voice sent shivers across my skin and a knot of fear into my belly. The line clicked off.

My gaze shot to Blaise who'd returned to my bedroom on the first ring.

"Nicolae?" he asked.

I nodded, one hand rising to the amulet I'd hung around my neck, as I hit the speed-dial button for Detective Thomas.

"Danske. Good. I was just about to call."

"Nicolae got away, didn't he?" I knew the answer before I asked.

"Yeah. A couple of large SUVs pinned the wagon and forced it into a wall. The drivers were killed and the demon got away." The detective sounded tired. "Is Michaels still with you?"

I glanced at Blaise. "Yes, he's here."

"Let me talk to him."

I handed the cell phone to Blaise.

He grabbed it and pressed it to his ear. "Michaels here."

All I could hear was the steady drone of a voice. I couldn't make out enough of the conversation to know what the detective was telling him.

"Will do." Blaise clicked the off button and handed the phone back to me.

"What did he say?"

Blaise shrugged out of his jacket and flung it across a chair. "I'm to stay."

"Why?" I sat up, my energy returning enough for me to lodge a protest. "I can take care of myself."

"Nicolae left a message that he was after you."

"So?"

"He used the blood of one of the transport officers to write it on a wall."

My heart sank into my stomach. "Bastard."

"Worse still, the man was alive while he did it."

A chill slithered across my skin, raising the hairs on my arms. "Why me?"

"I think it has to do with the amulet." Blaise reached out to touch the stone and flinched when he did, drawing back his hand. "Is it not burning you?"

"It's warm against my skin, but it's not burning me."

"Must be magical."

"The woman in the alley told me to grab it. That it was important to him."

Blaise's jaw tightened. "Important enough for him to kill to get it back."

Despite the tremors shaking my body, I protested. "You can't stay."

"I have orders from your boss to camp out here until they can locate and incarcerate Nicolae." He sat on the edge of the bed, a smile curving his lips. "We can make use of our time together, if you like."

I crossed my arms over my breasts, wishing I hadn't stripped so quickly upon entering my room. "No, I don't like." My mother had told me, and I had learned to believe her, that I was a lousy liar. This time was no different.

Blaise slid a finger along the curve of my calf and over my thigh.

I jerked the leg up against me, scooting back against the headboard. "If you're staying, you'll have to sleep on the couch. I'm serious. You distract me too much. And no one will take me seriously as long as we're sleeping together."

He tsked, that sexy smile all but melting my bones. "I thought you didn't care what others thought of you."

"I don't. Except when they think I'm sleeping with a member of the team. If one can sleep with the little female cop, they all think they can sleep with me." I frowned as deeply as I could. "I'm not a damned pinup girl or a porn star. I'm a cop, and a damned good one."

Blaise reached for my ankle and lifted my foot, massaging the inside arch with his thumb. "No one can question your ability and determination. You've proven yourself time and again. Tonight was a great example. What you did in that warehouse was beyond amazing."

I nodded, my brows pinching. "Too amazing, if you ask me." Almost as remarkable as it was to have my foot massaged by a very sexy demon. My fingers wrapped around the amulet. "Was the amulet responsible for opening those locked doors?"

"Could be. And probably flinging me against the wall." Blaise rubbed his elbow, his lips twisting. "I've seen similar amulets."

"You have?" I leaned forward. Mistake. I could smell his skin, the light scent of leather and soap and the musk of lust. My insides sizzled, my pussy creaming. Damn. I'd sworn off fucking the demon and had only lasted a couple of freakin' hours before my body turned traitor on me.

"The amulet is only as good as the innate power of the wearer. It can amplify, not create."

I shook my head. "I don't have any powers other than a super sensitive sniffer."

"You underestimate you abilities, my dear." He lifted my hand and pressed a kiss to my palm. "Are you sure you're not a demon?"

I laughed. "You'd think I'd know something important like that, wouldn't you?"

"Your powers could be latent. Most demons know who they are and start flexing their demon skills long before puberty. When their hormones kick in, their powers surge.

They are taught to recognize and understand their powers in order to use them properly."

"Are you insinuating that I might be a demon?" I snorted. "Get real. I'm as plain as apple pie and hot dogs. My mother never crawled inside anyone's head as far as I know or threw a fireball or whatever demons do." I pushed off the bed, heading for the shower, growing unease settling in my gut. I stripped out of my panties and bra, uncaring if Blaise watched. Hell, he'd seen everything in minute detail over the past couple weeks we'd been partners on the PIT crew and in bed.

Blaise followed me, leaning against the bathroom doorframe, his gaze slipping across my skin like a warm hand.

I ignored the tightening in my loins, and stepped into the shower.

Warm water sluiced over my head and breasts.

The damned demon couldn't let it go. He pulled the curtain back. Water sprayed out on the tile floor. "What about your father? You didn't even know him. You could be a halfling."

Chapter Four

I stood still, water pounding against my skin not nearly as hard as my heart pounded. "Leave my father out of this. I'm not a halfling. You're wrong."

"But he could have been a demon."

Blood thundered in my ears and I raised my hands to cover them. "I don't want to talk about that man. He deserted us when we needed him most. Or wait." I flung my hands wide. "Is that what demons do? Abandon the people they're supposed to love?" Tears welled in my eyes and I blinked them back. "Is that what you'll do?"

"Katya, demons, like humans, are not all the same." He stepped into the shower, fully clothed and lifted my hand to his lips, water soaking his shirt and trousers.

No matter how badly I didn't want it to happen, I couldn't stop the tears from coming, mixing with the shower's spray. "Damn it! Damn it all to hell! I swore I'd never cry again and look at me." I pulled loose from his grip, backed against the wall and slid down the tile, wrapping my arms around my knees. "I'm tougher than this. I don't fall apart. What's wrong with me? I've never been so emotional."

"Baby, you've held it together for a very long time." Blaise grabbed my hands and tugged me to my feet and into his arms. He leaned back, fingering the amulet around my neck. "I think this amulet is enhancing more than power. It's amplifying your feelings."

As soon as he said the words, I could feel the truth in the way my body melted against his damp clothes. Every nerve, every ounce of blood moving through my system jittered, my hands longing to touch his skin, the apex of my thighs burning, my channel aching for him to fill me.

With shaking hands, I ripped at the buttons on his shirt, tearing them loose from their holes, pushing the material back over his shoulders and down his back. I unbuckled his belt, and slipped the button loose on his trousers, sliding the zipper down with more desperation than care.

Finally his cock sprang free into the palm of my hand and I caressed its hard, smooth length. Each stroke only stoked the fires burning deep inside me. I had to have him. Caution, thought and reason all flew out the window.

His hands caressed my ass and he lifted me, wrapping my legs around his waist. Positioned over his throbbing cock, I edged downward, eager to have him inside, stroking, pumping and thrusting deeply.

"Not yet." He kissed my neck and pulled his wallet from his soaked back pocket, handing it to me. "Behind my credit card."

I fumbled, my mind awash in a haze of lust, my fingers moving jerkily until they curled around a foil packet.

"Even demons can get a woman pregnant without contraception." His wickedly sexy smile sent shivers of anticipation skittering across my breasts.

My clumsy fingers tore at the foil and I growled my annoyance.

Blaise leaned me away from him so that I could slip the condom over his length. I rolled the rubber down to the base.

Once cloaked, he shoved my back against the cool tile and thrust into me.

I moaned, my pussy clenching as his girth stretched me so deliciously tight.

He moved in and out, setting the pace.

My body tensed, my legs tightening around him, every cell buzzing with the impact of everything he was doing to me. I moved to meet his every thrust, to absorb as much of him as my body could take. When he thrust one last time, I catapulted over the edge, energy pulsing from every pore of my being. A rush of wind blasted through the room as if a door had opened in a hurricane, ripping the curtain off the rod and sending the shower's spray across the tiny bathroom.

When I could think again, I stared around the room at the damage. "What the hell just happened?"

"Baby, you got more than you bargained for with that amulet." Blaise lifted me off him and set my feet on the floor of the tub. He stripped out of his shoes and trousers and grabbed the bottle of my favorite body wash and squirted a healthy dose into his palm. "Let's work on controlling the energy, channeling it into something more positive than destroying your apartment." He smoothed the soap across my breasts, working the liquid into a bubbly lather, his hands swirling around my nipples.

For the first time in my life, I was glad I was female. Not just a cop with tits, but a real, feminine woman, with soft and sensitive skin.

Warm, coarse fingers smoothed over every inch of my body, washing me then rinsing the suds away. I closed my eyes, to the unbearable heat radiating out of me, forcing myself to calm in the eye of the storm of longing, threatening to overwhelm me. A power from within pushed to get out, the same flash of energy that had blown the curtain away.

I fought to control, to direct the force inward and contain its effects.

"That's better," Blaise murmured, his hand sliding down my belly toward the core of my being that pulsed and throbbed, eager for more.

Instead of burying his fingers in my pussy, Blaise reached around me and turned off the water, swung me up into his arms and set my feet on the bath mat. Grabbing a towel from a shelf, he went to work drying my body.

"I can dry myself, you know." I couldn't keep my hands off him, my fingers sliding across his naked chest, edging downward toward the dark, crinkly hairs at the base of his cock.

The demon's skin stretched taut over solid muscle.

"Are all demons built like weight lifters?" I grasped his cock in my hand, my breath catching, my control slipping.

A waft of a breeze lifted my hair and spun it around my face.

Blaise leaned close, his lips grazing my earlobe. "Control, my sweet."

His breath on my skin fanned the flames inside.

"And no. Only demons who work out are built like weight lifters."

The heat burning my insides sent blood racing through my body, and my breathing grew labored. I had to have him again. Soon, or I'd explode into a million horny pieces. My leg circled his, hooking around the back of his thigh. "Are you going to make love to me again? Or do I have to throw you on the ground and get the party started?"

He chuckled, the sound a bit strained. "I think the amulet is influencing your desire and mine. It's like a drug to your system. I don't think you would be saying what you're saying or doing what you're doing if you weren't wearing it. I don't want to take advantage of the situation."

"A noble demon?" I snorted. "I don't care what's making me hot and horny. I want you. Now if you don't want me, I'll try to understand." I struggled to wrap my mind around the possibility of not making love again with the demon. Another growl rose up my throat. "The hell with that. Are you or aren't you going to make love to me?" I pushed his chest, forcing him through the doorway into my bedroom.

He let me, capturing my hand as the backs of his knees bumped against the mattress. "Think about it, Katya. Earlier, you didn't want anything more to do with me. Now you're ready to jump me for sex." Blaise grasped my arms and spun me around. I tripped and fell on my back on the bed. Blaise leaned over me, pressing his legs between my thighs. "I want you more than I've wanted anyone...ever. Don't temp me when you're not in your right mind."

"I feel like I'm in my so-called right mind for the first time in my life." I grabbed the front of his shirt and yanked him down on top of me, my lips slanting over his, my tongue pushing past his teeth to stroke.

The tension eased from his shoulders and he sighed into my mouth. He pulled back enough to stare into my eyes. "I can't fight you."

My brows rose and I gave him a lopsided smile. "Why are you, then?"

He pressed his cock between my legs, nudging at my entrance. "Take off the amulet and see if you still feel the same."

My hand closed around the smooth, stone amulet, its warmth seeming to flare with my touch. Maybe me demon bodyguard knew what he was talking about. I lifted the strap over my head and dropped the amulet onto the nightstand. "Happy now?"

His eyelids drooped over deep brown eyes. "Yes." Blaise thrust deep, filling me, driving deeper with each stroke.

I wrapped my legs around his waist, digging my heels into his buttocks, urging him closer and deeper until our bodies felt fused as one. My breathing became sporadic and hitched when the tingling started in my fingers and toes, racing inward to my core. I spread my thighs, my heels falling to the mattress, my back arching away from the comforter as I pitched over the edge. "Blaise!"

The light bulb in the lamp on my nightstand exploded, spraying glass across the sheets and floor. I didn't care.

Blaise rose to his knees, shoved a pillow beneath my bottom and he rode me hard, pumping in and out until his final plunge, deep, hard and forceful. His body tight, he held my hips steady as his cock throbbed against the walls of my channel.

When the tension left his shoulders, he dropped to the mattress beside me, hauling me into the curve of his body, spooning me like a lover.

"You exhaust me," he whispered into my ear.

I yawned and stretched out my arm, my skin coming into contact with the delicate shards of light bulb glass. "What just happened?"

"Sweetheart, you blew it again." He smoothed the hair away from my temple and brushed a kiss to the spot. "Apparently, the amulet has bonded with you. As long as it's near, it will enhance your powers."

"I told you, I don't have powers. It's all in the amulet." I turned in his arms. "I need to get rid of it before someone gets hurt."

He nodded, touching the tip of my nose with his lips. "We will. We'll have it placed in the Tribunal's secure vault. Until it's contained, it will be a target."

"Think we should go straight there?" I yawned again, my eyelids drifting closed.

"We'll go...later." His arm slid around my middle and he pulled me against his chest.

The light beneath my eyelids and the sounds of the city faded as I drifted off to sleep. Thoughts of the amulet and its former owner spun around my head.

Nicolae was after the amulet. Once it was in the protective vault, he'd no longer have use of me. I wouldn't need Blaise to play bodyguard. I could banish my sexy, resident demon and get back to serious cop work and repairing my reputation among the PIT crew.

"Katya, wake up!" Blaise shook me.

My eyes popped open and I struggled to remember where I was. The room was dark, the only light from the streets and signs outside, shining through the thin curtain over my bedroom window. I sat up, pushing a mass of hair back off my face. "What's wrong?" I sniffed. "Smells like dog."

"Exactly." He stood beside the bed, shoving his feet into his damp trousers, tossing his shirt over his shoulders and his leather jacket over it. "Get dressed. I believe we're about to have company." He tossed my jeans and a T-shirt in my direction and hurried toward the window overlooking my fire escape. "Shit. There's a dozen or more werewolves gathering on the street below.

I leaped from the bed and dressed in the jeans and shirt and shoved my feet into my boots. "What should we do?"

"We can't go down the stairs or the fire escape. They'll be watching them." Blaise eased the curtain to the side, careful not to give the crowd below any indication we were on to them. He moved the curtain slowly back in place. "We go up." The demon headed for the door to my apartment.

I grabbed the amulet from my nightstand and slipped it over my head, running to catch up with my bodyguard. "We're trapped."

"We'll go up to another apartment and borrow their fire escape and get down that way."

"If there are so many of them, how will we escape notice?"

"We won't, but if we lead them on a chase, we can divide them and only have to face a few, rather than the whole pack."

I nodded. "Why don't we call for backup?"

"By the time they get here, we'd be dead, Nicolae would have the amulet and all hell would break loose."

"Good point."

Blaise eased the door open and peered out into the hallway. "We'll go for the stairwell. Be quiet in case that's the way they're coming up."

"Got it."

The demon led the way, running lightly down the tiled hallway, the sound of his shoes muffled by carpet.

I held my breath and followed, my ears straining for any indication the werewolves were near. I could smell them as much as I had when they were on the street and I was on the third floor of the building.

The creak of rusty metal hinges cut through the silence.

Coming to a halt, I cringed and opened my ears, expecting to hear a shout.

Instead I heard footsteps on the stairwell, heading up.

"Hurry," Blaise whispered, waving me forward.

I entered the stairwell and started up, taking the steps two at a time, trying to remember to breathe as I passed the fourth floor and fifth. When I reached the fifth floor landing, I pushed the door open and stepped through.

Blaise bumped into me, inching the stairwell door closed behind us. "Why this floor?"

"I know someone who lives on this floor. He'll let us into his apartment. As long as he's home. What time is it?"

"After seven."

"Holy hell. We were supposed to go back to the station at five for the debrief on Nicolae's capture and escape."

"I'm not worried about being late. Right now I'm more worried about being killed. Which apartment?"

"Apartment 546." I led the way to the correct door. Thankfully it was on the opposite side of the building from mine. Hopefully, whoever was ganging up on us would have their sights trained on my apartment. I stopped in front of Randi Saltmarsh's door and knocked lightly, my body jittering, the amulet warm against my chest.

Fifteen seconds passed and no response. I raised my hand to knock again.

Blaise brushed my hand aside. "We don't have time for this." He twisted the handle. The door remained firmly closed. "We'll have to break it down." The demon backed away and leaned his shoulder forward, bracing to hit the solid wood barrier.

"Wait." I held up my hand. "Let me try." With one hand on the amulet and the other on the doorknob, I closed my eyes, concentrating on the locking mechanism.

The lock snicked and the knob twisted easily in my hand. "I don't know what kind of mojo this necklace has, but it's pretty handy. We'd better hurry. I smell dog." I entered first, going straight for Randi's fire escape where he'd invited me to sit and drink a glass of wine with him one night. Had he had ulterior motives, I'd have turned him down. Thankfully, Randi was gay, which made him a great bro-friend for me to hang out with. He gave me advice on girlie clothes and I enjoyed not being mauled.

Blaise's hand on my shoulder stopped me before I pulled

the curtain aside and peered at the landing. He held a finger to his lips.

The sound of feet on the metal grates of the fire escape echoed off the brick buildings lining the alley.

I nodded and edged the curtain open enough to look down.

Darkness had settled on the Manhattan alley. I couldn't make out much through the shadows and fire escape landings until the climbing werewolf turned and started up the next flight.

My pulse hammered against my eardrums.

The werewolf was only two flights down from where we were and two columns over.

"Why the hell is he on this side of the complex?" I whispered.

"They too have super-sensitive sniffers, like you. He might have picked up your scent." Blaise inhaled, his eyes closing briefly. "And it's intoxicating."

I backhanded him on his chest, my pussy clenching at his murmured words. Now was not the time to make love. Not if they wanted to live.

The werewolf made quick work of the climb, easily taking the steps two at a time.

"He stopped on the third floor."

"Should we wait or make a run?" I tensed, ready for anything. "Or risk it since there's only one of him and two of us?" I patted my shoulder holster. "I have my gun."

"Make a break for it. The others will have made it to your apartment by now and could be following our trail." Blaise stepped in front of me and unlatched the window, easing it upward.

I sucked in a deep breath and braced myself.

"Ready?" Blaise glanced at me.

My gaze met his and I nodded. "Let's do it."

"You go first. When you hit the ground, run as fast as you can." Blaise lifted my hands. "If they shift into wolves, you won't stay ahead of them long."

Again I nodded. "I have my gun."

"They have the numbers." Blaise's lips claimed mine in an intense, brief kiss, then he was lifting me out the window. "Go."

I dropped onto the grate, the ensuing boots-on-metal sound making me cringe. If the werewolf hadn't already pinpointed my location, he soon would.

Halfway down to the fourth floor landing, I froze.

The werewolf on the fire escape two columns over raised his face to the sky and let out a long, loud howl.

Blaise pounded down the stairs, shouting, "Go! Go! Go!"

Chapter Five

Startled out of my stupor, I continued down the stairs.

On the fire escape two over from where we were, the were-wolf leaped down the steps, much more surefooted than me. With one flight head start and his speed and agility, he'd hit the ground well before we would.

Blaise pushed past me and leaped over the railing of the last landing, dropping to the pavement below. He barely had time to straighten when the werewolf plowed into his chest, knocking him flat on his back.

Leaning over the top of the landing, I pulled my gun and aimed at the demon with a huge mottled gray-black wolf bearing down on him. If I took the shot from where I was standing, the bullet could easily miss the wolf and hit the demon. I wasn't sure demons could die from bullet wounds, but I wasn't willing to find out. Holstering my gun, I ripped the amulet from around my neck and hung it on the railing. Then I grabbed the retractable ladder and jumped, riding the ladder to the ground, landing with a thunk that knocked me on my ass.

"Run!" Blaise grunted, shoving the wolf's snarling snout upward. "Run, damn it!"

One thing I'd learned as a cop, you never left your partner behind. Even though he was a demon and probably perfectly capable of taking care of himself, I couldn't run away from my responsibility to him. And I didn't want to. He'd saved my butt on more than one occasion. And despite all my noise to the contrary, I had a thing for the demon, a fact I refused to acknowledge on a good day.

Casting a glance over my shoulder, the alley was clear. I jumped to my feet, pulled my gun and aimed.

The two on the ground, rolled and a twisted.

I couldn't get a clear shot. Frustration mounted. Another howl filled the night air, rising above the honking taxi cabs. If we hoped to escape, I had to do something quickly. My gaze panned the immediate area, searching for anything I could use to hit the wolf. Of all the alleys I had to choose, this one was the cleanest I'd ever run across.

The wolf growled, ripping at Blaise's leather jacket, tearing into flesh.

My heart pumped so hard, I could barely hear over the blood pounding in my ears. I had to do something…but what? I flung my hand out. "Get away from him!" I shouted.

The wolf flew to the side, hit a brick wall and bounced back onto his feet, charging straight for me. He leaped into the air.

With barely any time to react, I dropped and rolled away from my attacker. I sprang to my feet and pulled my weapon from my shoulder holster.

The wolf reared and spun toward me.

I pulled the trigger and plugged him with a silver bullet to the heart.

The werewolf jerked backward and fell to the ground. Dead.

My relief was short-lived as half a dozen wolves and men rounded the corner, bearing down on me and Blaise. I aimed my gun at the closest one.

"Who wants to be next?" I challenged, bracing my feet wide, ready to take down as many as I had silver bullets for.

Blaise lurched to his feet and stood at my side. "You don't want to end up like your buddy."

One of the werewolves that hadn't shifted, stepped forward. "Give us the amulet and we'll leave."

I shook my head. "I don't have it."

"You lie."

I pulled the linings of my pockets out of my jeans. "I don't have it. And we called for backup." I bluffed. "If you don't want to stand before the Tribunal and explain yourself, I suggest you get the hell out of here."

Their leader's eyes narrowed. "We don't give a damn about the Tribunal. Give us the amulet."

Sirens wailed in the distance and I almost laughed. Talk about timing.

I stepped forward, faking a cockiness I wasn't exactly feeling. "They're coming and they're bringing the wagon to collect your asses."

As the sirens neared, the leader straightened. "Nicolae doesn't give up. We'll be back." Then he turned and ran from the alley, his associates close behind.

Blaise and I didn't wait around. When the sirens didn't stop at my apartment building, the werewolves would discover they'd been tricked and be back.

"Come on." Blaise hooked my elbow and dragged me toward the street. "Your apartment isn't safe."

"I can't leave until I get the amulet."

"I thought you were bluffing?" He turned her toward him, staring at her neck. "Where is it?"

I smiled. "Not far."

The ladder I'd ridden to the ground had sprung back up to the landing above. "Give me a boost."

Blaise glanced up. "It's up there?"

"I knew that's what they wanted. I couldn't let them see it on me."

The demon shook his head, a smile curling his lips. "Smart as well as beautiful." His hands spanned my waist and he raised me high enough to snag the ladder and pull it down.

He climbed up, retrieved the amulet and tossed it down to me. "Now, let's get the hell out of here before anything else happens." Blaise moved out at a smart pace, heading for street.

"Where are we going?" I panted, jogging to keep up with his long strides.

"My place."

I ground to a halt. "No way. We have to find Nicolae before anyone else gets hurt."

"In case you haven't noticed, I'm bleeding. I could use a fresh change of clothes and a rather large bandage." Blaise held up the forearm he'd used to fend off the wolf. Large gashes oozed blood, dripping onto the ground.

"I thought demons were invincible." I ripped the hem of my shirt all the way up to my midriff and wrapped the strip of material around his wound.

"We can't stay here."

"Okay. We'll go to your place. But no hanky-panky."

Blaise grinned. "I make no promises."

I crossed my arms over my chest, more to cover the tight peaks my braless breasts made against the soft jersey fabric of the T-shirt. "Then go on without me. I have work to do."

The sound of footsteps in the alley behind us made me jump and left my pulse pounding.

His lips firming into a thin line, Blaise grabbed my elbow and herded me down the street toward the subway entrance. We caught train heading away from the Fifth Precinct and toward Manhattan.

When we emerged at Grand Central Station, I still wasn't convinced leaving with Blaise was a good idea. Though the sun had set, Grand Central teemed with commuters, eager to get to and from the city.

My nose twitched at anything even slightly resembling the scent of dog. Some of the people I passed carried the strong odor, but most of them hurried by, just like any other human, anxious to get home to loved ones after a long day's work, or entering the city to attend one of the many cultural events available every day of the week.

I kept my head down and hurried though the station, feeling decidedly exposed in a sea of humanity and inhumanity. The lights and openness of the main lobby of Grand Central didn't prepare me for stepping out on the darker streets, where people pushed along the sidewalks.

Blaise's hand clamped on my elbow and he barreled through the masses, his gaze swinging right and left, eyes narrowed, his mouth set in a grim line.

As the crowd near the station thinned, Blaise ducked down one street after another, checking to our rear for any indication we were being followed.

I alternated between walking, jogging and skipping to keep up with the long-legged demon, wishing I had equally long legs so that matching his pace wasn't an issue. I took care of my body and prided myself on keeping physically fit. But by the time Blaise turned down yet another deserted alleyway, I breathed like a marathon runner in the last yards of a race.

"Are we there yet?" I gasped.

"Soon." Another glance over his shoulder and he leaned his hand on a brick wall.

She was about to pass out and Blaise hadn't even broken a sweat, yet he leaned against the wall, apparently unconcerned by the delay.

I sucked in huge gulps of air and then spoke. "We need to keep moving. If I stop, I'll—"

Before I could finish my demand, the wall shifted and moved inward, brick scraping against brick as a gaping door appeared in the brick's solid face.

"Stay close." He grabbed my hand in his and entered a dark hallway.

Like a lamb to slaughter, I followed, my mouth gaping. "I thought secret passageways were something legends were made of, not real." As soon as I cleared the doorway, the brick wall slid into place behind me tapping my ass in the process. I jerked forward and teetered on the edge of a step, darkness gripping me like an iron fist.

"Blaise?"

"Hang on." His hand tightened on mine and a light from an incandescent bulb dangling from the ceiling flickered, then shone, illuminating just enough of the stone steps we could navigate without falling.

The staircase spiraled down, down, down into what felt like was a bottomless pit. I sniffed. The stench of decay, oil, rot and sewer grew stronger as I descended into the bowels of the island.

Finally we stepped out into a tunnel that was as wide as a city bus. Dim yellow lights, spaced at long intervals, gave the passageway an eerie glow.

My eyes rounded, my pupils dilating in an attempt to see into the near-darkness. "Where are we?"

"In the catacombs below New York City." His voice echoed softly, almost muffled by the closeness of the walls.

I'd read about the tunnels beneath the city of Chicago and how they'd tried to build a rail system to transport cargo, but the only tunnels I knew about New York City were those used for the subway. Interesting. A strange breeze, smelling of stagnant water and damp earth, wafted through the passageway, lifting the hair off the back of my neck, sending a trickle of apprehension across my spine.

"You live down here?" I wrapped my arms around my middle, too tired and now cold to care if my dubiousness showed through in my tone. "What? You couldn't afford an apartment in Manhattan?"

He shrugged. "You could say I enjoy my privacy down here."

"I'm sure it discourages solicitors." I was careful not to rub against the tunnel's sides, afraid of whatever diseases I might catch touching the damp stone-lined walls.

"Come." He left me standing at the base of the steps as he disappeared into the murky shadows between the less than adequate wall sconces.

A spike of fear sent me racing after him.

You don't have to be afraid as long as you're with me. His thoughts pushed into my head, without a word being spoken aloud.

I'm not afraid.

Liar.

Get out of my head, demon. I didn't like it when Blaise pushed into my mind and spoke to me without moving his lips or vibrating his vocal chords. Then again, I'd responded to him without speaking aloud. That was a first. After we'd gone several hundred yards, I stopped, my fingers curling around the amulet, now cold and impersonal. "This is ridic-

Demon's Embrace

ulous. I need to get back topside and go after Nicolae before he gets away."

Blaise halted a yard ahead and turned to face me, his expression dark, his brows dipping low over his incredibly black eyes. "You don't get it."

"That he wants the amulet and will kill me if he has to in order to attain it? I get that part." She waved a hand at the tunnel. "I don't get why we're burying ourselves, hiding from Nicolae. If he wants the amulet, shouldn't we offer it to him? Maybe he'll come and collect it himself. That's when we can nab the bastard and hand him over to the Tribunal to dispose of properly."

Blaise shook his head. "He's one of the most powerful demons of the underworld." My demon partner sucked in a breath and let it out slowly. "He made the mistake of underestimating us last time. He won't make the same mistake again." Blaise turned away and continued following the tunnel.

"Okay, I get it. He's dangerous." I trudged after Blaise. "Look. I'm not a complete idiot. But we won't catch him if we're hiding in the sewer while he's topside, collecting his next bevy of hoes for sale to the highest bidders."

The demon ignored my outburst and stopped in front of a stone column that looked like the others spaced evenly along the tunnel's walls as additional support beams. Blaise pressed his palms to the stones at chest level.

The way he caressed the stone reminded me of when he'd captured my breasts in his hands and squeezed gently. My nipples puckered. I discounted it as an effect of the cool air in the underground sanctuary, but that didn't account for the rush of heat building inside, nor the sudden dampness between my legs. "Why are we stopping here?" I barked, my voice a little hoarse, lust choking my words. Damn the demon!

The stone wall pushed inward revealing an entranceway to a compartment carved out of the rock.

"After you." Blaise waved me forward.

I ducked to enter, passing through a low, narrow entryway, straightening once the ceiling rose high enough. "Nice. You really should have that door enlarged…" My words faded as I took in the granite-tiled floors, the Victorian-era furniture that looked too good to be knock-offs. "Holy smokes! This room is ridiculous." It made my squalid apartment look like a broom closet in a homeless shelter.

The white granite and artificial lighting illuminated the room, giving it a large and spacious appeal worthy of something out of an architectural magazine.

"You're not coming to my place ever again." I rolled my eyes. "How can you lower yourself to step foot in my hovel when you have this?"

He smiled. "It's taken me years to make this as it is. But I prefer your stimulating company over my…accoutrements. Come." Blaise held out the hand of his undamaged arm. "I could use some help getting out of these clothes."

"Uh, no." I refused to take his hand, knowing that touching him only made me that much less in control of my own actions. He was like a date-rape drug, erasing all my self-imposed reasons for abstinence. "We'll only end up in bed."

"And is that such a bad place to be?" He winked.

"Damn it." I stomped my foot, something I never did, but that this demon had me doing on a regular basis. "Do I have to slam your face into your granite tile to get you out of my system?"

"No, but perhaps making love will help." His grin faded. "Really, I could use your help. The blood on this shirt has dried to my skin. A demon's body recovers on its own, but it takes time and this clothing will not repair itself."

The sudden stab of guilt reminded me that he'd taken on a wolf for me. The least I could do was help him out of his shirt. "Fine."

As I stepped closer, his unique scent wrapped around me, drawing me closer. "But no funny stuff."

He held up his hands in surrender. "I promise...no funny stuff."

I made quick work of sliding his jacket off his shoulders, the black leather sporting a dark stain over the rips in the arm. Careful not to disturb his wounded arm, I eased the sleeve off and tossed the ruined garment to the floor. His shirt hung open. In our rush to leave my apartment, he hadn't had time to button.

As I smoothed the fabric over his chest, his breath caught and held. Not until my hands pressed into the solid muscles of his shoulders did I realize I wasn't breathing as well. "This is crazy."

"The lust building inside or you undressing me? Your thoughts are as conflicting as your actions." His good hand rose to capture my waist. "And you smell amazing."

"Oh, you like the stench of female perspiration?" I laughed shakily, pushing the shirt down his arm. When it stuck on the dried blood, that nudge of guilt overrode the way my pussy clenched. "We'll need to get this wet to get it off."

"The shower is through that door." He nodded toward a darkened room.

"Could we do this over a sink?"

"I'd prefer to get the disgusting odor of werewolf off my entire body. A sink won't do that."

I sighed. "You're killing me." But I let him lead the way toward the dark doorway, knowing once inside the demon's lair, I was a goner.

Chapter Six

As we entered the bedroom, subtle lights came on along the baseboard, illuminating our way.

"Nice." I swallowed hard, kept my gaze ahead on the bathroom door and ignored the king-sized bed in the center of the room. A man could seduce several women in that. "I suppose you never bump into furniture in the dark."

"Not unless I want to." The bathroom light sprang on. It, too, was a subtle glow, not a full-out glare. "Interesting image you have going there."

His grin spiked my anger, a welcome respite from the pounding urgency of lust making me want to experiment with the firmness of the mattress. "I'm leaving." I turned and would have walked out of the bedroom, but for the hand that grasped my arm and pulled me back against his naked chest.

Alarm bells went off in my head. "Let go of me," I whispered. The longer I leaned into him, the less resistance I could muster, the stronger my desire grew. "I have to get back to work."

"I know you want me." He spoke the words aloud, the rumble in his chest vibrating all the way through mine.

"So? I can control my desire." Another lie. I could no more control the flood of desire than I could stop molten lava from flowing downhill.

"Can you?" he challenged, his good hand slid up my arm to pull the hair back from over my shoulder, exposing my throat to the cool air and his warm breath.

"Yes." My head tipped, allowing him better access, belying my affirmation.

He bent to press his full, sensuous lips against my skin.

My knees buckled and all resistance fled as he turned me and kissed me full on my lips, capturing my breath, my imagination and locking me in for the duration.

His tongue slipped between my teeth and thrust along mine, his fingers tangling in my hair, drawing me deeper into his web.

With no more strength to defend against his onslaught, I leaned into him, my hands spanning his waist, slipping around to caress his tight buttocks, pressing him closer, his cock nudging my belly.

Adrenaline leapt in my veins, molten hot blood roaring through my body, pooling low, igniting a flame I could not deny. I had to have him. There in the bathroom. Soon. Or I'd explode with need.

"What are you doing to me?" I whispered. My fingers searching for and finding the button on his jeans.

"Nothing you don't already want." His lips caressed my temple, my cheekbone, brushing my eyelid.

The rivet slid through the button hole and I had the zipper down, and shoved the waistband over his hips in record time.

His cock sprang free, engorged, heavy and hard, bumping against my bare midriff.

Too many clothes. I had on too many clothes.

Take them off. A voice urged inside my head. Was it his or mine?

Did it matter?

I tore the remainder of my shirt over my head and tossed it to the floor, the amulet dangling between my breasts. I leaned against him, the heat of his skin against mine searing a path straight south, generating a rush of liquid. With shaking hands, I shoved his jeans down his thighs, my fingers trailing over taut muscles.

One foot rose and I pushed the jeans off, taking his leather shoe with it.

He shook off the other shoe and stepped on the denim, removing the last of his jeans.

Blaise stood naked but for the shirt stuck to the blood on his arm. The breadth of his shoulders filled the room, each muscle firm and defined.

Deep scratches slashed across his chest, the blood already dry, the edges of his skin well on its way to mending.

I trailed a finger across the scar. "Must be nice to heal so quickly."

"It has its advantages." He slid a hand between my skin and the waistband of my jeans. "But I'm not without limits." With deft movements, he flipped the button free and dropped my zipper.

"You take too long." Beyond impatient, and past caring that I had broken all my newly formed rules, I ripped off my jeans and boots and reached behind him to turn on the shower nozzle. "Get in."

He grinned, his dark eyes gleaming. "Yes, ma'am." He stepped into the large, granite-lined shower, taking me with him.

I didn't argue, figuring the sooner we did the nasty, the

sooner I'd be free of my desire for this demon and ready to focus on capturing the evil one.

Water sluiced over his shoulders, soaking the shirt, dried blood loosening its hold on fabric and skin. In seconds, the garment slid away, dropping with a plop to the shower floor.

I kicked it aside and stepped into Blaise's arms. "Let's do this."

Blaise's brows dipped. "You think it will be that easy? That quick?"

"It has to be. We have a baddie to catch before he ensnares more women as sex slaves." Though my words were blunt, my body felt anything but hardcore. Water lubricated our connection, making my hands glide over the planes of his chest and downward to the erect shaft prodding my belly.

My fingers circled him, rising up and down, pumping him hard, as if he needed his engine primed. Which he didn't. He couldn't possibly get bigger or harder.

The gashes on his injured arm had already started to heal, the crusted blood washing away with the water's spray.

I circled his calf with mine, pulling myself closer until my pussy rubbed against the coarse hairs of his thigh. A moan rose up my throat and I set it free, the sound echoing off the walls.

Blaise reached beneath my buttocks and lifted me, wrapping my thighs around his waist, his cock poking my entrance.

I wanted him inside me so badly I ached.

But he held off. Balancing me with one hand, his other reached for a ledge above the showerhead, returning with a foil packet.

A burn of jealousy made me stiffen. "Bring women here often?"

"No, but I've been thinking about you every night. Hoping I'd have you to myself. Here." He handed me the packet.

I hated myself for believing him, but ripped the condom free and slid it over his penis, eager to consummate this little get-together.

No sooner had the condom covered him then he was inside me, thrusting hard and fast.

I grasped his shoulders, pushing myself up and sliding down, matching his movements, wanting him to go faster, to drive harder.

He turned with me in his arms and pushed me against the granite, his hands gripping my thighs as he thrust one last time, bending to take one of my breasts between his teeth as his cock throbbed against the walls of my vagina.

"See? It didn't take long," I said, my breath coming in short gasps.

"We're not nearly done." He lifted me and carried me dripping through the bathroom and laid me out on that decadently huge bed, the satin comforter cool against my heated skin.

"I really need to be topside," I muttered, unable to make a move with Blaise pressing me into the mattress, his body settling over mine.

"Not yet." He pushed up on his hands, his muscles flexing as he bent to capture my nipple between his teeth. "Let them think you've disappeared."

"But this is all wrong." My back arched off the bed, pressing my breast deeper into his mouth.

"All wrong," he agreed, his breath skimming along my ribs, working his way lower to that triangle of hair guarding my most sensitive zone.

I drew in a shaky breath, capturing my bottom lip between my teeth, my hands digging into his full, thick hair.

"Oh, boy." As if perched at the top of a steep drop on a roller coaster ride, I waited, unable to release the air.

His fingers threaded through the curls, parting my folds to expose that thick sliver of skin, the bundle of nerves throbbing in anticipation of his touch.

As his face leaned close, my heels dug into the comforter, lifting me upward.

His tongue flicked my clit, sparking a string of electric shocks pinging throughout my body. He swirled, laved and lapped at the center of my desire, sending me rocketing to the edge.

When he pushed his fingers into my wet entrance, I came apart, my hands convulsing against his scalp, urging him closer, pushing him away with each wave of ecstasy washing over me.

He tortured me, strumming me like a harpist, the melody building to a crescendo, the blankets and sheets whipping around the two of us as the tide swelled, carrying us along in its wake.

At the peak, I dropped over the edge and fell into a bottomless abyss, my mind spinning. I squeezed shut my eyes and held on, riding the storm to the end.

When I returned to earth, I opened my eyes.

Blaise lay on his side, propped on an elbow and gazing down at me. A smile curled the edge of his lips, his longish black hair stood on end and there was a light slash of blood across one cheekbone. "You really have to channel the energy of the amulet before someone gets hurt."

"How did you get that cut?" I reached up and caressed his cheek, the movement of my body against the satin comforter, stirring me to life yet again. Forcing myself to focus on him and the room around me, I pushed to my elbows and gasped. "What the hell happened?"

The room was a disaster. The extra throw pillows that had been on the bed were strewn across the floor, the chair in the corner lay on its side against the far wall and the dresser had moved three feet away from the wall, the decorative statue that had graced its shiny surface lay in a broken tangle of sheets and clothing across the room.

Blaise frowned. "You don't remember?"

"Nothing after you got me off…" I could feel the heat of a blush rising up my neck, filling my cheeks. I'd never spoken so openly about sex with a man. Then again, Blaise wasn't just a man. He was a demon. One I'd sworn off and hadn't been able to leave alone.

"Sweetheart, that amulet has your own powers so hyped up, you don't know your own strength."

"I told you. I don't have powers. You're the demon. I'm human."

"Whatever you choose to believe. But when it comes down to it, use your powers to protect yourself." He kissed my lips, the caress sizzling but brief, then he skimmed his fingers across a nipple. "We need to go." Blaise rose from the bed and strode naked across the huge bedroom into a closet.

As if the rug had been ripped from under me, I sat up. "That's my line. We'd have gone a lot sooner had you not dragged me into your cave."

I wrapped the sheet around my body and scooted to the edge of the bed. Holding tight to my toga, I dashed into the bathroom and snatched up my damp jeans, shoving my feet into them. I lifted my tattered T-shirt from the puddle where it lay on the floor and shook it. Not much left after ripping the hem off to stop the blood flowing from Blaise's arm.

I shivered at the recollection of the wolf tearing into him.

"Here." Blaise wrapped a dark cotton long-sleeved shirt around my shoulders and pulled me against him. "I'm fine.

Demons heal quickly." He turned me to face him and buttoned the shirt up my front, his lips curling upward. "You look like a lost child in this shirt."

A glance in the mirror confirmed his assessment. Not only was the shirt big enough to fit two of me inside, but my hair stuck out like that of someone from a horror movie. "Great." I wet my hand and finger-combed my hair, but no amount of damage-control was helping.

I jammed the tail of the black shirt into my jeans, the wads of fabric bunching against my skin. Too bulky to zip, I yanked it back out and tied the tails in a knot around my waist and folded the sleeves up until I once again had use of my hands.

"Ready?" Blaise stood in the doorway, looking as well-put-together as a *GQ* model.

Which only made me feel even more like a drowned kitten. Thank goodness I didn't give a damn about my looks. "Ready." I stepped into my shoes and we headed for the underground entrance.

As Blaise reached out to pull the heavy metal door open, it smashed inward, a strong burst of fetid air blowing in with it, knocking me back as easily as a if I'd been struck by a bullet.

Chapter Seven

A man ducked low and entered Blaise's home.

Blaise had staggered backward, but remained on his feet.

I pulled myself up off the floor. "What the hell?"

Shoving me behind him, Blaise's chest puffed out and his demanded, "Who the hell are you?"

The man glared at Blaise. "The man about to save your sorry ass. Hurry. We have to get her out of here." He nodded toward me.

"I'll decide when I need to come and go."

"If you want to overtaken by a pack of angry werewolves in animal form, stay. Otherwise, follow me."

I refused to take a step. "You haven't told us who you are. Why should we follow you when you could be leading us into a trap?"

"I knew your mother. She would have wanted me to make sure you survived."

All the wind left my lungs as if I'd been punched in the gut. "What do you know about my mother?"

"Plenty. She loved you and wouldn't have wanted you

to die needlessly." He held out his hand. "Are you coming, or not?"

"Not." I stood with my arms crossed over my chest.

"Suit yourself, but the wolves have explosives and plan to use them."

Blaise glared. "How do you know this?"

"Let's just say the otherkin grapevine has many branches."

"You're one of us." Blaise stated. It wasn't a question.

The stranger nodded.

"And that's supposed to make us feel better?" I laughed. "Nicolae is a demon and he's determined to bank on his power. How do we know you aren't in on his plan?"

A shout echoed in the distance outside the entranceway.

"Because I don't care about the amulet. He does, and he won't let anything or anyone stand in the way of him retrieving it."

"If you don't care about the amulet, why are you here?"

His gaze bore into mine and silence stretched for long moment. "No time to argue. I'm leaving. Follow me if you want to live." The stranger ducked out of the low entrance.

Something about his face niggled at the back of my mind.

"What do you want to do?" Blaise asked.

Tension knotted the muscles in my gut. It was as if I teetered on the edge of a great discovery, but couldn't quite put my finger on it.

"Katya!" Blaise grabbed my shoulders. "We have to go."

"You're right. We can't stay here if they're bringing explosives. We could be trapped in here for days, if not forever."

"I have another way out." Blaise closed the metal door and waved toward the bedroom.

"We don't have time to play around, Blaise. We have to get out before the wolves get in."

"Then hurry. We don't have much time."

Blaise led the way through his bedroom into a small study lined with bookcases. He poked through the books, running his index finger across the spines until he reached a small red, leather-bound book. When he tipped the book out of the shelf, the ground vibrated and the shelf became a doorway, opening onto a steel ladder, leading upward into a dark hole.

I gulped, swallowing fear at the darkness of the passage. "You're kidding, right?"

"It's not lit, but it will take us up to the surface."

Pounding on the metal door made me jump and I moved toward the ladder. "Will it close behind us so they won't be able to find us?"

"It'll close, but they might sniff us out. The sooner we reach the top, the better. It's a long way up. Get started."

"What about the stranger?"

"The wolves aren't after him. He'll be okay."

The closeness of the escape portal gripped me as soon as I crawled up inside the chute, my fingers searching for the rungs of the ladder. Once I had a grip, I pulled myself upward, my back skimming against the dank walls.

"Are you sure we can get out at the top? It doesn't come out in a parking garage where I car is parked over it, does it?"

"We'll come out in an alley. Don't worry. I checked two days ago. Nothing blocked it then."

"Two days? It could be blocked now. If we get to the top and can't get out, we'll be trapped."

"We're trapped if we try to go back the way we came. The wolves are too close and move faster on foot than we can. If they have to climb a ladder, it will take them as long, if not longer than it takes us. They will have to shift to human form to do it. No go." He smacked my bottom.

"Okay, okay, you don't have to be so pushy."

"Yes, I do," he muttered, pulling the bookshelf door closed behind him.

Pounding sounded on the metal door at the other end of his spacious apartment.

I shot upward like a scalded cat, pulling myself up the ladder hand over hand, one rung at a time, my feet taking each in stride.

Below me, Blaise followed.

Darkness surrounded us. All I could do was keep moving, try to block out the fact that I was encased in what amounted to a long, narrow tube. Should it be blocked at either end, I could be trapped and die inside it.

"You're not going to die and we won't be trapped. Just keep moving." Blaise's voice urged me on.

My thighs and arms burned with the effort. Since it was dark outside on the streets of Manhattan, I couldn't expect to see light shining down from the top, giving me a feeling of endlessness that almost scared me more than the werewolves or even Nicolae.

When I thought my legs and arms could take no more, I dragged myself up one more rung and banged my head on a heavy metal plate. "Ouch!" The sudden pain made me lose my grip and I fell back a step.

If not for Blaise being directly below me, I'd have plummeted to the bottom.

He grabbed me, bracing his back against the wall, his arms securing me in his embrace, one hand gripping the ladder. "You okay?"

"I'm fine. Oh, by the way. We're at the top."

His chuckle warmed the cool air. "I gathered that."

"Thanks for breaking my fall." His nearness revived my senses, spurring my insides to life.

"Later, sweetheart." He kissed me and shoved us both up

the rungs until he could lift the manhole cover and fling it to the side.

"Show off," I mumbled, scrambling over the edge to drop to my hands on the pavement.

We were in a dark alley, where, I didn't know. But by the sounds of car horns honking and traffic on the street at the end of the alley, we had to be in Manhattan. The noise never died down as if Taxi drivers considered it their duty to keep up the din.

I rolled onto my back and let the blood return to my arms and legs and the pain recede.

"We can't stay long." Blaise rose like he'd just gotten out of bed, not a long climb up a narrow tube.

"I know." I groaned and sat up. "Where to?"

"The precinct."

"Sounds as good as we'll get. Maybe they can come up with a way to catch Nicolae. I'm fresh out of ideas."

"You're going to give me the amulet and leave it up to me and Detective Thomas to get our man."

"Like hell."

"He's too dangerous."

"You forget. This is my job. You can't go all protective on me. I'm in this position for a reason."

"I won't let him hurt you."

Having seen what could happen when a werewolf attacked a demon and having gone up against Nicolae once already, I nodded. "I'm okay with that." My shoulders straightened and I gave Blaise one of my eat-shit-and-die stares. "But don't get in my way of hurting Nicolae. I mean to bring the bastard down."

Blaise chucked me under the chin like a favored child. Then his fingers slipped to the back of my neck, tilting my head up. "Anyone ever tell you that you're beautiful when you act all tough?" His lips brushed mine.

"I *am* tough," I whispered, my mouth reaching upward for his, craving more. Holy shit, he was impossible to resist.

"Yeah. I get that a lot."

"Bastard."

He kissed me, his tongue thrusting between my teeth.

Several seconds slid by as time seemed to stand still around us.

My leg curled around his, my fingers loosening a button on his shirt. I would have stripped him naked, had he not grabbed my hand and held it away from his skin.

"Later." The one word held promise.

I struggled to tamp down the flame that licked at my insides. Now wasn't the time.

A guttural growl echoed out of the depths of the tube.

Blaise shoved the cover over the manhole and held out his hand. "Let's get out of here."

I grabbed it and ran.

We caught a ride to the precinct in a kamikaze taxi cab. Still fairly new to the city, I gripped the arm rest, my fingers digging into the cracked vinyl. "Do you ever get used to the way the cabbies drive?" I asked beneath my breath, afraid to offend the driver.

"Close your eyes," Blaise urged. "We'll be there soon."

Too tired to argue, I did as he said, my heart starting and stopping each time we jerked to a halt and the driver laid on his horn. Finally, I gave up and directed my attention to my partner. "Who was that man in your hideout?"

"I was hoping you'd know, since he mentioned your mother."

I squinted, dragging up a shadowy image of the stranger

in my mind. "There was something familiar about him, but I couldn't put my finger on it."

"Could he be a friend?"

"Mom didn't bring any of her friends around us. As far as I know, she didn't have any. It didn't cross my mind then, but now I think it's kind of odd she didn't have friends."

"How many friends do you have?" he questioned.

"Counting Randi?" I laughed. "One."

"What about me?" Blaise tapped his chest.

I studied him. Partner, yeah. Lover…whew…I was trying to change that, but yeah. "Friend?" I shook my head. "I don't know if we can be friends. I mean, you're a demon. Can a demon and a human have a meaningful relationship?" I snorted. "What do we have in common?"

"A desire to defeat the bad guys, for one." He lifted my hand.

For once, I didn't pull away. "That would be me and all the cops in the precinct, and I'm not friends with them."

"You could be…if you let them in." His thumb rubbed the back of my hand. "Why do you push people away?"

A sharp pain edged into my heart, and I glanced out the window. "I don't push people away."

"You call slamming a man's face into the concrete a way to make friends in the department?"

I glared at Blaise. "He patted my ass. What was I supposed to do?"

"I don't know, but you have the rest of the men afraid to work with you in case you misread their intentions."

"The bastard deserved it."

"Probably. But all you do is go to work and go to your apartment. You never stop by the pub and have a beer with the guys."

"These…" I cupped my breasts and lifted. "They never

look past my breasts. How can I strike up a conversation with men who can't look me in the eye?"

"What are you really afraid of? That you might like someone? That you might put down roots, make connections, get close like family with the people you work with?"

"Shut up." I crossed both arms over my chest and faced the street. "You don't know anything about me."

"I know that you don't like to show your emotions. That you don't like to talk about your mother and brother, and that your father left you when you were a child. You've told me enough that I know you're afraid to love. Afraid that whomever you choose to love will leave you."

"You're wrong. I'm not afraid of anything." A single tear slipped out of the corner of my eye and traveled down my cheek. Thank God it was on the cheek farthest from Blaise. He'd never see it, if I had any say in the matter. With a casual swipe, I eliminated the evidence of the chink in my armor.

"You don't have to be afraid." Blaise touched my cheek. "I've got your back."

"And that's supposed to make it better?" I shook my head, still refusing to make eye contact lest he see the tears welling in mine. "Look at you. You're not even a permanent member of the force. You could leave at will. Why should I trust you to be there for me?"

"Because I care." His hand gripped my chin and turned my face toward him.

"I don't need you to care. I don't need anyone." I sniffed. Damn.

"I know you don't need anyone. Maybe that's what I love about you. That you're tough. Determined. And so beautiful that you take my breath away."

"Blah, blah, blah." I jerked my chin free and resumed

staring out the window. "Words are just that. Words. People leave. They die. They go away."

"And you'd keep them at arm's length to avoid the pain." Blaise pulled me into his arms, refusing to let me keep him away.

I resisted. Well, sort of.

"Baby, you might be avoiding all the pain. But you're also avoiding all the joy that loving another person can bring."

I tried to push away. When he wouldn't let go, anger bubbled up and spilled out. "I've lost everyone I've ever loved." I smacked a hand to his muscular chest. "Damn it! It hurts too bad to ever go through that again."

"I know. But it hurts because you experienced the joy of knowing them. If you could forget everything about those people, would you?"

"Yes!" All the fight leached out of me and I pressed my forehead into his shirt. "No." My whisper was absorbed in the fabric. I never wanted to forget how it felt to be held in my mother's arms, the feel of my little brother curling up next to me like a puppy seeking warmth, or how safe I'd felt sitting in my father's lap when I was a little girl, scared of the boogey man hiding under my bed. "Why are you tormenting me?"

"I care."

The taxi slid to a stop in front of the precinct building, cutting off further conversation.

I scrubbed at my face with the sleeve of the oversized shirt Blaise had given me, determined to remove all traces of tears. I'd established myself as a bad-ass. I couldn't lose ground. The men of the precinct couldn't know I had feelings. Feelings I'd buried for so long I didn't know how to handle them.

Damn Blaise for being right. Damn him for bringing back all the good memories I'd packed away in the recesses of my mind.

We entered the building and headed straight for Detective Thomas's office. A man stood with his back to us, his stance familiar.

I gripped Blaise's arm. "It's him."

Blaise's lips thinned into a firm line as he stepped through the open office door. He nodded at my boss. "Detective Thomas."

"What the hell is he doing here?" I jerked my head toward the stranger.

The man who'd appeared in Blaise's lair before all hell broke loose turned to face us, his face grim. "I'm trying to help you. You have no idea what you've gotten yourself into with Nicolae."

"Then tell us." I crossed my arms over my chest. "And while you're at it, tell us who the hell you are."

He stared straight into my eyes. "I'm Ivan Danske." The determined set to his jaw slackened, the hard look in his eyes softening, almost to sadness. "Your father."

Chapter Eight

I would have been so proud of myself, if a single thought could take root at that moment. I stood perfectly still, absorbing the impact of those two short, seemingly insignificant words, sure I'd been hit by a twenty-ton locomotive.

Your father.

For a long moment I continued to stare at him, schooling my face to poker stiff. *Show no emotion,* echoed through my thoughts so loud I couldn't hear Blaise close the door behind me.

"Detective Danske, take a seat." My boss's brow furrowed, and he hurried around the desk to pull a metal chair forward.

"No." I held out a hand. "I've got this." I stepped forward, my eyes narrowing to slits. "How do I know you're telling the truth? I haven't seen my father since I was twelve."

"You have my eyes and your mother's hair." He reached out.

I jerked back. "Leave my mother out of this," I bit out. "Not that I believe you, but what the hell do you want?"

"To save your brother."

A well of emotion hit me like a tsunami, striking a heavy

blow to the shield I'd erected around my heart. This time I did step back, cocked my arm and unleashed all the pent-up hatred, anger, hurt and sorrow I'd ever locked away in a punch aimed for the stranger's face.

He caught my fist, absorbing all the power, bringing my arm to such a complete and painful stop, my body lurched backward.

If not for Blaise, I'd have landed on my ass. He steadied me, his arm going around my waist, holding me up when I should have fallen.

"My brother is dead," I said, my voice low and hoarse, the wad of emotion stuck in my throat, refusing to let me sound normal and in control.

"No, he's not." The man claiming to be my father shoved a hand through his hair, pushing the salt-and-pepper strands back, making them stand on end. Despite the haze of red-hot anger glazing my vision, I had to admit the man was handsome. I could see how a woman could fall for those devilish good looks.

"Look, I don't have time to explain away the past and why I left you, your brother and your mother, but know that if I could have come up with any other way to keep you safe, I would have."

"Safe? You left us in the rattiest neighborhood in Chicago with no money. My mother slaved away at two jobs just to keep a roof over our heads and food on the table."

"I know." Ivan's head dipped. "And I couldn't help."

"Why?" I pushed away from Blaise. "Why couldn't you help the woman you supposedly loved and married, the family you helped create?" I snorted. "I'll tell you why. You're a goddamn deadbeat. That's why. You weren't worthy of kissing the ground my mother walked on." By this time I stood toe-to-toe with the man, my anger burning in my cheeks.

He grabbed my arms. "I wanted to be there, but I couldn't. It was too dangerous. I had to leave so they wouldn't trace me back to my children. They would have found you."

I knocked his hands away. "They?"

"Nicolae and his demon followers. He's more dangerous than you can begin to understand."

I stood my ground, refusing to let the man's words get to me. "He doesn't scare me."

"He should." Ivan Danske spoke in a soft whisper. "I've been trying to capture him for years. Ever since he stole your brother away from our home in Chicago."

The blow hit hard. My chest felt crushed with the weight of this news of my little brother, whom we assumed wandered away from the house and been snatched by a sadistic killer, never to be found. "Stolen?"

"Yes, stolen." Ivan raised his hands, palms upward. "I tried to keep him away from your mother and you kids."

"Why was Alex taken? He was only five."

"When I heard Nicolae was stealing children for his special army, I knew I had to leave. He targeted half-human, half-demon mixed races, plucking the most promising children from their parents' arms. He raised them as protégés in an army of demons."

I tipped my chin, eyes narrowing. "That doesn't explain why he would come after Alex."

"Alex was already emitting a very strong aura of power."

"What the hell are you talking about?" My head spun, my pulse racing through my body. I wanted to press my hands to my ears to block out what my father was saying.

"Nicolae and I came from the same clan of the underworld demons."

My heart sank into the hollowness of my belly. "You're a demon?" I closed my eyes, bracing myself for his response.

"Yes." The one word set my mind into a tailspin.

Blaise's hand around my waist was the only thing holding me up. I swallowed hard past the constriction in my throat and reopened my eyes. "And Alex and I?"

"Are halflings. Half demon, half human." My father took a step toward me.

I held steady, more because I didn't think my legs would cooperate and get me anywhere after Ivan's revelation. "My mother knew about you before you married?"

He nodded. "She accepted me for what I was." His words were a challenge to me.

My lip curled into a snarl. "I could accept that you're a demon. I can't accept that you deserted us."

"As I told you, I had to leave. Being with you made you all a target. I left you, cut all ties that could lead Nicolae back to my family."

"I don't understand why."

"Nicolae hated that I always bested him at anything magical—moving objects, throwing fire, generating electromagnetic pulses...I was really good at it all. Nic lagged behind in his development and took a lot of bullying and abuse from some of the other young demons. He left the underworld and struck out on his own, vowing to be great someday. He'd get his revenge on those who'd hurt him or laughed at his attempts."

"Apparently he found us." My head had a hard time absorbing what my heart was telling me was true. I didn't want it to be true.

"I've been searching for Alex since he was taken. I'd always suspected he had snatched the child, but I couldn't find where he'd hidden him."

"And now you think you can find Nicolae's lair?"

"No. But I got word Nicolae wants to make a trade."

My hand went to the amulet hanging around my throat. "He wants the necklace."

Ivan nodded. "Apparently, it's the key to his power. Without it, he's just another demon, with mediocre power."

I looked up at the man who called himself my father. "Nicolae has Alex?"

Again, Ivan nodded. "Nicolae is willing to trade Alex for the amulet."

"Then we make the trade." I started to pull the amulet over my head, a surge of hope filling my senses. I wasn't alone. All of my family had not left me. My brother was out there somewhere and I held the key.

Blaise's hand stopped me. "If Nicolae gets hold of the amulet, he'll rule the underworld again."

I shook off his grip, anger and desperation making me tense. "He has my brother. I'd give my life for him."

My father gripped my arms and forced me to stare up into his eyes. "He's not the same boy you remember."

"He's the only family I have left in the world." I forced the words out between gritted teeth.

Ivan Danske winced and drew in a deep breath. "I want him back, too. But this is a trap."

"I don't care." I jerked backward, out of Ivan's hold. "We have no idea what Alex has been through. No matter what, I still love him."

"Nicolae has had him since he was five. He won't remember you, me or your mother. He's been trained by Nicolae and his followers to hate and kill."

"He's Alex."

"Not anymore." Ivan stood with his hands at his sides. "You can't make that trade."

I drew myself up to all five feet three inches of female wrath. "I can, and I will."

Detective Thomas, who'd stood patiently in the background throughout the interchange, stepped forward. "I can't let you do that."

My chest tightened until pain radiated throughout my body. "I have to."

Thomas shook his head. "It would be too dangerous." He held out his hand. "It might be best if we destroy it to keep it out of Nicolae's hands."

I moved back, toward the doorway. "No. It's my only chance to get Alex back. I have to make that trade."

The detective's lips firmed and he nodded toward Blaise.

Blaise's hands clasped my arms in an iron hold. "Sorry, sweetheart. I agree with the boss. We can't afford to let that amulet fall back into Nicolae's hands."

I stared across the floor at my father. "You say I'm a halfling?"

He nodded.

"Just how much demon power does a halfling have?"

"Every demon and halfling has his or her own level of power. A halfling can be every bit as powerful as any full-fledged demon. I wasn't worried about you being stolen because you hadn't shown any signs and you weren't emitting an aura like your brother. His was so strong, any demon within a city block could pick up on it."

Oh, but I had been showing signs. Signs I'd ignored. I hadn't told my mother about the items shifting in my room. I'd attributed the movement to breezes or miniature earthquakes caused by the fracking going on in the Chicago suburbs in an attempt to find oil deposits. Deep down, I think I'd sensed I wasn't like anyone else.

Blaise's hands squeezed my shoulders. *I sensed it, too.*

I held up a hand. *Don't.*

The fingers dug into my shoulders. *You can't let Nicolae have that amulet.*

My father's eyes narrowed as he stared at me then Blaise.

Forcing my thoughts into an imaginary closet in my mind, I closed the door and faced my father and Detective Thomas. "I have to handle this the only way I can." If the amulet was truly a power enhancing agent, I had only one shot at what I was about to do. "Let go of me," I said out loud.

"I can't and you can't do what you know you shouldn't." Blaise's body stiffened behind me, his hands like manacles on my arms.

I concentrated, resurfacing the same powerful emotions that I'd experienced in the basement of the warehouse when Blaise had been in my line of fire. I touched the amulet, focusing on its smooth, stone center, making it my center.

A surge of power rose up within me. My hair lifted off my shoulders and swirled around my face. Fissures of electric shocks slithered across my skin and out the tips of my fingers.

"Hey!" Blaise's hands let go of my arms and he slammed back against the wall behind me.

"Katya, don't let it control you." My father's voice came to me as if muffled in wool.

I opened my eyes and gasped.

"What's going on?" Detective Thomas, eyes wide and worried, stared around the room.

Books floated off shelves, papers rose into the air and the air felt charged.

"Focus, Katya," Ivan said.

"Oh, I'm focused."

"The power is dangerous." Ivan's shaggy gray hair stood on end. "You could kill anyone of us with a thought."

"Then don't make me mad." I backed toward the door.

"Don't go, Katya." Blaise pushed away from the wall,

reaching out for me. "Nicolae is a demented demon. You can't go it alone."

"He can't touch me."

"You're not invincible. Look at how easily you took the amulet from him."

"He wasn't paying attention." When my hand touched the door knob, a spark flew out. I gripped it anyway and twisted. "I'm going after my brother. Don't try to stop me."

"Then let me come along as your backup."

"I don't need backup."

"Yes you do. If not because you give a rat's ass about your own hide, you know it's procedure, Detective Danske." I almost laughed at my boss's attempt to wield his authority over me.

I was past caring about my job.

"Listen to him. You need backup." Ivan moved toward me. "Nicolae has years more experience than you do. He's known he was a demon all his life."

I ignored Ivan and stepped across the threshold, concentrating the power building in me on the door. It swung closed between me and the others in the room and the lock twisted.

Fists pounded on the wooden door as I turned and ran through the office and down the staircase into the parking garage.

Still high on adrenaline and a power surge like nothing I'd ever experienced, I jumped into the nearest cruiser and touched my finger to the ignition. The engine turned over, grating with the over-revving it received without my having to press a foot to the accelerator. I was out of the garage and on the street in seconds with no idea where to go. But I'd start with the warehouse where we'd found the women. Nicolae could have constructed hidden corridors in the sub-basement where he'd kept the women. I had no doubt that the energy levels I was now emitting would draw Nicolae out of his hiding place. But just in case he didn't, I sent a mental message through the city, telling Nicolae I'd meet him at the warehouse. Whether or not my message went out to the demon remained to be seen. If he showed up, I'd know. Then the real negotiations would begin.

Chapter Nine

Surrounded by yellow crime scene tape, the warehouse that had housed a brothel of drugged women stood silent on the dark street. Not a single streetlight shone, lending to the air of dark foreboding filling my heart and mind. I had to focus on my brother. On getting him away from Nicolae and to somewhere safe where he could be reprogrammed.

I didn't have any doubt Alex would be one messed up teen. After spending most of his life brainwashed by an evil demon, he was bound to be a disaster. But I would never forgive myself if I didn't at least try to rescue him. As his sister, I'd let him down by taking my eyes off him when he'd been playing in the yard. That's all it had taken, and Alex had been spirited away, never to be seen or heard from again. Until now.

My pulse pounded against my ears, drowning out other sounds. If Nicolae got my message, it could be only a matter of moments before I'd be reunited with my last living relative. At least one I could claim. Ivan Danske was still on my shit list of deadbeat fathers. His flimsy excuse of staying away so that we would not become targets didn't hold water in my book. If he'd cared at all for his family, he'd have stayed and fought to protect us.

The back door leading into the warehouse had been wired shut, the doorjamb and hinges bent back in place. Had I done that? Damaged the door so badly it couldn't be closed properly? All because of a little flare of demon power?

It hit me again.

I am a demon.

I sucked a breath into tight lungs and blew it out. What had Ivan called me? A halfling? Based on the energy-boosting effects of the amulet, I had some inherent talents I never knew I possessed. I twisted the wire loose and opened the door without using any demon magic. I wanted to save my strength for the coming confrontation with Nicolae. If I had to dig up the pavement of Manhattan, I'd find the bastard who'd stolen my little brother and ruined my family. There would be a convergence of myself and Nicolae that night, if I had a say in the matter.

I'd had the foresight to grab a flashlight from the glove box of the unmarked police cruiser I'd appropriated from the motor pool. As I followed the narrow beam down corridors and into the room that had been filled with sex slaves just a short time ago, foul aromas filled the air, threatening to choke my sense of smell. The room reeked of filth, semen, blood, sweat and fear, all warring for top billing in my head. I held a finger to my nose and performed a thorough search of the area, testing the walls and floors, hoping to find a hidden panel or doorway. Alas, the room was all that it appeared—a hellhole for the helpless women who'd been imprisoned and forced to perform disgusting sexual acts for the depraved *patrons* who'd paid top dollar to partake of the forbidden fruits.

I shuddered and moved on to the hallway leading away from the makeshift whorehouse. Rooms led off the hallway, each containing a bed the higher class patronage would appreciate—empty now but for the horrifying memories left in the girls' minds.

I checked each room, disappointed when I didn't find anything. At the end of the hallway, a staircase led up to street level and down into another level of the basement. I chose to go down.

At the bottom, a metal door opened when I pulled the handle, and I stepped through. As soon as it closed behind me, a lock clicked into place. I swung around and pushed on the lever, the door didn't budge.

I found myself in what I would call the boiler room of the old warehouse, the place where all the heating, cooling and electrical connections culminated in an array of pipes, ducts and wiring harnesses.

A sinister laugh echoed against the rusted metal of long dormant steam pipes.

"Nicolae," I called out.

Nothing.

He wasn't going to meet me, he wanted me to go to him. I could feel his thoughts, the hint of triumph for having lured me into his web.

I forced the fear from my mind and stepped forward, ducking beneath an overhead pipe and dodging a large tank-like fixture. I smelled the strong odor of dog and tensed, one hand curling around the amulet. "I'm here to negotiate the release of my brother."

"You are in no position to negotiate." Nicolae Dragomir stepped out of the shadows, into the beam of my flashlight.

"I think I am." I stood ready to move quickly if necessary, my mind moving around the room, while my gaze remained on the demon in front of me.

Movement behind him resulted in half a dozen werewolves lining up on either side of Nicolae.

"As you see…" the demon spread his arms wide "…you are outnumbered. Coming alone was a rookie move, was it not?"

I was beginning to agree with him, but damned if I'd let him know. I pushed my internal thoughts into that closet in my mind and slammed it shut. I didn't want the bad-ass demon reading my mind like Blaise did and anticipating my every move.

Given enough time, I'd master my inner demon. But that time wasn't now. Now I had to bluff my way through this exchange, grab my brother and get the hell out with the amulet. Like the others had said, under no circumstance could I let Nicolae have the magic stone, tucked beneath the fabric of the shirt Blaise had loaned me that still held his incredibly delicious scent. As much as he hovered and made me crazy, I wished he was there with me. I'd been rash to think I could do this on my own.

Part of the reason I had decided to go it alone had to do with self-doubt. I wasn't certain I could control the amount of power that emerged from within with the help of the amulet. If I got out of control, I didn't want the rest of my team to get caught in the aftermath.

I squared my shoulders. Time to get this show on the road. "Where's Alex?"

"Nearby." Nicolae's arms crossed over his chest. "The amulet?"

"It's around."

The demon nodded to one of the werewolves. The creature slipped into the shadows behind Nicolae and emerged dragging a lanky teen, with longish black hair, tattooed arms and an arrow-tipped barbell piercing through his left eyebrow. His forehead wrinkled in a frown and he glared at me. "Why am

I here?" He shook off the hands of the werewolf and stood with his feet planted wide, his hands resting on his hips.

Gone was the little boy with the rumbled dark hair, sleeping in my lap. Gone was any resemblance to the brother I'd loved. And gone was the innocence.

My heart broke at the young, defiant man who glared at me and asked, "Who's the bitch?"

Nicolae smiled. "She says she's your sister."

The surprise in his face was real. "I don't have a sister."

"She insists you do." Nicolae's smile turned into a sneer. "She wants to take you home."

"Bullshit."

If I couldn't see the resemblance between him and my father, I would never have believed this stranger was my brother. Everything about him reeked of Danske, from his dark hair to the ice-blue eyes and the breadth of his shoulders, despite his youth.

"Alex?" I called out. "Come with me. I can free you from this demon."

"Free me?" The teen snorted. "I'm free to go wherever I want. Why would I need you to free me?" He stepped close to Nicolae. "Nic is my brother."

I shook my head, realizing how hopeless it was to try to sway him in front of the demon. "Your name is Alex Danske. Nicolae stole you from your real family when you were five years old." I moved closer. "I'm your sister. I was there when you were born. I changed your diapers, I read to you and sang you to sleep. Our mother loved you more than life." My words bogged down in my constricting throat. "I love you and want you to be part of my life."

"That's a bunch of crap." Alex snarled, his fists balling. "My mother abandoned me, didn't she, Nic?"

"Not according to her." Nicolae turned to Alex. "Question

is, who do you believe? Your true brother…or a stranger who didn't bother to find her missing brother."

"Don't listen to him, Alex. He's lying. We searched. Our mother spent every bit of her savings and worked additional jobs to hire investigators to search for you when the police couldn't help. We never gave up hope. You don't give up on family." My words faded. If I was honest with myself, I was wasting my breath. All of Alex's memories of me and my mother had been erased, swept away by the evil that was Nicolae. But I couldn't give up. Focusing on Alex, I channeled the power of the amulet, all my love, and all our mother's love into getting through to him. Softly at first, then growing louder, I hummed the song I used to sing to him at night when he went to sleep. The song I'd used to frighten away the monsters beneath his bed, the song he used to sing with me.

The teen's eyes narrowed, his fists clenching and unclenching, his mouth set in a grim line. "Stop."

I couldn't. Once I'd started, I had to finish. It was my last hope to get through to him.

Alex clamped his palms over his ears. "Stop it, damn you!"

Nicolae flung out a hand, the force of a major league baseball bat punched me in the chest and sent me sprawling on my backside, sliding across the concrete. Pain radiated upward from my tailbone. As soon as I caught my breath, I hummed again, pulling myself to my feet, my legs shaking.

Nicolae's face wavered in my peripheral vision, as I focused all of my attention, thoughts and love on my brother. But I could see his hands flick out on both sides.

Werewolves inched closer, hugging the shadows outside the glow of my flashlight shining across the floor where I'd dropped it.

I didn't move from where I stood, repeating the song.

Alex swayed, his eyes glazing over, his hands pushed

through his hair. "Tell me she's lying, Nic. Tell me she's not my sister."

"He can't. Because it would be a lie," someone said from behind me. With the song in my head, reminding me of my past, and the family I'd loved so deeply, I recognized the voice immediately as my father's. I was a little girl again, surrounded by the love of my mother and father, holding my little brother in my arms.

Tears swelled in my eyes and spilled onto my cheeks. I stared at my brother, willing him to remember.

His gaze finally connected with mine and I could tell the moment he remembered. His eyes widened, his mouth opened and he held out his hand.

I reached out. Then everything happened at once.

"Take her!" Nicolae shouted.

The werewolves who'd closed in on me while I'd been in my singing trance, rushed forward.

"Katya!" Blaise's cry pierced the gloom.

My song ended when a werewolf plowed into me like a linebacker, trapping my arms against my sides, lifting me off my feet.

My father and Blaise raced toward me, too late to stop my attacker. Other werewolves met them and a struggle for survival ensued. Demon versus werewolf, each powerful in their own way.

I fought to free one of my hands so that I could curl it around the amulet, sure that it was the key to surviving the attack. But I couldn't move.

As the werewolf carried me toward Nicolae, the amulet shook free of my shirt and dangled around my neck.

As soon as I was close enough, Nicolae yanked the amulet from my neck and raised it into the air. "Now witness the power!" he shouted above the melee.

Nicolae raised his other hand, his fingers curling in the air.

My air was cut off. I struggled to breathe past whatever closed around my windpipe. The werewolf released me and I rose from his arms, hanging suspended in the air.

"Stop fighting or I kill her now," Nicolae called out, his voice ringing off the concrete walls.

Blaise stepped back, my father with him.

The two remaining werewolves, that hadn't been knocked unconscious, formed a barricade between them and me.

My gaze went to Alex. He was closest to Nicolae, the only one who had a chance to stop the demon from following through on his promise to kill me.

Without the amulet, I couldn't communicate with him, couldn't insinuate my thoughts into his mind and I couldn't speak to urge him to do the right thing. My only hope to survive was drying up like the oxygen to my brain. Gray haze closed in on my peripheral vision. *Help me, Alex.*

"Let her live, Nicolae." Alex spoke in a soft, urgent tone. "She's not a threat to you without the amulet."

"Oh, don't be so sure." Nicolae laughed. "Keep your friends close, right, Alex? And kill your enemies closer. That's our motto."

"Let her go." Ivan Danske stepped toward the barricade of werewolves. "I'm the one you hate. Not my daughter."

Werewolves grabbed his arms.

Alex's gaze shifted from me to my father, his eyes widening.

"Take your revenge out on me." Ivan struggled against the beasts' hold. "It's what you've always wanted."

"Oh, but I am. And what better way than to watch you suffer as your family dies around you." Nicolae flipped his hand toward Alex and my brother slammed backward, hitting his head against a metal pipe and slumped to the floor.

I kicked out, fighting to maintain consciousness. I had to help Alex. If Nicolae hated my family this much, he wouldn't stop until he'd killed us all.

"Take me." Ivan stepped closer, holding his hands out to his sides.

"I will. After I've killed your daughter and son. I want to watch you suffer."

As my father moved toward Nicolae, Blaise inched closer to werewolf nearest to him.

Blaise lunged for the werewolf at the same time Ivan dove for Nicolae.

The grip on my throat released and I dropped to the ground.

Then my father rose off the ground, his hands clawing at his throat.

"So you want to go first?" Nicolae laughed. "Have it your way."

For a moment, all I could do was breathe in blessed air, my muscles completely useless.

Blaise knocked one werewolf into the other and sent them both crashing into low-hanging rusted pipes. After a brief struggle, he'd subdued both and went after Nicolae.

I couldn't let the evil demon kill Blaise and, despite my animosity toward my father, I couldn't let the demon kill him as well. I staggered to my feet as Blaise threw himself toward Nicolae.

The demon stopped him with a raised hand and held him alongside my father, suspended in the air.

Nicolae laughed. "Try anything and I'll hang you as well." He laughed. "You might as well give up. You and your family are going to die today."

"Not if I can help it," said Ivan Danske. A streak of what

looked like lightning shot out across the room, hitting Nicolae in the wrist of the hand holding the amulet.

The amulet flew from his grip and landed on the floor in front of him.

Blaise and Ivan slumped to the floor, gasping for breath.

Too far away to grab the necklace, I ran and did my best slide into home, kicking the amulet out of Nicolae's range and right into my brother's hands.

He raised the amulet into the air, his face set in hard lines as he stared across the concrete at Nicolae. "You're not my brother."

"Yes, yes. I am." The evil demon waved his hands at the teen. "Give me the amulet."

"You wouldn't have slammed me into the wall, if you were my brother," Alex said, his glaring at the now less powerful demon.

A werewolf who'd recovered consciousness rose up behind my brother.

"Alex, look out!" I shouted.

Ivan Danske threw himself at the werewolf, tripping him. But he caught Alex as he went down, taking the boy with him.

Alex lay beneath the heavy werewolf, the amulet lying on the ground, inches from his fingertips.

Nicolae dove for the magic stone.

Together, we can take him. For once, I appreciated Blaise's thoughts intruding in on mine. He gave me strength and bolstered my courage and determination. I focused on Nicolae, picturing a giant hand smacking him down like a pesky fly.

The demon's dive was arrested in midair and he dropped to the floor, bouncing hard, his head connecting with concrete where he lay still.

Ivan grabbed the werewolf by the back of his collar.

As the creature transformed, Ivan slammed a fist in his half-human face.

The transformation stopped and the man slid to the ground.

With Nicolae and the werewolves out of commission, I rose to my feet, every bruise and mauled muscles screaming at me. I pushed my aches and pains to the side and stared across at the boy with the tattoos and piercings, holding the amulet in his hand, his gaze on Nicolae. "He's not my brother."

"No." Ivan stood and closed the distance between himself and Alex. "He stole you from your family out of revenge, not love." Ivan held out his hand. "Can I have the amulet?"

The boy curled his palm around the stone and shook his head. "It has power. I can feel it."

"Yes, but it also carries a curse. The bearer becomes more evil every day he wears it."

"I don't care. It's mine now."

"Alex." I stood where I was, my heart filled with the joy of finally finding my brother. "You're not evil. I can feel it. And you don't need the power boost of the amulet. Your own abilities are strong."

Ivan nodded. "She's right. I've never sensed a stronger demon than I sense in you."

"But I'm not a demon. I'm human." The teen shook his head side to side, a frown marring his smooth brow.

"You're a halfling," I told him. "Like me." My gaze went to my father. "And this is our father."

A scuffle drew my attention behind me.

"Ah, what a happy little reunion." Nicolae had recovered and grabbed Blaise from behind, holding a wicked knife to the demon's throat. "The amulet, or your boyfriend dies."

A trickle of blood oozed from where Nicolae pressed the sharp knife to my demon's skin.

My heart stopped. Was throat-slashing one of the ways to

kill a demon? Now I wished I had asked Blaise. Not because I wanted to kill him. I never had wanted to murder my partner in the first place.

The damn demon had slipped beneath my radar. No, he'd bulldozed his way into my life, refusing to take for an answer from me. Now, when his life hung in the balance, I realized I didn't want to live without him. I didn't want to go home to my apartment without him in it.

In the few short weeks he'd been my partner on the force and in my bed, he'd come to mean more to me than I'd cared to admit.

Blaise smiled, the movement turning into a grimace as Nicolae pressed the knife closer. *I love you, too, babe. But don't let him have the amulet.* Blaise didn't say a word, his thoughts curling around mine, reassuring me.

I held out my hand to my brother. "Please, Alex. We can't let him kill Blaise."

My darling demon frowned. *What are you doing?*

Trust me. Whether he could hear my thoughts or not, Blaise was in no position to argue with me. I had to free him by any method possible.

Alex curled his fist around the amulet. "No. It's mine now."

"You aren't evil, Alex. You used to carry the spiders outside to release them rather than kill them." I smiled at him. "You can't change the person you were born to be. Please, let me have the amulet."

The boy held on a little longer, then handed the necklace to me.

As soon as the amulet rested in my palm, a channeled the building energy, focusing all my anger and frustration on the demon holding Blaise. "Let him go and I'll give you the amulet."

"Let me have the amulet first. Then I'll let go of your boyfriend."

Don't do it, Katya. We can defeat him together, Blaise entreated.

That's what I'm counting on. I held out my hand and dangled the amulet in front of Nicolae, just out of his reach.

His eyes widened and his lips curled back in a feral grin. "It's mine." He lunged for the amulet, his grip on the blade loosening.

Blaise drove his arm up through the curve of Nicolae's and knocked it away. The knife sailed through the air, burying itself into the wall.

Nicolae grabbed for the amulet.

I jerked it up into my palm.

When his hand touched the smooth stone, flesh sizzled and he screamed, yanking his hand away. "Bitch. It's mine. Give it to me."

The sickening stench of burning flesh almost made me gag. "No, I think you've done enough damage."

"You don't know the damage I can do."

"I have an idea."

Nicolae raised his hand, his fingers squeezing into a fist.

My throat tightened enough that I struggled to get air to my lungs.

But my feet were solidly on the ground.

I had this. This demon didn't scare me. I channeled all the anger I'd felt for my father into one surge of emotion and aimed it square in the demon's chest.

He slammed backward, hitting the wall behind him. He slid down and slumped to the side.

Blaise held out his hand.

"I'm not giving you the amulet."

He chuckled. "I don't want it. However, I'll take your zip ties."

"Here." I handed the amulet to my brother. "Guard that with your life. We have a demon to secure."

Alex frowned. "You trust me?"

My father laid a hand on the young man's shoulder. "We're family. And though I haven't been around much, I hope to remedy that."

"What about the others?"

Ivan frowned. "The other children Nicolae stole?"

My brother nodded. "What will happen to them?"

"We'll find help for them," I promised. "But for now, I have a demon to deliver to the Tribunal." I raised my eyebrows toward Blaise. "What do you say we deliver him ourselves?"

Blaise grinned, tossing Nicolae over his shoulder in a fireman's carry. "I'm sure they'll be happy to lock him up and toss the key."

"Should we worry about his werewolf following?"

"Remove the head of the organization and the rest crumbles."

"Sounds a bit gory if you ask me." I led the way to my self-appropriated undercover car and unlocked the trunk.

Blaise tossed Nicolae in and slammed the lid.

"I hope this is the end of this particular assignment."

"I was enjoying playing bodyguard." Blaise smiled at me. "You all girly and scared. Me the macho demon, there to protect."

I snorted. "Yeah. Right."

After we'd personally delivered Nicolae and the amulet to the Tribunal holding facility, the lieutenant gave us the rest of the night off. "You two work great as a team. Now go get some rest."

We settled my brother in the hotel in which my father was staying, then Blaise and I caught a taxi to my apartment.

Standing beside the cab, I rubbed my suddenly damp palms against my jeans. "You don't have to walk me to my door. I'm a big girl. I can make it on my own now that Nicolae has been contained." Once again, I was pushing him away. Only this time, I didn't want him to go.

Blaise leaned into the taxi and paid the driver. "I know you're a big girl, but let me walk you to your door. Then I'll be on my way to my home."

Relieved that my ploy to blow him off hadn't worked, my pulse quickened and I scrambled to find a way to ask him in without seeming too eager. Hell, I'd pretty much told him I didn't want him staying with me anymore. What kind of flake would he think I was if I asked him to stay now?

Not a flake at all.

"Shit, Blaise. Did you read all my thoughts?" I had to get a better handle on my emotions if I planned to have any kind of relationship with this demon.

So now we're in a relationship?

I ground to a halt and pointed a finger at his chest. "If you're going to push words into my head, make them count, will ya?"

"And how will I do that?" His gaze slid over me, all smoldering heat and lust.

My eyelids drooped to half-mast. *Make them sexy.* I turned and walked away, swaying my hips the best way I knew how. It felt kind of good to act like a vamp, all girly and alluring.

What will the guys on the force think?

I propped my fists on my hips and tossed an exasperated

frown over my shoulder. "Okay, that's not sexy, and I don't give a damn what they think."

That's my girl. Blaise scooped me up from behind and took the steps up to the third floor, two at a time.

I laughed and held on, loving the way I fit against him. My soft curves against his hard muscles. I loved even more how hot he made me when we lay naked together.

Blaise carried me across the threshold and tossed me on my bed. Then his hands were on the buttons of his shirt.

My heart fluttered and I practically drooled in anticipation of running my hands across his body. Partnership with a demon wasn't all that bad after all.

Remember, you're part demon, too. Blaise stripped and lay down beside me.

Oh, yeah. And there was that…

* * * * *

MILLS & BOON®

Want to get more from Mills & Boon?

Here's what's available to you if you join the exclusive **Mills & Boon eBook Club** today:

✦ *Convenience – choose your books each month*
✦ *Exclusive – receive your books a month before anywhere else*
✦ *Flexibility – change your subscription at any time*
✦ *Variety – gain access to eBook-only series*
✦ *Value – subscriptions from just £1.99 a month*

So visit **www.millsandboon.co.uk/esubs** today to be a part of this exclusive eBook Club!

MILLS & BOON®

Maybe This Christmas

Author of *Sleigh Bells in the Snow*

Sarah **Morgan**

Maybe this Christmas

COMING SOON
OCTOBER 2014

* cover in development

Let Sarah Morgan sweep you away to a perfect
winter wonderland with this wonderful Christmas
tale filled with unforgettable characters, wit,
charm and heart-melting romance!
Pick up your copy today!

www.millsandboon.co.uk/xmas

MILLS & BOON®

The Little Shop of Hopes & Dreams

* cover in development

Much loved author Fiona Harper brings you the story of Nicole, a born organiser and true romantic, whose life is spent making the dream proposals of others come true. All is well until she is enlisted to plan the proposal of gorgeous photographer Alex Black—the same Alex Black with whom Nicole shared a New Year's kiss that she is unable to forget…

Get your copy today at
www.millsandboon.co.uk/dreams

MILLS & BOON®

Why shop at millsandboon.co.uk?

Each year, thousands of romance readers find their perfect read at millsandboon.co.uk. That's because we're passionate about bringing you the very best romantic fiction. Here are some of the advantages of shopping at www.millsandboon.co.uk:

* **Get new books first**—you'll be able to buy your favourite books one month before they hit the shops

* **Get exclusive discounts**—you'll also be able to buy our specially created monthly collections, with up to 50% off the RRP

* **Find your favourite authors**—latest news, interviews and new releases for all your favourite authors and series on our website, plus ideas for what to try next

* **Join in**—once you've bought your favourite books, don't forget to register with us to rate, review and join in the discussions

Visit **www.millsandboon.co.uk**
for all this and more today!